Heather,

Wish come true

The Blogger Diaries Book 3
by
KD Robichaux

♡

KD Robichaux

Published by © KD Robichaux
Wish Come True
Copyright © 2015 KD Robichaux
All rights reserved
https://www.facebook.com/authorkdrobichaux

Edited by: Becky Johnson with Hot Tree Editing
http://www.facebook.com/hottreeediting

Cover Photography by: Mike Fox Photography
https://www.facebook.com/
mikefoxphotographybeauty

Cover Design © Sommer Stein
with Perfect Pear Creative Covers
https://www.facebook.com/PPCCovers

Formatted by: Author JC Cliff

Chapter Headings Designed by: Author Danielle
Jamie
https://www.facebook.com/AuthorDanielleJamie

COPYRIGHT

The Blogger Diaries Trilogy

STOP! STOP! STOP! STOP!

PLEASE, FOR THE LOVE OF COFFEE, DO NOT START READING THIS BOOK WITHOUT READING BOOK 1, _WISHED FOR YOU_, AND BOOK 2, _WISH HE WAS YOU_, FIRST.

These books are NOT standalones and must be read in order.

Reading order:

Wished for You
Wish He Was You
Wish Come True

Now that I've had a panic attack thinking about someone reading this book first, you may proceed, but only if you've READ BOOKS ONE AND TWO FIRST!
Love,
KD

PR♠LOGUE

Kayla's Chick Rant & Book Blog
December 20, 2007

So I got this book called *Sex Lover's Book of Lists*—a super fun read about the history of sex all around the world—and it has me a little worried. Supposedly, they used to think you could go blind by masturbating. I mean... I can see that. The toe-curling, mind-blowing, eye-crossing, self-induced orgasms I've been having the past two weeks would definitely lead me to believe I'll eventually do physical harm to myself if I keep it up. But something tells me that's not going to slow me down.

I'm having better sex over the phone with Jason than I ever had actually doing the deed with Aiden. *snort* OMG, I'm so going to hell for saying that. But it's true! I had never had phone sex before Jason suggested it. I was so embarrassed at even the thought of it... until he started talking. Dear God. I swear the man could read me the phone book and I'd come in seconds. When I told him I got my first vibrator, he was like a dog with a bone, hounding me until I confessed all the details of my little buddy. I have named him Dean, by the way, after Dean Winchester on *Supernatural*. Now, *that* man is sex on a stick. I'm a Dean girl, but I'm definitely Sam curious. Mmmmm... Wow, I think I've been reading too many Kresley Cole books. Nix is rubbing off on me. Squirrel!

Back to what I was saying.

After that first phone call from Jason on Thanksgiving about a month ago, we've talked literally every single day for hours on end. It only took a week to be back in Jason's imaginary bed, half a country away. I know, I know... I'm such a ho. But whatever. He's... different. I was leery he'd up and "pull a Jason", as we now call it, referring to how he would completely, unexpectedly disappear. But I really believe he's not bullshitting me this time. Why?

Well, the conversation went a little like this...

CHAPTER One

December 8, 2007
Two weeks ago

I glance at the clock, counting down the seconds until my phone will ring, the same time it has every night since Thanksgiving. 10:00 p.m., that magical moment when it's 9:00 p.m. in Texas and we can talk on our cells for hours without being charged for it. I'm grateful to whoever came up with the "All calls free after 9:00 p.m." rule, because heaven knows I'd be spending a fortune on my phone bill otherwise, devoting so much time talking to Jason.

I have about ten minutes. I take my cell with me to the kitchen, setting it on the counter while I make myself a ham sandwich, grab a handful of sour cream and onion potato chips to go along with it, and then a Gatorade out of the fridge. I snatch my phone up, tucking it under my arm as I pick up my plate and my soda, and then walk back to my bedroom, closing the door with a backward shove of my foot.

I place everything on my nightstand and reach to turn up the baby monitor. Josalyn's already been asleep for two hours. I swear she's the easiest baby in the world. Her internal clock is locked, never veering off schedule, not even by minutes. And I think it's actually trained my body, because I usually wake up mere seconds before I hear her start to move around in her crib, and I make it to her to nurse before she even has a chance to cry. I wonder if all mothers have such a wondrous bond with their child.

I hop into bed with an excited bounce, cross my legs, pull my covers up, and hunch over my phone, elbows-to-knees, chin propped on my knuckles, and wait for the little gadget to light up. And at the exact moment the green neon numbers go from 9:59 p.m. to 10:00 p.m., my cell starts playing the lyrics to "Helena" by My Chemical Romance. That song never gets old.

With a thud of my heart and a face-splitting grin, I answer after Gerard sings, *'Things are better if I stay'*. "Hello."

"Hey, beautiful," comes his usual opening, which makes my cheeks warm and radiate downward to set off the roller coaster hill-drop in my belly. "What are we having for dinner tonight?"

"Just a sandwich and chips. I had to finish up a paper, so I didn't really have time to cook anything," I tell him. I love that we already have a routine. He picked up right away on the fact I eat dinner after I put Josalyn to bed. Probably not great to wait so late to eat, but with my metabolism, it doesn't really affect me. I silently thank my mom for her genes. "What about you?"

"Mom made her smothered steak. I'm so full I had to just come prop myself up in bed," he sighs, and I grin, imagining him rubbing his belly. I've been in that bed, so I can picture it perfectly.

"So anything exciting happen today?" I prompt then take a bite out of my sandwich.

"Well, it hasn't happened yet, but I'm seriously thinking about quitting my job."

"What?" I exclaim with my mouth full. I quickly swallow and then ask, "Why would you quit? I thought you loved your job. Getting to travel all over the place and building windmills... did something happen?"

"Well, it's a family business, and I'm not family. I get the feeling they're going to fire me soon to let one of the relatives have my job, so I figure I'll beat them to it. I was thinking about going ahead and doing it in time I could maybe get back in school this coming semester. I still have a couple of weeks I could register right down the road at San Jac," he explains.

"Have you talked to your parents about this?"

"Oh yeah, my mom is all for it. She never wanted me to quit school to take this job, so she's ecstatic over the possibility," he replies, as I take a sip of Pepsi.

"What does your dad say?"

"He had a good idea, actually. Instead of going for a four-year degree like Mom has been pestering me about since I was old enough to know what college was, he suggested I go for a certification. I like that idea much better. At least then I know I'll be able to use the damn thing. Gavin got his degree and all that shit, and he's still working at the fucking furniture store. I'm looking into drafting, learning AutoCAD."

I hear him shifting in his bed and then his echoing footsteps as he walks down his hallway. The telltale sound of his backdoor squeaking lets me know he's going on his patio for a smoke. Memories of all the time we spent back there fill me with warmth.

"You're speaking in a foreign language. Break it down for me," I say through a giggle.

"Drafting, like drawing but on a computer. AutoCAD is the program I'd learn... kinda like blueprints, only I'd know how to do everything from simple drawings all the way up to like 3D shit."

"Ah, very cool. That sounds perfect for you. I'm putting you on speaker so you don't have to have me chowing down on my chips all up in your earhole," I tell him, and do just that. I hear him chuckle and I smile.

"So what have you been up to today?" he asks, and then he blows out a long breath.

"Those things are going to kill you. Have you at least cut back on how many cigarettes you smoke in a day?"

"Yes, *Mom*. I only smoked half a pack today, thank you very much," he teases.

"Wow, impressive. That's way lower than the two packs a day you used to smoke. I'm so proud." I make sniffling noises like I'm so happy that it's making me cry.

"Oh, hush. I told you I would, so I am. You had a good reason to quit, having Josalyn and all. I don't really have one. I enjoy it too much. It's like an old friend I'm not ready to say goodbye to yet," he confesses.

"I'm just happy you're cutting back. As for my day," I begin, changing the subject back, "Aiden might be getting deployed again soon, so I'll be moving back into my parents' house sooner than I thought."

"Is that a good thing?" he asks.

"Like 90 percent yes. Since he'll have orders, we'll be able to get out of the lease without any penalty. I loved living with my parents after Josalyn was first born, and I spend a ton of my time over there anyways."

"So what's the 10 percent that's not good about it?" Jason questions.

"I don't know. Even though he's hardly present at all, I feel kind of bad moving Josalyn away from her father. At least now, she physically sees him here, whether he's paying attention or not. I just have a feeling that when we move out, he's not going to bother coming to see her."

"Well if he doesn't bother, then that's on him, not on you. You don't need to feel guilty about it," he says a bit heatedly. "I can't imagine being a dad and not wanting to spend every spare minute with my baby."

"I know. Ugh, whatever. I'm over it. Josalyn and I are going to move in with my parents and Granny, and it'll be awesome. I'll be able to leave her with them as usual when I go to work, without having to drive there every morning and then pick her up in the evenings. I'll just be able to come home. If I have schoolwork I need to get done, they'll be there to help me out. It won't be up to me to keep an entire house clean by myself while taking care of a baby with zero help. Oh, man, I'm gonna be spoiled rotten!" I laugh.

"See? There you go. Just count yourself lucky you have them. They'll probably be thrilled to have y'all there. Cure their Empty Nest Syndrome or whatever."

"True story. My mom didn't even want me to move out in the first place. Plus, she misses the animals. She's super attached to Jade, and Riley always snuggled up to her every day for a nap on the couch while Mom watched her 'stories'," I air-quote, even though he can't see me do it.

"I like this plan," he states.

"Oh, yeah? Why do you like it so much?" I ask with a smile in my voice.

"Because you won't be living with that jerkoff anymore, obviously."

I playfully make my tone husky. "And why don't you want me living with said jerkoff, Jason?"

"You keep making your voice sound like that and you're gonna make me put my dick in your mouth," he threatens, and I burst out laughing. When my laughter settles, he continues, "I'll admit it: I'm a little jealous knowing he's there."

"I told you he's hardly ever here. He goes to work about an hour before I get home from work, so we're like passing ships. Then he goes to bed a few hours before I get up and leave for the day. I only see him a little on the weekends, if I'm not hanging out at Mom's."

"I know, but..." he trails off.

"But what?" I prompt, holding my breath.

He takes a while to answer; I can hear him taking pulls off his cigarette and blowing it out. But when he finally does, my heart sings.

"Fuck it. I... I want you to myself. I don't like knowing there's another man there, even though I'm sure you're not doing anything with him. Just the fact he gets to share space with you makes me kinda insane. I want to be the only one sharing space with you."

His confession stuns me. Is this really the same Jason who never asked me to be his girlfriend? Even when he made the plans to come see me for his birthday before he disappeared, it was only platonic, coming to visit a friend. But this... this sounds way different. This sounds serious.

"What are you saying, Jason?" I whisper, brushing the hair out of my face as I stare at my phone like I would his beautiful brown eyes.

"I want you to be my girl. Like, for real this time. I let you get away, and I've told myself, ever since you said you were wishing for me, that I won't let it happen again. For some crazy ass reason, even after all the shit I've done to you, you still want my dumb ass. And I swear this time, I'm not going to disappear. The only reason I did before was because I thought I was doing the right thing. I thought it would be what was best for you. You don't deserve to have to put up with my bullshit." He pauses, and I hear him take a drag off his cigarette before the telltale sound of the glass ashtray moving against the glass patio tabletop as he puts out the butt.

He takes a deep breath then continues, "So I would just drop off the planet, thinking you'd forget about me if I'd just fucking leave you alone. And after the last time, when I had you take time off work, when I was gonna come see you for my birthday, I thought for sure you'd never speak to me again, and that's why I deleted your number. I thought you'd never call me again, so I made it impossible for me to call you too. But then you went and texted me. You texted me like it was no big deal I stood you up like a motherfucker. Sent me a message like no time had passed, like you did it every day. And as simple a text as it was, when I realized it really was you, I would have sawed off my arm to come have that Dos Equis with you. I couldn't fucking believe it was you, my sweet, beautiful girl, messaging me like you were right down the road, just any other day."

The words spilling from him turn into tears that fill my eyes. I can hear the pain in his voice, the guilt eating away at him. I know my Jason. I know what he's saying is his truth. I have no doubt that when he did his disappearing act, it was his way of trying to do what he thought was best for me. But what he doesn't realize is *he* is what's best for me.

"Jason, I'm going to tell you this, and I'm only going to say it once. So you better let it sink into that thick skull of yours. Got it?" I ask with more bravado in my voice than what I actually feel.

"Got it, babe," he replies.

"I am a grown woman. You do not need to decide what is best for me. I can make my own damn decisions. Before all the word vomit you just threw at me, I believe the first thing you said was you want me to be your girl. Is that correct?"

"Yeah, babe. I want you to be my girl," he says low.

I bite my lip and look up at my ceiling, trying to calm my racing heart and trying to commit this conversation to memory. I want to remember it always.

"How about you make that statement in the form of a question?" I look at my phone, waiting to hear the words I would have given anything to hear two and half years ago—what feels like a whole lifetime ago.

"Kayla... will you be my girlfriend?"

As simple as the question is, nothing has ever filled me with such happiness besides my daughter. With that thought, my heart skips a beat when I force myself to ask him a very important question. "Have you thought about this, Jason? You know it's not just me now. I'm a package deal."

"I started thinking about that when I learned you were pregnant. Yeah, it was just a fantasy I played out it my head, never thinking it would really happen, but it got me to wondering. You know how I can live in my head..." He trails off.

"Yeah, I know," I say, waiting for him to gather his thoughts and continue.

"The way it went in my fantasy... God, it's so fucked up," he cuts himself off.

I let out a small laugh to ease his tension, dying to know what he's thinking. "I promise I won't tell."

"I had this fucked-up thought. You know I'm not able to have kids of my own, so I always knew I would be adopting when I settled down, got married, and it was time for babies. Well, I thought... wouldn't it be something if all this shit happened for a reason? Maybe it was all part of God's plan that you went back to North Carolina and had a baby... for us."

My eyes widen at this. I let the scenario play out in my head. What if it really was like that Rascal Flatts song, "God blessed the broken road that led me straight to you". I mean, Aiden doesn't want hardly anything to do with her. And from the beginning, she was always *my* baby. He only agreed to get me pregnant in order to get me off his back. Was I meant to have all the heartbreak, the pain of losing Jason, to come home and have my baby girl, all so that Jason and I could be together in the end with Josalyn? If so, then that saying "The Lord works in mysterious ways" is hella true, and He certainly has a weird sense of humor.

"So in other words, yes, I know you come as a package, and Josalyn only sweetens the deal for me," he tells me, and I hear the sincerity in his voice.

But I still have to lay it straight. "If I say yes, you cannot pull a Jason again. You can't just disappear on me. If you start having doubts, you have to promise to talk to me. You can't just stop answering your phone and fall off the face of the Earth. It was fine when it was only me. I mean, it sucked, but it only hurt me. It's not just me anymore. If I agree, you can't do that shit, because it's me *and* Josalyn you'd be doing it to." Tears well in my eyes again at just the thought of losing him again. I want him to know exactly what he's getting into before I jump the gun and say yes, no matter how badly I want to dive in headfirst.

"Babe, I swear on everything I believe in I won't do that to you again. I have no doubts about us. But if some arise, I promise I will talk to you. I won't ever do that shit to you again. I know I can't take back what I did, but I can at least apologize, and then try my best to make it up to you."

"Holy shit," I whisper.

"What? What's wrong?" His voice sounds immediately

alarmed.

"Holy fucking shit," I say a little louder.

"Babe, what's the matter?" He sounds like he gets up from his chair, and I start to laugh, thinking about what exactly he'd do from Texas if something really was wrong here.

I giggle hysterically and fall over in my bed, pulling the phone closer to me. And then I squeal the one thing I've wanted to be true for the past three years.

"I'm Jason Robichaux's girlfriend!"

CH♠PTER *Two*

December 23, 2007

"Hey, kid," my big brother, Tony, replies when I answer my cell, surprised to see his name flashing across my screen.

"What's up, Nony?" I ask cheerfully, relieved when his tone isn't low and grumpy. Last time I saw my middle brother —I'm the youngest of four siblings and the only girl—he flew to Fayetteville to meet a newborn Josalyn. It had been a nice getaway for him, as he was going through a rough divorce. The divorce was a surprise to the whole family; I grew up adoring my quirky, scatterbrained, Venezuelan, fashion-designing sister-in-law, but as an outsider, you never truly know what goes on inside someone's private life, in their marriage.

"I have some news, and it's happy news. It's a lot, and it's probably going to catch you off guard, because it doesn't seem like a very Tony thing for me to do," he warns.

I let out a nervous but excited giggle. Anything that's bringing out this giddy schoolboy part in my brother, I'm anxious to hear. Tony is the Alpha-male of the family. Always levelheaded, my go-to sibling whenever I need advice on something serious. Don't get me wrong; he's not a square. He and the youngest of my big brothers, Jay, are my go-to guys for the all the best hard-rock and metal music, and he makes me die laughing whenever I get the pleasure of spending time with him. When he was here visiting last time, Tony, Jay, and I went to the hotel bar Anni works at for a drink, just the three of us.

I nearly pissed myself laughing at them as they very animatedly used the steering wheel and the dashboard to play a drum duet to "Enemy". Jay head-banging his shoulder-length blond hair and even pausing to wiggle his fingers like he was twirling a drumstick, Tony's face contorting as he screamed along with Lejon, I had to cross my legs to keep from having an accident in his rental. The cool thing about it though is both Tony and Jay are very talented drummers, and Jay is even in a super popular local rock band, so as funny as they look in the front seats of the car, they sound fantastic! When Jay told Tony he had to listen to this band he's now completely obsessed with, Tony begrudgingly gave in, saying, "Yeah, yeah..." not believing Jay when he said they were right up there on the list with Sevendust, our favorite metal band. As soon as the opening rift of "Arms of Sorrow" started coming through the speakers, I broke out with all-over body chills. And then the voice. Dear God, I've never heard a voice the likes of Howard Jones's. The tone covers you like a warm blanket at the same time every hair on your body stands on end.

Tony brings me out of the happy memory. "So, I met someone, and it's a really cool story, actually. Like one of those girl-books you like to read so much. We met on an airplane... after she was a complete bitch to me," he says through a chuckle.

"Oh, yeah? What did you do to deserve her wrath, big guy?" I prompt.

"Nothing! I just had knee surgery, ya know, and I still have the drain. I needed an aisle seat so I could stretch my leg out, and let's just say she was not happy when I asked her to scoot to the middle seat. But anyways, I don't want to paint her in a bad light. I just can't wait for you to meet her. You'll be shocked when you see her. She's the complete opposite of my normal taste."

Tony's normal taste in women is above average height—so he doesn't 'have to hurt his back just for a kiss', since he's almost 6'5"—with super short dark hair and big boobs. I take a guess. "So she must be short, with long blonde hair, and is a member of my Itty-Bitty Titty Club."

"Well... yeah... that's pretty much spot on." He lets out another chuckle. It's good to hear him so jovial.

"Well, what's her name? I'm excited to meet her!"

"Get this. Her name is Buffy," he says in all seriousness.

"Like... The Slayer?" I press my lips together. I can't

decide if that's the funniest or the coolest thing I've ever heard in my life. I was *obsessed* with that show. Spike was one of my very first crushes.

"Yep, and it's not even a nickname. She was named after a relative," he tells me almost proudly.

I can't help the laugh that comes out of me, but I swear I'm not laughing at this girl who has my brother sounding like he's sitting on cloud nine. It's a laugh of pure joy for Tony. He deserves someone who makes him so obviously happy.

"So when do you plan on coming out this way? You should bring Jossy to meet Alex and Amanda," he suggests. "And you need to come meet Buffy and her daughter Aspen."

"Oh, my God, Nony. Her daughter's name is Aspen? It's fate! All the kids have A-names!" I point out excitedly.

"I figured you'd catch that. So any plans to come to Texas soon?"

"Well, I was toying with the idea to come next month sometime. I sort of have some news too," I say cautiously. My heart thuds in my chest. I haven't told anyone besides my mom and Granny about Jason, since my divorce only just finalized.

"And what's that?" he prompts.

"Do you happen to remember my best friend in Friendswood? The one I used to drive every single day to see when I lived there?" My brothers never knew of my true feelings for Jason.

"Yeah, the one who rescued you when that lady rear-ended you, right?"

"The one and only. Well, I was thinking about coming to

see him. We're... talking. And I can't believe I just used that horrendous saying, but that's what we're doing. He asked me to be his girlfriend. And before you go crazy grilling me, yes, he knows Josalyn is part of the deal and he's thrilled about it, and yes, I know I just recently got divorced, but it's not just a spur of the moment, jumping into something type of thing. I've been in love with him for a very lengthy time, and the divorce was actually a long time coming."

I don't want to get defensive, but I know my brother. He's the type of person to question every tiny detail and weigh all the pros and cons, and I really don't feel like hearing someone try to talk me out of being with Jason. But his response surprises me. "Kid, my divorce was barely finalized when I met Buffy on that plane. My marriage was over a long time before that paper made it official. You've known this guy for a long while now. I'm actually kind of glad you've fallen for someone who began as a friend first. Means you got to know the real guy for once."

I breathe out a relieved sigh. "Thanks, Nony. I'll let you know as soon as I make official plans. I gotta get time off work, and time it for when I don't have any big assignments due at school."

"All right, just give me a heads up. You know you have a room here when you come," he offers.

"Okay, love you."

"Love you, too, kid. Bye."

I hang up and can't wipe the smile off my face the entire time I'm finishing packing up Josalyn's nursery. I'll be spending Christmas Eve tomorrow moving into my parents' house, hopefully for the last time. I won't be moving out again until either I want to live on my own, or if by some miracle, this whole thing with Jason works out, and we end up moving in together. But I'm not even going to think about that. I'm just going to ride this high my brother gave me with his encouraging words.

Kayla's Chick Rant & Book Blog

January 6, 2008

It's totally possible to have a heart attack at the age of 23. I'm sure of it. Because I'm pretty positive I'm about to have one. In a little over a week, I will be on a plane to Texas, going to see Jason for the first time in two and a half years. I can't even get my thoughts in order as I write this, y'all.

I never thought I'd ever see him again. As much as I longed for him, cried over him, loved him, I thought for sure I would never be with him. And now I have a flight booked for Mom, Josalyn, and me to go to Houston. It wasn't easy lining up the dates with work and school. I'll have to bust ass to get my assignments done before I leave, and one of my professors is letting me take a test early. My boss wasn't too happy about me taking a week off after we were just closed for a week for Christmas, especially since everyone and their brother is calling to book appointments to get their heater fixed. But Jenna stepped in, saying she'd be able to handle everything while I was gone. I think she's just as excited as I am for me to see Jason. Well... probably not, because I feel cardiac arrest setting in.

Holy hell! What is it going to be like laying eyes on him for the first time after all this time, after all we've been through? Will it feel like we're just picking up where we left off in 2005? Will it feel as comfortable as it does just picking up the phone and talking to him for hours?

Oh, God. I have to look him in the eye now after having phone sex with him! My face heats up just thinking about it!

Okay, changing subjects before I die of embarrassment before I even see him.

Holiday Updates:

Christmas:

Christmas was excellent. Josalyn and I got all moved into our old room at the parental units' casa, and we celebrated Josalyn's first Christmas with everyone we love. We ate great food cooked by Mom and Granny, and opened presents. My baby girl got spoiled rotten by everyone. She was fascinated by Jay's two and half year old, my nephew, Bret... yes, named after Bret Michaels. I told y'all about me catching Jay with my makeup when we were little, making the Poison singer's signature duck lips in the mirror, right? Yeah, he still hasn't grown out of that obsession—Poison, not the makeup. Anywho, she watched Bret's every move, giggling over his hyper antics. He couldn't get enough of her baby cackles, and looked as if he was King of the World when he got her screeching in laughter.

21

Aiden stopped by for a hot second just to drop her off a gift. He went all out and got her some bath toys. *rolls eyes

New Year's Eve:

My favorite holiday. Went to Paddy's Irish Pub. I was on the phone with Jason for my midnight, his 11:00 p.m., and we kissed over the line then, and an hour later, when it was my turn for the countdown. Cheesy? Maybe, but the fact it was his idea made me swoon.

I am super excited to meet Buffy. Oh! Surprise! A couple days after I talked to Tony, he called to tell us she's pregnant. He sounded ecstatic about it, so I just went with it. As much as I love a book with insta-love, who am I to think it can't happen in real life? I'm chalking it up to fate that they met on that flight, and I'm anxious to meet the woman my brother is head-over-heels for, and the mother of my future niece or nephew.

When I told Mom I was trying to figure out how to get to Texas, she immediately wanted to come along. She hadn't been to Texas in a while, and jumped at the opportunity, since she'd have someone to fly with. She doesn't like going alone. She talked to Marky and got me a buddy pass to fly standby. She doesn't need a buddy pass to fly standby, because she's his mom. The perks of having a flight attendant brother! Josalyn doesn't need a pass, because she's under two and can sit in my lap.

Okay... now I'm rambling just to keep my mind off what it really wants to dwell on. HOLY FUCKING SHIT! I SEE JASON IN 8 DAYS!

*faints

CHAPTER Three

January 14, 2008

My school assignments are complete. My bags are packed with outfits for every occasion, every scenario that could possibly happen on this trip, from lounging in Jason's room and watching TV, to a hot fancy date in downtown Houston. Josalyn's every possession is in a separate suitcase. It's the first time I've ever been on a trip as a mother, so I brought every damn thing I could think of that she could conceivably need.

Jason and I made plans to meet soon after my flight lands. He's going to drive up to Humble from Friendswood and meet me at Deerbrook Mall to see a movie. Whenever I let myself dwell on seeing him that first time, I feel both painfully excited and nerve-rackingly nauseous, so I quickly divert my attention elsewhere.

We're sitting on the plane, waiting for them to seal the doors. Josalyn is grinning with all four of her pearly white teeth, entertaining herself by pushing and pulling the window shade up and down. I ignore the pain in my knuckle each time she pulls the shade down on top of it where I have it propped at the bottom of the window, because at least I know she won't smash her little baby fingers.

As we're waiting, a smiling flight attendant comes by and asks if this is her first flight. I tell him yes and give him her name when he asks, and after leaving and returning once again, he brings her a certificate signed by the captain and a plastic pair of Southwest wings, their signature red heart in the middle. Little things like this make my soul happy. Call me a hoarder—I prefer 'sentimental collector'—but I keep any and all little mementos like these. I tuck the certificate and wings into the carry on under the seat in front of me after Josalyn uses her insane baby strength to pull my hand to her mouth to get a taste of the grey and red plastic.

Pulling her pink moccasin-covered feet underneath her plump little butt, she gets two handfuls of my long dark hair and pulls herself up into a standing position in my lap. I anticipate it and keep her balanced when she throws her full body weight to my left, into my mom's ninja-like reflexive arms. She's had lots of practice with four children and seven grandbabies. Just a few weeks ago, I swear she looked like a superhero as she dove across the living room from where she was sitting in her computer chair, catching Bret right before his head hit the hardwood floor when he came off the step wrong. It's the same step that gave me the scar on my chin when I was little. She literally caught the back of his white-blond head in the palm of her hand mere inches from the floor.

I let out a laugh as Josalyn gets herself a mouthful of MomMom's high cheekbones, and make a funny face at her when she cuts her gorgeous hazel eyes at me as she pulls away, a line of drool bridging the gap between her grinning rosy mouth and my mom's now wet cheek.

Finally, another flight attendant comes over the speaker and begins the safety instructions. Josalyn watches, fascinated, as the man who gave her the wings demonstrates how to use the seatbelt, oxygen mask, and life vest, and then he leans over and directs that in case of emergency, I'm to put my own mask on first, and then the baby's. My first instinct is to say, "Oh, hell no!" thinking I'd want to protect her first. Seeing the look on my face, he has obviously explained this to first-time flying mothers before, because he explains, "If you run out of oxygen, you can't help anyone else with their oxygen mask." *Makes sense.* I nod in acknowledgement.

I take Josalyn back from Mom and sit her in my lap facing forward, opening the shade so she can watch outside as we move slowly along the tarmac. As if by magic, as soon as the plane hits full speed and lifts into the air, she falls right to sleep. I nudge Mom with my elbow and glance down at the snoozing eight-and-a-half-month-old, and with a loving smile, she lays Josalyn's pastel-colored fuzzy blanket over us.

I find it impossible to sleep on flights unless I manage to score a whole row of seats to myself and can lie down. So, I quietly ask Mom to grab my paperback of Kresley Cole's *Wicked Deeds on a Winter's Night* from my carry-on, maneuver Josalyn to lie across my left arm, and immerse myself in the magical world of Mariketa the Awaited and Bowen MacRieve.

Josalyn doesn't wake up the entire three-hour flight, and after the two full cans of tomato juice I've drank, the only thing on my mind is getting to a bathroom as soon as the doors open. But when everyone stands, grabbing their bags from the overhead compartments, and we start filing out of the bird, the sentimental part of my brain perks up when I see the pilot step out from behind the cockpit's door. His grin is contagious as he looks at my daughter with wide eyes, asking her in his deep voice, "Is this the little one who earned her wings today?"

"Yes, sir," I answer, laughing when she reaches her arms out to him and makes grabby hands. He glances at me, silently asking for permission to take her, and I turn her toward him.

As soon as she's in his arms, she lays her chubby cheek against his chest and lets out a dramatic sigh, giggling when he tickles her floral pajama-covered belly. "Did you enjoy your first flight, little one?" he asks her in an excited, high-pitched voice.

She looks up at him and lets out some gurgling baby babble, smiling the whole time as if what she's saying makes perfect sense and expects a response.

The pilot doesn't disappoint. "Is that so? Well, I'll take that into consideration on the next leg. Did you know I've flown with your Uncle Mark? Yeah? He is quite the character, always rapping the safety instructions." Seeing the surprised look on my face, he explains, "We know when there are Southwest family members on the flight. Mark is a hoot."

"How cool," my mom says from behind me, and hearing her voice, Josalyn starts wiggling in the captain's arms, reaching for MomMom instead, apparently finished making friends.

When she takes Josalyn from him, Mom tells him, "Thank you for the smooth flight. Not a single bump."

"You're welcome, ma'am. It's a beautiful day today. Enjoy the nice weather here in Houston. You came during one of the only cooler months they get here."

I start edging down the hall, my bladder standing at attention once again. Mom takes the hint at my 'I gotta pee' dance, tells the pilot bye, and hustles to catch up to me. "I've got her if you want to run ahead."

"Ohmagosh, okay," I rush out, and step lively toward the ladies' restroom. I nearly collide with a woman as I round into the curved entrance, and call back an apology as I run and lock myself into a stall. I can barely keep myself from moaning aloud at the relief.

"We're in here, KD," I hear Mom say from inside the restroom. When I come out, I take Josalyn from her so she can have her turn, and then laugh when Mom doesn't control her own relieved groan.

After picking up our luggage from baggage claim, which includes three suitcases and Josalyn's car seat and stroller combo, we pick up our rental car, strap the baby in, and I pull out the directions I printed off MapQuest before we left that will lead us from Hobby Airport to Tony's house in Kingwood. He had offered to pick us up, but knowing I'd want to spend time in Friendswood, forty-five minutes south of where he lives, I decided to get the rental.

It's strange driving on the busy highways again, after living in Fayetteville for the past couple years with only its double-lane streets, but about an hour later, since we landed during rush hour, we pull into the driveway of Tony's massive two-story all brick house. It's 6:36 p.m. I'm supposed to meet Jason at Deerbrook at 7:30. It'll take about twenty minutes to get there. I timed it as we passed it by on I-59 on our way here. That means I only have a half-hour to do everything I need to before I leave.

Mom sees what must be obvious panic in my eyes, because as I round the back of the car to get Josalyn out of the back seat, she takes ahold of my shoulders and says, "Breathe, baby girl. I know you're excited and nervous to see him. Just take a deep breath. Let's get all our stuff in, meet Buffy, and then you can go fix yourself up before you have to leave. I'm not going to let you drive out of here unless you are calm."

My head gives a jerky nod as I do what she says. I take deep, soothing breaths as I pop the trunk and get the suitcases out, knowing Mom will be much better off getting Josalyn out instead of hauling the heavy luggage. I collect two of the three bags and I follow behind Mom as she hikes her granddaughter up on her hip and throws the diaper bag over her shoulder, making our way to the front door. Before we can even knock, the door is whooshed open, and standing inside the foyer is a golden goddess with long, glowing blonde hair and the brightest smile I've ever seen. I blink a couple times, wrapping my head around what I'm seeing. If Tony hadn't warned me of what to expect, I would swear Reese Witherspoon is greeting me into my brother's house.

"Oh, my gosh, you look just like Anthony!" she squeals, pulling me into a hug with an arm around my neck, and before my face is buried in her waist-length mane, I catch a glimpse of her eyes. They're two different colors, unique, but no less gorgeous. I let go of the suitcase handles and wrap my arms around her. A hugger. I love her already.

"Anthony? You call him by his full name?" I laugh.

"That's pretty cool, I think," my mom says, smiling at me when I turn toward her. "After all, I'm the one who named him."

Buffy lets me go and immediately reaches for Josalyn, stealing her out of her grandma's arms, but then pulls Mom into a tight, one-armed hug at the same time. "It's so great to finally meet you!"

I can only stand back and grin, and when Buffy finally lets Mom go, she turns to me and says, "Anthony calls me a baby stalker. If there's one in the vicinity, you can bet your ass I'm going to hold it and make it love me. I was so excited when he told me you and your baby girl were coming!"

Her enthusiasm and unashamed use of the curse word automatically puts me at ease. No stuck up goody two-shoes here. I should have known Tony wouldn't pick one anyway, but it's nice to see she is so down-to-earth.

"Well, you're more than welcome to hold her all you want. In the meantime, I'm going to go get the rest of the stuff." I scoot around Mom, who's still standing in the doorway, and go to grab the last suitcase, and also the car seat out of the backseat, just in case they want to go somewhere for dinner.

As I return to the front door, I hear Buffy saying, "Anthony had to work late, but he should be here within the hour."

"Okay, great." Mom turns to take the car seat out of my hand. "Is that it?" At my nod, she tells me, "All right, get your stuff and go freshen up. Don't worry about Josalyn. I've obviously got some good help while you'll be gone."

"Gone? Where are you going?" Buffy asks, confused.

"I'm meeting Jason at Deerbrook for a movie in like forty-five minutes." Saying it aloud causes my heart to thump frantically in my chest.

"Oh, okay. I knew you were coming to spend time with your guy, but I didn't think you'd be leaving the second you got here.

Makes sense though. If it was me coming to see Anthony, I'd do the same thing." Buffy gives me a smile and then turns to Josalyn to speak baby-talk to her, receiving a four-toothed grin and babble in return.

"Which room do you want us in?" I ask her.

"You and Josalyn will be in the room to the left at the top of the stairs. I've set up a Pack 'n Play for you in there beside the bed. And Ava, we've got you in Alex's room, since he and Amanda are at his mom's house this week. But don't worry, she knows you're here, so they'll be over to visit whenever you want," she reassures at Mom's disappointed look. My mommy loves her grandbabies.

I take hold of my suitcase, figuring Tony can haul Mom's up the stairs later, and drag it up the flight of carpeted steps. I heft it up onto the twin-sized bed, unzip it at lightning speed, and grab my toiletries bag from where it's nestled between several pairs of shoes. I had the mind to pack the outfit I wanted to wear tonight on top, so I snatch it out and head toward the bathroom.

Throwing my hair up on top of my head with a claw, I take the fastest shower in history, washing off the airplane funk and replacing it with my current favorite scent: Calvin Klein's Euphoria. I pull up my dark bellbottom jeans and yank on my hot pink three-quarter sleeve American Eagle Henley over the first sexy bra I've worn in a long time. Pregnancy and breastfeeding have confined me to comfy ones for over a year now. With that thought, I remind myself to set out Josalyn's bottle and formula for my mom. A couple of months ago, our pediatrician thought it would be a good idea to add a bottle of formula to her diet before bed to help raise her weight's percentile. My girl is long and lean like her mommy.

I brush my hair back out, using a bit of shine serum in the

bristles to get the frizz out, and then put on my makeup, my hand trembling as I painstakingly apply my mascara. Finally, I throw everything back in my bag, squirt one last shot of my perfume in my hair, and toss it all into my suitcase as I pass by the room and head down the stairs. When I enter the living room, where Josalyn is cruising the giant square leather ottoman between Mom and Buffy, I glance at the time on the cable box above the big screen TV. 7:05. My heart drops into my stomach and I feel myself wobble on my feet.

I turn back to my mom, and I don't even have to say a word. "We've got her, KD. Have fun." And I'm out the door.

I jump when my cell phone rings in my lap, and I glance down at the name on the screen, smiling when I see it's Jason calling.

"I'm almost there!" I say as my greeting.

"I might be just a few minutes late. The traffic was backed up at I-45 and 59, but I'm hauling ass now," he tells me.

"You don't need to haul ass. Be careful." After a beat, I admit, "I'm so fucking nervous. Why am I so nervous? It's you! I should just be super excited, right?"

"I literally just got off the phone with my buddy, telling him the same thing. I was like, 'Dude, my fucking heart is about to beat out of my chest.' He called me a pussy and set me straight. Still nervous, but past the terrified part."

His confession makes me laugh, releasing a bit of the tension in my shoulders, and I relax back into my seat, realizing I'd been holding myself close to the steering wheel.

"Okay, beautiful. I'll see you in a few minutes. Park at the JC Penney's. It's the entrance closest to the theater," he mentions helpfully.

"All right," is all I say before ending the call. I want to tell him how excited I am to see him, how I can't wait to hug him for the first time in so long, but it's like my brain is misfiring. The only thing broadcasting across my grey-matter is *Get to the mall... Get to the mall... Get to the mall...* scrolling on repeat behind my eyeballs.

By the time I pull into the entryway nearest JC Penney's and find a parking spot, my relief is completely demolished and replaced with a nervousness I've never felt in my entire life. I'm actually trembling, my breathing erratic, making me dizzy as my lungs dance to a completely different beat than my heart, my stomach clenching to add to all the crazy feelings going on involuntarily inside me. I don't know which will happen to me first; will I pass out, puke, or have a heart attack?

I think I'm about to completely lose it, and then my text message tone goes off, and I let loose with an all-out scream inside my rental car. I look around to make sure no one heard me as my face heats at my ridiculousness. I shake my head and look down at my phone.

Jason: *I'm here. Meet you at the door.*

Oh, shit. Oh, God. I can't do this! I have to do this. Holy fucking hell. I can't even get my seat belt off! Okay, it's off. Open your door. Where's the goddamn handle? Oh, my God, it's like that Dane Cook comedy skit, where the girl gives him a blow job and then can't find the handle to spit it out. Fuck! Oh, there it is. *Stand up, Kayla.* Close the door. *Wait!* You forgot your purse. Open the door. Lean in, but don't hit your head. That's the last thing you need, a big fucking bruised knot on your head. That would be a lovely first sight of you in two and a half years. *Fucking... strap... hooked on... buckle.* Come here, you fucker! *Got it.* Okay, shut the door. Lock it with the remote. Now... the hard part. Walk. Through the darkness, lit only by a few streetlamps scattered throughout the parking lot, I see a tall, masculine figure making its way toward the door from a few rows over from where I've parked. All the emotions swirling around inside me are becoming overpowering, and unbidden, my eyes well up with tears. I'm about thirty feet away from where the manly silhouette has stopped, leaning against the side of the building next to the entrance. I press my lips together and take a deep breath, because I know, not by sight, but because my soul is telling me, reaching greedily for its other half it's missed so much, that it is Jason waiting for me.

That's when every other feeling aside from love, comfort, and *home* evaporates from inside me, and I'm filled to the brim with happiness. The last ten feet are closed in a heartbeat and I'm in his arms. I'm surrounded in his familiar scent. My face is buried in that perfect place between his shoulder and his neck. I'm enveloped in the only arms I've ever dreamed of being wrapped in. My wish has come true. My Jason is here, and he's finally mine.

We stand like that for... I don't even know how long. I can't pull away, and it feels like he's experiencing the same urge to never let go. Without removing me, he whispers, "Do you feel that?"

"Yeah," I breathe.

I feel him nod, the short scruff on his face tickling my cheek, setting off intimate memories of other places I've felt it against and I shudder. He pulls back then and looks down at me, his dark eyes swallowing me up. The whole world has disappeared from around us. All that exists is the two of us, and the feeling is both wonderful

33

and overwhelming. I don't even know what to say, and as always, he rescues me before I panic.

"How about we go get a drink before the movie? There's another showing that starts in about forty-five minutes. This is... intense. I could really go for a Seven and Seven." He chuckles and puts his palms on the upper part of my arms, sliding them down, up, then all the way down to hold both of my hands. He brings them up to his perfect lips, and I feel them gently press against my knuckles, and it's like a defibrillator to my very soul. They send lightning bolts up through the blue veins in my hands, up my arms, and down into my chest, where they kick the once dead parts of my heart back to life. Just a few short minutes in his presence, and I'm fully alive again.

"That sounds perfect," I agree, and he keeps hold of one of my hands as he leads me across the parking lot. When we reach a fern-green Nissan Altima, we cut between it and the truck it's parked beside, but instead of him opening the passenger-side door like I expect, I suddenly find myself pressed against it. I have the fleeting thought of 'caught between a rock and a hard place' before I'm surrounded once again, cloaked in all things Jason. His black Henley's sleeves pushed up to his elbows, he rests his tattooed forearms where the top of the door meets the hood of the car on either side of me, caging me with his tall, sculpted body. He's close enough I can see that his eyes are dark chocolate, not pitch-black like most people think, and my breath hitches in my chest as he closes the gap.

Time stands still when his lips press to mine, and I whimper. I could cry it feels so wonderful to touch him once again. He's *here*, actually touching me, awakening things inside me I thought I would never feel again. This isn't one of the fantasies I've played out in my head over and over for the past thirty-one months. This is truly happening. With that realization, I deepen the kiss, pressing forward against him, trying to force every square inch of my front to make contact with his.

His response doesn't disappoint. With his right hand, he cups the back of my neck before he slides his spread fingers into my hair then tightens his grip on my scalp. I couldn't move away if I tried, but I never would. There is no better feeling in this entire world than Jason Robichaux going primal on me, possessing me as his tongue finally dips between my lips, and when it swirls gracefully around the tip of mine, I'm a goner.

But as suddenly as it began, the kiss ends, and he's pulling me away from the car so he can open the door. I sit and pull my legs in without using any conscious part of my brain, reaching up to run the pads of my fingers along my swollen lips as he closes the door, walks around the back of the car, and gets into his side.

"There's an Olive Garden across the street," he says in a voice that definitely sounds affected by our first kiss as a real couple. I'm just impressed he can speak at all, because the only thing I can do is nod in reply.

It takes no time crossing over FM1960, and we pull into the parking lot just as a light drizzle starts to come down. We rush inside, knowing a Texas raincloud can show up in the middle of a perfectly sunny day and flood an entire neighborhood without the sky even darkening before it's gone again moments later. It reminds me of movies I've seen where people dump their full pots out their windows several floors above the street. Comes out of nowhere. Hopefully it'll be over before we leave again. I don't want to sit in a cold-ass theater when I've just been rained on.

We tell the hostess we'd like to sit in the bar area, so we don't have to wait with the couples and families standing inside the entrance who are waiting for a table in the main restaurant. We slide onto the high barstools, and immediately order our drinks, him a Seven and Seven—whatever that is—and me a glass of the Chateau Ste. Michelle Riesling my friend Katie turned me onto last time we went to the Olive Garden in Fayetteville a few months ago.

"What's this drink you're having?" I ask him as I watch the bartender pour dark liquid over ice in a tumbler, and then tops it off with carbonated clear liquid.

"It's Seagram's Seven, which is a whiskey, and 7-Up. Nice and smooth. You should try it." He looks at me like he knows there's no way in hell I'm putting whiskey anywhere near my taste buds... unless it's coming directly off his.

"I'll pass, thanks. I can't even stand the smell of Jack Daniels, if you recall."

"Oh, I remember."

There are a few moments of silence as I sip on my glass of white wine. It's not uncomfortable, but it's tension-filled.

"I don't know what to say. We don't really have any catching up to do, because we talk literally every night." I let out a nervous laugh. "How 'bout them Yankees?" I blurt.

I've never watched a baseball game in my life.

He chuckles, shaking his head, and then leans forward on his stool where he's facing me, whispering in my ear, "We have a lot of catching up to do, but none of it involves talking." His cool, whiskey-scented breath sends a chill down my neck, along with the images that immediately pop into my gutter-residing mind. I cross my legs to soothe the ache that began building between them the moment I spotted him crossing the mall parking lot.

He notices, and when his eyes lift from my dark jeans and meet mine, there's an almost wicked gleam in their depths before he winks at me. God, I had forgotten how easily he affected me. One bat of those ridiculously long, black eyelashes of his and I'm a puddle. *Do with me what you will!* my lady bits scream, and I clench my thighs more tightly together to shut the tramp up.

He glances down into his drink with a smirk pulling at his lips, giving me a brief reprieve before I embarrass myself by pouncing on him in the middle of a busy restaurant.

"So what's this movie we're going to see? I don't really care what you picked, as long as I got to see it with you," he tells me sweetly.

"*Enchanted*? Oh, it's... well, I'm not sure either. I know it's a princess fairy tale, but it has McDreamy in it from *Grey's Anatomy*. That's really the whole reason I wanted to see it. I'm obsessed with that show," I declare.

"I know you are. You still believe they're your imaginary friends?" He grins.

"Drop the 'imaginary' part and you bet your sweet ass I do! Have you still not watched it?" I chide.

"Nah, I don't really like hospital shows."

I gasp dramatically and look him in the eye as I implore, "It is *not* just a hospital show! You... I can't... ugh! Just freakin' watch it. I can't even explain. Just trust me."

"I hate starting shows in the middle of a series. Didn't you say you have all the seasons so far on DVD?"

"Yep," I reply, popping the P.

"Well, whenever I come to see you, I promise to watch at least the first episode of the first season. We'll see how it goes from there," he tells me.

My heart thuds at the thought of him coming to see me in North Carolina and my eyes widen at his proclamation.

"What? You didn't think I'd come visit you or something? I told you I'm in it for real this time, babe. You've come to see me, and next time, it's my turn. I've already set aside the gas money for spring break." The more he talks, the more my head feels like it's going to explode. Is this really happening? Or have I dozed off after my Thanksgiving meal in a tryptophan-induced coma and just dreamt up the happenings of the past two months? God, how devastating would *that* be?

He snaps me out of my nightmarish thoughts by running his fingertip along my jawline, lifting my chin so I'm looking him in the eyes again. "I'm not going anywhere. I told you, there's no getting rid of me now." He smiles gently and then kisses me briefly on the lips before taking another sip of his drink. He changes the subject, pulling me out from under the cloud I was beginning to soak under. "So I have a few things planned for us to do while you're here. When do I get to see you this week?"

"Well, my mom has offered to be my babysitter for basically the whole week, so whenever you want," I reply.

"But you'll bring Josalyn with you sometime too, right?" he asks, and he looks so worried over the thought of me not bringing her along that it makes my chest swell.

"If you want me to. I didn't know if you were ready for that or not. And… I was being sorta cautious… because, uh… I didn't know if I was going to get here and you'd be like, 'Oh, J-K. I just wanted to bang you again.'" The hurt I see on his face makes me immediately regret my words, but when I go to take them back, he stops me.

"No, I totally deserved that. It was absolutely fucked up what I did to you the last time I saw you. I mean, who sets up a nice, intimate dinner and makes love to a girl the night he plans on dumping her? I deserve a lot worse than your doubts about what I'm telling you. And then add to that the times I up and disappeared on you after you moved. I'd find it strange if you completely trusted me after all I've done to you. But, I fully plan on earning it all back. It'll have to be through my actions, but you'll see eventually that I'm all in, babe."

An overwhelming urge to comfort him consumes me. Before I'm aware of what I'm doing, I'm pulling him to me by the unbuttoned neckline of his black Henley, hooking my thin arm around the back of his neck, and sealing my lips to his, kissing the hell out of him until my breath is coming out in short pants and he's laughing against my lips. The laugh makes me want to hear more of it, because it fills me with pride that I can make this normally broody guy sound so spirited, changing what was supposed to be a passionate, loving kiss into a mischievous one. So I lock my arm more tightly around him and move my head in a sideways figure-8 over and over again, my lips still pressed against his, letting out a theatrical moan that has me grinning when he starts to laugh heartily, gently pushing against me to break the playful embrace.

"Down, woman! Save that for later," he cajoles through his chuckles. I flirtatiously use my knuckle to clean up the gloss around my lips, intimating it's something else entirely. "There's my girl." He leans forward to peck me on the lips and catches my wrist before I can lock it around him again, tutting at me with a sexy smile. "Nice try."

And just like that, we're the old Jason and Kayla. The tension that had been surrounding me has lifted, replaced with a feeling of rightness. It had felt strange being anxious around him, especially when he's the one person I've always been able to be completely open and free with. A little piece of that shattered part of me reconnects itself, locking back into place like a jigsaw puzzle.

"Well, I feel better. You ready to head back to the movie?" he asks, shaking his glass a little to rearrange the ice cubes, finishing off the last little bit of liquid left.

I down the rest of my wine in one gulp and grab my purse, hopping down off the stool as he signs the receipt for our drinks. "Yep, I hope it stopped raining. I don't want to freeze in the theater. Thank you for the wine."

"Of course. I'll pull the car around if it hasn't, and you know I'm good at keeping ya warm during movies," he teases with a wiggle of his eyebrows. "Just the tip... just to see how it feels," he whispers in my ear as he wraps his arm around my waist and pulls me against his side.

I playfully smack him in the chest with the back of my hand as we come to the front doors of the restaurant. It's stopped drizzling, so we continue on to the car, his arm still wrapped possessively around me. "As if I'd fall for that again," I gripe.

"Hey, I didn't hear any complaining coming from your end. I kept waiting for you to stop me, but you never did," he muses, referring to one of the many times we went back to his place after a night of playing pool at Legends Billiards. On that particular occasion, I could've sworn I would be too sore to make love after having marathon sex the night before. After working me into a complete frenzy with his mouth and fingers, there was absolutely no soreness when he offered to put in 'just the tip, just to see how it feels'. The following day had resulted in me walking funny, hoping no one noticed.

At my glare, he tickles my side, sing-songing, "I straight up murdered that puuuuussaaaaaay!"

I can't help but throw my head back and laugh until I'm coughing, trying to catch my breath. *And there's my Jason,* I think happily.

Jason gets our tickets with a severely tense face as I try to make him squirm by pinching the place where his ass meets his thigh, the girl in the booth having no clue why I'm giggling up at him as his eyebrows lower, making his face quite scary to anyone who doesn't know him. When she hands him the tickets, he turns toward me abruptly, removing the offending hand from his delightfully muscular ass as he steps closer, looming over me. I let out another girly giggle as he suddenly wraps both of his sinewy, tattooed arms around my waist and picks me up over his shoulder, hauling me over to the escalator to the second level of theaters like a sack of potatoes. I lift my head enough to see the surprised, dreamy smile on the teenaged employee's face before I reach down Jason's back and smack him on the ass.

When we reach the top of the escalator, he sets me on my feet and then spins me toward Theater 18, where our movie is about to start in just a few minutes.

"Go find us some seats. I gotta use the restroom. You want anything from the refreshments?" he asks.

And when I answer, he says the response in unison, "Chocolate-covered almonds," making me smile and my chest swell once again. I can't believe he would remember something so insignificant as my favorite movie theater candy.

With a quick swat to my ass, he sends me in the right direction as he heads to the men's bathroom.

The theater is completely empty, a perk of coming to a late showing during the workweek. A few minutes later, right before the room goes dark, I see Jason come around the corner and look up the stadium style seating until he spots me at the very top in the middle of the row. My heart beats rapidly as I watch him climb the steps, drawing closer and closer to me. Even though I've spent nearly an hour with him already, it's still crazy to actually see him with my own eyes, physically in my presence. It's not a picture I'm looking at of him on MySpace. No, it's really him. Flawless flesh and blood.

He plops down into the seat to my right, gives the cup holder armrest a very intimidating look before lifting it from between us, and then hauls me into his lap, looking into my face before handing me my box of chocolate-covered almonds. I smile and snatch them from his grip, ripping open the top of the thin cardboard, tearing open the clear bag inside it, and pouring a few of the nuts into my hand. I put two in my mouth, crunch down, and lift one to his lips. He opens his mouth and then closes his teeth gently around the tips of my thumb and forefinger holding the candy, scraping lightly along my flesh before taking the chocolate from between them. My eyes go half-mast. Jesus, everything he does is purely sexual. If anyone else would have done that, I would've been like, *Ew*. Jason does it, and I have to keep myself from tackling him down on a row of these theater seats and sitting on his face.

CHPTER Four

We watch the previews, me eating the candy two at a time—a quirk of mine, I have to have a piece on each side of my mouth before I bite down... is that OCD? *Squirrel!*—and feeding him one until the box is empty. Then, I don't know what to do with my hands. He must see I'm going into awkward Kayla mode, because just as I reach up to twirl a piece of my hair nervously, he catches my hand and laces his fingers through mine, wrapping our arms around my waist as I stay seated comfortably on his lap. I relax against him turning slightly so my back is pressed to his front, and I drape my legs over the chair-back in front of us.

The movie begins, and I'm happily watching it, somehow concentrating on the storyline, even though I have Jason's delicious hard body beneath me, that is... until I make the mistake of squeaking and wiggling when Patrick Dempsey's beautiful face finally pops up on the screen. *Oh, McDreamy, how I love thee...*

Was that a growl? I could swear I heard a feral sound coming from behind me, and I turn and look into Jason's face, seeing the heated look in his eyes. *What did I do?*

"If you don't hold that tight little ass of yours still, I'm going to end up in jail for public indecency," he prophesies.

"I... uh... sorry. That's my favorite doctor on *Grey's,*" I cite lamely, and face forward. But there is no concentrating on the movie for me after that, because all I'm focused on is not only the hard body underneath me, but the fact my seat has grown noticeably less cushioned. No longer is my backside supported by the relaxed thick muscles of his thighs; there is now something large and stiff behind the rough fly of his dark blue jeans.

And just like when something clearly states, Do Not Touch, it's like a damn magnet for my curious digits. I gotta touch it. Plus, I don't like being told what to do unless I'm naked. I do the complete opposite of what he warned me from. There's no way I can sit still now. I make a conscious effort not to move, I really do! But it's like I have no control over my deceitful body. It's been too long since it's been valued, too long having been neglected by an appreciative man's touch, and like a demanding feline, it wants to be petted. Right meow.

I suddenly have a case of restless legs syndrome and have to move them every few seconds to stay comfortable. I feel his breath on my neck and it makes me roll my back, and when my hair falls into my face, I arch as I bring my hand up to push it behind my ear, bringing his face more into focus in my peripheral vision. His thighs flex beneath me, his chest expanding against my back as he takes in lungsful of air, his arms tightening and relaxing around me, his fingers tensing between mine.

By this point, I've lost all sense of what this damn movie is about. All I'm aware of is Jason. And as he always was before, he is completely attuned to me, and his self-control snaps. Before I know what he's doing, he's reached over and lifted the armrests on both sides of us, and then I'm being moved as if I weigh nothing. When he's done arranging our bodies, we are lying stretched out across several seats on our sides facing each other, his back to the seatbacks, and his arm wrapped around my waist to keep me snug against him so I don't fall off the edge of our makeshift couch. My head rests on his other forearm as he props himself up on his elbow, elevating me to the perfect height that all he'd have to do is lower his face a couple of inches, and I could easily kiss the life out of him.

He pauses, though, and it gives me a rare moment to take in my surroundings. Looking past his handsome face, I see the beaming light of the movie projector, illuminating the particles swirling in the air. Below me, I'm surprisingly quite comfortable, the cushions supporting our sprawled position. Behind me, I turn my head slightly to see the next row of seats is the perfect height to hide us from anyone who might walk into the otherwise empty theater. And then in front of me, the person who claimed my heart and soul years ago, and I realize in this second, I have never been happier. I take a high-resolution snapshot of this moment with my long-term memory, because I'm sure I will tell this story one day, and I want to remember every detail.

"What are you thinking about, beautiful?" Jason whispers, running his finger along my hairline and pushing strands away from my face.

I shake my head, not wanting to voice anything that would freak him out and make him run, but he's having none of it.

"No secrets between us. Tell me what's going on in that head of yours." He touches his fingertip gently to my temple before trailing my cheekbone, down the bridge of my nose, and then tracing the outer edge of my lips.

His touch is hypnotizing, and I find myself spilling everything. "I was trying to take in every element of this moment, because it's like something you'd read in one of my romance novels. I want to tell my kids this story one day, when Mommy was young and in love and did something crazy, like that time she made out with her boyfriend in the back row of the movie theater, even though she knew there were night vision security cameras watching." I snicker.

He leans down and barely touches his lips to mine as he whispers against them, "Who knows? Maybe you'll use this as a scene in a book you'll write one day. Because if I have anything to do with it," he finally presses a kiss to my mouth before continuing, "you're going to fulfill your dreams. You've always talked about writing, but there's always something standing in your way." He kisses me again. "But if one day it's up to me..." Another gentle press of his lips. "...the only thing you'll be worrying about when our kids go to school and I leave for work is how many words you can type out until we get home." Kiss.

"What studly muscle-man you'll use on your book cover." Kiss. "If you'll be able to find a bigger grammar-Nazi than you to proofread it." Kiss. "And what color picture frame I'll use to put the *New York Times* best-seller list with your name on it up on a wall in our house."

I stare at him with wide eyes, letting the fantasy wash over me. Goddamn, that was better than the phone sex we have. And the best part? There's not an ounce of teasing in his tone. He's dead serious. Not to mention that part about 'our kids' and 'our house'. I don't know how to respond, so in typical Kayla fashion, I go to snort and say, 'Yeah, right,' but he cuts me off before I can even take in the air to let out through my nose.

"It's going to happen. Mark my words," he declares, and then his lips are on mine and there's no more discussion.

We make out like teenagers, with wandering hands, heavy breaths mingling, and words of intimate appreciation.

"I've missed your lips."

"You fit so perfect against me."

"My heart is pounding."

"Your skin is so soft."

"You smell so good."

"Can we stay here forever?"

"Can I keep you?"

"Yes."

In what seems like a blink of an eye, the theater lights come on, and we look up to find the credits scrolling up the screen. My heart sinks, knowing it's time to leave. I'd give anything for this night to never end, but I know I have to get home to my little girl. I wonder if this is how Cinderella felt when she realized it was midnight and she had to leave her prince. I try to shake off my disappointment as Jason gets to his feet and then pulls me up, wrapping his arms around my waist when I stand and pressing one last kiss to my lips before he takes hold of my hand. After I grab my purse, he leads me down the row, down the stairs, and then to the escalator.

I feel like dragging my feet, taking baby steps so the walk through the parking lot takes longer. When we had come back from our drinks at Olive Garden, he was able to park next to my rental, so we trudge hand-in-hand toward our cars, neither of us saying a word. Does he feel the impending sense of loss too?

Instead of walking to my driver side, he pulls me over to his passenger side door, opens it, and gestures for me to sit. I start to tell him I don't have time to go anywhere tonight, that I have to get home to Josalyn, but he closes the door as I take a seat, cutting off any protests I might've made.

When he sits down behind the wheel and closes the door, he cranks the car and turns on the heater, and then I'm being hauled over the center console and into his lap. I smile, because it really seems like Jason can't keep his hands off me. It's quite a heady feeling, and it makes me feel loved, taken care of, and even a little sexy that this man I'm so infatuated with can't stop himself from touching me, wanting me as close to him as physically possible... well, with clothes on, that is. For now.

"I know you have to get home to Josalyn, but I just can't let go of you yet," he mumbles against my neck, making me shiver. He wraps his arms more tightly around my, rubbing mine to soothe away the goose bumps.

"Maybe saying goodbye tonight won't be so bad if we know

exactly when we'll see each other next," I suggest, the Virgo in me wanting to make a solid plan.

"How about tomorrow? I get out of class at one. You could bring Josalyn to my house, and then I could take y'all out for dinner." He lifts his eyebrows, seeming nervous about my answer.

"That sounds perfect," I reply, and I feel him physically relax beneath me. "Will your mom and dad be there?"

"Dad will be, since he just retired, but Mom still has a few months left at United Space Association, so she won't get home until around six. Depending on how long you decide to stay on my side of town, we could go back to my place after we eat so you can see her."

"I definitely want to see her. I don't know about driving home too late though. Makes me nervous driving on the highways, especially with the baby in the car," I confess.

"Well, one of these nights I'm going to come get you then, because I want to take you out. That way I can bring you home and you won't have to worry about driving, especially since I plan on getting you tipsy and taking advantage of you," he says with a sexy smirk.

I cup his cheek and coo, "Aww, silly boy. Don't you know you don't have to get me drunk to do that?"

He turns his face into my hand and places a kiss in the center of my palm, his scruff tickling the sensitive flesh there. When he returns his gaze to mine, the fire there is hotter than the heat coming from the vents, warming me from the inside out. "Oh, I assure you I'm all man now, and you definitely shouldn't have said that," he asserts, and I feel his hand at the button of my jeans.

As much as I'm turned on at this moment, my nerves get the best of me and I grasp ahold of his wrist, stopping him from dipping inside the denim covering me. The last time I was touched intimately by another person was the sex I had to conceive Josalyn. Over a year and a half ago. I'm suddenly filled with overwhelming self-consciousness, completely embarrassed by the thought of Jason actually touching—or heaven forbid, *seeing*—me. My body isn't the same as it was the last time he saw me. I know for sure it doesn't *look* the same, but even more nerve-wracking, what if it doesn't *feel* like it did before I had my baby?

I wouldn't know. I don't touch myself down there. Call me weird, but female anatomy grosses me out. It's why I've always used massaging showerheads and my vibrator to take care of myself. What if I'm not tight down there anymore? What if my newly acquired softness around my middle turns him off? And why the hell didn't I think of these things before this very moment? Thank goodness I didn't, or I might not have gone through with meeting him tonight.

He must sense my growing panic and my fight or flight instinct going off, because he doesn't try to press farther into my jeans. Instead, he turns his hand over and laces his fingers with mine after I let go of my death grip on his wrist.

"Hm, seems my girl's bark is bigger than her bite. I thought you said I could take advantage of you," he teases. He nuzzles his nose against my neck, and I relax minutely in his arms, feeling sure I don't have to worry about him pressuring me into something I'm quickly realizing I'm not ready for. "What's wrong, baby? We don't have to do anything you don't want to, but you've gotta talk to me."

I pull back and fold under the force of his intense gaze, breaking eye contact, looking down at our interlocked hands instead. "I... I haven't been touched by anyone since I had Josalyn. I don't have that hot twenty-year-old body you remember. God only knows what perfection you've been with since we were together, and now here I am with my mom-bod, and you're going to think, 'Why the hell am I settling for this shi—'"

Jason seals his exquisitely firm lips to mine before I can finish my self-deprecation. His kiss feels almost angry, as if he's punishing me for the critical words I used against myself. I know my analysis of his intensity is correct when he speaks his next words, tearing his mouth away from mine.

"God, for such a smart girl, you can be so stupid when it comes to me."

Tears instantly fill my eyes at his harsh words and I go to pull away, but he locks his other hand in the back of my hair and forces me to look at him when he continues. "Do you think I give a fuck that you might not have a perfectly flat stomach anymore? Do you think that even registers as a conscious thought, when you're here in front of me, in my arms, where I can see you, feel you, kiss you? Yeah, I've been with other women since you moved back home, but *perfection*?" He sneers the word as if it tastes bad. "Hardly. None of them could be classified as perfect, because every single one of them was always compared to you, and not one of them measured up. And I didn't just compare them to your body; they couldn't equate to everything that makes up... *you*," he says hoarsely. "They couldn't make me feel the way you do. They couldn't provoke the... *fuck*... the emotions, the desire, *the anything* in me. It's like I wasn't alive, just... existing until I held you for the first time tonight. And now, I feel everything again."

More tears fill my eyes, but instead of ones of hurt, they're from being touched right on my very soul. He felt exactly what I was feeling the moment I fell into his arms. And now I feel silly for thinking something so trivial as a few extra pounds and stretch marks might have any effect on the way he sees me, because God knows that would *never* make me look at Jason any differently. The depth of my love for him erases any importance on things like physical perfection plays, because in my eyes, he *is* perfect, no matter how his body might change.

I attempt to look at him through critical eyes, trying to see if I can spot any differences from the last time I saw him. His hair is just slightly longer on top, gelled, instead of being buzzed like it was before. His face is a little fuller, his ears not seeming to stick out as much as they used to. He's got a few scars on his forehead and temples from blemishes he used to have that he couldn't leave alone, but none of these differences even registered in my mind before I went looking for them, and they certainly don't make him any less attractive. If anything, he's even more handsome than before, growing finer with age as men do.

Is that what he sees when he looks at me? Does he still see the old me, just tiny inconsequential tweaks? I guess I just feel so different from that old me that I thought it would've somehow manifested into something corporeal, visible, tangible. There are ugly parts of me now, from what I went through in my marriage, my heartbreak over Jason; I feel like they could be perceived by the naked eye. But what I didn't grasp until now is one: they can't be, and two: even if they could, it wouldn't matter. He apparently never wanted me just for my young, tight body. He wants me for the same reasons I want him, because we each have a half of the same soul.

I let go of his hand and wrap my arms tightly around the back of his neck, hugging him fiercely. There's nothing sensual in this embrace; it's purely for showing him my love, for showing him I understand what he told me, and for healing, apologizing without words for thinking he'd care about something as irrelevant as some physical changes.

"I'm sorry. It's just... been a while. For some reason, making out with you for the past two hours didn't set off any alarms, but you went for the pants and I panicked. The only physical affection I've gotten in the last eighteen months are slobbery kisses and cuddles from my daughter," I murmur into his shoulder.

I can feel the warmth of his palms through the fabric of my shirt as he rubs them up and down my back. "Don't apologize. Talking to you every day over the phone, for a split second I forgot we haven't been together all this time. No pressure, babe. I completely understand what you're saying. I'm just happy you're here."

He holds me like that, in his lap in the driver's seat of his Altima, for the next fifteen minutes before I finally give in to the guilt I'm experiencing not being home with Josalyn. I'd spend the entire night here with Jason if I could, but the niggling feeling of selfishness becomes too powerful. Knowing my baby's schedule, I'm sure she's asleep, passed out in a milk coma, and won't wake up for another three hours to be nursed, but if by chance she happens to wake up, it makes me a little crazy to think I won't be there for her.

"I've got to get back to my brother's house," I say, shifting to get back into the passenger seat, but he tightens his arms around my waist, making me laugh. "Are you holding me hostage?"

With one last heaved sigh into my neck, he finally lets me move across the center console and into the seat. "So tomorrow, right? You'll be at my house when I get out of class?"

"Yes, I'll be there. Oh, do your parents, like, *know* about us? Or is it going to be me visiting as a friend?" I ask, hardly believing I hadn't thought to ask this sooner.

"It's funny. Maybe a month before you sent me that text at Thanksgiving, I was talking with my mom. She had asked if I was dating anyone, or had met anyone I was interested in, and I told her that I was done dating for a while because no one was comparing to the person I called my Great White Buffalo, my one who got away."

My eyes widen. "What did she say?"

"Well, she asked if it was someone she had met, who I was talking about," he drawls.

"Oh, my God, you're killing me, Smalls. What happened? Your parents never knew we were more than just friends back then," I squeak.

"I told her it was you, and she was definitely surprised, but she didn't seem disappointed in the least. She always loved you.

She did bring up the fact you were married with a new baby, asking me how I felt about that. So when I told her in December that your divorce was final, she wasn't too shocked when I confessed we were talking long distance."

"I mean, she wasn't shocked, but did she seem, like, unhappy about it?" I prompt. My heart pounds in my chest. I *love* Jason's mom. The woman used to keep Lactaid in her fridge for me because she knew milk upsets my stomach. She told me with as much chocolate as we ate in her house, she felt she had to keep the drink stocked for me, her brownie eating partner. As much of a health nut as that woman is, all rules were lifted and forgotten when it came to chocolate. I would be devastated if she wasn't happy about Jason and me dating.

"No, she wasn't unhappy. She was her normal sensible self, bringing up pros and cons, asking me questions about what I thought dating a woman with a kid would be like, how a long distance relationship would work. She was actually worried about you too, grilling me about if I thought I could stay faithful, knowing what a player I've always been. That kinda hurt a little, seeing how I've never cheated on anyone before. I might have been a manwhore, but if I was in a relationship, I never messed around on them," he asserts.

"You know your mom, though. She doesn't just look at both sides of the coin. She breaks out a microscope and runs a full analysis on it. As long as she doesn't hate the idea of us being together, I'm good. Okay, I really have to go now. I will see you tomorrow." I lean over and press one last kiss to his lips and swat at his hands as he tries to reach for me again, pulling the door handle and hopping out of the car with a laugh.

"Bye, beautiful," he calls before I close the door and make my way to my rental.

It's a weird feeling, being torn in two different directions. It actually hurts to walk away from Jason, at the same time I'm being pulled to rush home to my girl. My mommy intuition isn't going off. I don't feel like anything is wrong with her, but with her being in a place she's never been before around people she's never seen, I want to be there for her, so she doesn't feel like I abandoned her. I'm sure this is my first-time mom craziness going on, but I don't care.

I'm just glad I know exactly when I'll get to see Jason again and that it's so soon. Not knowing and sitting around wondering would make me crazy.

CHAPTER Five

The next morning, I'm woken up by the smell of coffee and the sound of my brother's voice as he comes through the front door, calling out, "Kolaches and donuts! Come get 'em before I eat them all."

I smile and stretch, looking over to my left to find a grinning Josalyn peeking at me over the side of the Pack 'n Play. "Well, good morning, sweet face." I lean over to kiss her forehead, and she plops down onto her diaper-cushioned butt, giggling when I pop my head over the side to look down at her. I pull back, wait a few seconds, and then sing, "Peekaboo!" as I pop over again, loving her precious laughter when I do it a few more times. She grips the padded edge of the portable crib with her dimple-knuckled fingers and pulls herself up to standing again, so I reach in and pull her out, peppering kisses all over her neck as she throws her head back and cackles. My girl is always in such a good mood in the mornings. Makes waking up way less sucky.

I lay Josalyn down between my legs and place my right hand on her stomach so she won't roll and crawl away, and reach down with my left to the floor to pick up the diaper, wipes, and outfit I sat there last night when I came up to bed. I get her all changed and dressed and head downstairs to the kitchen, where Mom, Buffy, and Tony are sitting at the table.

My brother wipes his mouth on a napkin and then claps his hands at Josalyn where I have her hiked up on my hip, spreading out his hands to her, which she immediately throws herself into. I lean down and kiss my mom on her head before sitting down on the bench with Buffy, next to Tony.

"We've got sausage and cheese, ham and cheese, and sausage, jalapeno, and cheese kolaches, and then a shitload of different donuts. Grab what you want, kid," Tony points out.

I pull a paper plate off the stack in the middle of the table and pick out a sausage and cheese kolache and a blueberry-filled frosted donut. Before I dig in though, I go over to the counter and fix Josalyn's breakfast of rice cereal mixed with banana baby food, sitting back down and placing the bowl next to my plate. Tony has her facing the table, sitting on his knee closest to me, so I Velcro her bib around her neck and spoon her some of her sweet concoction, taking a bite of my own food while she chews.

"So how was it?" Buffy asks excitedly. She was already in bed when I got home last night, so she didn't hear the recap of my date with Jason when I told it to Tony and Mom, who were sitting in the living room chatting when I came in. Josalyn had been as I thought, fast asleep, but instead of in the bedroom, she was drooling face down on Tony's chest. I scolded him for it, telling him he was going to spoil her and throw her off her routine, and he fired back, saying by that time, we'd be headed back home and it would be me who had to deal with it, not him. Ass.

"It was awesome. It was a roller coaster of feelings the whole time, bouncing between feeling just like old times, and then the newness of being a couple after not actually seeing each other in so long. But it was amazing. He's still my Jason, still my best friend, and still a fan-freakin'-tastic kisser."

I smirk at Tony when I say the last bit, who shakes his head and complains, "La-la-la-la-la... I can't hear you!" Josalyn turns her head and looks up at him after she jumps at his antics, and he coos down at her, "Your Uncle Nony doesn't want to hear about your mommy getting it on with her boy toy. She's still his baby sister, no matter how old she gets." Josalyn's eyes sparkle as she giggles up at him like she knows exactly what he's talking about.

"Hey, I didn't get it on with him! We just made out like teenagers; that's all." I lean over to stage whisper to Buffy, making sure Tony can hear, "But I couldn't tell you a damn thing about that movie," and he starts shaking his head again while Buffy lets out a loud and boisterous laugh. It's infectious, and everyone at the table ends up laughing along with her, Josalyn's surprised face looking at each of us, trying to figure out what all the ruckus is about.

"Damn, he *must* be a good kisser if he was able to distract you from your McDreamy fella," Mom interjects, snickering when Tony starts his *La-la-la*-ing again.

"So when do you get to see him again?" Buffy asks, taking a bite of her donut.

I feed Josalyn the last of her cereal and wipe her mouth with a damp washcloth, replying, "Today. He gets out of class at one, so I'm going to leave here around noon. He and his parents really want to meet Josalyn, so we're going to spend the day down there. I'll probably head back around seven so I'm not driving in the dark."

"Why can't you drive in the dark?" Tony questions, leaning down to inhale the top of Josalyn's head. He loves that clean baby smell; he did it several times last night too while she was sleeping on him.

"Ever since I had her, for some reason, driving at night messes with my eyes. It's like I have no depth perception anymore. Headlights look like big starbursts, and I can't tell how far away cars are. I think it's called being night blindness," I explain.

"Have you been to an optometrist for it? You need to get that checked out, sis."

"I don't have any insurance anymore. I don't really go places at night anyways, so it's no big deal." I shrug. "Jason said he wants to take me out sometime while I'm here, so he's going to come and get me then bring me back, but tonight we're just going to hang out at his house and get some dinner."

"If your eyes get any worse, just let me know. I don't mind paying for you to get your eyes checked, kid. You kinda need them," he offers, and I nod.

I clap my hands at Josalyn and she reaches up to me as I stand. "Let's go wash that cereal down with some milk, big girl," I tell her, holding her on my hip while I gather up my trash and her empty bowl. I rinse the bowl and spoon off in the sink, throw away my paper plate, and then head upstairs to nurse her. No matter how cool my brothers and I are, it's still weird to breastfeed her in front of them. Even if they don't look, it's awkward. So I grab my book out of my bag and read while sitting up in the bed as she tops her fat little belly off with her morning meal.

After a few hours of hanging out with Tony, Buffy, and Mom, it's finally time to start heading to the south side. As much fun as I've had conversing with them, getting to know Buffy, and telling pregnancy and baby stories about Josalyn, time has crawled waiting for the clock to strike noon so I could leave and see Jason again.

I've spent the last hour getting ready, packing up Josalyn's diaper bag, and making sure I have everything I need for the day. Mom, in her usual way, is running off a verbal checklist, double-checking what I've already triple-checked myself. By the time I'm headed out the door, I'm so freaked out that I'm ready to leave everything here and run. I'll just buy whatever I need when I get there. But seeing she's making me nervous, Mom stops her pestering, gives me a hug and Josalyn a kiss on her chubby cheek, and tells me to be careful as I hop in the car.

It's surreal driving my old path to Jason's house after this long. God, I used to drive this forty-five minute route every single day, just to see that boy. How did I do that? Nowadays, I can't even stay up very late without feeling hungover the next day, even if I don't drink! How the hell did I used to drive down there, stay out playing pool until the bar closed at 2:00 a.m., spend like an hour at IHOP sobering up enough to go back to his house and make love, and then drive all the way back home, putting me in bed at 5:00 a.m. before having to be in class by eight? What in the world was I thinking?

I smile a secret smile. I was in love. That's what. And as I take the exit for Dixie Farm Road, I get an overwhelming feeling of coming home after a lengthy time away. Everything looks exactly the same, and as I pull into the Robichauxs' driveway, I can't help the happy tears from welling up in my eyes. I've missed this place and the people inside so very much, and for a long time thought I'd never see them again.

I glance into the backseat and peek over the back of Josalyn's carrier, seeing she is fast asleep. There are a couple of SUVs in the garage, but Jason's car isn't here. Looking at the time, it's a quarter 'til one. The school is just five minutes away, so I decide to wait for him to get here instead of going inside without him. I have just enough time to feed her before he gets home. I love his dad to death, but I think it would feel too awkward showing up without Jason here. Plus, I want Jason to be the first one to meet Josalyn.

I get out of the car and walk around to the passenger back door to gently wake my daughter up. She makes the most adorable scrunched faces as she stretches herself into consciousness, and then looks at me with glazed hazel eyes. I unbuckle her, close the door, and carry her back to my driver seat. It's actually really comfortable breastfeeding in cars, because you have the armrest to prop your elbow on while the baby nurses.

Just as she's finished and I sit her up, Jason's car pulls into driveway, and he parks next to me. I quickly rearrange my bra and straighten out my shirt, pulling everything back down into place. He opens my door for me just as I've covered up my stomach. I grip Josalyn as I stand up out of the car, and the way I had to tilt her and then pull her back upright, she lets out a gigantic belch, and Jason bursts out laughing.

"Oh, my gosh, baby, that was so not very lady-like!" I chuckle then kiss her cheek. At least she didn't spit up all over the place the first moment Jason met her. It's a little chilly, so I pull the hood of her pink cherry-print zip-up sweater over her head, making sure her ears are covered.

"Hey there, Tooty." Jason leans down, smiling into her happy face, and my heart swells at his use of her nickname. I've called her that since the day she was born, because the tiny girl can rip ass as loud as a grown man. I told Jason about it when we first started talking again, and he thought it was hilarious, sounding quite proud of her, especially the first time he actually heard it over the phone. Gassy little thing. "Let's get y'all inside. It feels like the temperature dropped," he comments, and he leans into my rental and pulls out my purse and the diaper bag from the passenger seat without me even asking.

What is this sorcery?

I follow him to the door inside the open garage, having flashbacks of the first time I walked up the driveway and spotted him as he came out from underneath his truck, covered in streaks of oil and cursing up a storm. God, he was breathtaking back then, and still is as he hitches both the bag and my purse up on his shoulder, giving zero fucks of what someone might say. Not that anyone would dare make fun of Jason for anything—not if they wanted to keep all their teeth.

As he opens the door, everything looks exactly the same. We enter into the utility room, which houses the washer, dryer, and the extra refrigerator his mom always kept stocked with her wine and the guys' beer, passing by the half-bath I used to run to during our poker games on the back porch while the boys always just relieved themselves in the yard.

Walking through the doorway, the dining table I had many a dinner at still sits, surrounded by its six green-checkered cushion-seated chairs, and the kitchen straight ahead. But we turn right through the archway, and there, in the same squeaky green-leather recliner, sits Steve Robichaux, Jason's wonderful dad, who hops up when he hears us walk in and immediately wraps Josalyn and me in his strong arms. When he pulls back, he's smiling ear-to-ear, and he pets Josalyn's plump cheek with the side of his pointer finger. "Well, ain't you just the cutest?" he clucks at her. "Gosh, you look just like your momma, you pretty thang."

She grins and then goes off on a baby-babble tangent, ending with a loud, "Ma-ma-ma-ma-ma-ma-ma!" as the three of us laugh at the serious face she makes when she's done.

"And how you doing, baby doll?" Steve asks, giving me a quick peck on my cheek before reaching up to pull Josalyn's hood off her head, running his big hand over her soft hair. It warms my heart seeing him be so comfortable and affectionate with her. His dad has a ton of nieces and nephews, so it's not surprising, but it makes me feel good that he'd be that way with my daughter too.

"I'm fantastic," I beam, looking up at Jason.

"Well, I'll let you get all your stuff put down and relax for a little bit after that drive. I was just watching one of my episodes of *King of Queens* I recorded. If you need anything, just ask Junior there." He winks, lifting his chin at his son and making me giggle. He sits back down in his chair and turns the TV back up, effectively relieving us of small talk so we can head back to Jason's bedroom.

We walk through the foyer, and visions flash through my mind of Jason and me sneaking down this very hallway in the pitch-black hours before dawn. Unable to keep our hands off each other, we tried to be as quiet as we could as we'd make our way to his room, always starting the festivities with him tossing me onto his queen-sized bed before he'd close his door. My face heats and I smile, remembering how wonderful it felt every time he'd grip me by the ankles, haul me to the edge, and then lay himself between my legs, kissing me fiercely before deciding what he'd do to me that night. It was always different, always an exciting surprise to see what he'd introduce me to each evening, never ending until I was completely satisfied.

As we turn left at the end of the hall into his bedroom, I have to stop in the doorway and take it all in. It's arranged differently than the way it was before. His bed is up against the far wall, the one with the window, with his TV on his dresser facing it from the left of us. On the right wall is a long black leather sofa, the other end of it stopping just at his walk-in closet's doorframe. Jason sits the bags down on the sofa, takes off his black pea coat, and then turns to face me, still standing with Josalyn on my hip and looking around his room. Even the smell is bringing back blush-worthy memories. I'm so glad he still wears his Realm.

"I haven't worn it since you left," he says, my eyes snapping to his. Did he read my mind? "You used to close your eyes and inhale deep like that all the time back then. I could never bring myself to wear it without you here to tell me how *intoxicating* I smelled," he emphasizes as he paces toward me, using the word I always had to describe his scent. I could happily drown in the dark depths of his eyes as they twinkle down at me, but then he breaks the spell when he turns his gaze on the little girl in my arms. "God, she looks just like you, babe. Can I hold her?"

"Of course you can," I breathe, shifting Josalyn off my hip to face forward so Jason can take her easily.

He slides his hands under her armpits and lifts her into his embrace, and she instantly latches onto him with her pudgy fingers. Grasping his faded black T-shirt, she leans back to look into his face, giving him a thorough once-over. Then, letting out a long stream of intelligible words, she lets go of his shirt with one hand and grabs ahold of his nose.

I lunge forward, about to remove her grip, but he takes a step back and shoots me a look that tells me he's fine, shaking his head gently so she doesn't let go.

"You like that nose, pretty girl? It's big, huh? You gotta thing for big noses like your momma?" he asks her lightly, raising his deep drawl slightly.

She smiles and growls out, "Ma-ma-ma-ma-ma-ma-ma," once again, and turns to cheese at me.

"You wanna sit down?" Jason asks, and pivots to carry

66

Josalyn over to the bed where he takes her into his hands and flies her to the center of his mattress. She giggles as she lands gently on the soft comforter. The opposite side of the bed is up against the wall, so I sit on the edge to make sure I can catch her if she decides to take a crawling leap.

She grabs ahold of Jason's finger and ungracefully pulls herself up into a seated position, and he slides himself down until his knees are on the floor but his torso is still on the bed. I watch, fascinated at their interaction, a smile stretched across my face I wouldn't begin to know how to wipe off.

Josalyn lets go of his finger and claps her tiny hands, watching Jason expectantly. When he doesn't do what she apparently wants him to do, she takes hold of his pointer finger on each of his hands and brings them together, apart, and then together again, lets go of him, and then claps her hands once more. When he claps by himself this time, she erupts into a fit of giggles and looks up at me with her eyebrows raised, as if to say, "Look what I taught him, Mommy!" It's all I can do not to burst into tears at the scene, and I grab my camera out of my purse quickly to snap a picture before tossing it back on his couch.

To get ahold of myself, I use distraction, leaning over to unzip Josalyn's hoodie and pull it off her. Leaving her in a baby pink onesie, the cherry sweater's matching pants, and fluffy socks with grippers on the bottom. She's really starting to get the hang of cruising now, holding onto furniture while she walks along wobbly, so I got her these new socks so her little feet don't shoot out from under her.

"So what do you want to do today?" Jason asks me,

continuing to clap his hands lightly for Josalyn.

"Isn't there a TGI Fridays close by? I've been seeing an advertisement for fried green beans from there that look delicious, but I've never been to one before."

"Yeah, there's one over by Baybrook Mall. Are you hungry now? I haven't had any lunch yet since I've been in class since eight." He looks at me hopefully.

"I'm starving. I only had a kolache and a donut early this morning, and I definitely need to eat. Don't know if this is too much info or not, but I still nurse Josalyn, so I eat like a pig," I confess.

"Why would that be TMI? Babe, there's nothing you can't share with me," he assures seriously.

"I just... have you ever dated anyone with a kid before? Or, more specifically, a baby? I didn't know if you were one of those people who think breastfeeding is gross."

"No, I've never dated anyone with a kid before, and no, I don't think breastfeeding is gross. I mean, I wouldn't want you to just whip your boob out for the whole world to see when we're out in public, but that's just because they're mine and I wouldn't want to kill anyone for looking." He gives me a grin that immediately puts me at ease and makes me laugh.

"Actually, they belong to her for three more months, and then you can stake your claim. I'm gonna stop when she turns one." I reach over and tickle her belly, loving the giggle she lets out. "I normally time everything around feedings though. If I get desperate and have to feed her in public, I usually do it in my car, or at least find a secluded area and cover up with one of her baby blankets. You can't even tell I'm doing it with the clothes I wear. It just looks like I'm holding her while she sleeps."

"I'm not worried about it, babe," he says, getting to his feet. "So, TGI Fridays? I haven't been there in a while. Sounds good. You want me to drive?"

I stand as well and then put Josalyn's hoodie back on her. She gets frustrated, swatting at me and whining after I just took it off her, but it's gotten too cold outside to let her go without it.

"Yeah, I just need to grab her car seat out of my car," I reply, picking her up after I zip her sweater.

"Okay, you do that and I'll get your bags. You have everything you need in the diaper bag?" he checks.

Instead of getting annoyed like I would with my mom, him double-checking makes me smile. It amazes me how naturally all this is coming to him. "Yep, I brought Miss Tooty some carrots for lunch!" I say excitedly, bouncing her on my hip and blowing a raspberry against her cheek to pull her out of her suddenly grouchy mood. I swear the child would love to be naked all the time if I let her.

"Well, that just sounds delightful," Jason says, sarcasm dripping from his voice as he gestures for me to lead the way out of his room. "Dad, we're headed out for some lunch. Be back in a couple hours. We may get into something after we eat, but we'll be back. Kayla wants to see Mom before she leaves later."

"Good, Barbara would be pissed if she didn't get to see y'all, knowing you were coming to visit today," Steve tells me, and it makes me smile knowing Jason's mom is excited to see me too.

"Say bye-bye, byyyye-bye," I prompt Josalyn, and she grips

and ungrips her hand toward herself instead of at him, making us all laugh. "We'll keep working on that."

I open up the back passenger door of my rental and buckle her into her carrier, adjusting the handle so I can lug her over to Jason's backseat. She's getting too heavy for me to carry her around this way. I thread the seatbelt through and fasten her in, and then get into the passenger seat, Jason observing me the whole time.

"What?" I ask when he smiles at me.

"I just like watching you in mommy-mode. You look so happy doing the simplest tasks, taking care of her," he states, reaching over to tuck a piece of hair behind my ear.

"I finally found something I'm good at, I guess." I shrug. "Of course, she's the easiest baby on the planet."

"What do you mean 'finally found something you're good at'? I know lots of things you're, like, pro-status." He gives me a playful, lascivious look and I smack him on his bicep as he backs out of his driveway. "Hey! Driving precious cargo here." He smirks, and I growl at him, crossing my arms over my chest.

We arrive at the restaurant about fifteen minutes later, taking a little longer than I remember, but it could be because Jason was driving more carefully than I've ever seen him drive before. I'm definitely enjoying this more mature version of the man I fell in love with, but happy he still has his playful, naughty personality.

He walks around and pulls Josalyn out of the backseat in her carrier, holding the handle easily in his grasp like it weighs nothing. I grab my bags out, and we head inside the restaurant, where they seat us immediately. It must be a good time of day to come, in between lunch and dinner hours, because the place isn't very busy.

"Do you want a high chair for the baby?" the waitress asks Jason, who looks at me for the answer.

"No, thank you. Will you just slide her all the way into the booth? Like, sideways, where she'll be facing me when I sit," I instruct, and he does as I ask then takes a seat across from me as I slip in.

"What are you having to drink?" she asks Jason, smiling at him as she faces her body fully toward him, giving me her back. I cock my head at the back of her head, narrowing my eyes.

"I'll have Coke," Jason answers, seeing the look on my face and smirking. "Baby, what would you like?" he asks me after a few empty moments when the waitress makes no move to.

Is this chick serious?

I clear my throat and take a deep breath to control the rising tempo of my heart. "I'd like ice water, pl—" Before I can even finish the word, she walks away, swishing her hips as she passes Jason.

Dis bitch...

I scoff, looking at Jason through wide eyes, who pulls his plump bottom lip between his teeth, trying not to laugh.

"Did you see that?" I exhort disbelievingly.

"I don't know what you're talking about." He swipes his palm from his nose down to his chin, fighting to keep his composure.

I shake my head and narrow my eyes, pulling my menu to me from the end of the table, which makes me realize she had actually handed Jason's to him, causing me to squeak at the back of my throat. I inhale deeply and breathe out again to release some of the growing stabbiness inside me.

"What looks good?" Jason asks over the top of his menu, seeming to enjoy watching me squirm.

I sigh, trying to concentrate on the descriptions and pictures in front of me. "I definitely want the fried green beans I heard about, but that's just an appetizer. This chicken dish looks good, smothered in cheese. I wonder if they could give me some tortillas to make soft tacos out of it," I think aloud, and just then the server returns with our drinks. She sets Jason's carefully next to him, and then plops my water down on the table, some sloshing over the brim, making my eye twitch.

"Do you need another minute?" she directs at Jason sweetly, moving her body closer to him.

My grip tightens on my menu, my fingertips turning white as my hands tremble. *If this chick doesn't back the fuck up off my man...*

"No, we're ready. Go ahead, baby," Jason offers, seeing I'm really starting to get upset and trying to defuse the situation.

The waitress pops her hip as she begrudgingly faces me, pulling a pen out of her half-apron and looking at me expectantly, a bitchy expression on her face. Apparently this cunty asshole doesn't care about getting a good tip.

I clear my throat so I don't spew the words I have for her floating around in my mind. "We'll take the fried green beans as our appetizer, and I'll have the smothered chicken. And can I get a side of tortillas, please?"

She doesn't answer, just turns back to Jason with I guess what she thinks is a sexy smile. I raise an eyebrow at the red lipstick smeared on her front teeth, letting out an audible snort as I fold up my menu.

Jason disguises a laugh as a cough behind his fist and he sits up straight, lowering his eyebrows as he relocates what he wanted to order. "I'm gonna have the bacon cheeseburger plain and dry."

"Do you want fries or a different side with that?" she breathes, leaning over him to flip the page of his menu, pressing her body against his arm. I nearly choke on my spit as I gasp. "You can choose anything from this section here."

"Fries are fine," Jason says, pulling his arm away and shoving the menu at her to push her away.

She looks dejected as she spins to walk away, but I call out, "Excuse me!" and she turns back with a scowl.

"Yes?" she prompts shortly.

"Can I get a small cup of warm water please? I have to mix our baby's food up," I add, my voice dripping with fake sweetness, throwing the word *our* in there to mark Jason as my territory, since I think it would probably be frowned upon if I walked around to his side of the booth and peed on him.

"The water that comes out of the fountain is already cold," she spits.

"So you're telling me there's no way to heat up the water?" I admonish.

The waitress begins to shake her head, but Jason interrupts her, all of the humor on his face from before completely gone, replaced with almost scary seriousness. "Ma'am, this is a restaurant that serves—get this—*hot* food. I'm sure you've got this brilliant invention in the kitchen called a microwave that one can—listen carefully—*heat up* a cup of water. And seeing how it's for that precious little girl sitting right there, if I get any suspicion that you've done anything to it, I will get your ass fired so fast it'll make your head spin, probably whipping that red crap right off your teeth." At this, she gasps and covers her mouth with her hand, and I see her chin move side to side beneath it, like she's trying to lick the lipstick off her chompers. "So, please, if you'd be so kind, bring my wife some warm water as she requested."

Two things happen in the next moment; one, I gasp sharply at his use of the word *wife*, and two, she nods and spins away again to go fill our order. My gasp causes Josalyn to jump next to me and I look over at her, determining if she's going to cry. But instead, she lets out a stream of baby babble, blowing a slobbery raspberry at the end, making me laugh as I turn my gaze back on Jason.

"Wife?" I smirk at him, raising an eyebrow.

"What? You called Josalyn *our* baby, so I figured girlfriend wouldn't have the same effect as 'wife' would," he retorts.

I can't wipe the smile off my face, my mood immediately lifting as his words echo through my mind. Going from longing for him to ask me to be his girlfriend to him freely pretending I'm his wife is kind of shocking, but it makes me feel like a giddy schoolgirl, not a grown-ass woman with a baby of her own.

I let out a small chuckle as a memory hits me. "I remember you going off on that lady who rear-ended me. You have a distinctive way of defending my honor, dear sir." I take a sip of my water, using a napkin to wipe up the mess the horrible waitress had made.

"I thought it was funny at first, your green-eyed monster rearing its adorable head when the waitress was flirting with me. But when you obviously fuck with my girls, your lazy ass not wanting to take the time to heat up some water for a *baby*? Oh, fuck that. Funny time, over." He shakes his head.

God, I love the way he calls us his girls. Just this conversation can salvage the lunch the bitchy server had begun to ruin. A few minutes later, a man in a nice dress shirt and slacks brings me a mug of steaming water, and another glass of water with no ice.

"Hi there, folks. I'm the manager here, and one of our waiters came and told me your waitress wasn't being very professional or hospitable. He overheard you needed some warm water for your baby, so I brought you some hot water, and some cool water, so you could mix it to the temperature you need. I'll be taking care of you for the rest of your meal, and I'd like to offer you a dessert on the house if you have room for it after you're done with your lunch," he extends.

"Thank you. I'll definitely take you up on that," I reply, pulling Josalyn's bowl and spoon from her diaper bag, along with the box of cereal and jar of pureed carrots.

"We'll have your meals right out," the manager says, and nods at Jason before walking away.

I peek up to see Jason watching me closely as I mix some of the hot water from the mug with the rice cereal in the bowl. There's no need to add any of the cold water because it'll be cool enough after stirring it all together. Then I empty the carrots into the bowl, combining it into a concoction Josalyn seems to love. She hates the rice by itself, but has no qualms chowing it down when it's flavored with her baby food.

I lift a spoonful of the mixture to my lips, touching it to my sensitive flesh to make sure it's not too hot, feeling that it's the perfect temperature to feed her. Her hands and feet are squirming and kicking, her mouth already wide open as I turn toward her, and I hear Jason chuckle when I swoop the spoon in her direction with my flying sound effects as I give her a bite.

She hums as she chews, the same way I do when I'm eating my favorite chocolaty desserts, and soon her mouth is open again, ready for her next spoonful.

Jason surprises me then, asking, "Can I try?" as he leans forward to see around the handle of her car seat.

"Really? If you want to," I concede, sitting the bowl back down on the table and sliding out of the booth so he can take my spot. Just then, the manager brings out the fried green beans, and I thank him as I slide into the seat Jason just vacated, grinning when he picks up the spoon.

I pick one of the appetizers up and dip it into the ranch that came with it as he carefully tries to fill the spoon with the exact same amount as I had, taking my first taste, and he wipes the bottom off on the rim of the bowl before cautiously feeding her a bite. His expression looks as if he just won a gold medal in the Olympics as she makes her appreciative humming sound again, just as I make the same noise over the fried green bean, and he chuckles as he turns to fill the spoon once more. This continues until her bowl is empty and he looks up at me with a slight furrowing of his brow.

"Is that it? Does she get any water or something to wash it

down with?" he asks worriedly.

"If you reach down into the side pocket of the diaper bag, there's a mini-bottle of filtered water. She usually won't drink it after she tastes it's just water, but you can give it to her if it makes you feel better." I smile.

He leans down to grab the bottle out of the bag, tugs the cover off the nipple, and places it at her lips. She takes a couple pulls from it, wrapping her hands around it, but as always, when she discovers it's not milk, she yanks it out of her mouth with an audible pop and shoves it back into Jason's hand.

He chuckles and shakes his head, looking up at me admiringly.

"What?" I grin, sitting up straighter.

"It's just amazing how perfectly you know her. It's like you can foresee her next move. I saw it when you were holding her, like you'd counter her every movement without even having to think about it. You know the tiniest thing to do to snap her back into a good mood when she gets a little fussy. And you do it all seamlessly, almost unconsciously. It's just awesome to watch," he explains, and I blush at his obvious approval.

"She's changed you. In a good way," he adds. "You have a confidence with her that you never had before. You do everything with her with a sure hand, never seeming to question yourself when it comes to what she needs."

"Like I said, she's the easiest baby on the planet. And it's mostly instinct. I just do what my gut tells me to. I've learned her different cries, so I know when she's hungry, or needs to be changed, or if she's just being a little bitchy." I shrug. "You want your seat back, or...?"

"Nah, I like sitting here. That way I get the perfect view of both my girls," he coos down at Josalyn, who kicks her feet and reaches for his nose, and Jason places his mouth against her palm instead, nibbling the center and making her giggle.

Cue Kayla swooning into a puddle under the booth.

Finally, our food comes, and seeing my tortillas are missing —the bitch probably didn't even put the order in for them— Jason asks the manager to bring me some. It's so nice having someone look out for me for a change. His consideration doesn't seem fake at all. He genuinely *wanted* to feed Josalyn. He didn't do it just to impress me. That's not who Jason is. He doesn't do things to look good for other people. He only does something if he really wants to, out of the goodness of his heart.

The rest of the meal is perfect, and we follow it up with dessert before Jason pays the bill and we stand to leave. I hand him his black pea coat from beside me, and he puts it on before sliding Josalyn's carrier out of the booth. I follow behind them and my heart clenches at the sight. Quickly, I pull my digital camera out of my purse and snap a picture of the sweet scene: Jason looking manly and sophisticated in his structured wool coat, contrasting adorably with Josalyn's baby pink car seat as he carries her effortlessly with one hand.

I pull my jacket more tightly around me, and when I glance up to see Jason has turned to reach into the diaper bag hanging on my shoulder to pull out Josalyn's blanket, I come ridiculously close to crying as he tucks it around her. As if I could love him any more than I already did, I feel my heart grow an extra chamber for paternal Jason. After watching over his shoulder as he buckles her into the car flawlessly, when he closes the door, I grab him by the bicep, turn him around, and use every ounce of my much smaller body to shove him up against the car. I feel absolutely savage as I wrap myself around him, and within seconds, I don't feel the slightest bit chilly. I kiss him with a passion I'd forgotten I could possess, throwing every bit of the new level of love I feel for him into the embrace.

I don't let him go until he finally starts to gently push at my shoulders and begins to chuckle, and when I do begrudgingly release him, I'm breathing heavy, little puffs of white forming before me with each exhale.

"Woman, if you don't control yourself, I'm going to end up bending you over the trunk of the car, and that's not the way I want to have you for the first time as my girl. Plus, the baby is rear-facing, and I don't want to scar her for life," he jokes, bending his head down to kiss me lightly on the lips before sliding out from between me and the door. I watch him circle the car, feeling like a cat ready to pounce, but as he opens his door and disappears inside, I snap out of it and get in my side.

CHAPTER Six

We spend the next couple of hours walking around Baybrook Mall, Jason carrying Josalyn most of the time since I didn't think to bring her stroller. The view is an ovary explosion. There's nothing sexier than my hot-ass boyfriend holding my sweet-faced baby girl.

There's no hesitation from either of them. Josalyn has taken to Jason like he's been around her every day since the day she was born, and Jason holds her with a confidence I don't think even he realized he had. I say this, because when we were standing in line for a pretzel and lemonade, he told me, "I'm usually kinda nervous holding people's kids, but I really like carrying this little turd." And then he pressed his lips to the side of her neck and blew a raspberry, making her cackle and wiggle in his arms. "Plus, she smells really good."

"I use Johnson's lavender bubble bath on her. I catch myself doing lines of baby smell off the top of her head all the time." I grinned when he laughed heartily. It always feels so accomplishing whenever I can make Jason really laugh.

But now, as we pull into his driveway and I see his mom's maroon Toyota Highlander in her garage bay, my heart thumps with a mixture of anticipation and nervousness. Will she treat me as she always had, welcoming me into her home with open arms? Or, now that I'm dating her son, will she be more critical of me? I haven't made the brightest decisions over the past couple of years. Will she judge me for them?

Jason reaches over and squeezes my knee, seeing my hesitation. "She's really excited to see you, babe. Don't worry."

I nod and let out a breath, opening my door and moving to get Josalyn, but Jason playfully jumps in front of me, shuffling backwards bent at the waist to move me away with his ass. "That's my job." He winks at me over his shoulder and the butterflies in my belly take flight. I could definitely get used to this.

Before we even reach the door inside the garage, it swings inward, and there stands his mom, in all her barely five-foot glory, looking exactly the same as she did years ago, her hair in its pixie cut, her makeup all done, and still dressed in the nice business casual outfit she wore to work. With more strength than you'd think her tiny body would have, she pulls me in for a giant bear hug, squeezing the breath right out of me.

"It's about time you got here, girl. I snuck out early, because I couldn't wait to see you and the baby!" She lets me go and turns to Jason, who's holding Josalyn's carrier on his forearm, making faces at her and then returning her smile. "Now let me see this precious little thing."

Within a few seconds, Mrs. Robichaux has Josalyn unbuckled from her car seat and in her arms, propping her up on her hip and turning to walk back into the house. I glance up at Jason and give him a relieved smile. Like the whirlwind I remember, by the time Jason and I get all the bags and the carrier set down in his room and return to the living room, his mom already has Josalyn out of her hoodie and is dancing around the coffee table with her, oldies music playing over their surround sound as his dad taps his foot to the beat in his recliner.

I grin at Josalyn's open-mouthed smile, her giggles doing even more to fill me with relief. She's usually pretty friendly with strangers, but there's not even a smidge of shyness in her demeanor as Mrs. Robichaux spins her around the room to "Hooked on a Feeling" by Blue Swede.

Jason takes my hand and tugs me over to the long green couch facing the TV, plopping down then pulling me down next to him, securing me to his side with his arm around my shoulders. It feels surreal sitting with him like this in the first place, but doing it in front of his parents? It feels even crazier. I mean, we were always pretty openly affectionate in front of them before, but nothing platonic friends wouldn't do. A hug here, playful wrestling there. But snuggled up tight against his delicious body, his arm possessively holding me to him, that's a different story. From the outside, there would be no question if we were together, a couple, not just friends. Surprisingly, I don't feel awkward in the least. It feels too amazing for Jason to openly be staking his claim on me to feel anything but loved.

Jason's dad starts up a conversation with his son about some rifle he's thinking about adding to his collection, and I take in how relaxed and normal this all feels, watching his mom continue to dance with Josalyn as Blue Swede ends and The Marvelettes begin singing "Please, Mr. Postman".

After a couple more songs, Mrs. Robichaux drops down onto the couch beside me and sits Josalyn on her knees facing her, holding onto her hands and bouncing her legs. The baby giggles as I start singing, "Ride, ride, ride that horsey..." as Granny always does, and Jason's mom leans forward and leaves a coral lipstick kiss mark on her plump cheek.

"So how was the trip?" she asks, still bouncing Josalyn on her knees.

"A lot less stressful than I thought it would be. She slept the whole time, out like a light as soon as we took off," I tell her.

"What have y'all been up to today? Did you get here pretty early?"

"I got here right when Jason got out of school. We went and had some lunch at TGI Fridays and then just walked around the mall. It's so much bigger than the one in Fayetteville. Way more stores. I had to contain myself." I laugh.

"Jason said you'd be leaving before dark, so I tried to get here as soon as I could so I could spend some time with this sweet baby I keep seeing pictures of," she says, tickling Josalyn's belly and making her cackle. "And of course you, my dear." She reaches over and pats my leg.

"Oh, don't worry. I'm used to being an afterthought nowadays. Everyone always goes straight for the baby, and then

I get the consolation hugs."

"I remember it being that way too when we finally got Jason. We tried so long to get pregnant, and then when we adopted him, everyone was so thrilled to have another baby in the family that they were always fighting over who got to hold him," she replies, stretching her arm behind me to tug on Jason's ear.

He swats at her hand playfully, growling, "Stop that," when she pulls a few more times.

I glance at the time on the grandfather clock against the far wall, seeing it's 4:30 p.m. I should probably feed Josalyn again before we leave in about an hour. I don't want to wait until we get to my brother's, because I don't want her to be fussy on the drive back. She'll more than likely fall asleep after I feed her, since she hasn't taken a nap since we got to Friendswood.

"Can I use your room to nurse Josalyn?" I ask Jason quietly. I don't want anyone to feel awkward by breastfeeding her in the living room.

"You don't have to hide, babe," Jason tells me, but seeing the uncomfortable look on my face, he nods. "Of course you can use my room, but I'm coming with you. You're not leaving my side the whole time you're here. I don't care what you say."

"What if I have to pee?" I joke, standing from the couch and grasping Josalyn under her arms when Mrs. Robichaux lifts her up to me.

"I'll be there to squirt soap into your hands, like one of those bathroom attendants at the bar," he asserts, making me snort.

"That's not creepy at all," I say sarcastically, but I can't help the smile pulling at my lips that he wants to spend every minute he can with me, because I feel the same way. It's how I always felt when I lived in Texas too. It's why I never thought twice about the long drive every day to come see him. It was worth every second of the stressful route, every cent I scraped together for gas, and every hour of sleep I lost going home at such a late—or technically early—hour before having to make it to school shortly thereafter. I would do it all again in a heartbeat, even knowing how things ended up, because this moment makes it all worthwhile.

"Do you want to sit on the bed or the couch?" Jason asks as we enter his bedroom.

"I'll take the couch," I reply. The armrest looks plush and comfy. It'll be nice to rest my elbow on while she nurses. Plus, a part of me wants to save his bed for just us, to keep it for more intimate and fun activities.

"Do you need anything?" he asks, seeming a little lost as he turns around in circles, not knowing where to look.

"Could you hand me the baby blanket out of her car seat?" I can't help the smile tugging at my lips as I sit down on the far end of the couch, next to his closet. He looks adorable as his slight awkwardness turns into relief, having been given a task. Sitting Josalyn on my lap, I unbutton the four buttons of my thermal Henley and then reach through the open neckline to pull my sports bra's elastic above my right breast, keeping myself still completely covered with the fabric of my shirt. When he hands me the blanket, I lie Josalyn back into the crook of my elbow, cover us up with the soft cotton material, and then using my left hand, I move my shirt out of the way, feeling my girl immediately latch on, never exposing even an inch of skin. We might have had a rough start with the whole breastfeeding thing, but we have it down to an unconscious science now.

I scoot my butt down a little on the black leather cushion and get comfortable, knowing I'll be here for the next twenty minutes, and then glance up at Jason, who is still standing next to me, a confused look on his face.

"What's wrong?" I ask him, glancing down to make sure she hasn't pulled the blanket out of the way. The little turd has done it before, so I hope she spares me the embarrassment this time. I know I shouldn't feel any type of shame for feeding my daughter, and I really don't. But I'm the girl who used to dress out for gym in school in the girls' bathroom because I was too shy to do it in the locker room. I can count on one hand how many people have actually seen my boobs, even though my sexual partner count is a couple hands higher than that. It's the part of my body I will probably always be self-conscious about, no matter how cool it is I've been able to keep a baby alive with them for nearly nine months. Super useful as they are, I'll never be happy with the way they look, so covered they will stay. Jason's the only person who even remotely made me feel comfortable with my small breasts, so I want him to continue to see them as a sensual part of my body, not as a functional one.

I'm still draped with the baby blanket, so I look back up to him with a questioning expression.

"That's it?" He tilts his head to the side, lowering his brow.

"What do you mean?"

"Like, I expected the set up and stuff to be a lot more difficult and to at least catch a glimpse of a titty. That took like two seconds, and you can't see a thing. What's the big deal?" he asks.

I force myself to stifle the laugh wanting to burst out of me. I don't want to startle Josalyn and make her unlatch. "Sorry to disappoint. It just makes some people uncomfortable being around it, so I spare everyone the awkwardness and do it privately. Even when they can't see anything, just knowing it's happening can freak people out." I shrug my left shoulder, since she's cradled in my right arm.

"Fuck those people. Let anybody say anything to you about it while I'm around," he grumbles, making me grin.

"That's exactly why I do it in private, so I don't ever have to worry about that. Plus, there's the added benefit of getting some quiet time. If I get overwhelmed and just want to be alone, then all I have to say is I gotta go feed the baby. Boom, instant scapegoat. Sure, I'm not really alone," I pat Josalyn's diaper-covered bottom, "but it's close enough."

"You okay with me sitting beside you, or should I get on the bed?" he asks cautiously.

"Of course you can sit next to me, silly," I giggle.

"Good." He sits as close to me as possible without actually sitting on my lap, sliding his arm behind my lower back and using his strong hand to cup my right hip and pull me against him once again. He uses the remote to turn on TruTV, and we spend the next fifteen minutes laughing at *The World's Dumbest Criminals*. It takes me a while to realize Josalyn has stopped suckling, enjoying the relaxed easiness of being snuggled up to Jason and doing something so domestic as watching TV while feeding the baby. But when I do, and I pull my sports bra back down beneath my shirt and remove the blanket, I see Josalyn has gone into a milk coma, breathing deeply, her mouth wide open, milk dribbling out of the corner of her lips.

I giggle, pulling Jason's attention from the show, and when he sees what I'm softly laughing at, he leans closer to look down into her sleeping face. "She looks shwasted," he whispers, making me cover my mouth with my palm so I don't wake her up. My body shakes with my laughter, but I manage to keep from making a sound. "Do you want to lay her down?" he asks quietly.

I nod, and he takes my left hand and pulls me up from the couch. I lay her in the middle of his bed on her side, and then smile at Jason's fascinated face when I slide one of his pillows under his fitted sheet, creating a makeshift bumper so she doesn't roll off.

"You seriously know all sorts of tricks, huh?" He sounds proud as he pulls me down onto his lap on the couch.

"You learn things to make life a little easier after you have a baby. But then there's all sorts of shit you think you need before you have them, and then never end up using it too, though. Like a baby bathtub? I got one for my baby shower, and ended up only using it once. It's much easier, and a lot less painful for your back, just to bathe them in the kitchen sink."

He threads his fingers into my hair and pulls me down for a kiss, and as if we do it every day, he turns our bodies and stretches out, and we finish watching the rest of the show.

When it's over, Josalyn is still sleeping deeply, so I set up the baby monitor I had stuffed into her diaper bag before I left

Tony's, taking the white handheld device with us as we go into the kitchen, where his mom is fixing dinner. Glancing out the window, I see it's already starting to get dark, but I just can't bring myself to leave yet. I might as well wait until it's late enough so not that many cars will be on the road. Plus, I can always drive in the far right lane; that way, the headlights coming from the opposite direction won't mess with me so much.

"You better get t'goin', honey. It's almost full dark already," Mrs. Robichaux says as she opens a can of corn and pours it into a pot on the stove.

"Josalyn is taking a nap right now. I think I'll be fine as long as I wait until rush hour is over. With the concrete wall between north and southbound, headlights shouldn't bother me too badly," I reply.

"Well, call your momma and let her know, since she's probably expecting you to be home soon."

"Yes, ma'am." I smile at Jason, seeing him roll his eyes. I use the phone on the kitchen counter to call her quickly, telling her I'll be home later than expected. After repeatedly assuring her I'll be fine in the dark, I finally have to cut her off, telling her dinner is ready and I have to go. I swear to God she makes me feel twelve, when I'm a twenty-three year old woman with a child of my own. But at the same time, I wouldn't have her any other way. She's the best mother anyone could ever ask for.

"Are you guys hungry?" his mom asks.

"I'm still pretty full from lunch, and then we had the big pretzel at the mall. Thanks, though, Mrs. Robichaux."

"Oh, stop it with all that Mrs. Robichaux nonsense. Call me

either Barbara or Mom. I've known you too damn long for you to be so formal," she reprimands, making me grin up at Jason again, who leans down to kiss my cheek before moving to the refrigerator in the utility room.

"You want something to drink, babe?" he asks, bending down to grab himself a Coke from the bottom shelf.

I peek around him to see what they have and ask him for one of the Gatorades in the door. I haven't had a soda since before I found out I was pregnant. The carbonation gives me heartburn just thinking about it now.

We sit down at the kitchen table to sip on our drinks, and when Barbara is finished stirring each of the three pots heating on the stove, she comes to sit with us, wiping her hands on a dishtowel.

"So, little lady, imagine my surprise when my womanizing son here told me he had asked you to be his girlfriend," she exhorts, making me choke on my Gatorade. My eyes cut between her and Jason then back again, not knowing how to reply. "I remember y'all being very close, the best of friends, but never once did I ever catch wind of you having feelings for each other. Did you date when you lived here?"

"Mom, we've been over th—" Jason gripes, but his mom cuts him off.

"I know your side of the story, but now I want to hear hers."

I swallow, feeling a little panicky, because I'm not positive what Jason has told her about our past. I shoot him an anxious look, but all he does is shrug. What the hell does that mean?

"We didn't *date*, exactly. Um... we, uh... I had a huge crush on him, and he was my best friend, and we... um—"

"Y'all were friends with benefits," she supplies, and I feel my face grow extremely hot.

I clear my throat and shift in my seat. "I would have given anything to be his girlfriend, but he never asked, so I took what I could get, yes," I confirm.

"When you first started coming over, weren't you dating Gavin?" she inquires.

"I went on a couple of dates with him, but I wouldn't say we were dating. We weren't an exclusive couple or anything. And to be perfectly honest, I only talked to him for as long as I did so I could hang out with Jason," I confess. "But then Gavin pulled that crap, telling me I wasn't allowed to come see y'all."

"Oh, I remember that now. Is that why you and Gavin stopped talking for a little bit after she moved back to North Carolina?" she asks Jason.

"Partly," he replies. "I was hung up on her, and it felt really strange, for the both of us, for me to be down in the dumps over a girl he had gone out with, so we kind of stopped hanging out for a while."

My head snaps up in his direction. This is all news to me.

Barbara catches my surprise and confirms, "Oh, yeah, honey. He was miserable to be around when you left. I thought he was just sad to have his friend move away, or that maybe he and Gavin had a fight or something, but it makes much more sense now, knowing it was because the girl he was in love with had moved home. We could barely stand to be around him. Worried us for a little while, going out and drinking all the time. And then he met that awful girl—"

"Mom," Jason growls, interrupting her.

"What awful girl?" It slips out without my permission. I don't really want to know anything that went on during the time we weren't together. Even though I was married to someone else, I don't want to think about Jason being with other people.

"Don't worry about it, babe. None of that matters now," he says, reaching beneath the table and squeezing my knee.

I change the subject. "Do you have a piece of paper I can use? I have something to show you. I don't think even Jason has figured it out yet." I give him a nervous smile as Barbara grabs a pad of paper and a pen from the kitchen counter. I take the pen and write out Josalyn's name in all caps, and underneath it the same way, I write out Jason's. I set the pen down and turn the pad towards them, holding my breath while they read what I wrote.

His mom slides her glasses onto her nose from where they dangled on a chain around her neck, taking the edge of the pad in her hand to tilt it at a better angle. I don't even have to look at Jason to know he's staring at me. I can feel the heat of his gaze boring into me, making my neck grow hot and tingly. He finally spotted it.

"I guess I'm not figuring out the puzzle, sweetie. What is it?" Barbara asks.

"You might not have known this before, but I've always loved your son, since practically the day I met him, and every single day since. Even when I thought I'd never see him again, and definitely never thought I'd get to be with him, I wanted a piece of him with me always. If you look at the letters in Josalyn's name, you'll see Jason's rearranged," I reveal, my voice cautiously low, unknowing what her reaction will be. I still can't bring myself to even glance at Jason quite yet.

She takes the long nail of her pointer finger and slides it across the paper, matching each letter up between the two names, and then looks up at me, pulling her glasses off her face. Her face blank, she stands, and my heart drops. I brace myself as she walks around to my side of the table, and flinch when she shakes the pad of paper out of my hands, it landing on the table with an audible plop. But then she takes my hands in hers and, with that same surprising strength in her half-foot shorter body, pulls me out of my seat and wraps her arms around me.

I breathe out a sigh of relief and return her hug as I feel her tremble against me and hear a light sob. After a few moments, she pulls back and kisses me on the cheek, smiling as the tears fall down her made-up cheeks.

"I really had no idea. Y'all hid your feelings really well. But all I've ever wanted is for my boy to find a good girl who truly loves *him,* so what better person for him to be with than his best friend?" she surmises, and all I can do is smile.

I'm scared to death to look at Jason. His mom's reaction was exactly what I was hoping for, but I have no clue how he's taking it. Does he think I'm a creeper for naming my little girl after him? Does he find it in bad taste that I named another man's child after the man I truly wanted to be with? I mean, I didn't do it as a 'fuck you' to Aiden or anything. I did it for the exact reason I just told her, because I had wanted a small part of my soul mate to be with me, even if it was only in a name I'd say daily. It had been my little secret up until now; it wasn't something I flaunted. So I hope he knows that he was that important to me, so significant to me that I'd name my own flesh and blood after the man I loved with every inch of my heart.

But as always, he can read me as easily as a large-print book, and the next thing I know, I'm spun out of his mom's embrace and enveloped in the one I never want to leave for the rest of my life. With seemingly no care given for present company seeing the affectionate display, he cups my jaw in one of his hands, tilts my face up to his, and kisses me, right in front of his mom. I can't help but giggle, because I, on the other hand, am painfully aware of the other person in the room, and so I break the kiss and tuck myself shyly against his chest until my embarrassment fades enough that I can breathe correctly again. I'm just relieved he evidently likes the little secret I just revealed to them.

Barbara pulls two tissues out of the box on the counter, lifts her glasses off her nose, and wipes under her eyes, sniffing once before letting out a short laugh. She moves back over to the stove, and after stirring one last time, she turns the burners off, yelling to Steve, "Dinner's ready!" then turning to ask me, "You sure you don't want anything? There's plenty."

I come to stand beside her, taking a peek at what she had fixed. I sniff, and it smells delicious, but I have no idea what it is.

"It's shrimp creole," she supplies, but at my still-iffy face, she elaborates, "It's a little spicy, but not too hot, because I can't eat stuff that's too spicy. It's tomato based, and you serve it on top of rice."

"I've never tried it. I'll take a little bit. I'll try anything once,"

I say. Even though I wasn't hungry before, the scent is making my stomach growl.

"If you like it a little spicier, like Steve does, we have a bunch of different hot sauces in the door of the fridge," she offers.

"Oh, no thanks. I'm like you. I can't handle spicy. I craved spicy chicken sandwiches from Chick Fil A a couple times while I was pregnant, but let's just say that didn't end well," I tell her, shaking my head.

I end up scarfing down two giant bowls full of the Cajun dish, Steve chuckling when I asked if I could have seconds. "No one can ever resist Momma's shrimp creole. Have all you want."

Jason also goes up for seconds, adding a little bit of hot sauce to his. Even without the added heat, I've gone through a couple tissues, my nose running and the back of my neck sweating, making me giggle. "I guess I'm not much of a masochist." At Jason's questioning smile, I explain, "I learned in my college course that liking spicy food is psychological. People who love it actually get pleasure from the pain."

We both laugh when we glance over at his dad as he shakes a ridiculous amount of hot sauce onto the top of his freshly filled bowl. When he looks up, continuing to cover the food in red sauce, he quips, "Oh, I've always enjoyed a good spanking," and I nearly fall out of my seat from laughing so hard.

Suddenly I hear Josalyn start to make little dinosaur noises as she wakes up from her nap, and as I stand to go clean out my bowl, Jason rests his hand on my wrist, telling me he'll take care of it while I go get the baby. I catch a glimpse of his mom's pride-filled face before I leave the kitchen.

I walk into his room just as Josalyn tries to sit up in the middle of the bed, but it's so soft that she topples back over, making her grunt in frustration. I reach out and pick her up, placing her on my hip and kissing her when she looks up at me with a sleepy smile.

Carrying her into the kitchen and sitting back in my chair, when she sees Jason next to us, she reaches out and makes grabby hands, and my heart swells when he hurriedly takes our bowls to the sink then comes back to us, picking her up off my lap and folding his arms around her. She lets out a dramatic sigh and lays her head on his shoulder, blinking down at me, not quite fully awake yet. He turns his head to press his nose into her hair, and I hear him breathe deeply. I lock gazes with his mom, and I can tell she's feeling as deeply moved by the scene as I am. This has got to feel just as surreal to her, seeing her bad boy son melt into a puddle at the feet of an eight-month-old. She doesn't say anything, probably not wanting to break the moment, but she reaches out and pats my cheek before standing to take her own bowl to the sink.

About an hour later, I think it's probably safe for me to make my way back across town to my brother's house. We make plans for Jason to come pick me up tomorrow after he gets out of class, but he refuses to tell me what we're going to go do. He tells me to just dress in jeans, nothing fancy, but that's the only clue I get.

After strapping Josalyn into the back seat of my rental, Jason kisses me before I get into the driver seat. He tells me to call him as soon as I get to my brother's house to let him know I made it.

Forty-five minutes later, I pull into Tony's driveway. I call Jason as promised, tell him I can't wait until tomorrow, and then we hang up. It was much different spending time with him with Josalyn present. She seemed to help tame the crazy sexual tension between the two of us, keeping us in check. But God only knows what it'll be like tomorrow, when I'm baby free and all his for an entire afternoon and evening.

CHAPTER Seven

My heart pounds when I see his Altima pull into the driveway outside my brother's house. Not only am I excited-slash-terrified of this evening's activities, but this is a big moment in itself. Jason is about to meet part of my family.

I watch from the living room as he exits his car and passes by the front windows, and then hear him knock on the door. I jump up to let him in, not able to make him wait, anticipation be damned. When I pull open the door, I take in all his Texan badass glory, from his scuffed and broken-in brown cowboy boots, up his dark blue jeans barely containing the muscled thighs beneath the rough fabric, over the soft-looking red plaid shirt that wraps snuggly around his tattooed biceps, and finally land on his scruff-covered handsome face.

Clench.

"Um, babe. Can I come in? Kinda chilly out here," he says through a smirk.

"Oh! Yeah, sorry. You just look... yeah." I step back and open the door wider, allowing him into the foyer before I close it behind him. When I turn around, he wraps his arm around my lower back, pulling me to him.

He sighs into my neck, "Mmm, you're warm. And you smell good."

I don't care what anyone says. It's way hotter getting complimented on your scent than on the way you look. There's something so carnal about someone liking your aroma so much that they take the time to comment on it. Maybe I'm weird. Wait... that's already established.

"Thank you. Now, c'mere. I can't wait for you to meet my mom!" I pry him off of me, giggling when he tries to wrap himself back around me, but then he gives in and lets me take his hand to lead him into the kitchen, where Mom, Tony, and Buffy are sitting at the dining table nibbling on some fresh fruit. It was seriously the first time I'd seen an actual pineapple get cut up before. Buffy laughed at me while my mouth hung open in fascination as it went from giant spiky fruit to little yellow chunks of tangy deliciousness. I always just had the canned kind.

When we enter, Mom turns around in her seat and looks up at us, a smile splitting her face. She stands and comes to wrap Jason up in a tight hug, pulling back to tell him, "It's so nice to finally meet you." Then she rears back and punches him in the arm, making me yelp, "Mom!" as Jason rubs at the spot on his bicep.

"That's for breaking my baby's heart, you devil," she growls with narrowed eyes, poking her finger into his chest that's at her eye-level. And then she gives him another hug, conceding, "But I've never seen her happier than in the past couple of months. So I guess I forgive you."

"Wow, that was the strangest meeting of The Mom I've ever been through," Jason says with a chuckle then reaches out to shake Tony's proffered hand.

"Good to meet you, man. My sis talked about you all the time when she lived here," Tony tells him then turns to the blonde next to him. "This is my girlfriend Buffy." Jason shakes her hand and then they all sit back down in their seats.

"Where is Josalyn?" Jason asks, glancing around the kitchen.

"She's in the playpen in the living room," I reply, hitching my thumb over my shoulder in her direction, and I smile when he immediately heads that way. I follow him, my heart thumping as he walks up to the Pack 'n Play and gets down on his haunches to be face-to-face with my babbling baby girl. When she sees him, she crawls the short space over to the side, reaches up to grip the top, and pulls herself up to stand right in front of him.

"Hey, pretty girl," I hear him tell her, and I laugh when she starts bouncing, bending her knees and standing up straight over and over again as she lets out a shrill squeal before plopping down on her diaper-cushioned butt.

"Well, alrighty then. Does that mean you're happy to see me?" he asks her, standing and reaching in to pick her up. And just like yesterday, she grips the collar of his plaid shirt, leans back to get a good look at him, and then reaches up to latch onto his nose. He laughs and then makes a loud elephant sound with his mouth, making her jump. I brace myself, waiting to see which direction she'll go, either bursting out into tears or laughter, and I grin when she chooses the latter.

I come to stand next to them and lift up on my tiptoes, leaning in to give her kisses on her cheeks and mouth, using the back of my hand to wipe off the drool left on my lips. "You be a good girl for MomMom, okay? Mommy will see you for your 3:00 a.m. feeding," I coo at her, and she answers with, "Ma-ma-ma-ma-ma-ma," while flapping her hands, settling down enough to grasp ahold of Jason's nose again.

He sets her on her feet inside the playpen and waves at her, and she does her backward wave in return, saying, "Baaaa-ba. Baaaa-ba."

"That's right, Tooty. Bye-bye," I say, and we go back into the kitchen to let everyone know we're leaving. Tony gives me a key to get back in the house in case they're already in bed when I get home tonight, and then we head out the door.

"So now will you tell me where we're going?" I ask Jason, tucking one leg up underneath me in the leather bucket seat.

"First, we're going out to eat. Then we're going to our old haunt and playing a couple games of pool. But the rest is a surprise," he teases, and I shake my head, giving him a mock-pout. I look at the time, seeing it's only 2:30 p.m.

"It's kind of an odd time to eat. Do you want to kill some time before dinner?" I ask.

"What did you have in mind?" he rumbles, lifting his eyebrow and cutting his eye over to me briefly as he merges onto 59 South.

"I don't know. Maybe watch a movie at your house or something until around five-ish?" I suggest.

"If I take you back to my house to watch a movie, it's going to end up like every other time we tried back in the day. I'll end up pulling the 'just the tip' trick, and then after you've had about five orgasms and gain your composure, I'll get blamed for making you miss the movie." He smirks.

"But it is your fault I miss the movie. If you would keep those talented idle hands of yours to yourself, we wouldn't have to play it twice in order to watch it once!" I scoff. When he looks over at me, I grin, letting him know I never minded one bit when showtime went from meaning when the film would begin, to when a whole different kind of action started. "Okay, probably bad timing for that, being in the middle of the afternoon and all. Sooo... how about we go see one, like at a theater?"

"And what happened last time we tried to see a movie in a theater, babe?" He chuckles.

I narrow my eyes, boring a hole into the side of his handsome face. "I ended up missing that one too, because we made out like teenagers in the back row the whole movie."

"So the lesson of the story is...?" he prompts.

"It's pointless for us to try to watch movies together?" I fill in.

"Ding-ding-ding! So, what else do you want to do?"

"Ugh! Well, I guess let's just stick to your original plan and go eat, and then go play pool super early. It's going to be weird getting there at like six. Are they even open then?" I question.

"Babe. Calm. Just relax. You don't have to plan everything out. Let's just have a good time and see where the night leads us," he drawls deeply, reaching over to rest his hand in the crook of my folded leg.

I sit back in my seat and let out a huff of air. I hate it when people tell me that. I don't have it in me not to try to schedule everything. I might be able to control not voicing it, but my brain doesn't know how to just 'go with the flow'. In my head, if there are things I definitely want to do, if I don't set up allotted times to do them, then I could miss getting them done. Like on vacation, I like to have an itinerary. If we're at the beach, but this place is only open for certain hours, I'm going to be pissed if I miss getting to go there, just because I was being forced to relax and not plan things out. But for Jason, I will let him take the lead. It doesn't sound like we're doing anything that needs to be put on a tight schedule, and I'm baby free for the rest of the day, so I decide to do my best and relax.

We pull into Chili's right across the highway from Legend's Billiards in Webster about half an hour later, and after a few drinks, some salsa and tortilla chips, and a bacon cheeseburger later, we head to our favorite pool hall.

It's still light outside, so it's very strange when Jason opens the big wooden door and we walk in, seeing it looks exactly the same inside as it does late at night. A couple things have changed, but not much. There is a new arcade game when you first walk in, and to the right, they've added a new big-screen TV. Looking at the tables, I have a flashback of Jason and me sitting at one, talking about his doctor appointment he'd had that day, long before we had taken our friendship to the next level. The PA had hit on him, asking him for his number. I played it cool, asking if he thought she was cute and if he had given it to her. I sniff out a silent laugh remembering his answer. "Nah, too skinny. You know me. I like my girls thick."

The fucker.

I didn't have a clue. He had me going for so long, believing I never stood a chance, that he'd never find me attractive, because I'd never be the body type he was attracted to. Until he finally confessed it was all bullshit, lies he fed me so he wouldn't steal me from his best friend. And little did he know at the time that he had stolen my attention the moment I met him.

Jason laces his fingers through mine, pulling me back to the present and toward the bar. "What do you want, baby?"

"I think I'll stick to what I was having at Chili's, if they can make it," I reply in front of the bartender.

"What were you drinking over there? I can pretty much duplicate anything if you know what was in it," the bartender offers.

"I was having the Tropical—"

"Tropical Sunrise? On it. It's my girlfriend's favorite, so I had to figure it out for her," he says, already three ingredients into making my drink before he finished his sentence. A few seconds later, he shakes it up and pours it into a large glass, topping it off with a straw and a slice of orange. "Try that. See what you think."

I take a sip and moan, "Nailed it," nodding and taking another swig.

The bartender smiles and slaps the top of the counter in triumph. "What about you, Jason. Same as always?"

"Yup, I'll take my Seven, please, and a rack of balls," he responds, and with his drink in one hand and the tray of colorful pool balls in the other, we make our way to the left side of the bar, sitting everything next to a pool table I've never played on before. We always used to play on the right side of the bar for some reason.

"God, I haven't played in forever," I confess, chalking up the end of the cue Jason hands me.

"Yeah, me neither," Jason says dryly.

"*Psh!* I know your games, you hustler. Plus, the bartender knows you by name." If I have any chance of winning, I'm going to have to break out my old tricks of distraction; otherwise, there's no way he'll miss a shot unless he does it on purpose, which he knows makes me crazy.

I swish my ass as I round the pool table, and when I turn to face him, propping my hip next to one of the corner pockets, it's my turn to smirk when his eyes lift from my tight destructed blue jeans to my face, heat sizzling in their chocolaty depths.

Momma's still got it.

He keeps his stare locked with mine as he bends forward and lines up his cue, landing the shot blindly, never once glancing away from me. I bite my lip, remembering the times he used the Drive-and-Stare on me. Dear Lord, he's sexy as fuck. And right when I put a score mark under my name in this silent little game we're playing, Jason one-ups me yet again.

"Oh, yeah, you're so rusty. Maybe you should take a couple practice shots," I snark, rolling my eyes and trying to look cooler than I feel, because on the inside, I feel my temperature rising to a level I can't ignore.

With my back to him as I take a sip of my drink at the small bistro table against the wall while he takes his next shot, I reach down into my pretty pink bra and lift my boobs up inside the cups, making cleavage, showing off the little bit larger-than-normal tatas I've had since breastfeeding. They're not nearly as big as they were when I was pregnant, but they're a full cup larger than what I had before that though, so I plan to use them to my advantage while I still have them.

I turn back around to face him, arching my back and not making eye contact with him as I pull my long dark hair high up into a ponytail, feeling the heat of his stare the whole time, and then a volcano blast of sexual tension as I tug my V-neck heather-grey T-shirt back into place. I toy with my necklace as an excuse to look down and make sure the tops of my girls are in plain sight, smiling to myself when I see they are in perfect position.

You're going down, Robichaux.

Just then, he tries a bank shot that narrowly misses going into a side pocket, and the cue ball rolls until it stops right in front of Jason.

Perfect, I think smugly, and I stroll over to him, my stick in hand, slide between the pool table and his front, and bend over, using my ass to back him up so I can line up my shot. I feel his hand come up to squeeze my left hip and hear him groan, making the little devil on my shoulder smile with glee, but then he moves away, going over to take a sip of his mixed drink. I sink one of my solids, but miss the next shot. I've always sucked at side pockets.

I walk over to where Jason still stands by the table holding our drinks, and that's when I notice the pack of cigarettes in his hand. Groaning, I sink down into one of the chairs. I saw this standup show once, where comedian Rob White talks about drinking and smoking. He made the perfect analogy. He said it was just like pooping and peeing. You can pee without pooping, but you can't poop without peeing. Just like you can smoke without drinking, but you can't drink without smoking. Vulgar, but oh so very true.

With the tequila running through my veins at the moment, his cigarettes are looking mighty nice. I haven't had one since I found out I was pregnant with Josalyn, but as he lifts one to his sexy lips and lights it, blowing out a stream of smoke toward the ceiling, I have absolutely no willpower to fight the urge. I reach out and steal the cigarette from between his fingers, placing it to my lips. Dear God, it's exquisite.

Hello, old friend. How I've missed you.

"Sorry, babe. I tried. But the drinkin' we're doing... I can't *not* smoke," he tells me regretfully.

"It's no big deal. I have friends who only smoke when they drink. I'm gonna have to scrub every inch of myself before I hold Josalyn, but I'm sure I'm going to need a shower after tonight anyways," I allude, lifting a brow in his direction.

"Oh, yeah? Why's that?" he coaxes, lighting himself another cigarette since I'm not giving him this one back.

"Because I plan on getting very dirty with you," I breathe, and I manage to hold a straight face for a full ten seconds before I burst out laughing. "Oh, my God. That was so fucking corny. I should be ashamed of myself. I need another drink." I swallow the last of my fruity drink, making a loud sucking sound when my straw hits nothing but ice and air. He chuckles and lifts my glass out of my hand, leaving me long enough to return with it freshly filled.

"You always were my favorite," I say, taking a swig of the yummy concoction. I hollow out my cheeks, shaking my head and squeezing my eyes shut tight. "Hoo-ahhh... that's much stronger when it doesn't have melted ice diluting it. That, and this is the most I've had to drink in almost eighteen months. Looks like my little one will be getting a bottle in the middle of the night."

"Yeah, that's going to be your last one for a while. It's barely dark outside, and we still have a whole night of fun to get through," he tells me, and I squint one eye as I look up at him, take a dramatic pull off my cigarette, and blow it up in his direction.

"It's your turn, sugar tits," I chide, and he laughs and bends down, mumbling against my lips, "Hey, that's my line," before going to make his shot.

CHAPTER Eight

The next couple of hours continue this way, only he refills my cup with ice water instead of alcohol. He's actually impressed with the amount of water I take down, considering before I got pregnant I drank water only if I was about to die of thirst. I couldn't stand that crap. We flirt openly the whole time, which is a new experience in itself, since we used to hide our affection for each other when we'd go out. And by the time he pays for our pool time and our tab, I'm ready to molest him in his car.

I lunge across his center console, locking my thin arms around his neck and forcing him back against the headrest as my lips seal themselves to his. I ungracefully manage to get my right knee on the other side of his hips and pull my left leg over to squeeze between his and the belt buckle. It's a tight fit, but as he reaches down beside his door and pushes the button to make his seat lie back, the steering wheel removes itself from my back and I'm able to get comfortable.

His hands grip my hips and then slide up underneath the hem of my shirt, coming to rest on the sensitive skin of my sides. The heat radiating from his palms both soothes and entices me, causing me to grind against him. I can't even remember the last time I was this turned on.

His lips feel perfect beneath mine, and his hands begin to stroke up and down my spine, causing goose bumps to spread across my flesh. The seam of my jeans rubs against my already soaked underwear, rubbing that perfect spot, and I have the fleeting thought that I'm going to leave a wet spot on the front of his pants and make him look like he peed himself, causing me to sit up on my knees and let out a sound between a gasp and a laugh.

"What's wrong?" Jason rumbles, pulling the tie from around my ponytail, threading his fingers up the back of my hair, and trying to pull me back down to kiss him, but my legs are pretty strong and I lock them in place.

"I... uh, where are we going after this?" I prompt.

"You're on top of me in my car, dry humping me until my eyes are rolling back in my head, and all of a sudden you want to know where we're going next?"

"See, um... that's the thing. It's not... uh. It's not technically *dry* humping." I lean down and, embarrassed, whisper in his ear, like someone outside the car might hear me, "I'm like... really, really wet, like soaking through my clothes." I feel my face heat. "I don't want to make you look like you pissed yourself." I cover my mouth with my hand, so mortified, but still finding the situation hilarious. Thank God for the alcohol in my system or I might not ever be able to look him in the eye again.

But instead of laughing at me or throwing me off of him, he reaches between my legs and presses his fingers to my denim-covered center, causing my hips to jerk forward and a shudder to wrack my whole body. I wobble on my knees, unable to keep still. His touch weakens the strength in my legs, and finally, I sit back down.

He pulls my face to his with the other hand still tangled in my hair and whispers against my lips, "Is this all for me?" and I nod before kissing him thoroughly, dipping my tongue in to stroke the tip of his when he opens his mouth to me. He sucks my bottom lip between his teeth and I moan, pressing myself down onto his massaging fingers.

Suddenly, out of nowhere, my body detonates, sending bright lights through my vision as I look down into his gorgeous eyes, seeing a look of surprised triumph in his gaze before I curl forward, pressing my forehead against his shoulder as I ride the wave rolling through me. When he lightens his touch and I'm finally able to catch my breath I sit back up and look at him questioningly, my brow furrowed.

"What is it, baby?" he prompts, nothing but love in is happy expression.

"How the hell did that happen?" I squawk, throwing my hands in the air.

"Um..." He chuckles, obviously not knowing how to answer.

"No, you don't get it. I'm the chick who couldn't come to

save her life until I was twenty and met you. Then, I go the last two and half years with only self-induced orgasms to tide me over, and then the second your hand barely touches my hoo-ha, it's like Orgasm City without even having to go to Pound Town! What the fuck?" I end my rant by quoting one of our favorite comedy skits by George Lopez, which he sent me the link to on MySpace, "I swear to God, if you leave me, I'll kill you," and he bursts out laughing. I double over, giving into the fit of giggles I've been holding in.

He helps me into my seat, instructing me to buckle up, and then backs out of the parking space.

"Are you telling me where we're going yet?" I sigh, reaching over to play with the super short hair at the back of his head.

"Nope," he says, popping the P. "But it's not far, so you won't have to suffer for long."

I glance at the clock, seeing it's almost nine. Wherever he's taking me, I hope he doesn't plan to stay too long. I'm feeling brave enough now that I could pretty much throw him down and ravage him without a second thought of self-consciousness.

Not even five minutes later, we pull into a shopping center and find a parking spot.

"Are we going to IHOP?" I ask with a short laugh, seeing the brightly lit restaurant on the end of the building. Fitting, I admit, but this isn't *our* IHOP. That one is close to his house.

He chuckles. "Nah, maybe after we leave the club I'll take you to our old one, but I'm taking you over there." He points in the other direction, and that's when I see the neon sign in the corner of the shopping center that says Big Texas Dance Hall and Saloon.

"We're going dancing?" I squeal excitedly, but then I look down at myself, seeing my holey jeans and T-shirt. "I didn't really dress to go to a club."

"You're dressed perfectly for this one. It's a country bar," he tells me like that explains anything.

We show our IDs to the doorman and step inside, and the atmosphere is similar to the Palomino club Anni and I go to, with neon beer brand signs, dark wood bars, and country décor. We got here early enough there's no cover charge, so we walk right up to the bar and order some drinks.

The place is huge, like four times the size of the club in Fayetteville, with a dance floor to match. I can't wipe the smile off my face, watching the men in cowboy hats twirl ladies around the floor, people in the center of the circle dancing more slowly than the ones doing intricate spins and turns on the outer edge, but everyone moves in the same counterclockwise direction.

We find two stools open along the wooden counter that surrounds the circle and doubles as a guardrail, so I have the perfect view to watch with bright eyes and mouth gaping at some of the moves these couples are showing off. You'd never expect to see some of these partners. There's a gentlemen well into his seventies dancing with a girl my age, but you can see the pure joy on her face as he spins her, throws her into a dip, and then—I shit you not—falls into a graceful split, gyrating his hips on his way back up to stand before twirling her once again. How the hell a man his age, in tight Wrangler jeans no less, could pull that off, I have no idea, but he looks badass.

There are the sets of best girlfriends giggling in the center of the circle, of course, trying to figure out how to two-step as they watch the couples around them. Then there are the partners who you can just tell are madly in love in this moment, holding each other as close as possible, her eyes closed, head pressed against his chest, trusting him to keep her safe as he leads her around the floor.

I'm so transfixed with what I'm seeing that I actually jump when Jason leans close to my ear and says, "I don't normally like dance clubs, but I'll come here anytime you want. There are never any fights, no shit-starting. People come here just to have a good time. Anyone—and I do mean anyone," he nods at the old man still getting his groove on, "will come up and ask you to dance, whether you're single or taken."

"And guys don't get pissed off when other men come up to ask their chick to dance?" I ask, astonished.

"Nope, it's like an unspoken rule. I mean, the girl can always say no, but it's all in good fun, so you'll see all sorts of mismatched dance partners out there." He smiles. "Do you know how to two-step?"

"I know a ton of line dances, but not how to two-step." I shake my head then take a sip of my drink.

"Well, when a slower song comes on, I'll teach you. It's hard to learn during one of these fast tempo songs," he explains.

"You know how to two-step? I didn't peg you for the dancing type."

"Do you know who my mother is? She was on her local *American Bandstand* type show when she was young. That woman can dance. And Dad is badass too. It's that generation, I think. They swing dance and know all these crazy moves you see out there. My mom put me in ballroom dancing lessons when I was little, and then taught me a ton of stuff right in our living room."

I look at him with my head tilted, trying to picture Jason ballroom dancing, and 'Does Not Compute' scrolls behind my eyes. It's just something I'd have to see to believe.

"Oh, this one is perfect," he says excitedly, taking my drink out of my hand and setting it next to his on the counter. He then threads his fingers through mine as he leads me onto the dance floor. We move to the center, where it looks like the beginners seem to migrate, and he pulls me close with one arm behind my lower back, keeping a hold of my hand. "Okay, loosen up your shoulders. Relax. I'm going to lead you, so all you have to do is let me guide you. You're going to take two steps backward with your left foot first, then one with your right. So it'll be left, together, left, together, right. Left, together, left, together, right. Got it?"

"I think so," I reply, and with a "Ready?" and nod, we move. His right foot steps forward and my left one moves back, and it's as if I don't even have to think. With slight pushes to my hip with his hand around my waist, and little tugs to my hand in his, he moves me around the floor effortlessly. The only thing I have to pay the slightest bit of attention to is keeping up with the footwork pattern, while he spins me, rocks us in the opposite direction for a beat, and then switches us up. Our feet are backward, me moving forward now, but I still feel his tiny guiding movements as he continues to lead me. It reminds me of the way he used to take control of our lovemaking, even when he was on the bottom.

The song ends, and a more upbeat one begins, and I laugh as he spins us once again and I try to make my feet go fast enough to keep up with the tempo. Soon, I'm out of breath, so he pulls me to him for a lingering kiss in the center of the moving circle, couples twirling and laughing all around us, before walking me off the floor.

I hop onto my stool with a sigh then take a sip of my drink. It's a little easier to picture Jason as a good dancer now that I've experienced how great of a lead he is. I took tap, ballet, and jazz for nine and a half years when I was young, and I'll be forever grateful to my instructor, Miss Kim, for teaching me how to control my otherwise long, gangly limbs. I was not a graceful little girl until she got a hold of me and taught me how to hold my tall and skinny form with much better posture and elegance.

We sit and watch everyone dance for a few country songs, and I'm surprised that I don't mind the music. I usually can't stand country, but having the dancing couples to watch makes it bearable, and I even end up liking a few songs, typing the titles into my phone to remember to download them. That's when I hear it, the opening notes of "Copperhead Road", and I let out a squeal and jump from my stool. "I love this one!" I call to Jason over my shoulder as I scurry to the opening to the dance floor, following the counter back down until I'm directly in front of him still sitting in his seat.

"You wanna learn?" I shout to him over the music, stomping my foot along with everyone else on the floor, waiting for Steve Earle to sing the first line, our cue to start the steps to the intricate line dance.

He shakes his head with a sexy smirk. "I've got the perfect view. I'm just gonna watch you."

"That doesn't make me nervous at all." I smile shyly and look down, watching my foot stomp one last time before moving into the actual dance. I can't help the grin that spreads across my face as everyone nails the choreography at the same time, aligning just right with the song. After each set of steps, the crowd turns a quarter of a circle, and as I turn to face Jason once again, I glance up to see he hasn't taken his eyes off me. Normally, I would feel self-conscious with someone watching me so closely, but his eyes are dancing with a mix of happiness and heat, causing me to stand up a little straighter and put a little extra roll to my hips.

I spread my fingers and run both hands through my hair at my scalp, lifting it off my neck as I make another quarter turn, peeking at him over my shoulder and seeing his eyes have moved to my ass. It's empowering realizing he can't look away, especially with all the pretty girls around me, wearing cute dresses and cowgirl boots. But somehow he makes me feel like the sexiest person on the floor, even in my ripped-up jeans and plain grey T-shirt. I'm just glad I decided to wear my brown ankle boots. Otherwise, all this line dancing and two-stepping would've been nearly impossible.

As the song winds down to its final cords, and I turn to face Jason fully once again, my brows lower when I see his stool is empty, and I jump when I feel arms lock around my middle from behind. But one glance down at the tattooed forearms lets me know my man has decided to join me on the dance floor. Surprisingly, it's a hip-hop song that comes on, and Jason smiles at the pleased look on my face.

"That's usually how it goes here. They'll play like five or six two-stepping songs, then a line dance, and then a set of like three what I call booty-shaking songs. I figured you'd like that," he says, moving his hips against my ass as I start to sway. The deejay has mashed 50 Cent's "In Da Club" with Nine Inch Nails' "Closer" and the remix is sexy as hell. "Closer" is baby-makin' music to begin with, but by adding the harder bass of the hip-hop track to the rock song, it manages to make it even hotter.

Jason grabs a hold of my waist and turns me to face him, and I wrap my arms around his neck, sliding my fingers up the back of his short hair. As we rock and grind to the beat, I unconsciously close my eyes and bite my lower lip, feeling his muscled thigh press between my legs at their apex. As amazing as he is in bed, I should have known dancing with him would be a sexual experience in itself. The remix ends, but we continue moving together as it bleeds into Usher's "Yeah", snapping me out of the rapey mood that consumed me for the past three minutes and into a goofy one.

I throw my head back and laugh, calling out, "Oh, my God. Prom, class of oh-three, baby!" I turn around and bend over, shaking my booty against him, and I feel his hands clamp onto my hips. I'm grateful for the extra steadiness they provide as the alcohol I've been consuming starts to catch up with me. He spins me and pulls me upright, leaning in for a kiss, but I cut it short, making him laugh when I grab my small boobs in both my hands, pouting while I sing along with the featured rapper, "Ludacris fill cups like double-Ds," making Jason burst out laughing.

The hip-hop set ends with Flo Rida's "Low", and after following the singer's instructions to, "turn around and give that big booty a slap," Jason doesn't allow me to dodge his kiss, locking his strong arms around me while I giggle. I've never had this much fun at a club without my girlfriends, and I find myself looking forward to future times he and I get to come back to this one.

We stay for a few more rotations between two-stepping songs, line dances, and hip-hop tracks, and by the time we leave, I'm ready to jump on Jason right there in the middle of the dance floor. I feel like I'm about to spontaneously combust I'm so freaking turned on. When we get in the car, I mentally threaten him, thinking he better take me straight to his house, or if he tries to take me somewhere before then, I'm gonna have a female-equivalent-of-blue-balls-fueled hissy fit.

He must receive my telepathic message, because twenty-three minutes later, we pull into his driveway. As they always used to be at this time of night, all the lights inside the house are off, and the garage doors are closed, so we take the walkway to the front of the house, entering through the front door.

Jason slides his boots off inside the foyer, and I mimic the action, knowing our heels would make too much noise on the laminate floors and could possibly wake his parents up. I can't help but grin, feeling like that same twenty-year-old girl who used to sneak into his room with him, back when he wanted to keep our feelings for each other a secret. I grab hold of his hand and shuffle my socked feet down the hallway, gasping when my feet almost shoot out from under me, but he catches me with his other arm and then carries me into his room.

With a backward shove of his foot, he closes his door and tosses me on his bed. I land with a little bounce and watch, trying not to laugh as he gets behind his black leather couch and shoves it against the door. "What are you doing?" I whisper.

"When my parents replaced all the doors as an upgrade, they put on knobs that don't lock. I'm just making sure they can't come busting in here when I'm trying to please my lady," he explains, unbuckling his belt, pulling it out of the loops of his jeans, and tossing it on the couch.

"If I had a dick, that would definitely make me go limp," I say with a chuckle as he reaches down, pulling the socks off my feet.

"You have no idea," he grumbles, and I start to ask what he means, but that's when he goes for the button of my jeans, and all thoughts flee my mind except for what he's doing.

My heart thumps behind my ribcage, and I bite my lip in anticipation. I'm nervous, but I don't feel the urge to stop him like I did the other night in his car after the movie. This tension comes from not having been intimate with anyone in over a year, not from being self-conscious of my body. The way he danced with me and looked at me like he could eat me up did away with any of that. Or maybe it's just the anticipation of finally getting to be with Jason, knowing the mind-blowing things he can do to my body.

He pulls the zipper down then places his hands beneath me, grabbing a hold of my jeans and working them over my hips and down my legs. Shockingly, when he goes for my cute white boyshorts, he doesn't pull them off, but straightens out the hem and waistband, putting them back into place after the denim had rolled them down a bit. He stands up straight and takes off his shirt, baring his toned, tattooed chest, covered with a light, soft layer of dark hair, and his flat stomach. I lay back and take in the way his shoulder muscles move as he pulls the shirt down his arms and tosses it on top of his belt.

He places his knee on the mattress between my legs, places his calloused hand behind my neck, and pulls me up to meet his feverish kiss, the perfect distraction as he takes hold of the bottom of my shirt and swiftly lifts it over my head, leaving me only in my pink push-up bra. But when he reaches around my back to unhook it, I shake my head and use my elbow to push his arm away.

"What is it, baby?" he breathes against my lips.

"I gotta keep it on," I whisper, not wanting to go into detail and ruin the mood.

"You know I love your bod—" he starts, but I cut him off.

"I know. It's not *that*," I emphasize, hoping he'll understand. I don't want to have to explain that since I'm breastfeeding, they don't feel like a sexual part of my body right now, and worse, they could make a mess, and then I'd be mortified.

"I know what you're worried about, but if I promise not to touch, will you let me take it off? I just want to see you. All of you," he adds, kissing down my neck.

How can I possibly say no to that? With a sigh, I nod, and he unhooks it with one hand, letting the cups fall to my lap. Not able to look him in the eye, I tell him, "Fair warning, they could...leak. I have no control over it. It just happens."

"You're worrying about shit that doesn't matter again, baby. Get out of that head of yours, and just *feel*." He accentuates the last word with a stroke of his fingers up the seam of my panties, making me shudder.

Soon, my breasts are the last things on my mind. Instead, I'm focused on the nibbling at my hipbones, the firm kneading of my ass cheek, and the gentle caresses at my clit through the white cotton.

Kissing his way lower, my breath hitches, knowing what's to come. I hook my fingers in the elastic at my waist, starting to tug downward. "Leave it," he growls against my core, sending a shockwave down my legs and up my torso. I peek down at him questioningly and meet his intense gaze. "It's hot, keeping a little wrapping on my gift." He kisses the inside of my right thigh. "Like you want me so bad..." He kisses down to where the leg of the boy shorts is snug against me. "...you don't even want to take the time to pull them off. So you pull them to the side..." His finger mimics his words. "...just enough so I can get to my present."

The first lap of his tongue up my center has my back bowing and my hands digging into the sheets. It doesn't take long before his hands are hooked under me, holding my hips in place as I try to simultaneously grind against him and move away from the overwhelming sensations as lights explode behind my eyes.

I hear movement, fabric falling to the floor, and then feel the bed dip as his hot skin comes to press against mine, the hair of his legs giving me goose bumps as it brushes the sensitive flesh of my inner thighs.

I expect him to pull my underwear off, the novelty wearing off, but again, he pulls the fabric to one side, aligning the crown of his erection with my opening. Balancing with an elbow on either side of my head, he leans down to kiss me. I'm completely surrounded by him, his muscled biceps working as blinders to bring Jason's face into perfect focus above me. God, he's so handsome, and the look of both lust and love in his dark eyes makes me push my hips forward, wanting to feel him inside me.

"Careful, baby," he groans in my ear. "It's been a long time. I don't want to hurt you."

I know he's right. A year and a half without sex combined with the size of him could do me some serious damage, but after the swift climax in the car, and the one I just had by his mouth has me ready to throw caution to the wind. He already knows I'm on the pill, so there's nothing to wait for. I start circling my hips against him, trying to feel as much of him as I can with what little he's allowing me to have.

"Please," I beg up to him. "I need more." My eyes close as I try to focus my attention where our bodies are barely connected. I feel his biceps harden against the tops of my shoulders, bracing himself so I can't thrust up toward him. When I look up at him again, his face is like stone, a mix of concentration and sternness, showing self-control I know I won't be able to break. He is hell-bent on going slow, and it makes me calm a little, allowing him to take care of me, since I see how important it is to him.

I relax beneath him, and he rewards me with another inch, pulling out and pushing into me a few times, coating himself in my wetness before giving me a little more. Achingly slow, until I'm at the point where I'm trembling I want it so badly, he continues this process, until finally—thank you, fucking Lord— he buries himself to the hilt, filling me so exquisitely I'm actually thankful he took so long to do it. As he moves, there's not even a twinge of discomfort. I feel stretched to the max, but it's pure pleasure as he rocks in and out of me, and I reach up to grasp his rippling arms, turning my face into one and inhaling his scent. It goes straight from my nose to my pussy, and I feel myself clench around him, hearing him groan.

He feels amazing, even better than I remember, but something is bothering me, and I can't figure out what it is. It's nothing he's doing. God knows he's doing *everything* right. But something is distracting me just enough that I'm not able get *there*. He must sense my frustration, because he leans down to kiss me, and whispers, "You with me, baby?" swiveling his hips.

"Yeah, I just..." I don't know how to reply, but my hesitation is answer enough. I brace myself for his disappointment, but when I look into his face, there's not a speck of it visible, only determination. He pushes up onto his hands, straightening his arms, and when the cool air hits my skin, that's when I feel it. I glance down to see if it's sweat covering my upper body, but discover it's exactly what I was afraid would happen. With his light chest hair stimulating my nipples as he thrust against me, it caused milk to release from my breasts, and I cover my face with both hands, horrified.

The way our bodies had been moving together, it's even ran down to soak the top of my panties. It's no wonder I couldn't concentrate on reaching my orgasm; I'm fucking drenched.

Jesus, could anything be more embarrassing? Here I am, finally with the man of my dreams, who is so goddamn gorgeous and sexy, and what do I do the first time we make love as a couple? I fucking bathe us in breastmilk. As I pray the mattress will open up and swallow me *Nightmare on Elm Street*-style, I feel him pull out of me. Oh, God. He's so disgusted he doesn't even want to be inside me anymore. I finally got my soul mate back, and now I'm going to lose him because of my leaky boobs.

I'm seriously about to start crying from mortification, but then I feel his hands at my hips, tugging my saturated panties over my ass and down my legs. I still can't look at him, so I try to decipher what he's doing with all my other senses. I hear movement, a drawer opening and closing, and then he returns. And that's when I feel his hot tongue against the soft skin of my stomach. I gasp and then bite my lip, squeezing my eyes more tightly closed behind my hands. I don't know what to do with myself as he laps at my belly button and then moans. He sucks tiny pinches of skin between his lips on his way up my body, and I whimper when he comes level with the pair of troublemakers that created this whole mess. What he does next changes my mind completely on my breasts not feeling like a sexual part of me anymore.

Licking along the crease beneath the swollen orb, he then trails tiny nibbling kisses up to my nipple, swirling his tongue around the darker circle before sucking it gently into his mouth with a moan. Behind his teeth, I feel him flick it with the tip of his tongue before rolling it between his lips, causing my back to arch and my arms to come down around his shoulders, holding him gently to me. He pays my other breast the same attention, making masculine sounds of appreciation before leaning up to kiss me, and I taste the sugary sweetness of the milk he cleaned from me as I feel him run something soft over my chest and stomach. When I look down, I see he's drying me off with one of his white T-shirts, and when he's done, he runs it over his own torso before placing it on the pillow beside us, I assume for easy access in case we need it again.

There is absolutely nothing he could have done to disable the bomb that was my shame any more gracefully and caringly, making me love this man even more. He knows exactly how to handle me in every situation. No matter how far gone I think I am, he not only brings me back, but lifts me higher, pulling me from the brink and making me feel better than ever before. Moments before, I had never been more embarrassed in my entire life, and he managed to turn it around, making me feel like a goddess, like he couldn't get enough of me.

With my panties finally off, he slides into me with one smooth thrust, and I clamp my legs around his hips, lifting up to meet him. With the high he has given me, and without the niggling distraction of the wetness between our bodies, it's not long before I feel the building tension inside me. I zero in on it, everything else around us disappearing, and all I concentrate on is his every movement as he hits that oh-so perfect spot.

The explosive orgasm hits me forcefully, stealing my breath so swiftly I don't even make a sound. Every muscle in my body tightens and flexes at the exact same moment, and Jason gives one strangled grunt before I feel him pulse rhythmically inside me, the hot liquid soothing my core.

He doesn't pull out right away, lingering for a while to pepper kisses over my face and neck, and for the first time in person, as I'm wrapped in his strong arms, still full of him, he looks down into my half-mast eyes and whispers, "I love you, baby."

My gulp is audible through my dry throat, and I don't know if I'm going to cry, laugh, or both, but I manage to get out, "I love you, too," before lifting my head to press my face into his chest, breathing him in. His aroma is no longer all Jason, but a sensual mix of the two of us, and I find I love that even more, knowing he's covered in me.

CHAPTER Nine

Kayla's Chick Rant & Book Blog
January 20, 2008

My last three days in Houston were amazing. I spent every day with Jason, twice with Josalyn, and the other alone with him, celebrating his birthday early in style. He took me to a Brazilian Steakhouse, where each person gets a coaster, green on one side, red on the other, and the waiters walk around with different kinds of meat on skewers. If your coaster is on green, that means you want them to slice you off a hunk of the meat onto your plate; red means you're good for now. We ate so much it hurt, and we ended up going back to his house and watching a movie, like old times, ending the same way it always did, with him giving me mind-blowing orgasms.
He drove me home, just like he had the night we went out

dancing, and ended the night with sweet kisses and words of love. It's so different than the way nights used to end with him, with awkward smoke breaks, him not wanting to show me any affection or get too close. Looking back, I understand it now. Sharing these special moments at the end of the day makes me fall more and more in love with him, and him distancing himself back then was his way of staving off these feelings. It makes me appreciate them even more now.

He pulled up a calendar on my last day with him, and we picked out the dates he'll be coming to see me. He's bound and determined to drive, instead of just flying, but he's going to stay for four days instead of just a weekend, so I'm making no complaints.

Now it's back to my normal routine, working during the day, schoolwork at night. Hopefully the next seven weeks will pass by quickly before I get to see Jason again. Until then, I have lots of new books to read from my used bookstore to get through. Watch out for those reviews!

March 6, 2008

I haven't slept in two days. I'm so excited to see Jason. He's supposed to get in sometime tonight, and I'll be meeting him in the morning after he gets some sleep. He's been calling me throughout the day, letting me know when he reaches each state line on his drive from Texas. He slept all day yesterday and left at 8:00 p.m. so he could arrive tonight and go straight to bed.

I've tried to pass the time today with my mom. It's her birthday, and Josalyn and I took her gallivanting. We went to the mall and bought her some new super soft pajamas at Victoria's Secret, and of course I picked myself out a little somethin'-somethin' to wear for Jason.

We went to lunch at K&W Cafeteria, one of the restaurants I missed terribly during the semester I lived in Texas. I could pretty much live off their turkey and dressing smothered in gravy. I always buy way too many side dishes, because I can never choose between all the country-style vegetables. Mashed potatoes and gravy, turnip greens, cabbage, collards, sweet potato casserole, mac-and-cheese... and don't get me started on their desserts. I always get a slice of their sweet potato pie and their chocolate cream pie, take a couple bites from each, and then take the rest home.

Mom got her New England dinner—don't ask me what's in it—the orange Jell-O with the fine slivers of carrots she loves, and a slice of coconut cream pie as her 'birthday cake'. Little Tooty had bites of everything off our plates. Turns out my little southern girl loves the greens just as much as I do.

I can't believe she already turns one next month. We stopped breastfeeding a few weeks ago. She all of a sudden lost interest, preferring her bottle instead, since the milk comes out a lot faster, I assume. Sooner than I planned to stop, but the bright side is I won't have to worry about soaking Jason again. Also, she's sleeping through the night now too, not even waking for a bottle in the middle of the night anymore.

These several weeks went by a lot faster than I thought they would. I've stayed busy with work and school, and have talked to Jason on our lunch breaks and every night on the phone. My boss wasn't too happy about me taking tomorrow and Monday off from work so I could have the four-day weekend with Jason. He's been a real douchebag to Jenna and me lately anyway, griping about stupid shit we have no control over. We've been training his niece this week. I've seriously thought about quitting once she gets the hang of it.

I have a lot of guilt spending so much time away from Josalyn. I know it's a normal thing for both parents to work nowadays, but I grew up with my mom raising me, and looking back, I wouldn't change that for anything in the world. Maybe we didn't have as much spending money as we would if she had a nine-to-five job, but there wasn't anything more I could have wanted than that time with my mom. Even those years she had a secretary job at Granny's church, she was able to take me with her. I can remember bringing pillows and blankets to prop up in her office and read and color. And I was even allowed to walk around to all the Sunday school classrooms and draw on their chalkboards as long as I cleaned them after I was done. Sometimes, the church's organ player would be there to practice, and she'd let me sit on the bench next to her while she played. I always thought it was so cool when she'd let me play the foot pedals.

My dad didn't really care for all the pageants and extracurriculars I was in, having raised three boys before me, so it was up to my mom and me to pay for them. Mom had her little part-time jobs, like the one at the church, and then merchandising once I got into school, and then I raised money for things like pageant dresses and training by selling candy. We would go to the fundraiser place and buy a box of chocolate bars for fifty cents apiece, and then sell them each for a dollar. I would go into car dealerships around town in my little tap shoes, impressing them with a dance, and most of the time they'd buy a whole box to turn back around and sell for themselves. I got a lot of sponsorships that way too. I wonder if the Ford dealership still has my autographed picture with my crown on my head still up on their bulletin board. Probably not —that was a decade ago.

As lucky as I am to have my mom and Granny to watch Josalyn, I wish I was home with her all day. Thinking about it, I get enough financial aid from school and child support that I could survive easily without the job. I've got a ton saved up right now, set aside for visiting Jason. And I would be able to finish up school a lot faster if I could take more than two classes per semester. It's just a hard decision, because I've never had a job with such great paychecks before. It's a rush every two weeks to open up that check and see forty hours a week at ten dollars an hour, when my biggest checks before were around two hundred bucks bi-weekly, since I was only part-time at

GNC, splitting shifts up between five different employees. It's nice seeing my savings grow and grow, but at the same time, that's not the only thing growing. My little girl is, and I feel like I'm missing it.

But that's a decision for another day. Right now, the only thing I'm thinking about is the text message I just received from Jason saying he had just gotten to the hotel. I told him specifically *not* to get one off Bragg Boulevard, but apparently my badass big-city boy was willing to risk safety for the much cheaper price, because lo and behold, the address was on that strand of strip clubs, pawn, tattoo, and gun shops, and questionable businesses. I only go over that way to run into Edward McKay's, my used bookstore, and the Krispy Kreme Doughnuts shop.

"Oh, my God, he's here!" I blurt out from where I'm sprawled on the living room sofa next to my mom, who is sitting in her computer chair, but turned around facing the TV. Josalyn is upstairs asleep in her crib. I look at the time, seeing it's almost 10:00 p.m.

"Wait for it..." Mom tells Granny, giving her a wink.

"What?" I ask, glancing between the two of them, and they share a secret smile, not answering.

I decide to ignore them, texting Jason back:

Glad you made it! Can't wait to see you tomorrow.

He replies quickly.

That was a hell of a drive. I'm going to take a shower

then go to bed. I didn't even stop to get anything to eat.

I send him one last text so he can get to bed.

*Well then, I'll take you to get some awesome breakfast
in the morning. I love you.*

Jason: *Love you to baby.*

I fight the urge to correct his message to 'too' and close out
my texts, placing my phone on the armrest behind me. I drop
my right foot down to the floor, my knee bouncing as I try to
focus my attention back on the show we're watching.

I look at the clock again. 10:02 p.m. God, I can't wait to see
him. This is a new form of torture, knowing he's in my little
hometown, breathing the same air. He's here, only a short
twenty-minute drive away. Not halfway across the country.
Jason is not only on the east coast; he's within my reach. And
here I lay, having to wait one more night to see him. How the
hell will I sleep tonight?

What seems like hours pass, and when I check the time on
my phone, I groan, seeing it's 10:14 p.m. My knee bounces
rapidly, and I run both hands down my face, begging my body
to settle down and feel tired enough so I can go to bed and wake
up to go see him. You'd think since I haven't slept well the last
couple nights I'd be exhausted, but no. Knowing he's near, it's
like my body is hyperaware of his closeness. My soul has woken
from her nap, stretching and looking around for her other half,
sensing his proximity.

"Three... two... one..." Mom counts down with a smirk, and at the exact moment she reaches zero, I spring from the couch, unable to take it anymore.

"I'll surprise him!" I say, almost manically. "He said he didn't eat, so I can pick him up something and take it to him. I could just come back home after he eats—"

Granny and Mom start laughing, cutting me off.

"I knew there was no way in hell you'd be able to stay put knowing that boy had arrived. I'll keep an eye on Josalyn, KD. Go see your honey. Just be careful driving. We'll see you tomorrow," Mom tells me, and I look at her with happy exasperation and lunge toward her, wrapping her up in a tight hug, making her computer chair roll backward. I keep my toes planted on the floor, but follow the chair's movement with the rest of my body, ending up lying in Mom's lap as I squeeze her.

"Thank you, thank you, thank you, Mommy!" I squeak, hop up, and bolt up the stairs two at a time. I run into the bathroom, put on a fresh layer of deodorant, spritz myself with my perfume, and brush my teeth. I brush out my hair then pull it up into a much smoother ponytail, deciding to go makeup-free so I don't wake up with raccoon eyes next to my man in the morning. That thought makes me meet my own reflection in the mirror. Holy shit. I'll be sleeping with and waking up next to Jason for the very first time. I mean, we stayed at that beach cabin in Galveston, but we didn't do much sleeping. We stayed up drinking, just the two of us, making love all night and into the next day. But this will be my first time actually falling asleep with him as his girlfriend. After my heart gives a tremendous thump, I spring back into action.

I slip into my room and look down into Josalyn's crib, seeing she's sleeping on her front, her knees up under her, her chubby cheek smooshed against the mattress, making her perfect little lips form an O as she snores away. I kiss my fingertips then run them through her ash-blonde hair before grabbing my hoodie off the foot of my bed and my purse from where it hangs on my doorknob. The baby monitor is downstairs, so they'll still be able to hear Josalyn if she wakes up.

I control myself enough not to use the handrail to slide down the stairs, even though I'm about gleeful enough to do just that. I run over to Mom, smacking a kiss on her forehead before doing the same to Granny, and then I'm out the door. It's pitch-black outside, but for once, I'm not petrified walking over to the wooded side of our yard to my car.

Normally, even at twenty-three years old, I have my mom stand in the doorway and talk to me while shining a flashlight in my direction if I come home when it's grown dark, after calling her and letting her know I've arrived. I think it's some sort of post-traumatic stress disorder, after my evil-ass big brother hid in the woods one night, when he knew I was due back home from my first job at the car dealership when I was eighteen. That asshole had put on his *Friday the Thirteenth* hockey mask—he thought it was funny since his name is Jason too—and when I got out of my car, he started making the infamous *Ch-ch-ch* sound, then burst out from the tall oaks and pines, waving my dad's chainsaw around like a nutcase as he ran toward me.

My throat hurt for three days I'd screamed so loud, and to

make things worse, when he caught up to me—I'm not a runner, and if you ever see me running, you better run too, because that means something is after me—he set the chainsaw down and tackled me to the ground, tickling my sides until I peed. Yep, eighteen years old, and my stupid big brother held me down 'til I pissed myself. Fucker.

I back out of my parking spot and swoop onto the main road stunt car driver style, zipping through my neighborhood and out into Hope Mills in record time. This late, there aren't many cars on the road to mess with my vision. I make it to Bragg Boulevard five minutes faster than I ever have before, hoping it's just because I've been lucky with hitting all green lights instead of unconsciously speeding like a maniac. I stop by the McDonald's closest to his hotel and grab him a quarter-pounder with cheese, plain and dry, and myself a chicken nuggets meal with sweet-and-sour sauce.

I pull into a parking spot, my stomach giving a colossal swoosh when I see his green Altima. I check my texts again to see what room he's in, and then grab my purse and the bag of food, plus the large sweet tea out of my cup holder.

I climb the stairs, my heart racing from both the physical exertion and the fact Jason is only mere feet away. I pull open the glass door and walk down the corridor until I'm standing in front of room 328. Taking a deep breath, I lift the hand holding the bag of food and knock with my knuckles. My face feels hot, excitement and nervousness pressing down on me as I wait for him to answer the door. After a minute without him answering, I set the bag down and knock a little louder, but again, no answer. Maybe he's still in the shower, or already asleep. I knock one last time then grab my phone out of my purse, getting ready to text him, but finally the door opens as much as the chain lock allows, Jason's handsome but intense face appearing in the crack. He glances farther down than where his eyes initially looked out, in order to reach my smiling face, his expression softening the moment he sees it's me.

"Housekee-ping. You want me fluff pillow?" I ask, mimicking David Spade's high-pitched voice in *Tommy Boy*, making him chuckle and close the door long enough to remove the chain. He holds it open for me, and I come into the room, which I'm surprised is so massive for the price he told me he got it for, after grabbing the Mickey D's off the floor. I only catch a glimpse of his firearm as he puts it into the drawer of the nightstand by the bed, and then I'm in his arms. *Oh, my Texan.*

I rest my face against his neck, breathing him in. With my arms hanging at my sides, I tell him, "I come baring gifts," then lift the bag and sweet tea for him to see. "Sorry, I couldn't even function knowing you were here. Mom is watching Josalyn, so you're stuck with me for a sleepover. I forgot my sleeping bag though. You got one I can borrow?" I tease, surprised at how playful and composed I feel being in Jason's presence for the first time in almost two months.

He lifts the iced tea out of my hand and takes a long pull from the white straw, one of his corded forearms still wrapped around my lower back, holding me close. "No sleeping bag, but I think there might be a corner of that king-sized bed I'd be willing to let you have," he goads then leans down to press his

perfect lips to mine, sending a thrill down each of my
extremities.

After a few more kisses, he takes the McDonald's bag out of
my hand and sits down on the edge of the bed, toeing his boots
off, and that's when I see he's not wearing any socks. Then I
take in the fact his hair is damp, and I can see wetness coming
through his T-shirt. I wave my hand in front of him. "What's all
this? Have you taken a shower already?"

He looks down at where the center of his shirt is a darker
blue than the rest of it. "Yeah, I'd just finished when I first
heard a knock. I threw my clothes back on and grabbed my
gun, in case this part of town really is as bad as you said. But
instead, I found a little angel at my door," he says, taking a bite
of his burger.

I pull my nuggets and sauce from the bag after slipping my
flip-flops off my feet and sitting Indian-style in the center of the
bed. I can feel the silly grin that won't leave my face as I munch
on French fries, flattening out the paper bag and dumping the
salty potatoes on top of it between us so we can share. This feels
so... normal, so comfortable, like we do it every day. He feels
like home.

He moans as he chews, closing his eyes like it's the best
thing he's ever tasted. "I didn't realize how hungry I was
because I'm so tired. Thanks, babe." He leans over our
makeshift picnic to give me a quick kiss before devouring the
rest of his meal, washing it down with a swig of tea.

I ball up everything and take it into the bathroom to throw
away, returning to crawl into bed next to Jason, where he's now
under the covers in just his boxer briefs. He pulls me closer,

wrapping his arm around me and tucking me into his side, and my head rests comfortably on his chest. I trail my fingers up and down between his pecs, and with a kiss to my forehead, we drift off to sleep, and it's the best night of sleep I've had since before I got pregnant. Shit, even before that, when I used to fall asleep after drinking a bottle of wine, trying to drown out the looped thoughts of the man I'd give anything to be with, the same man who now holds me to him like his life depends on it.

CHAPTER Ten

Heated breath.

Delicate, wet strokes of a nimble tongue.

A strong hand gripping around my right thigh.

A sudden plunge of dexterous fingers.

A firm caress to that secret spot only one man has ever found inside me.

"Jason," I breathe, my hips circling as he continues his ministrations to my most sensitive place. I'm in that hazy state between dreaming and consciousness, but as he hooks his fingers, dragging it across the wall of my core over and over, and he sucks my clit gently between his teeth, I jerk fully awake with an orgasm that wracks my entire being.

I'm completely limp as he crawls up my body, and I'm so primed for his entry that he fills me in one smooth thrust. He braces himself on his elbows on either side of my head, surrounding me in that way I will absolutely never get enough of, and as he pistons his hips, his powerful thighs moving him in a technique that blows my mind every time, somehow he's still able to kiss me softly. He pulls my bottom lip into his mouth, letting it slide out between his teeth, the sensation shooting directly to my center, where I feel myself tighten around his hard length.

I have no control over the noises or words that pour out of me as he completely consumes my universe, but I have one conscious thought the whole time he showers me with pleasure only he knows how to give me. "I love you," I arch up to whisper into his ear before burying my face in the hot skin covering his collarbone, inhaling his intoxicating scent that both excites and soothes me.

My heart thuds in my chest at his immediate response, "I love you, too," and my hands reach up to grasp the sheets above my head, holding on for dear life as he suddenly pounds into me. My breath comes out in short, sharp pants, and everything inside me begin to tighten. I'm hanging on, hovering at the top of the roller coaster's first giant drop. As I look down my body, seeing his thick cock disappearing and reappearing over and over as he thrusts, my vision is then filled as he lowers his face to my breast, and then with his amazing eyes as he looks up at me from where he's taken my nipple into his mouth, watching my reaction.

I implode, my body latching onto him with every bit of strength I have in my much smaller body, and as suddenly as that tension hits me with all its power, it flips and changes, becoming an explosion, a relaxing shudder taking over my whole form. At the perfect moment, he pulls out and reaches between us to feel me come all over his fingers, the pleasure coming out in a hot gush of wetness.

He growls his approval, and feeling what he's made me do seems to renew and double his efforts, even though I feel like I can't take any more of it. He flips me effortlessly to my stomach, positioning my limbs the way he wants them because I have no strength to move them on my own.

He takes me savagely from behind, making me gasp sharply at the depth he reaches inside me. Not wanting to hurt me, he tilts my hips up in the perfect angle, and hearing my moan of ecstasy, he lets loose, hammering me with the sheer power of his muscled body. All I can do is breathe and relax, my front melting into the mattress as he takes from me what he wants, and I'm all too willing to give it to him.

I lose count of how many towering hills he pushes me up then drops me over the other side, one orgasm starting before the previous one ends, and soon I'm in an all-consuming state of floating, drifting, zero-gravity, until I hear his breath rush out of him in a whoosh, the only sound he makes, and I know he's finally gotten his own pleasure.

Next thing I know, I'm under the covers again, snuggled into the nook between his arm and chest, and I'm drifting off to sleep once more.

When I awaken again, light is filtering into the room where the two curtains meet over the window. I glance over at the clock radio on the nightstand and see it's only 8:00 a.m., so God only knows what time it was when Jason woke me for that round of amazing sex. Or was it a dream? I shift my legs, feeling the not unpleasant ache between them, and I know for sure it was not just a dream. I lift my arms above my head and stretch, arching my back as far as I can. I slept like the dead, and it feels almost as if I got too much sleep, since I'm so used to waking up two hours earlier than this for work or with Josalyn.

I look over at Jason and see he's watching me, his dark eyes dancing with humor.

"Good morning, beautiful," he says huskily.

"Morning," I reply, and sit up. My bladder is about to pop from all the sweet tea I drank before bed last night, so I get out from under the covers, and try not to look as awkward as I feel walking across the room naked. Lying close to him in bed is one thing, but prancing around on full display as he gets an unobstructed view of my nudity is another.

When I close the bathroom door behind me, I can hear the rustle of the sheets as Jason shifts in bed, which makes me frown. If the walls are so thin I can hear that, then that means he'll be able to hear me pee.

Oh, my God, Kayla. Grow up, I tell myself, but I can't help it. This is the first time I've woken up next to him, having always gone home after a night of lovemaking. I've never had to show him my human side, always tried to be perfect when I'm in front of him.

I bite my lip and look around. I flip the switch next to the one for the lights, and the fan comes on, and then I turn on both the sink and tub faucets. There, that should make enough noise to cover up the sound of me peeing. But just in case, I also flush the toilet while I go.

After using a washcloth to freshen up, I wash my hands, turn everything off, and go back into the bedroom, but stop in my tracks when I see Jason holding in laughter, propped up against the headboard, the covers barely covering his hips.

"What?" I look down at myself. I knew I should have wrapped up in a towel before I came out.

His voice tight, like he's trying his best not to burst out laughing, he asks, "What were you doing in there, sexy mama?"

My face heats. "I had to pee."

"Do you always create a sound barrier when you pee, or was that for my benefit?" His grin takes over his face when I fidget.

I don't really know how to answer without sounding ridiculous, so I just snap, "Shut up," and get into bed beside him. "Way to call me out, jerk," I pout, but immediately laugh as he quickly straddles me, holding my hands above me with one of his and tickling my ribs with the other.

I start squealing, trying not to scream, since we're in a hotel and I don't want our neighbors to call the front desk. "Stop! Oh, God! You're gonna make me pee!"

"You already peed," he reminds me, digging his fingers into my sides then dancing them upward to my armpits.

"I can't breathe! Please! Stop!" I beg, and finally, he ceases the torture, bending down to kiss away the laughter tears from where they've dripped down my temples and into my hairline.

He smiles down from his perch above me, and asks, "So what are we doing today?"

I catch my breath and glare up at him. "Nothing. You can go home, ass." When he raises his hands and wiggles his fingers like he's going to tickle me again, I cross my arms over myself protectively. "Kidding! I'm kidding! I was thinking—and tell me if this is too far away, and we can do something closer—but there's really not much to do here in Fayetteville. Do you want to go down to Myrtle Beach? It's only about a two and half hour drive."

"What would we do down there?" he asks, uncrossing my arms and threading the fingers of both hands with his, pushing them down into the mattress on either side of my head. He begins kissing his way from my wrist, down my forearm, my bicep, over my shoulder, and then buries his face in my neck.

I try to answer while his mouth does wicked things to the sensitive flesh there. "Well, there's... there's Medieval Times, and Barefoot Landing..." I have to pause to moan as he moves across my throat to the other side of my neck, where he nibbles up the column to my ear, making me shiver. "...which... which has lots of little shops, kind of like a K-Kemah on steroids." My hips give an involuntary thrust as he licks the sensitive skin behind my ear, and my nipples harden.

But then he sits up abruptly and lets me go. "Sounds fun. We bringing the baby?" he asks, like he wasn't just driving me mad with need.

When I gain my composure, I clear my throat and reply, "How about we spend day one just the two of us, and then the rest of the time with my mini?"

"Sounds perfect." He hops out of bed in all his naked glory and walks confidently over to his suitcase.

Dat ass.

Since he's pulled out clothes to get dressed for the day, I lean over the side of the bed to find where he might have tossed mine when he undressed me before he woke me with his mouth. It was just the pair of comfy pants and T-shirt I had been wearing last night while watching TV with Mom and Granny, figuring I could just bring Jason to the house to see them and I could get dressed there, wasting no time packing anything.

As we head out the door, Jason hangs the Do Not Disturb sign on the handle, I assume since he's left his handgun in the room, and I call my mom on our walk to the car and tell her our plans, confirming she's all right with keeping Josalyn for the day. I decided to drive, since he was on the road for so long yesterday. I asked him one more time if he was sure he wanted to make the trek down to the beach, and he swore it was fine by him.

Soon, we pull into my driveway.

We walk across the yard and in through the side door, and when we enter the living room, I can only stare in wide-eyed surprise as Riley prances up to Jason wagging his tail, not a single bark escaping his normally over-yappy mouth. Riley hates everyone.

Jason reaches down to pet him, and I quickly warn, "He bites! He'll act like he's being sweet, just gonna sniff you, but then he'll attack." But even as the words leave me, it's like Riley wants to make a liar out of me, because as sweet as a well-trained puppy, the little asshole lets Jason pet him, and then Jason picks him up in his massive arms. Riley lets *no one* but me pick him up. He'll let my mom and Granny pet and snuggle him, but he gets a little snippy if they try to pick him up.

And so, in awe, I watch as the Chihuahua having an identity

crisis licks Jason all over his face then turns to look at me like, 'You were saying?'

Hurriedly, I pull my digital camera out of my purse and snap a picture. That's definitely going on the blog.

"Granny, this is Jason," I say with a cheek-aching grin as he walks over to her where she's sitting at the kitchen counter, shaking her hand gently with Riley still nestled to his chest.

"Well, I'll be damned, KD. Would you look at that? They say dogs are a good judge'a character, and Riley doesn't like nobody," Granny says, her southern accent thick as she finishes the bite of Bojangle's biscuit she'd been eating when we walked in.

"Nice to meet you, ma'am. Kayla talks about you all the time. She sure loves her granny," he tells her, giving her his charming smile.

"You're damn right she does. That's my baby girl. And don't go breaking her heart again or I'll give you a ride on my foot," she threatens, narrowing her blue eyes on him and waggling a naturally long-nailed finger at him.

"No, ma'am. I wouldn't dream of it," he replies, taking the old woman's intimidation in stride, making me smile over at Mom, who's holding Josalyn in her lap on one of the barstools.

"Hey, Jason. Glad to see you made it safe, sweetie," Mom says.

"That was one hell of a drive. Think I'll be flying next time," he remarks, and it causes butterflies to set off in flight inside me, thinking about him coming to see me again. It's still surreal to me he's even here. It's hard to imagine him returning.

As Jason makes his way over to my mom, I tell them I'm

gonna run upstairs and change, and I catch a glimpse of Josalyn reaching up to him and him taking her in his other arm not holding Riley before I get too high up the stairs to see anymore.

It's still a little chilly, and I'm sure it'll be even cooler down at the beach, so I put on some jeans, a cami, and a hoodie. I freshen up in the bathroom, brushing my teeth and squirting some perfume on, and after using a washcloth on my face, I put on some moisturizer and my makeup before heading back downstairs.

We hang out for a few minutes with the ladies in my life, but knowing it's just going to be a day trip to Myrtle Beach, we escape quickly so we can go on our adventure.

The drive is fun, us play fighting over who gets control over the radio. I win when I tell him the line from one of my favorite shows, *Supernatural*, "Driver picks the music, shotgun shuts his cakehole." Our first stop is the box office of Medieval Times. We get the tickets to the 2:00 p.m. dinner show, which gives us a couple hours to kill, so we head to the beach.

We find a bar on The Strand, the shops and restaurants lining the road along the ocean, and we stop to have a drink, him choosing a Budweiser, and me a fruity concoction, feeling festive at the beach, though I'm cold, even with my hoodie on. Afterward, we walk hand-in-hand in the sand until I spot one of my favorite stores, a three-story beach shop with all sorts of souvenirs.

There's a pressed penny machine—I have a giant collection of the flattened and engraved copper coins—and I choose the one that says 'I love you. Myrtle Beach' with a heart in the center, cranking the handle twice so I can make him one too. He puts it in his wallet and calls it his lucky penny after giving me a kiss.

Soon, it's almost time for our show, so we drive back to Medieval Times and park. We're the first ones to arrive, so when we walk up the drawbridge across the mote and in through the massive doorway, I'm giddy as hell seeing I have full access to all the shops without having to wait in line.

I buy a souvenir program to add to my collection. I get one at every event and show I go to, from the *Stars on Ice* Mom, Granny, and I went to see at the Crown Coliseum a few years ago, to the one I got from *Phantom of the Opera* when it came to Raleigh. I also get a shot glass with the Medieval Times logo, and a magnet. Jason chooses a shot glass the size of five stacked on top of each other, which has a sort of ruler printed on it, measuring just how drunk you'd be if you filled it to a certain line.

When we enter into the main area, giving them our tickets, we're handed card-stock crowns, which are red and yellow striped, signifying which knight we'll be rooting for during the tournament. I don't hesitate folding mine together, adjusting it to fit my head and putting it on, but Jason just holds his in his hand.

"You have to put it on," I tell him, raising an eyebrow.

"Nah, I'm good," he replies, crossing his arms over his broad chest.

"You *have* to put it on," I repeat. "It's part of the fun. Don't act like such a hard-ass. Loosen up and put on the fucking crown." I put my hands on my hips and stare at him haughtily, giving him 'the look' until he finally rolls his eyes, adjusts the crown to fit him, and then places it on his head, which he shakes while trying to hide his smile.

"There, you happy?" he asks, looking adorable with the bright paper crown on his dark head, completely out of place on such a badass-looking man.

"Extremely." I grin and go up on my toes to smack a kiss on his full lips before turning toward the bar lining the entire left side of the room. "Want a drink?"

"Dear God, yes," he says dramatically, and I slap him on his arm before leading the way over to the bartender.

"What will ye be havin', milady?" he prompts in a fake British accent.

My eyes land on a souvenir glass the size of a freakin' fishbowl, and I turn with wide eyes to look up at Jason. He sees the look on my face then glances up to see what could've caused it, immediately spotting the glass. "Malibu and pineapple? We can share it. I know your tiny ass won't drink that whole thing, but I know you can't resist that glass," he states, making me smile. He knows me so well. I nod excitedly.

"Ah, the King's chalice. It's the equivalent of four individual drinks. Fine choice. Fine choice, indeed," the bartender continues to talk animatedly in character while entertaining us with some crazy tricks with two white bottles of Malibu rum. He tops off the massive glass with pineapple juice, ending with a flourish as he decorates the top with cherries and inserts two long black straws. I applaud the show as Jason hands him cash for the drink, a whopping fifty bucks.

We stroll along the perimeter of the room, which has

everything you'd see at a Renaissance Festival, sipping our giant drink. We walk through a maze of medieval torture devices, both of us giving each other wicked grins when we come to a set of shackles, which makes us burst out laughing at our similar lascivious thoughts.

A few minutes before it's time to go into the main arena to find our seats, the building is now busy, full of families excited to see the show. I spot a young woman in costume holding a huge, lethal-looking bird, and realize she must be a falconer, just like at the Renfest I went to in Raleigh on a high school field trip. I grab Jason's arm and pull him toward her, him holding back and making me work to haul him over.

"What's wrong?" I ask him with a giggle.

"Oh, nothing, just that that thing looks like it wouldn't hesitate to eat your face off," he gripes.

"Quit being a pansy. This is a family establishment. I'm sure it's well trained. Otherwise, they wouldn't have it here," I assure him. "Now go stand beside it. I want to take a picture."

Being silly, he makes an awkward face and takes hesitant, stiff steps sideways until he's beside the woman and the falcon, and I snap a photo of him staring at the bird as if waiting for it to attack. He visibly relaxes, letting me know he was just playing the drama queen the whole time, and I give him another *thwap*, this one on his chest. He makes me violent, apparently. He only grins and takes a big swig of our drink. As a small circle forms around the falconer, we listen as she gives us fun facts about what they used to use the bird for in history, and she lets us know that he will be playing an important role during the show. And with that, the big stone-looking doors open to the arena, and everyone starts filing inside.

Since we were so close to the doors when they opened, once we get to the red and yellow section matching our crowns, we got a front row seat in the stadium-style rows. Not that there would've been a bad seat in the entire house. In the center of the arena is a dirt floor, and at the other end are thrones, where the king and queen will sit. I remember this from when we came in middle school. At 71st Classical Middle School, our mascot was The Knights, so we had a field trip down here, I believe in the 7th grade. I also remember the food being absolutely delicious, so I hope that's still the case.

When we're all seated, a woman dressed in a barmaid costume stands in front of us and yells up to us in the first two rows, "Hello, everyone. I'm Franci, and I'll be your wench today! Anytime you need anything, a refill, a napkin, you name it, all you have to do is holler, "Wench!" and I will be at your beck and call." She does a curtsy as she says the last part. "Now, let's practice, shall we? Ready? One... two..."

She raises her arms in the air, prompting us to do as she said, and we all yell, "Wench!" causing a round of laughter through the crowd. All around the arena, we hear the echo of other groups giving their practice cry of summoning their waitress as Franci makes her way down our row, taking our drink order. When she's done, she stands back in front of us.

"Now, for those of you who have never been here before, and for those who don't know this, there were no eating utensils back in Medieval Times. Therefore, what we serve here can all be eaten with your hands. We've tried to keep the experience as authentic as possible... and yet... as someone of you just realized... we serve Pepsi products," she snarks, making us chuckle. It reminds me of the part in *Cable Guy,* when Jim Carey takes Matthew Broderick to this show and he questions the same thing. They must've added this bit to the wenches' scripts after that movie came out.

Franci leaves to go fill everyone's drink orders, and soon, all sorts of stuff is brought out and placed in front of us until our plates and bowls are filled. Tomato bisque soup, garlic bread, an herb-roasted potato, corn on the cob, and what looks like half a damn oven-roasted chicken! And it all smells heavenly.

Soon, the lights around the perimeter dim, highlighting the center of the arena as the knights in different colored costumes ride out on their horses. Each knight goes to their section, and our red and yellow one stops right in front of us, making his horse bow. We all clap and cheer, getting into the show as the king comes out and revs us up with his dramatic speech.

We eat our feast between screams, rooting for our knight as he battles the others in different events, from sword fighting to jousting, and we watch in awe during the intermission as the falconer puts on a show, the majestic bird ending the display by taking flight and making a full circle around the top of the whole arena.

By the end, we're in full-on nerd mode, feeling like we're truly back in time, rooting for our knight as it comes down to him and the blue one, yelling, stomping, clanging our plates and cups together, trying to distract the enemy so our hero can one-up him and win. And even though in the back of our minds we know it's all staged, our group freaks the hell out when our knight gets the upper hand and ends up winning the tournament.

It's 8:00 p.m. when we arrive at my parents' house that
evening. I called Mom to tell her to keep Josalyn awake as long
as she could, because I was going to swing by and grab her so
we could spend the night at Jason's hotel.

We load up the portable crib and everything she'll need the
next day as far as clothes and baby food go, and I pack myself
an overnight bag this time too. I have no doubt she'll fall asleep
on the drive.

When we get to the hotel and open up my back door, sure
enough, she's snoozing away in her car seat. I unhook her from
her straps and she doesn't even stir as I lay her head on my
shoulder while Jason grabs the bags and the Pack 'n Play out of
my trunk.

We set it up near the bathroom, behind the wall, so if she
wakes up she won't be able to see if any hanky-panky is going
on. She stays completely oblivious to the world as I lay her
inside and cover her up with her baby blanket.

My hair is in a windblown knot on top of my head, and I feel
sticky from our day at the beach and the five hours in the car, so

I give Jason a wicked look as I take hold of the bottom of my hoodie and lift it over my head then prance into the bathroom to turn on the shower. He takes the hint and follows me inside, and I ask him to leave the door cracked a little so we can hear if Josalyn wakes up as he goes to push it shut.

Josalyn may be almost a year old, but this whole sex thing as a mother is still brand spanking new to me. I've yet to have to sneak around my kid's back to get some action. She stayed with Mom the few times Jason and I went out in Texas, and then again last night. So this is a new experience. It feels both weird and exhilarating at the same time, like the excitement of being caught, but also feeling a little ashamed of doing the dirty with my daughter so close by. But here in the bathroom, at least there's a mostly-closed door between us, and she is asleep. Shower sex it is!

The next morning, we go to Krispy Kremes for breakfast down the road, but then hang out in the hotel together. Jason cuddles up with Josalyn on the bed and shows her YouTube music videos, and I can't help taking pictures of their adorable interactions. It's a very relaxed day of just lying around and spending quality time together, and it feels wonderful, like everything in the world is as it should be.

The following day is much the same, only we spend it at my house, going on a paddleboat ride, taking a stroll on the trail through the woods, and of course, I had to introduce him to Smithfield's Barbecue. We had the same argument again, over what barbecue really is, my side being 'pulled pork with vinegar sauce' and his side being 'beef with red sauce', but after his first taste of North Carolina style barbeque, there was no more arguing. He thought it was 'Good... damn good.' My face hurt from grinning at my triumph.

The next day would be our last together, which was going to be cut short since he was going to leave that night, so Josalyn spent the night at home with Mom so I could have Jason to myself. We spent the evening making love, and slept for a good portion the following day, and before I was ready, it was time to tell him goodbye.

This time was a little harder, since I didn't know exactly when I'd get to see him next. It had been hard enough getting these past few days off from work, so I didn't know when it'd be wise to try again. But with one final kiss and a hug I didn't want to end, he got into his car and headed back to Texas.

I cried the whole way home.

CHAPTER Eleven

Kayla's Chick Rant & Book Blog
December 12, 2008

 I've pretty much kept up with all my book reviews for you
ladies, but I've neglected the 'Chick Rant' portion of my blog.
Probably because there really hasn't been anything to rant
about. The last several months have been a blur, between
multiple visits with Jason, alternating between him coming to
see me, and Josalyn and me flying to Texas to stay with him. If
anything, I should change the name to 'Rave', because it's been
nothing but good things happening. Let me catch y'all up.

April:
I decided to quit my job to focus fully on my degree and
Josalyn. With the upcoming visits with Jason, there was no way

my boss would've been okay with me taking a week off basically once a month, so I went ahead and threw caution to the wind, quitting after saving every penny of my last few paychecks so I'd have a nice cushion.

Josalyn's first birthday party was a blast. I took lots of pictures of her digging into her birthday cake, which ended up everywhere, mostly in her hair—of course. I got her a blow-up castle, and Aiden bought the colorful plastic ball-pit balls to go in it. It was the first time he'd come to visit her since Christmas.

May:

Josalyn and I flew to Texas and stayed with Jason this time. We timed the trip so we could attend Buffy's baby shower, both women and men attending, which I thought was super fun! They had games for everyone, including which man could chug beer fastest from a baby bottle. They didn't realize how slow liquid comes out through the nipples, so it was hilarious watching the grown men suck as hard as they could to get the alcohol out.

We went on an awesome little day trip to Galveston one day, and took Josalyn to Moody Gardens. Jason's parents came along with us, and we had a great time exploring the three pyramids, showing her the penguins in the Aquarium Pyramid, and walking through the Rainforest Pyramid. The last one held the IMAX theater, where we watched a cool 3D movie about ocean life. Josalyn wouldn't keep the 3D glasses on, but she was still really well behaved for the forty-five-minute show.

June:

This was an exciting month! Jason flew to Fayetteville this time, and Mom watched Josalyn for two days while we went up to Williamsburg, Virginia to visit Busch Gardens. Usually, when I go to the giant amusement park, it's a day trip there and back home, so I never realized how impressive the city itself is. We went to a winery and got souvenir glasses at our wine tasting, and ended up buying a couple of bottles we really enjoyed. Jason loved the dry red ones, while I preferred the sweet ones. When we got back to Fayetteville, I took him to my favorite tattoo shop, The Chop Shop in Hope Mills, where I've gotten all of my tattoos to date, because I don't trust anyone else. Jason shocked me, asking me if I wanted to get a tattoo with him, and we ended up getting kanjis. He got the one meaning Yin in the middle of his back between the tribal wings he has outlined, and I got the one for Yang on the inside of my left wrist above my Celtic trinity knot. We loved the meaning behind the symbols, Jason making me melt when he explained he felt I was the Yang to his Yin, the light to his dark, his opposite who completed and balanced him.

At first, I was a little nervous to get a matching tattoo with him, because I've always heard it's bad luck. But after learning the full meaning of Yang, it fit me personally, so I'm not worried about it.

The next day, we grabbed Tooty and went on an overnight trip to Myrtle Beach. (I know, I know! But it's soooo much fun down there!) I cannot even describe how awesome it was. When we first arrived, Jason pulled the new floaty we got her out of the box and blew it up, and I snapped the cutest pictures of her pudgy little self, sitting on the bed watching him as the yellow plastic expanded, her face mesmerized, like he was working pure magic.

The hotel we stayed at was awesome. It had an indoor waterpark, with a lazy river we floated in for a couple hours, a few kiddy slides Jason took her down, and even I had a great time in the water! Well... the pool, that is. I still didn't go into the ocean. But let me tell you, seeing Jason's tattooed sexy-ass body in his bright white swim trunks, holding my daughter in just her little swim diaper and a shitload of sunscreen as he introduced her to the ocean for the first time—OVARY EXPLOSION. If he could make babies, I would definitely give him one.

He had a late-night flight home that same evening, so when we got back to Fayetteville a couple hours later, we only had time for a short paddleboat ride around my lake before it was time to take him to the airport. It was much harder to say goodbye to him after each visit, since every minute spent with him I was growing more and more attached and in love with him.

End of June/ July:
This was quite a trip for us, because Josalyn and I ended up staying for two weeks! So much happened, all of it amazing. First, Buffy had my niece, which they named Abigail (they really love those A-names!) and we got to meet and snuggle her the day of my nephew Alex's birthday party. The baby had to stay in the hospital for a few extra days because she was severely jaundiced, but finally came home healthy and absolutely beautiful.

Also, we went to Beaumont for the 4th of July to spend the day with Jason's dad's side of the family. We had a huge barbecue, played in the pool (Jason even took Tooty down the waterslide!) and set off tons of fireworks. His—ridiculously good-looking—cousin Chad, a male nurse (something Jason gave him hell about throughout the entire day) made me both nervous and laugh hysterically. He was intimidating with his quick wit and sharp tongue, but then softened the teasing with drool-worthy smiles and a "I'm just playin', honey" said in his Texas drawl. Apparently the only girl Jason had brought around them before was the infamous 'awful girl' his mom had mentioned back in January, and everyone openly agreed they liked me way better. The comments made me happy, at the same time curious and jealous. He still hadn't told me anything about her. Though I finally found out her name was Lainey.

August:

August was extremely busy for the both of us, getting started with our fall semesters. I didn't get to see Jason this month, but oh, holy hell! If I wasn't head over heels in love with this man already, then this would have sealed the deal. *Acheron*, the fourteenth book in Sherrilyn Kenyon's Dark Hunters series, which I've been reading since the very first book *Fantasy Lover* was a new release, came out at the beginning of the month. Exciting in itself, I know. BUT WAIT! THERE'S MORE! I saw she would be doing a book tour, and one of the stops would be in Houston. I freaked out and told Jason about it, and without me even asking, he volunteered to go get me a signed copy!

He called me while he was there, at the Barnes and Noble store on the north side, at Deerbrook Mall, where we'd gone to see the movie when we saw each other the first time in over two years. Imagine my tall, dark, and handsome Texan badass boyfriend in a sea of housewives and goth-dressed teenage girls waiting in line to get their hands on the hardback Goliath of a book. I could feel his discomfort through the phone, but being the wonderful man he is, he asked me if there was anything I wanted him to tell or ask the author when he got up to her. I told him to ask her if Nick Gautier, one of my favorite characters, would be getting his own book. Turns out, Nick would be getting his own series!

Instead of worrying about my beloved book getting lost or damaged in the mail, I asked Jason to just keep it safe for me until the next time I saw him.

September:

We didn't see each other until the next month, when Josalyn and I made the trip to Texas. I take all online classes, but Jason goes to the actual school every day, and I didn't want him to miss class when he's been doing so well in his courses. So the next few trips were up to me to go to Texas. And what a trip this one was!

My big brother Jay, sister-in-law Renee, my oldest niece, fourteen-year-old Brooke, and three-year-old nephew Bret had moved to Texas a few months prior, so we picked Brooke up and took her to Galveston for a day at Schlitterbahn, a massive waterpark. Being petrified of waterslides, my ass was happy just hanging out in the kiddy area with Josalyn while Jason and Brooke went on the biggest and scariest slides. Brooke is normally pretty shy around new people, but she warmed up to Jason quickly, and even ended the day giving him an adorably nervous hug.

After the beautiful day in Galveston, you would never have guessed that Hurricane Ike would soon turn the rest of the visit into quite the adventure. Jason's parents evacuated to San Antonio, but the three of us decided to go to Kingwood and weather the storm with Jay and his family. I will never forget when the hurricane finally hit at two in the morning, and my crazy-ass brother got out on his balcony in his tighty-whities, yelling "WE HAVE DEBRIS!" the infamous line from *Twister*, as limbs landed on the floor of the patio. I was both terrified and laughing my ass off, shouting for him to get his ass back inside. He finally came in, telling us, "Those are hundred mile-an-hour winds for sure!" while I covered my eyes at his state of undress. The idiot. I love him.

The power went out, but we had plenty of light, thanks to Renee's obsession with candles, and we actually slept pretty soundly for the world to be seemingly ending outside. When we awoke the next morning, sure enough, it looked like we had been through the Apocalypse. Josalyn stayed with Renee, while Jason and I headed to Friendswood to assess the damage to his parents' house. It was surreal making our way south. The normal forty-five-minute drive took us three hours. The roads in Kingwood alone were a disaster, seeing how their motto is "The Livable Forest". Every square inch of free space in the suburb is filled with trees... except for the huge ones that had fallen across the main roads, forcing us to double back and find other avenues of getting out. When we finally hit the highways, it truly looked like the set of an end-of-the-world movie. The freeways, even the ones high up in the air, were flooded, causing us to take backroads and other routes, instead of our normal straight shot down 59 and 45. As we passed Downtown Houston, I got chills at the eerie sight of hundreds of windows blown out of the majestic skyscrapers.

When we finally made it to Jason's neighborhood, we got a laugh at someone canoeing down one of the roads, relief flooding us when we saw no damage had been done to his family home. There was debris everywhere, but nothing Jason and his dad would need help cleaning up themselves.

We got back a couple hours later, stayed one more night with my brother, then decided to make our way home. Jason's dad had bought two generators before the hurricane hit, so we felt like we were living like kings, while tons of other people went without electricity and hot water around us. Even though it was a complete disaster, I feel a little bad for saying it was also kind of fun. Not wanting to use up gasoline on things like television or computers, we spent our time playing board games and actually talking to each other. Although I feel terrible for the people who weren't as lucky as us in the outcome of the storm, it was an experience I'm glad we went through, because it brought us even closer together.

October:

Probably my favorite trip thus far visiting Jason, our October trip was awesome! We dressed Tooty up like Little Red Riding

Hood and took her around his neighborhood, his Mom, now officially named Mimi by Josalyn, proudly walking her up to her friends' doors to show off her adopted granddaughter.

But the best part of the trip: I finally got to meet Jason's best friend, Logan. He's the Marine who Jason had joined with. Up until now, I had never met him, because he was stationed at Camp Pendleton in California, or deployed overseas. He was home on leave, and I was super excited to meet him, since I'd heard so many stories of their misadventures as teenagers, and because I'd been friends with him on MySpace for quite some time now, after Jason told him we were getting serious.

My first thought when I'd seen his profile pic was "He looks like a douchebag." He was wearing a white wife-beater and baggy jeans and looked like he was trying to make an intimidating face. This was *not* the case when meeting him in person. Dressed in a nice polo shirt, jeans, and white K-Swiss shoes, his dark blond hair in a perfect high-and-tight, Jason's best friend was a hottie. Muscles... muscles everywhere.

Josalyn instantly latched onto him (God, she is definitely my daughter). And just like Jason, she immediately wrapped him securely around her little finger. She wasn't happy unless she was sitting on his lap. The boys got their amusement, learning she couldn't pronounce her R's yet, so they made her say the word *fork*, cackling like twelve-year-olds when her sweet baby voice sounded like she was saying *fuck*. Even I giggled when Logan took it to a whole new level, telling her to say mother-forker. She beamed at me when the guys exploded with laughter when she repeated it back to him.

Jason's parents watched Josalyn one night so we could go out with Logan, and it was so much fun hearing *his* side of the tales Jason had told me. It was a night full of laughter and good times, especially when after a few drinks, they decided they were awesome at doing the robot and had a dance battle. Also during the trip, it was Jason and Logan's friend Kano's wedding. I dressed Josalyn in an adorable baby pink velvet dress with grey polka dots and black patent-leather Mary Jane shoes, and we accompanied Jason to the celebration. When we arrived, Logan was there in his dress blue deltas, looking devastatingly handsome. It's a good thing Jason is not a jealous man, because I couldn't help drooling over the hunk. There is nothing like a man in uniform. Being from Fayetteville, I'd never been around a Marine before. Their dress uniform is definitely way hotter than the Army and Air Force ones I'm used to seeing. With Logan's bright blue eyes and amazing, contagious ever-present smile, it wasn't hard to understand why the two friends had been the perfect wingmen for each other back in the day. They were complete opposites, Logan with his boy-next-door, handsome, good guy, Captain America vibe, and Jason with his dark features and bad-boy thing going on, they made quite the pair.

On one of the last days there, we made the two-hour drive north to the Texas Renaissance Festival. Holy shitballs! If I thought the one in Raleigh was cool, the one in Todd Mission, TX... this was a case where 'Everything's bigger in Texas' was actually true! (Oh, Gavin. Nice truck, sorry about your penis. Hehe!) Squirrel!

The day before we left, Logan came over to Jason's house to hang out, not knowing Jason would be at school for a couple more hours. My periods had been super weird the past couple months, and at one point, my cycle was completely opposite— on my period for twenty-one days, then off it for only seven. I hadn't started my period when I was supposed to this month, and since I didn't have a car to drive, I awkwardly asked Logan if he'd run me up to the Dollar Tree so I could buy a pregnancy test. What was funny was there was no weirdness between us, and he didn't seem to think anything of it. I ran into the store and bought the test quickly while he waited in the car with Josalyn.

I took the test as soon as we got back to Jason's house, and not surprisingly, since Jason can't have kids, it was negative. This just meant I needed to go to the doctor whenever I got home to see what the hell was going on with my body.

And finally, November:

I spent a lot of time with Jenna last month. I'd missed her terribly after not working with her every day since I quit. One night, she called me completely out-of-her-mind excited, because some MMA fighter named Brock Lesner was going to be at Husk Hardware, a really nice bar and restaurant in Downtown Fayetteville, signing autographs after the fight at the Crown Coliseum. One, I had no idea who the dude was, and two, I didn't even know Jenna liked MMA, but nonetheless, it sounded like fun, so we got dolled up and went to see him. Holy giant, Batman! He was literally a half a person taller than me, and like five times as wide. Super sweet though, and gave one hell of a hug.

Jenna and I went to Chili's one night, something we do quite often, even if it's just to go eat chips and salsa and grab some drinks. But on this particular night, we were hell bent on going to get tattoos. We didn't care *what*; we just knew *where* we wanted them: behind our right ears. The Chop Shop was already closed by the time we had this grand plan, so we went to a place we knew off Yadkin Road that stayed open late. We went through all the posters on the walls, and she ended up choosing some cute little stars and hearts, and I chose a pink flower with a long green stem. Surprisingly, it didn't hurt at all. Just the sound of the tattoo gun right in your ear was really irritating.

On a different note, the doctors had no explanation for my periods being so off lately, and the only thing they could think to do to fix it was to switch my birth control. I got off my pills and switched to the NuvaRing, and thankfully my cycle was back to being predictable by the time Jason and I got to see each other again.

I got Mom and myself tickets to see Lisa Williams Live! Oh, my gosh! I had become obsessed with her show on Lifetime, her freaking me out with her amazing clairvoyant ability. I don't care what people say; that shit is real. And seeing her live was extraordinary. Originally, I had gotten Mom the ticket just so I wouldn't have to go by myself, but it turns out she's a believer too. She told me a story on the way to the event about how she'd gone to see a psychic soon after her little sister had passed away years before I was born. It was mostly to get closure, and I was happy to hear it when Mom said she'd found it by going to see the medium.

Speaking of the paranormal, I went and saw *Twilight* at

midnight when it released November 21st. I absolutely loved
the books and couldn't wait to see my Edward Cullen on the big
screen. I couldn't care less I was there by myself, because I
wasn't. I was there with a bunch of other girls with a love of
paranormal romance books, and I even told a few about my
blog. They said they couldn't wait to look me up so they could
read some reviews and pick out their next book.

A couple of days later, Jason came to see us, since he had time
off for Thanksgiving. By now, we had phone sex regularly, and I
was no longer shy about it. But we thought it would be a great
idea to hold out for like a week, not taking care of ourselves,
that way when we made love when he came to visit, it would
feel extra good. And damn if we weren't abso-freakin'-lutely
right!

Mom thought it was silly for him to pay for a hotel, because
we've now been together for nearly a year, so he just stayed at
our house. I had moved into my old bedroom the month
before, instead of staying in the same room with Josalyn, so we
didn't have to worry about the weirdness of sleeping together
next to a crib.

This was kind of a milestone-reaching visit for us. I had wanted
to get Josalyn's pictures made for Christmas cards, and when
we took her to Wal-Mart to get them taken, the photographer
asked if Jason and I would like a couple of the two of us. At my
expectant look, he agreed, and we ended up with some really
great shots that I bought several prints of. Jason asked if I'd
save him some to give his mom for Christmas, which I thought
was sweet.

We spent Thanksgiving at my Aunt Peggy's house, and Jason got to meet several of my cousins, including the one I had grown up super close to, Brittany, who announced she was pregnant! We filled our bellies and hung out for a long time before we went home, enjoying the time with my crazy family. This time wasn't so hard telling him goodbye, because I knew exactly when I'd see him again. Josalyn and I would be making the trip to Texas, flying out the day after Christmas, and we'd be there for New Year, my first time spending my favorite holiday with Jason!

So now you're all caught up on my adventures the past several months, and in a couple weeks, I'll be on my way to see my honey!

CHAPTER Twelve

December 27, 2008

Josalyn and I got to Houston yesterday, and then made the drive to Beaumont this morning to spend the day with Jason's mom's family. It was fun meeting them, especially since his gorgeous cousin Lisa had little girls close in age to Josalyn for her to play with while we were there.

We opened up presents, and I was surprised when a couple were handed to me from his mom. They were a beautiful pair of sterling silver earrings she and Dad got in Greece on their cruise a few months ago, and a matching necklace. Jason surprised me with tickets to go see the Trans-Siberian Orchestra perform at the Toyota Center tomorrow night. I was ecstatic. He couldn't have picked anything better than that. I just hope I'm feeling a little better when we go.

That morning, I told Jason I felt... weird. I wasn't sick, and it didn't even feel like I might be *getting* sick. I just felt off. Like my equilibrium wasn't quite balanced. Maybe it was PMS. I had taken my NuvaRing out so I could have my period, but it'd been four days and it still hadn't come. Maybe it was just the stress of traveling that had my body off, but I just couldn't shake the unbalanced feeling.

So, as we drive back to Friendswood, having left Beaumont about an hour and half ago, I ask him to stop at the Dollar Tree so I can get a pregnancy test. I've had to do this a couple times before. I don't know what it is, but the routine is: my period doesn't come for unknown reasons—stress, change in season, the moon and stars aligning funky, I don't know—but it waits long enough that I start questioning if I'm pregnant or not. Then, I take a pregnancy test, it comes up negative, and the next day, I finally start.

Josalyn rode home in Mimi and Papa's car, so Jason and I drove straight to the store and went inside. Having done this a few times now, I went directly to where they hung in the health and hygiene aisle and grabbed one.

"Just one?" Jason asks, taking another off the hanger and flipping it over to read the back.

"I mean, I know I'm not pregnant. I'm on birth control, and your swimmers are missing their fins, so this is really just a superstitious thing I do to wake my uterus up, like, 'Yo, bitch. We ain't pregnant. Hurry up and bleed already and get it over with, hooker.'"

He laughs and pulls me to him with an arm around my

lower back. "Oh, yeah, girl. Talk dirty to me," he growls playfully.

"You're like, the only guy on the face of the planet who doesn't get the least bit squeamish when it comes to period shit. I kinda love that about you." I smile and lean up on my tiptoes to kiss him before turning in his arms and getting in line to check out.

When we get back to his house, I head toward the back to his bathroom to take the test while he uses the one by the kitchen. He drank two Red Bulls and a Coke on the drive back and said he was about to explode. I'm doing the I-gotta-peepee dance myself, and when I sit down, I realize I forgot to grab anything to do my business in for the test. I look around for a second and spot the red Solo cup in the tub that Josalyn was playing with during her bath last night and reach in to grab it.

A few seconds later, I'm taking the dropper from the test package, collecting enough urine to drip into the little circular window at the far end of the white plastic test, and before I even have time to lay it flat, not having to wait the three minutes it says the test will take, the unthinkable happens.

Normally, when I take these things, you can see as the liquid is absorbed up the material of the test, and it skips the first line, which would tell you if you're pregnant, and only makes the Control line appear across the window, letting you know the test is complete. One line, letting you know you are not pregnant.

My test. My little one-dollar, superstitious, 'I only take you to jumpstart Aunt Flow's visit' test. My test?

Has two lines.

I stare at it for a solid minute, my jeans still around my calves as I sit on the pot, picking the test back up, tilting it toward the light, trying to make sure I'm not seeing things as the hysterical panic starts to gurgle and brew inside my stomach. My breath starts to come out in sharp pants and heat crawls up the back of my neck, into my scalp, making it tingle as my face flushes. Oh, God!

I go to hop up then realize I'm still in a state of undress. With shaking hands, I set the pregnancy test on the side of the tub and clean myself up before rebuttoning my jeans. And then... I collapse.

I sit in the middle of the bathroom floor, grab the towel hanging on the towel rack, and finally release the sob of overwhelming emotion inside me as I begin to bawl into the thick, soft fabric.

Oh, fuck. Oh, shit! What the fuck am I going to do? I'm *pregnant?* How the hell did that happen? I mean, duh. But Jason is infertile! Has been since he was twelve years old. Plus, I'm on birth control!

We live half a country away from each other. What about school? Oh, God. Josalyn. My poor baby! She's going to think I don't love her and am trying to replace her! She's my world, my everything. This baby... how am I supposed to love it enough, when all my love already pours into my daughter, and all the reserves go to Jason? I'm only one person. Do I have enough love inside me for everyone? Oh, sweet Jesus. What is Jason going to think? Is he going to think I cheated on him, since he's always been told he couldn't have kids, and here I am pregnant? He has to know I'd never do that in a million years. I fought too fucking long and hard, and put up with entirely too much shit to do something so stupid as cheat on my soul mate after I finally got him. He has to know. Right? *Right?*

A knock at the door sends me gasping and clutching at the towel in my hand like a life preserver. After a few seconds, it comes again, and I gather my wits enough to crawl on my hands and knees to the door to pull down on the handle enough to pop the lock undone. I don't have it in me to actually open the door. That would mean I'd voluntarily be giving up my solitude, here, hidden in the bathroom with my secret. But that privacy doesn't last even a moment longer as Jason pushes the door open and comes inside. Looking down at me, where I've backed myself up on my ass against the wooden cabinet beneath the sink, still clinging desperately to the towel, he quickly closes the door behind him then crouches down in front of me, reaching out to push my hair out of my face.

"Baby, what's wrong? What happened?" His deep voice flows over me gently as he tilts my face up to him.

I manage to look up at him, into those beautiful dark chocolate eyes I love so much, and I choke out, barely making it through the two words, "It's positive."

I hold my breath, waiting for the horrible reaction I know is coming, the bitch inside my head chanting, *He can't have kids. He won't believe you. He can't have kids. He won't believe you. He can't have kids...*

"The test? It's positive?" he asks, his voice steady, not angry, not disbelieving, just solid, trying to clarify what I'm telling him.

"Y-yes. It's on the tu-tub," I sob out, my heart racing at the thought of him getting up, walking over to the test, picking it up, and seeing it for himself.

Which is exactly what he does.

A part of me wants to giggle as he tilts the test toward the light, just as I had, but I think I'm in shock and can't do anything but stare at his face, waiting for his reaction.

He comes back over to me and sits down Indian-style next to me then opens his arms. "Come here, baby."

I launch myself at him, nearly knocking him backward, but he quickly recovers and wraps his arms around me and my towel, which I think has now cemented itself to me with the amount of snot I've blown into it. I'm sure I look *extremely* attractive at the moment, but I give zero fucks.

After a few minutes of him rocking me, he stops suddenly, tightens his arms around me, and says aloud, "I'm gonna be a dad," as if it just at this very moment hit him what my positive pregnancy test means. "Baby," he pushes his chest forward to sit me up then looks me dead in the eyes while holding my face in his hands, "I'm gonna be a dad!"

I bite my lip, cut my eyes to my far right, where he's holding the test against my cheek, and then with as much humor as I can muster, I look back into his awe-filled stare and tell him, "Babe... I just peed on that."

He looks at the test in his hand then swiftly pulls it away from my face, reaching above our heads to place it on the bathroom counter. "Sorry," he grunts, using his thumb to rub at the spot on my cheek the test had rested against.

"You're not mad?" I ask in a small voice, watching his eyes observe the movement of his thumb before they lift to mine.

"Mad? Baby, are you kidding me?" He shakes his head, a disbelieving look on his face. "I told you a long time ago that if I could, I would have a ton of kids."

"That's the problem, Jason. *If* you could. I'm scared you're gonna think I—" My voice breaks and I can't continue, not wanting to be the one who puts it in his head that I could've possibly cheated on him.

"Stop. Seriously? I *know* you didn't, baby. We talk every. Single. Night. For hours, on the phone. When you're not talking to me, you're raising that precious little girl of yours and working your ass off on your schoolwork. You live with your parents, and you never even stay out late enough when you go out for me to even waste brainpower on thinking you might be at some other guy's house. Plus, I don't think anyone on the planet makes their significant other feel as loved, wanted, and desired as you make me feel. I know you'd never do that to me. I *know* this is my baby. Our little miracle." And with that, he pulls me to him and kisses me like he's never kissed me before. Loving, tender, his whole heart pouring into it, with notes of possessiveness I'd never felt from him before.

When the kiss finally ends, my heart drops once more when something pops into my head, and seeing the panic in my eyes, he asks, "What is it?"

"Go get your mom," I state firmly.

"What? Why?" he asks, a tinge of panic lining his own voice now.

"Jason, go get your mother. We *have* to tell her," I implore.

"Can't we tell her later? I mean... we just found out like five seconds ago," he tries to rebuff, but I'm not having it. My mommy isn't here, and I need my stand-in. STAT.

"Jason Louis, you go get your mom for me right fucking now," I growl, and he pulls his head back, his brow furrowing.

"Okay, okay, geez, Satan. Pregnancy hormones already?" He shakes his head as he unwraps himself from around me and pulls himself up to stand. I scoot back against the cabinet once again, my heart pounding as I wait for him to come back with his mom.

When she sees me on the floor, just like her son, she gets down on her haunches in front of me and asks what's wrong. Instead of answering with words, I reach above my head, grasp a hold of the test, and bring it down in front of her face.

She pulls her glasses down onto her nose from the where they sat on the top of her head and looks at the rectangle of white plastic. After a second, she tells me, "Honey, I don't know what this is."

"It-it's a pregnancy test," I stutter. I had thought I'd just have to show it to her and that would be the end of it, but oh no. I guess God wants to play a little joke on me and make me spell everything out for her.

"And what does it say, baby doll? I never had to take one of these before," she adds, taking the test in her hand.

I had forgotten she'd never been pregnant before, never conceiving once, even after years of fertility treatments. "The two lines you see in the little window there," I explain, pointing to the little blue lines, "that means the test is positive."

As soon as the words process in her mind, she falls out of her crouch, plopping down onto her pajama-covered butt. "Oh, my gosh," she breathes. After a few moments, she asks, "How accurate are these things? Are you sure? When did you take it?"

"It's over 99 percent accurate, and the reason I took it is because my period is late and I've been feeling really weird lately, so I'm almost certain. And I just took it about ten minutes ago. I... I don't have my mom... so I asked Jason to run get you," I answer.

"Oh, honey." She leans forward and wraps her arms around my back. For such a tiny woman, she gives wonderful, fierce hugs, and I absorb all the comfort she's giving me. "We gotta tell Steve!" she exclaims, leaning back and grasping my forearms, not hesitating as she gets to her feet and yanks me up. She tugs on me until I'm out in the hallway, where Jason has been waiting, leaning up against the wall beside his bedroom doorway, and she tells him, "Y'all go sit at the kitchen table and I'll go get him."

"Oh, shit," Jason grumbles, but seeing the scared look on my face when I whip my head toward him, he gives me a sexy smile and leans down to kiss me. "Remind me to tell you a story after we tell Pop."

"Ooookay," I reply, taking a moment to peek in at Josalyn, where she's asleep in the middle of the full-size bed in the room next to Jason's.

We sit down at the kitchen table and wait for Mom to go to the shop out back to tell Dad we need to talk to him. When they return, the couple sits across from us, and his dad takes his ball cap off of his head, setting it next to him. "So what's going on?"

"Mom didn't tell you?" Jason asks, fidgeting in his seat, and I reach over and place my hand on his knee.

"No, I didn't tell him. This is all you, bud," his mom

interjects, giving Jason a haughty look.

Jason seems to have gone speechless, so I take a breath, clear my throat, gaining Dad's attention, and tell him, "Well... even though I was on birth control, it seems we've... um, well... you see—"

"We're pregnant."

The words burst out of Jason like canon fire, but I can't even move to look over at him as my eyes widen, watching for his dad's reaction, utterly terrified out of my mind. You can never, ever tell what Steve's reaction will be when it comes to *anything*. Sometimes you think he'll absolutely love something, but he ends up hating it. Food, movies, tools, politics... you name it. Whatever opinion or reaction you think he might have, it's almost guaranteed it'll actually be the opposite. Makes it hard to buy him anything for gifts, but in this instance, as I sit here scared to death he's going to hate me for ruining his son's life, it's a very, very good thing.

Steve stands up, pushing his chair back, walks around the table, scoots past his son, and obviously having seen the fear in my eyes, he takes hold of my hands and pulls me up into a bear hug. He then pats me on the back as he pulls away, and tells me with his contagious smile planted firmly on his face, "Well, welcome to the family, sweetheart."

The words send me launching back into his embrace and I squeeze him hard, so relieved that he isn't upset.

He must feel me trembling, because he tells me, his Texan accent strong, "What's all this about, girl? You thought I'd be mad atcha or something? Hell, y'all have been friends for how long? And you've been dating for about a year now. I've never seen Jason so hung up on a girl before. My boy loves the hell outta you. I mean, damn—we're Mimi and Papa to your youngin'," he adds, holding his hand out to Mom. "I knew those doctors were full of shit, tellin' us he wouldn't be able to have kids." He turns to face his son, pointing his finger and narrowing his eyes. "That's why I always told you to wrap your shit up." His face softens again when he turns back to me. "And it might be happenin' a little sooner than y'all planned, but there ain't nothin' to be mad about, babe." He gives me one last hug before making his exit, calling over his shoulder, "Going back to the shop, Mama," and we hear the back door close.

Well, I guess that's that, I think, letting out a relieved sigh before looking up at Jason, who has a stunned look on his face.

"He can think what he wants, but I say it's a miracle. Those doctors were certain you wouldn't be able to have kids. And you were on birth control, honey?" Mom asks, gaining our attention.

"Yes, ma'am. I had been on the mini-pill ever since I had Josalyn, since that's all you're allowed to take while you're breastfeeding, but then when I stopped nursing, my body went haywire, so they put me on the Nuvaring," I explain.

"See there? I mean, I'll take you somewhere to really get tested. I don't really trust this little thing anybody can buy at the store. But if you took the test because you're late and because you felt funny, then the test is really just confirming what you already knew. Whether you realized you knew it or not," she tells me, and I nod. "And of course this happens on a weekend. We'll go bright and early Monday morning. Sound good?"

"Yes, ma'am. Thank you."

With that, Jason seems to snap out of his stupor and wraps his arms around both of us, kissing his mom on the top of her head first before leaning down to kiss me on my lips. "Night, Mama," he tells her, and then he lets go of her before leading me out of the kitchen and down the hallway to his room.

I plop down on the foot of his bed, pulling my feet up underneath me after I kick off my shoes. I don't really know what to say. Besides the fact that went better than I could've ever imagined... I can't believe it happened in the first place.

I'm pregnant.

I'm pregnant with Jason's baby.

Jason and I are going to have a baby... together... that is *ours*.

Josalyn will be a big sister.

I'll be a mother of two.

Jason sits beside me on the bed, putting one of his muscular legs behind me so he can pull me to him. "You want to hear that story I mentioned before we told Pop?"

"Should I be scared?" I ask, still a little dazed over everything. I don't think it's fully sunk in yet that I'm pregnant... with Jason's child... at this very moment. It all feels so surreal.

"Nah, it's a funny story. Okay, you know the 'awful girl' my mom mentioned? My ex-girlfriend, Lainey, the one Chad said he much preferred you over?"

Now *this* gets my attention. I've never really asked Jason about any of the relationships he had while I was married to Aiden. Part of me tries to pretend they didn't exist, but another part of me, a weird, sort of morbidly curious part, wants to know every minor detail of what went on during that time period.

"Yes, I recall," I say sarcastically, and he squeezes me, letting out a chuckle.

"Well, she was a bartender up at Slick's, the pool hall I used to go to all the time. We started dating, and she came over one night. Without going into too much detail, Mom walked in on us."

My eyes widen and I jerk around to face him with a gasp. "No. Way." But then a creepy feeling comes over me and I look down and around me. "Oh, God!" I jump off the bed, out of his grasp.

"What?" he asks, a worried look on his face.

"Here? She walked in on y'all... in here?" I say, dreading his answer.

"Well, yes, in here. But you are the only person I've slept with in this bed, babe. I swear. I got this furniture after I dumped her ass." I don't miss the bitterness that enters his voice on that last sentence. "But anyways, Mom walked in on us —"

"How? Like she just came busting in? And where were y'all? What were you doing exactly?" The questions come out rapid fire, and Jason gives me a funny look.

"You sure you want to know all this? I mean, you are the most jealous woman on the face of the planet. So jealous that even though the entirety of your giant family has blue eyes, yours turned green," he jokes, but nothing he says will distract me from getting the information I'm now dying to get.

"Yes," I state with a short, concise nod.

"All right, well come here and relax. You look like you're about to attack me if I speak the wrong word," he says, holding his arms open to me.

I make my way back into his embrace and snuggle against him as he restarts his story.

"We were on the floor, because the bed I had at that time squeaked, and she was on top of me," he says.

"Like riding you?" I ask, biting my lower lip.

"Yeah. And Mom, being Mom, just came busting into the room without knocking."

"Oh, jeez." I shake my head. I would be absolutely mortified. Just thinking about it has my face heating up. "So what happened?"

"Well, there was this awkward moment where Mom just stood there, and it felt like a lifetime, but it couldn't have been more than a couple seconds, and then she turned around and left. And then I heard my dad coming up the hallway, and he stopped outside the door, not looking in, and told us he needed to talk to us out in the living room," he replied, and I can hear the smile entering his voice. What he's smiling about, I have no idea. I'm embarrassed for him and this girl just hearing about it.

"What was Lainey's reaction? I mean, was she absolutely dying? I would have wanted to off myself!" I question, my voice pitching higher and higher.

"She wasn't fazed." He shakes his head and shrugs.

"What?" I scoff. "What do you mean?"

"Lainey was a bitch. I mean, you know how when a girl does *one thing,* people will be like, 'Oh, she's a bitch', using the term lightly just because she might have made one bitchy move? That's not the case with her. She was. A. Bitch," he states, emphasizing each word. "She didn't just make a bitch-move every once in a while. She just was one. Twenty-four seven. To her core."

"Wow, sounds like you picked a winner," I snark.

"Hey, it was a rough time in my life. No judging. Anyways, so, we went into the living room, and Mom goes, 'Well, this isn't exactly the way I wanted to meet you the first time,' and after a little bit of awkward conversation, Lainey left. And finally, I come to the funny part. The part I really wanted to tell you," he says, his voice rising in energy as he shifts on the bed like he can't sit still. "When she left, Pop goes, 'Dang, son, looks like you've got yourself a sweller,' and I was like, 'What the fuck? What's a sweller?' and he said, 'That girl might look good right now, but if you knock her up, she's gonna swell right the hell up.'"

I can't help it. I know it's so super rude to laugh at someone picking on anyone for their size, but thinking about this super-bitch fucking my man and not even having the decency to be the slightest bit embarrassed about being caught doing the dirty in his parents' house, I let out a laugh from so deep in my gut that I have to jump up, grab my crotch with both hands, and run out his bedroom door into the bathroom across the hall, barely making it to the toilet before peeing on myself.

When I come back into the bedroom, Jason has a shit-eating grin on his face. "You all right, beautiful?"

"Yep. Have I mentioned I love your dad?" I smile.

"Yeah, but I didn't even finish my story before you hightailed it to the bathroom," he teases.

"The joys of motherhood. I can't even sneeze without—never mind. Finish your story," I say, cutting myself off.

"When you came over and brought Josalyn to see us the first time back in January, he told me, 'See, son, that's good breedin' stock there. Definitely not a sweller.'"

"Oh, my gosh. You're dad is hilarious. He just says the sweetest things." I say the last part in a breathy southern belle accent as I start taking off my clothes, watching Jason's eyes heat.

Before he gets any ideas, I quickly grab my pajamas off his leather couch against the wall and put them on. After our day of travelling, and then the emotional roller coaster I've been on since we got back home, I'm suddenly exhausted and would rather he just hold me while we watch some TV and fall asleep.

Taking the hint as I walk to the head of the bed and pull down the covers, he stands, only taking the time to let his jeans drop to his ankles, pulling his feet out of his boots and pants at the same time while lifting his shirt over his head, leaving him in nothing but his briefs.

"What?" he asks as he crawls up the bed and gets in beside me when he sees the amused look on my face.

"First thing I'm doing when we move in together is burning all your tighty-whities," I say through a giggle.

"I like the sound of that."

"What? Me burning all your old-man undies?"

"No, the moving in together part," he clarifies, and my face heats.

"I didn't mean... that just kinda came out. I didn't mean to assume we'd be moving in together now that I'm pregnant. I just—"

"Babe," he interrupts my rambling. "Of course we're moving in together. That was going to happen whether you are pregnant or not. We've talked about this."

We had, on several occasions, but we had never settled on a plan because everything was so up in the air. My life—my family, school, everything—is in North Carolina, and he had never lived anywhere but here in Friendswood. It was never really a question of *who* would move *where*. I always assumed it'd be me who moved back to Texas to be with him, since there was so much more offered in life outside of Fayetteville. I mean, even if I wanted to go shopping at a Hollister I had to drive two hours away to the mall in Raleigh. The only thing keeping me in Fayettenam was the people—mainly my mom and granny. I could always move my credits to a school in Texas. The question was always the *when*.

"Maybe this is a sign," he adds, sliding his arm beneath my pillow and tugging me closer, placing his other hand on my stomach. The feel of his warm palm through my nightshirt radiates through me, filling me up with his loving touch. "Maybe this little miracle was God's way of giving us a little shove in the right direction, hurrying all this along when only the man upstairs knows how long it would've been dragged out."

"You sure have been talking about God a lot since we got back together," I point out, and he gives me a contemplative look.

"What do you mean?"

"When we first got back together, you confessed that you thought maybe God sent me back home to meet Aiden so I could have Josalyn for you and me. And now this," I explain.

He thinks on that for a few moments, and then says, "I guess me finally getting to have you, it's made me believe He's got a plan for me. I've always believed He put you on this Earth for me. I was just stupid and let you go. And after I put that roadblock in its path, making you take a detour, He's now set the course straight again and upped the speed limit to hurry us along."

I can't help but smile at his reasoning. Leave it to him to explain his renewed belief in God with a driving analogy. Jason's always had a... different relationship with religion. He believes in a higher power; he just has a problem with organized religion, in the sense that he hasn't found one that he fits into like a jigsaw puzzle piece. I've tried telling him that I don't know anyone who believes and follows every single, solitary rule of whatever religion they fall into. But he's bound and determined in his belief that it's an all or nothing kind of deal.

He was raised Methodist, while I was raised Catholic. He still occasionally goes to church with his mom, and he participates in UM Army, a group from the church that spends a week somewhere fixing things for people in need. He did it last year, his first time as an adult leader instead of as a youth, and they went to Athens, TX and Alexandria, LA and built wheelchair ramps onto people's houses. He said he loved the building part, aiding people who needed it and wouldn't have otherwise been able to get the help, but said he was super uncomfortable at the end of the day when it was time for 'all the Bible reading and singing shit', as he put it.

Asking him one time what his biggest turn-off was from the Methodist church, which he had grown up going to every Sunday since he was born, he said, "It's my African fisherman." After letting out a laugh of surprise, I asked him to explain.

"My African fisherman. I was taught in Sunday school that the Bible says the only way into Heaven is through Jesus. My teacher said that if you don't believe in him, then you can't get into Heaven when you die. Even when I was little, my question was what if you are somewhere you never even heard of Jesus. Like my African fisherman. He's just a sweet, little old man who spends his days fishing to bring home food to his wife he's never cheated on, his kids he's never raised a hand to. He's been the epitome of a good man his entire life. Never stolen anything or killed anyone. Okay, are you telling me he doesn't get to go to Heaven, just because he lives somewhere they might never have heard of Jesus before? But some asshole, who has murdered a bunch of people, suddenly finds religion in his prison cell and asks for forgiveness gets to? I don't fucking think so."

"Well, personally, I think we all believe in the same person; we just call him something different. I call him God, someone else calls him Buddha, another dude calls him… I don't know… what's another one? That turtle… Anyways. All the same dude, different name. Because if you look at the main set of rules in each 'handbook'—the Ten Commandments in the Bible being ours—they're all the same. Lying, killing, cheating, all that shit —bad. Kindness, generosity, helping fellow man—good. So getting back to your African fisherman. He more than likely has his own religion, which calls Jesus or God by a different name, but he's going to end up in Heaven. It's just going to be *his* Heaven."

I thought I'd made a pretty damn good argument, but he still wasn't having it, so I gave up on trying to make him feel better about his little African fisherman.

But now, lying in bed with him, his protective hand warming my belly, hearing him talk about us being on the right path God had set for us, it makes me happy he seems to have found a bit of peace with Him. It's one less thing for my otherwise broody boyfriend to worry his over-analytical mind about.

We watch a little bit of TV, and soon, as my eyes get heavy, I roll over to be the little spoon, and he keeps his hand right where it is all night as we fall asleep.

CH♠PTER *Thirteen*

Two days later, Jason stays home to watch Josalyn and to help his dad with a project in his shop while his mom takes me to Planned Parenthood for a 'real' pregnancy test, as she calls it. She wanted to take me to her doctor's office, but since I don't have insurance, it would have cost a fortune, so this was the next best option. I had never even heard of this place, but as I read the posters on the wall and the little brochure I picked up when I signed in at the window, checking the box for pregnancy test and paying the $30 fee, I learned it was a place you could get birth control, annual women's wellness appointments, and STD and pregnancy tests at low cost if you don't have insurance.

We were the first ones here, so it's only a few minutes before I'm called back. I wanted Mom to come with me, but the nurse said she wasn't allowed for the testing, but that she could for the results. She has me step up on a scale to find out my weight, and then I sit in a chair for her to take my temperature and blood pressure. After writing my name on a clear cup with a green lid in Sharpie, she hands it to me and points me toward the restroom, telling me to set it inside the metal window after I fill it to the line, and then I can go back out and have a seat when I'm done.

I'm only in the waiting room for five minutes before Mom and I are heading back to the nurse's office to get my results. Even though I *feel* pregnant, and had my at-home test confirm I'm positive, I'm a little nervous. Yesterday, we spent the day talking and daydreaming about nothing but this little one growing inside me, Jason even taking a moment to get on his knees and kiss my tummy before I slid on my little black dress I was wearing to our Trans-Siberian Orchestra performance, and it gave me a chance for it to really sink in this was really happening. It would be absolutely devastating to find out that it was just a false positive and something else going on with my body.

With my heart pounding in my ears, I sit down in one of the two chairs facing the nurse's rolling one, Mom sitting in the other, holding her purse in her lap. I watch as the woman in pink scrubs pulls out a piece of paper from the manila file folder in front of her.

She looks at it a split second before turning to me with a smile on her face. "Your paperwork says you have one child, a girl, who is twenty months?" She poses it more as a question, even though she can clearly see that's what I wrote down.

My nerves are making me grumpy and impatient, so I have

to force myself to leave the "Duh" out of my voice when I answer, "Yes, ma'am," as I wait for her to get the hell on with it.

"Well, congratulations. In nine months, if all goes well, you'll be a mommy of two little ones," she says pleasantly, obviously gauging my reaction and purposely keeping a happy tone in her voice to offset if I were to have a bad one.

A gust of breath leaves me, and my face splits into a grin as I look over at Mom, who nods at the confirmation, a small smile on her lips.

"So let's find out your due date, shall we?" the nurse prompts, and I watch her take out some kind of paper wheel with a bunch of numbers and dates on it. "When was the first day of your last period?"

"Oh, hell. I have no idea. My cycle has been so screwed up since I stopped breastfeeding that I don't know when it's coming. But there's only one week I could have possibly gotten pregnant in the last couple of months. My boyfriend and I date long-distance. I live in North Carolina and he lives here. In the last two months, meaning November and December, I only saw him for the week of Thanksgiving before coming to see him this past Friday. It had to have happened that week, because I had a period before he came, but not since," I explain.

She nods and turns the wheel around on itself, and when she has it aligned the way she wants it, she looks at it closely and says, "Alrighty, that's means this baby is due August 28th," making a note on my paperwork. She checks a few things on the form and then tears the copies apart, handing me the top portion and keeping the bottom to put back into the manila folder. "The building directly behind us is where you'll go next." She smiles and stands, nudging the rolling stool out of our way.

"I'm sorry, what?" I ask, confused about why I need to go anywhere else, since we came to find out for sure I'm pregnant, and she already confirmed that.

She gives me a perplexed look before hooking her toe on the caster of the stool and pulling it back toward her to sit on. "Well, I assume since you're here that you don't have any health insurance, correct?" I nod and she continues. "Did you have insurance with your last child?"

"Yes, ma'am. I was a military spouse," I clarify.

"Ah, okay. So since you don't have insurance, the building behind us is where you will go to register for Medicaid. Once they see if you qualify, that will be your insurance provider, and then you'll be able to find an OB."

"Oh. I hadn't even thought that far ahead," I say quietly. I've been military my whole life. All I've ever had to do is walk into Womack Army Medical Center, and no matter what my ailment, they'd just send me to whoever I needed to see within the same hospital. There was no having to seek out my own doctor.

Mom reaches over and pats my leg. "No need to worry about all that. I'll teach you everything you need to know." Then she turns to the nurse with a serious look on her face. "Just out of curiosity, what is the difference between the pregnancy tests y'all give, the ones at a true doctor's office, and the over-the-counter ones like she got from the dollar store?"

"Honestly, nothing. In fact, I worked at a doctor's office before I moved here, and when we ran out of pregnancy tests, they sent me to the dollar store to load up on some until our shipment of the exact same ones was due to come in the next day. All it is, is a little strip that will be activated to change color if the hormone HCG is found in the urine. So whether you pay a dollar for it there, or thirty dollars for the fancy ones, they're all the same. One is no more accurate than another," she replies, standing once more. "Do y'all have any more questions?"

"I don't think so," I say, and with a nod, she opens the door for us, and then I hear her go into another room as we walk out into the waiting room and then through the front door. We drive around until we see the large brick building that houses the Medicaid office.

The next hour is spent filling out a ton of paperwork, but then we discover I have to have a valid Texas ID in order to get Medicaid, because each state has their own program. We take a number in line in order to ask the person in the window some questions, and when it's our turn, Mom doesn't hesitate in asking anything and everything she can think of, including her last question, which I've heard her ask different people before. "All right, I've asked everything I can think of. Is there anything else I should have asked that you can tell me?" Such a smart lady.

"It'll take approximately three weeks for her to get on Medicaid once she turns in all her paperwork with her valid Texas ID." He turns to me. "If I were you, I'd go ahead and get your Texas driver's license while you're here. That way you can go ahead and start the process, instead of waiting until you actually move here."

My heart gives a tremendous thud thinking about all this.

It's all happening so fast. I just found out I'm pregnant two days ago. And now, in what seems to be a blink of an eye, there's all this talk about moving to Texas as soon as possible. I mean, yes, awesome, super happy I'll be with my Jason. But holy shitballs. I haven't even told my mom I'm pregnant yet! I can't just go planning this huge change in my life, uprooting Josalyn and myself and leaving my mom and Granny, when I was just supposed to come to Texas on one of our normal visits, where we'd fly back home and wait until the next time we'd go for a visit, doing it all over again, always going back home. This would be different. Next time I went home, from the way things were sounding, it would be to pack up our stuff and move here.

I thank the man who answered all of our questions and start heading toward the door, needing some fresh air. When Mom catches up to me, she tells me I look pale and asks if I'm okay.

"Just a little overwhelmed. And I think I need to eat something. I'm getting that weird, off-balance feeling again," I reply, and when we get into her Highlander, she takes me to Saltgrass Steakhouse and makes me eat a big house salad with Ranch dressing, plus a six-ounce sirloin steak to make sure I have a good amount of iron in my system. When we leave, I feel ten times better, and we head home.

Kayla's Chick Rant & Book Blog
March 24, 2009

Finding out I'm pregnant threw a little wrench in my New
Year's plans to go out dancing with Jason and get white-girl
wasted. Instead, we ended up going back to Beaumont for his
Aunt Melissa's surprise birthday party her kids were throwing
her at the boat docks. They had tables and chairs set up all over
the pier, a table of food off to the side that I took full advantage
of, realizing how different this pregnancy already is from
Josalyn's, and even had fireworks set off.

There were tubs of beer and bottles of wine next to the table of
food, and I was happily impressed with Jason when his cousin,
Lisa, offered him a beer and he told her, "Sure, but just the
one." His cousin, however, was flabbergasted.

"Just the one? First, your girlfriend here turns down a glass of
wine, and now you're only going to have one beer...on New
Year's? If it's the drive home you're worried about, don't. You
can always stay with us," she told him.

And that's when it seemed to dawn on her. I could almost see the little light bulb go on over her pretty blonde head. "Oh, my God. You're pregnant, aren't you?"

I'm the most horrible liar on the planet. Even if the lie were to come out of my mouth, you'd never believe me, because I have absolutely no control over what my face does when I react to something. I felt my eyes bug out of my head as I turned to look up at Jason, who had a shit-eating grin on his face.

Lisa's smile lit up her whole face and she gave us both a big hug. We told her I just found out the night we came to Beaumont the weekend before and that no one knew except Jason's parents. "Well, better you than me, girl. I don't think I want any more kids, at least not right now. Two little girls is enough."

As I type this, I'm laughing my ass off, because little did she know a few weeks later, not only is she pregnant, but Jason's other cousin, Dianna, who was also at the party, is as well!

When I got off the plane in Fayetteville with Josalyn, I didn't even have a chance to say hardly one word to my mom before I shoved Josalyn's stroller at her and ran into the bathroom, my hand clamped firmly over my mouth. As I puked my brains out, I heard Mom come in behind me and coo at Josalyn, "So, guess who's going to be a big sister? Youuu are!" And between heaves, I had to wonder how the hell my mom could possibly know. I mean, I could just be nauseous from the flight. How did she guess I was pregnant?

When I swayed out of my stall after catching my breath, I looked at my mom with a questioning look. "I had my suspicions before you left. This just confirmed it," she told me with a smirk. "I think you should name him Jensen. Jensen is a fine name."

She's convinced it's a boy. She was dead-on with Josalyn, knowing super early it was a girl, but I have no idea. That was the first time I'd gotten even a little bit nauseous during this pregnancy, when I could barely keep down water with Josalyn's for the first trimester. Maybe it is a boy, and that's why this time feels so different.

We told Granny when we got home, and then I let them know what Jason, his family, and I had been discussing while I was there. They weren't happy Josalyn and I would be moving away, but they understood there were many more opportunities in Houston than in little Fayetteville. The Robichauxs offered for me to move in with them until Jason and I could get a place of our own.

During this same conversation, I told them the whole story of how I found out I was pregnant, from the initial feeling of just not feeling right, all the way to the part when Steve gave me the big hug that put my mind at ease. Mom stopped me when I told her about how I was so scared Josalyn would think I'm trying to replace her, and that I wouldn't love this baby as much as her. She asked me, "KD, do you think I love Tony any less than I do Mark?" I shook my head adamantly. "Do you think I love Jay any less than I love your other two brothers?" I shook my head again, tears filling my eyes. "And do you think I love you any less than I love the three of them?" This one made me snort. "Of course not. They're always picking on me, saying I'm your princess and the favorite, and I came last," I replied.

She wrapped me up in her arms, where I sat next to her on the couch with Josalyn on my knees, who was reaching up and

putting clips in my hair. "You don't have to worry about any of
that, baby doll. Josalyn will have a sibling to play with and grow
up having her best friend live with her. And as for you, you
don't run out of love. Your heart just grows." As if that line
wasn't enough, she hit me with some truth. "Plus, this is Jason's
baby. Do you really think you wouldn't love the child you
created with the man of your dreams?"

I can be a real turd sometimes.

This is why I'm a momma's girl. After that, I had no fear.
Jason got a job at Friendswood Roofing a couple of weeks ago,
the work perfect for his mathematical brain. He gets up on
people's roofs, measures them, comes up with all the square
footage and whatnot, and then prices them out for the
customer. With so many homes still damaged from Hurricane
Ike last year, there is plenty of work to be done. I offered to get
a job as well, but Jason told me no, to focus on my schoolwork.
He wasn't going to allow anything to get in my way of finishing
my degree I was so close to completing. This would be my last
full year of school if I kept going the pace I was at, and I could
graduate at the end of the winter semester.

We went the rest of January and half of February without
seeing each other, and Jason had basically been insane not
being able to be around us. To the point that he bought a plane
ticket and decided he was coming to see us for a four-day
weekend for Valentine's Day. He got here super early the
morning of the fourteenth.

And I don't know what it is about Jason coming to visit turning
into a traditional trip to Myrtle Beach, but that's what
happened. Before he booked his ticket to come, Mom and I had

booked ourselves a hotel room down at the beach because she had 'a hankerin' to go see Brookgreen Gardens' as she put it. Finding out Jason would be visiting, she offered to cancel, but he told her to do no such thing, that he would love to see the beautiful sculpture garden and wildlife preserve. So, he found out what hotel we were staying at and reserved us another room.

The trip was a ton of fun. The first thing we did after checking into our hotel was go straight to the gardens and spent a few hours taking pictures and admiring all the giant sculptures, topiaries, and the maze you could walk through. There weren't a lot of flowers blooming because of the time of year, but it was still beautiful. Josalyn liked the huge fountain and threw every coin all three of us owned into the water, until we finally had to tell her we didn't have any more.

When we left, we went to Calabash Seafood Buffet, which had all-you-can-eat snow crab legs. Boy, I bet they didn't know what hit them when we walked in the door. Between us three adults, no lie, we probably put away about fifteen pounds of those suckers. Even little Josalyn ate a couple, Jason cracking them open and dipping them in a little butter before handing them to her. Even as full as we were from the crab legs, we still managed to try just about everything on the dessert buffet before we hobbled our fat asses out of there.

For Mom's birthday on March 6th, Jenna and I took her to Paddy's Irish Pub. I don't think my mom had ever even been in a bar before, but she thought Paddy and Bill were hilarious and loved watching them perform all the songs on the guitar and electric violin. I told Paddy it was her birthday, and after flirting with her from the stage and having everyone in the bar sing her Happy Birthday, he asked her if there was anything she'd like them to play. I had been telling her how awesome they were when they sang "Take On Me" for almost two years now, so she chose that, dancing in her seat. Paddy couldn't get her to come up on the platform, so he handed her the tambourine to play from our table, which was right up next to the stage. I had called and reserved it for us when I had the idea to bring her. By this time, Jason was done. He could not take being away from us any longer, especially knowing I had his child growing inside me. There had been rough days, talking to him on the phone, him being in a pretty low mood. At one point, he even confessed that his buddies at work were getting to him, when they were joking around and saying there's no way this kid could be his. He told me he knows in his heart it is and that I'd never cheat on him. And the guys haven't fucked with him ever since, seeing how Jason had flipped over his desk and left work for the rest of the day without a backward glance. They must have confessed it was their fault, because he said the next day the boss didn't mention it, and everyone else acted like it never happened.

And on that same day, official plans were made to move Josalyn and me to Texas. Jason and my sister-in-law Renee would fly from Texas to North Carolina, and while Jason drove the moving truck with all our stuff in it, Renee would help me with the drive back to Texas in my car. This all happens in about two weeks, so I need to get packing as soon as I have a spare minute.

Jenna's birthday is on Saint Patrick's Day, which was last

Tuesday, so Paddy's had their big shindig on Saturday the 21st.
I told Jenna we had to leave at 11:30 p.m., one: because my
pregnant ass didn't want to be out at a bar too late, even though
I was just out celebrating my friend's birthday with her, being
her DD and sipping on my Shirley Temples. I didn't want Jason
to worry. And two: I had to be at Wal-Mart a couple minutes
before midnight. I was bound and determined to be the first
person to get my grubby little mitts on a DVD of *Twilight*!
I pulled her out of the bar at 11:35 p.m., after having to argue
with her to get her ass in the car or I'd leave her there.
"Why are we going to Wal-Mart this late at night again?" she
huffed.
"We're going on a fucking *adventure*!" I squealed, and
reminded her I wanted the DVD of the book-turned-movie the
very moment it released.
"I don't get you and these vampire romances. I mean, you know
I love reading as much as you do. I've read practically every
romance they have at Edward McKay's. But vampires? Really?
I don't get it."
"I've been trying to get you to read one for years. Just try one,
and then you will see what the hell all my fuss is about! I mean,
you loved *Buffy*. You saw the romance between her and Angel,
and then her with Spike. Now put it in book form and give the
heroine a happily ever after, and bam! Those are my
paranormal romances." I grinned like a loon over at her in my
passenger seat.
In the end, I watched them open the cardboard box and hand

me the very first copy. Yes, it was the first copy sold at that Wal-Mart out of the gajillions of stores selling it, but in my head, I had just been the first person on the planet besides Stephenie Meyer herself to hold *Twilight* on DVD in my hands.

CH♠PTER
Fourteen

Kayla's Chick Rant & Book Blog

August 14, 2009

Holy crap, has it really been five months since I posted anything on my blog? Epic fail, Kayla. Jeez. Are any of y'all still around? I'm still alive, I promise! God, where do I even begin to update everyone? Okay, let me think. Last post, I was about to move to Texas, so let me start there.

April:
Jason and Nay flew into Fayetteville, we went and got the moving truck from the rental place, and then we started loading it up. There was a little bit of my crap in an old storage unit I had with Aiden, and at first I almost decided to just say fuck it and leave it, but I remembered it had a bunch of my old

pageant trophies and my big pretty dresser in there. I didn't have a key to the lock, so (awkwaaaaaaard!) we met Aiden there and grabbed everything we needed, Jason mumbling what a piece of shit he was the whole time, since he'd made the effort to see Josalyn only a handful of times since our divorce over a year ago. I was able to shush him and keep him from making a scene, whispering he'd 'upset the baby' in his ear while pushing my little bump into his abs through my oversized hoodie. Aiden didn't know I was pregnant. I didn't feel it was any of his business. He wasn't fighting me in any way about the move. I mean, he really wouldn't have a leg to stand on anyway, considering how he never came to see her while living fifteen minutes away, so why would he care if she lived across the country? But I didn't want to say or do anything that might change that.

That night, after all the work of packing everything into the van, Jason and I treated Renee to a night out at Paddy's. She had never been before, and I wanted to go one last time to hear them sing my songs.

The next morning, Jenna came over for the big farewell. Josalyn and I hugged and kissed her, Mom, Granny, and Dad, me bawling my eyes out as I got in my car and began backing out of the driveway. Jason had Riley in the front of the moving truck with him as his 'companion', but Mom wouldn't let me take Jade. She said I could have visitation rights to the cat whenever I came home to visit.

We stopped frequently, between me having to pee, changing Josalyn's diaper, having to gas up, me having to pee again, letting the dog pee, and stopping for food. We stopped in

Alabama overnight, and then finished the rest of the drive the next day, meeting my brother Jay in Baytown late that night so he could take Renee home to Kingwood.

A couple of weeks later, we had Josalyn's birthday, my brothers and their families coming for the event, filling up the Robichauxs' entire huge backyard, which I had decorated and scattered water toys, from sprinklers and water guns to slip-and-slides. We got an awesome picture of all three of my siblings and me, my little bump protruding proudly like the baby wanted to be in the photo too.

Okay, y'all. I'm going to try something out. I have to write a short, true story for my creative writing class, so I'm gonna tell you what happened to me after Josalyn's party and then turn it in as my assignment. My professor is a really cool, artsy-fartsy poetic type, and thankfully, she doesn't mind the use of adult language in our writing. Let me know in the comments what you think!

Being Texas, the mosquitoes were horrible, but I made sure to cover Josalyn's body, clad only in a swim diaper, in bug spray, but one managed to bite her right on her eyelid, obviously the one place you can't protect from the little fuckers. It swelled up, making her look like she'd went a round in a boxing ring, so Jason called her his 'Little Boxer' for the rest of the day.

The next day, on the way to the grocery store, I looked in the rear-view mirror to find her scratching at it. Turning around in the driver's seat to pull her hand away from her eye, since she wouldn't stop just from me telling her to, I wasn't paying attention and went right past a stop sign that wasn't there when I used to drive to come visit Jason every day. Random stop sign, completely useless, making you stop for seemingly no reason—and lo and behold, I happened to look up at that exact moment, and of fucking course there was a cop sitting a few car-lengths back on the street.

I barely had time to say, "Oh, shit," before he pulled out onto the road behind me and turned on his lights. When I pulled over and he came up to my window, I looked up to find a super-hot romance novel cop—not the Fatty McFattersons we have in Fayetteville. And damn my uncontrollable facial expressions, my jaw must've literally dropped, because he smiled as he asked, "Ma'am, do you know why I pulled you over?"

The sun reflecting of his perfect white teeth must've jerked me out of my drooling state, because the next words out of my mouth were, "I went right through that damn stop sign! I can't believe I did that. It didn't used to be there, and I just moved back here from North Carolina, and I was turned around yelling at her to stop scratching her eye," I word-vomited, hitching my thumb over my shoulder at the little booger in question. He bent at the waist and looked in my window at Josalyn. "Da'gone mosquito bit her right on the eye yesterday and she won't leave it the hell alone. And I can't stop cussing for some reason. I'm sorry. I'm the daughter of a sailor. I can't help it. Oh, my God, I'm going to shut up now."

With a smirk, he asked, "License and registration, please," and watched as I leaned over to reach into my glove box. As I opened it, an old CVS Pharmacy bag fell out onto the floor, and the policeman held out his hand. "Can you hand me that please, ma'am?" At my questioning look, he explained, "Any visible prescription drugs in a vehicle must be checked during routine traffic stops."

I shrugged and handed it over. "It's just my old birth control pills. Obviously they didn't work," I said with a snort, rubbing my baby bump.

Seeming to notice for the first time that I'm pregnant, the officer smiled and asked how far along I was as I got my wallet out of my purse and handed him my new Texas Driver's License.

"I'm twenty-four weeks, so a little more than halfway done baking."

He lifted his chin at my wallet and handed me back the pills. "Is that a military ID?"

"Yes, sir. I just moved here from Ft. Bragg. I was born and raised there," I replied.

"Good ol' Fayettenam. I was at Cherry Point at the Marine base. We used to go to Ft. Bragg for training all the time," he said almost excitedly.

"You're a Marine? My boyfriend's best friend is a Marine. He's at Camp Pendleton though. Do you know Logan Cachete?" I asked eagerly.

"Name doesn't ring a bell. Did he go to school here?" At my nod, he asked, "What year did he graduate?"

"Hmmm, I think he's a year older than me, so 2001 maybe?" I shrugged.

"Ah, a few years younger than me then. Well, I'm gonna go run your stuff. Sit tight," he told me, and when he walked back to his cruiser, I turned to look at Josalyn.

"You little stinker. You made Mommy get in trouble," I whispered, but then smiled to let her know I wasn't mad at her. "No more messing with your eye, little girl."

"It's itchy," she complained in her sweet little voice, using the back of her fist to rub at it this time, instead of her fingernails.

"As soon as the nice policeman comes back, we can go get you some medicine for it, and it'll feel a lot better. But no more scratching. You don't want to leave a scar on your pretty face."

A few moments later, the officer came back to my window and handed me my cards. "I'm going to let you off with a warning this time, but please be aware of the traffic signs. We recently had a change in speed limit down the road too, so careful down that way. Congrats on the baby, ma'am. And welcome back to Texas."

"Thank you so much. Have a good day," I breathed, relieved I was not getting my first ticket. And we went on our merry way, my hands strictly at ten and two.

The End

May:

My summer mini semester started, and trying to stay on schedule to graduate in December, I took on three classes: Computer Presentations, which focused on Microsoft PowerPoint, and had to actually go to the school for it. It was strange sitting in a classroom after all these years, but it was pretty fun. Yes, I was one of the oldest students in the class, besides the middle-aged woman who had decided to go back to school after her kids finally went off to college themselves, but I liked interacting with all the new people, since I didn't have any friends in Texas, yet again. (*Let's do the time-warp agaaaaaain...*) The other two classes were online, and were pretty damn hard, but luckily Jason had just taken the Excel class himself and could help me with it, and I eventually got the hang of Access. By the end of all this, I'll be a Microsoft Master! Barbara, being the forward-thinking woman she is, signed us up to go speak to a couple's counselor. She said they might give us some helpful advice on transitioning from our long-distance relationship, to all of a sudden being an insta-family. Mostly, I think she wanted to make sure her son wouldn't be overwhelmed by all the changes, so I just went along with it. And I'm actually glad I did.

The counselor, learning Josalyn called Jason by his name, told us it would be much better if she called him Dad, Daddy, or whatever he decided to be called, because children view those names as words of authority. By using his first name, he was telling her that she was on the same level as he is, an equal instead of father figure and daughter. It had made him uncomfortable when I had previously brought up the idea of her calling him Dad, because he didn't want to take anything away from Aiden. But after the counselor pointed out how Jason had been in her life, teaching her the things a father should be teaching her, not Aiden, I could see the pride building in his eyes.

When we got home that evening, when Josalyn ran to him yelling, "Jason!" and he picked her up, he gave her a squeeze then leaned her back to look her in the face, and told her, "How about, instead of Jason, you call me Daddy, big girl?"

She tilted her head to the side and grinned, and like it was no big deal, shrugged and said, "Okay, Daddy. Can I have some juice?" And that was the end of that.

June and July were pretty low key. OH! I'm totally lying. June is when we finally got to get the ultrasound of our little nugget! My Medicaid got approved back in May and I went to my first doctor appointment for this pregnancy at twenty-five weeks. It was well past the time to get an ultrasound to find out the sex of the baby, so they set me up with an appointment pretty quickly. Jason and I sat in the waiting room with Josalyn for about an hour, anxious for our turn, playfully bantering about whether our kid would be a boy or girl. Mom had gotten in my head that it was a boy, but at the same time, I *felt* like it was a girl while Jason thought for sure that it was a boy. Josalyn started getting antsy, so Jason stood up to let her hold his hands, walk up the front of his legs, and then flip over. After a few times, she let go of his hand too soon and dropped right on her head, and my pregnant ass hopped up with a squawk, freaking out while Jason laughed. The way he'd been holding her, she couldn't have been more than a foot off the ground, and realizing she not only wasn't crying, but she was reaching up for another flip, I decided not to stab him for dropping my baby... on her head no less. He even made me laugh by telling her, "When you're older, and you ain't acting right, we'll remember this moment, and you can blame Daddy by saying he dropped you on your head as a baby." Then he looked at me and said, "At least if she'd gotten hurt we're already at the hospital." I smacked him on the chest for that one.

When the ultrasound technician called us back, Josalyn sat

wiggling on Jason's lap while I lay down and lifted my shirt over my growing bump. The tech tucked a paper gown into my waistband to keep the clear gel off my pants, and immediately started taking screenshots of the baby. She made her measurements and told me our little nugget was right on target, and then asked if we wanted to know the sex. We yelled, "Yes!" at the same time, making her laugh, and she set to work trying to find a good angle with the wand to see the baby's private area.

"Come on, little one. Show us your goodies," she said quietly, but the baby wasn't having it, keeping its legs locked firmly together. After a few moments, the tech told us, "Let's try one last thing. Mom, roll over on your side. We'll see what this little rascal does when you flip 'em over."

She helped me roll onto my right hip, facing her, and then placed the wand back to my belly. The next thing we saw, it's like the baby said "Tada!" spread its legs, and pushed its ass right up to the screen for the whole world to see.

"Congratulations, guys. Another beautiful baby girl!"

I turned to look at Jason, and I couldn't decipher the look on his face. But then he breathed, "Daddy's girls," looking down at Josalyn and then up at the screen, and my heart melted at the smile that spread across his face.

We've decided on the name Avary. My mom's name is Ava, which is Josalyn's middle name, but it's gotten so popular lately so we chose to change it up a little, but keeping it spelled with the second 'a' instead of 'e' like the usual way. Her middle name is going to be Dorothy, Granny's first name, and my middle name. It was actually going to be Avary Dorothy Carol, after

Jason's mom's middle name, but she said not to burden the poor kid with four names, but that the thought was very sweet.

Which brings us to this month. We had our baby shower over at Mom's best friend's house, who Jason called Aunt Pat, and since we'd had so much fun at Buffy's, including the men, we decided to make it for everyone too. I learned a very important lesson about being a Texan that day. Under strict orders to do absolutely nothing, I sat on a stool at the kitchen counter munching on fresh broccoli dipped in ranch dressing while everyone set everything up around me. After Jason got all the sodas in from the car, he said, "Okay, I'm gonna go make the beer and wine run. Any requests?" looking at his mom.

"Wait, this is a baby shower," I scoffed, looking at him questioningly.

"Yeah... and?" he prompted.

"It's a freakin' baby shower. What do you need alcohol for?"

"Much to learn you have, beautiful. This is Texas. Anything involving two or more people is a call for alcohol. That's not to say everyone gets hammered drunk, but it's just a social thing. We hang out, have a couple beers, and have a good time," he explained, and then leaned down to kiss me on my lips before heading out the door with a, "Be right back."

"Two or more people?" Aunt Pat's husband huffed beside me on his stool. "Shit, sometimes ya don't even need that many!" He cackled, making me burst out laughing.

He smelled strongly of cigar smoke. The scent wasn't unpleasant, even to my sensitive pregnant nose. He must smoke the same kind my Uncle Dan used to enjoy, which filled my nose when I'd give him a big hug. I grew up with him coming to visit Mom and Granny every morning. He lives on the other side of our lake, so he'd make his morning walk over the dam for a glass of sweet tea. Eventually, he got himself a golf cart, which he uses to help haul the stuff he picks out of his garden.

I got everything I wanted for the baby shower, including the Moby wrap Buffy uses with Abigail. I never knew about them when Josalyn was a baby, so I always just hauled her around in her car seat. But a few weeks ago, when I'd gone to visit them up in Kingwood, Buffy showed me how to wrap it around myself and put the baby in it, freeing my hands to do whatever I needed to. Abigail is big enough now that Buffy wraps her up and puts her on her back, and she gets all of her housework and stuff done with no problem.

Jason's cousin, Chad, the hot one from Beaumont who gives me anxiety, asked Jason when he was going to 'wife me up'. I told him he wasn't allowed to ask me to marry him until we've been together for two years. He thought that was hilarious. I told him I also didn't want to get married anytime soon, because people would think we were getting hitched just because of the baby.

Logan was home on leave last week. We couldn't go out partying, obviously, so he very sweetly chose somewhere we could all go and have a good time, instead of me having to stay home. We went to Cork Wine Bar, since my doctor said it was perfectly fine for me to have one glass of wine. I wore a cute red sundress I had found at a baby and maternity thrift store, the

Texas heat carrying through long after the sun had gone down. As usual, the moment we sat outside on the patio at one of the bistro tables and I got comfortable, Avary started doing her aerobics inside my belly. I'm so little, and all baby, that she can literally move my whole body when she gets to dancing around. Seeing the uncomfortable look on my face, Logan asked if I was okay, probably worried I was going into labor. When I told him Avary was doing her nightly jiujutsu, he asked Jason first if he could feel her kicking. With an "Of course!" from his best friend, Logan then turned his questioning look to me. In response, I grabbed his massive mitt of a hand and laid it on the side of my stomach, where I felt her kicking the hardest moments before. I pressed my palm to the back of his hand, letting him know to push in a little, and Avary immediately gave him a high-five... with which body part of hers, I have no idea.

The big Marine jumped in his seat but didn't remove his hand for several more kicks, breathing, "That's crazy!" his bright blue eyes wide with amazement.

"Yep, that's why when they tell me there's a baby in there, I tend to believe them," I joked, smiling at the gentle giant's awe-filled face.

He let us know that night he was getting deployed again, this time to Afghanistan instead of Iraq. And as Jason and Logan bantered and reminisced, I rubbed my belly and said a silent prayer that Avary's 'Uncle Logie', as Josalyn calls him, would make it home safe to meet her.

So now we're just waiting on little Avary to arrive. My fall semester starts the same week as her due date. I've already signed up for my classes, so we'll see how it goes. I have to take two electives, my Microsoft Word class, a class on filing, and lastly, a business letter writing course, and then I will finally be done!

I feel uncomfortably big, and I'm ready to serve this baby her eviction notice. I'm having trouble sleeping at night.

OH! That reminds me. Funny story.

I had insomnia one night, and Jason was just a'snoring away beside me. Sex while pregnant has been great. I never had it when I was pregnant with Josalyn, so I had no idea how amazing it felt. And I never slept better than after Jason made love to me. He wasn't one of those men who worried about poking the baby. He always makes me feel like a goddess, taking the time to kiss me all over, removing any of the fear I have that he doesn't find me sexy when I feel like a stuffed cow. Anyway, on this night, I was tossing and turning, unable to get comfortable, even with my giant body pillow, so I rolled over and started stroking my fingers up and down his chest. He seemed to wake up, and asked, "What is it, baby?" in his sexy, sleep-filled voice.

"I can't sleep," I answered in as sultry a tone as I could muster, hoping he'd get the hint as I trailed my fingers down to his boxer brief-covered dick.

But instead of coming more fully awake and giving in to a little midnight nookie, he sighed and said, "That sucks. Sorry, babe," rolled over, and started snoring again. After frowning and staring daggers into the back of his head, I decided to read for a while until I finally passed out. When I told him about it the next day, he laughed his ass off, because he didn't remember it at all. And then he proceeded to make up for it.

I slept fantastic that night.

CH♠PTER *Fifteen*

August 21, 2009 *2:16 a.m.*

I wake up, a weird feeling coming over my whole body. A chill runs up my neck, and I have the thought, *Maybe that fire sauce at Taco Bell before bed was a bad idea*, and I struggle to sit up so I can go to the bathroom. After what comes out of me, I go back to bed having no doubt that's what was wrong, and I fall back to sleep.

I couldn't have been unconscious for more than twenty minutes before I wake up with the weird feeling again, but this time, my stomach isn't upset. Soon, the feeling dissipates, but I don't have time to fall back to sleep again before the discomfort returns.

"Jason," I whisper, nudging him with my elbow.

"Yeah, baby?" he sighs, and I can tell he's answering me in his sleep.

"Jason, wake up. I need you to time this." I rub my hand across his face, and when he still tries to ignore me, I pinch his nose closed until he finally gasps through his mouth, startling fully awake. I pull my lips between my teeth and try not to giggle as he sits up and looks around as if looking for the person who was trying to smother him in his sleep.

"I need you to time this," I repeat, and he turns and looks down at me. "I think I might be having contractions, but I'm not sure. It doesn't feel like it did with Josalyn."

"Really?" he breathes, his eyes widening. "Okay, baby." He grabs his phone and looks at the time. "Let me know when you feel it again. Here, roll over and I'll scratch your back. Grab the remote and find us a show."

I do as he says, appreciative of his idea to distract me. A rerun of *Supernatural* is on, so we watch it for a few minutes before the feeling comes back, this time a little stronger than the last. Another one comes not too long after, and glancing at his cell, he tells me they were twelve minutes apart.

"I think I'm in labor," I say with a smile, rolling over to look up at him.

"Are you sure? I imagined... I thought it'd be a lot worse than this. You don't seem to be hurting." His brow furrows.

"I mean... if they are coming at a steady pace, not just one and then a couple hours later, that means they aren't those Braxton Hicks thingies. It doesn't *hurt*. It's just really uncomfortable," I explain, and he nods.

"Okay, well, at our class, they said we should get up and

start moving around," he reminds me, talking about the six-hour labor class we took at the hospital. It was for his benefit, since I had already gone through this before. Seeing how my labor with Josalyn was such a traumatizing experience, I'm surprised at how calm I am right now.

He comes around the bed and helps me stand, and then holds my hand as we walk down the hall and into the kitchen. "They said you won't be able to eat after you get checked into the hospital, and that you should eat before we go, so what can I make you, baby?"

"Well, before I woke you up, I went to the bathroom with an upset tummy, so I'm really not all that hungry," I tell him, but he starts shaking his head before I even finish.

"No, you gotta eat something. How about some toast? Will you at least try to eat some toast for me?"

The worried look in his eyes tells me that eating the damn toast is important to him, so I nod, giving in and eating the lightly buttered bread after he sits it in front of me with a kiss to my forehead. Halfway through the second slice, a contraction hits me, this one way stronger than the others. He sees me grip the side of the table with both hands, and quickly stands and pulls me up to him.

"Wrap your arms around my neck, baby. Just like they showed us in the class," he says soothingly, wrapping his own arms tightly around my waist, starting to sway us side-to-side. I press my forehead to his chest and breathe deeply like they taught us, and as I inhale Jason's familiar masculine scent, a sense of calm washes over me, even through the discomfort as everything in my center tightens. As he feels my arms relax around his neck, he loosens his grip around my waist, and I pull back to look up into his eyes.

"That's not so bad," I whisper, and he leans down to kiss me gently. "Oh, shit."

"What? What's the matter?" he questions anxiously.

"I haven't shaved in like a week. I can't go to the hospital like this," I reply, starting to move toward the bathroom.

"Babe, no one cares if you have a little stubble on your legs. You're about to have a baby. No one is going to be paying attention to any of that."

"I'll know. And I won't be able to concentrate on pushing this baby out when I'm worried about my vagina looking like the one that was on that nasty childbirth video they showed us at the hospital," I state, and with that, I hurry into the bathroom, hearing him call out, "No shower! And yell for me when you're done so I can help you out of the tub!"

I can't help but giggle to myself as I turn the water on and wait for it to heat up. About a week ago, Jason and I were taking a shower together—he hadn't let me shower alone since watching the episode on *Grey's Anatomy* where the pregnant girl slipped in the tub. I had gotten a new facial cleanser and wanted to try it on him. He argued that he had already washed his face with his lava soap, and that you shouldn't mix anything with it since it's so abrasive, but I wasn't hearing any of it. I was gonna wash his face with my fancy new cleanser whether he liked it or not.

So, I lathered up my hands, feeling his wrap around my back to hold me close. And as soon as I laid my soapy hands against his cheeks, he let out a manly yet blood-curdling scream, making me jump, gasp, and then cry out, "What? What's wrong?" my heart about to beat out of my chest.

"It burns!" he howled, but then immediately started laughing harder than I've ever seen before.

Realizing he was playing a trick on me, when I finally caught my breath, I reached around and pinched his ass cheek as hard as I could, making him laugh even more.

"You asshole! You could have sent me into labor!" I yelled, rubbing my belly, but his laughter was infectious and I couldn't help but join in.

Feeling the water has reached the temperature I want, I quickly strip out of Jason's T-shirt and my panties, the only thing I've been able to comfortably sleep in for the past two months, and carefully get into the tub. After bathing myself hastily, having one more contraction inside the water, which seemed to lessen the discomfort, I call for Jason to come help me.

"I just need to sit on the side of the tub so I can shave. I can't squat inside the water like I do when I don't have this giant belly," I tell him, and he has me wrap my arms around his shoulders so he can grip me around my back to lift me up. I settle my bottom on the wide porcelain lip of the tub and reach for my body wash and razor.

"Tell me when you're done so I can help you dry off, baby," he says, and then leaves the room, but I hear him return almost immediately and turn to look over my shoulder, seeing he has his digital camera.

"What the—? What are you doing?" I ask, turning back around to face the wall. I can only imagine what I look like, my wide ass perched on the edge of the tub, one leg up as my toes press against the other side while I shave my leg. Hearing him chuckle, I lift my left hand, the one not holding the razor, up so he can see it over my shoulder and flip him the bird, and that's when I hear the camera shutter go off.

"That'll be a nice one for the baby book," he says through a chuckle. I roll my eyes then try to shave everything from the waist down before another contraction hits.

I call out for him once more, and he comes to hold my hands as I rotate and then stand up on the bathmat, and then he grabs the towel off the rack and wraps it around me. Used to this recent routine, I allow him to dry me off from neck to toes, smiling as his head disappears below my protruding belly. As he stands, he kisses my tummy on his way up, and a contraction immediately takes my breath away.

When it ends, I pull my face from his neck and tell him quietly, "I think it might be time to call the doctor."

"On it," he replies, and he helps me to our room, grabbing the phone from its cradle on the dresser.

I hear only one side of the conversation.

"Hi, this is Jason Robichaux. My girlfriend is in labor... Yes, she's been having contractions for about an hour and a half now... Ten minutes apart... Yes, ma'am. Oh, hi, Doc... Really? In the class, they told us to wait to call you until they were ten minutes apart... Right now? Okay, I'll grab our bags and we'll see you in a little bit. Thanks." He hangs up.

"What did he say?" I ask, my brow furrowed.

"Apparently, we were supposed to call him at the first sign of a contraction, not wait like the nurses in the class told us to.

He said get our asses to his office STAT," he answers, getting our hospital bags out of the closet, where I've had them packed and ready for the past month.

"Shit. Okay, well, go wake your parents up and let them know we're leaving, and I'll finish getting dressed."

With a nod, he jogs out the door and I hear the garage door open. And as I put my arms through the straps of my sundress, I hear him return and then knock on his parents' bedroom door. The four of us meet in the living room, his mom pulling her robe around her and tying it at the waist, his dad tugging a shirt down over his head.

"You all right, babe?" Dad asks, giving a gentle squeeze to my shoulder.

"Yeah, it's been fine so far. Nothing like Josalyn's. So we can stick to our plan. We'll go see the doctor now, while y'all watch Josalyn. We'll call when he tells us what to do, and then you can come on up to the hospital whenever you want. I have no idea if I'm even dilated at all, since I didn't on my own last time, so who knows how long this is going to take?"

"Okay, hun. Just give us a call when you know what's going on," he replies, and they give us each a hug and we head out the door.

I have four contractions in the car on the drive there, but when Jason starts to speed going down 610, I grab a hold of his wrist and tell him to slow the hell down. The anxiety he's giving me weaving through the cars is worse than the labor pains. When we take the exit for Fannin Street, I breathe a sigh of relief knowing we're almost there. The doctor's office shares a parking lot with The Woman's Hospital of Texas, where I'm delivering, so we park directly in the center, not knowing where we'll end up at the end of this. With my luck, they'll probably send us home saying we're not ready yet.

I waddle into the exam room, and the nurse helps get my ankles into the stirrups, not worrying about changing into a gown since I'm wearing a dress. When she checks me, her eyes grow wide, and she throws a "Be right back" over her shoulder as she hustles out the door. When it reopens, it's Dr. Chavez, his quiet calm immediately blanketing the room when he walks in, making me feel a lot better after the nurse's hasty exit.

"Let's check you out, Mom," he says as he sits on his rolling stool between my legs, and Jason reaches for my hands and squeezes it while we wait to see what the nurse had discovered.

"Dear girl, you are already at four centimeters," he says in his soothing tone. "All those worries about scar tissue like with your last one were for nothing. You're gonna have this baby girl no problem. Right now, I need y'all to head across the parking lot and get checked in at the hospital. I'll be over there shortly."

"That's it?" I ask, surprise filling my voice.

"Hun, if you sneeze wrong, she's going to fall into my lap. Now get your tuchus over there and get checked in." With that, he stands, pats me on the knee, and then holds out both his hands to help me sit up. He pushes the metal stirrups back into their hidey-holes and then pulls out the step at the bottom of the bed to help me get to the floor. "I'll call them right now and let them know you're on your way."

"Thank you, Dr. Chavez," I say, almost dazed. I can't believe this is all happening so fast. I was in labor with Josalyn for four days! I just woke up a couple hours ago with contractions, and now I'm already about to be checked in at the hospital? What is this sorcery?

Jason holds my hand while we make our way, slow but steady, across the parking lot, and enter through the front doors of the hospital. When we reach the front desk, we tell the woman I'm in labor, and she asks us to wait while she gets a wheelchair.

"Actually, I think I'm okay to walk," I stop her. "I mean, they said it helps the baby get into position when you're standing, and gravity pushes their head against your cervix, helping it dilate, so I think I'm good."

"Are you sure? It's no trouble to get you a wheelchair, ma'am," she asks.

"Really, I'm all right. It only hurts during the contractions, and even those aren't that bad while I'm upright," I say, turning to look up at Jason, who nods.

"I'll keep a hold of her. If she says she's good, then she's good," he backs me up, and with a nod, she reminds us which floor and points us in the direction of the elevator. We had taken a tour of the hospital during our labor and delivery class, so we were able to find it no problem. On the ride up, a strong contraction grabs hold of me, and we assume our middle-school-slow-dance position, him rocking me side-to-side while I breathed through it. The car stops before our floor, and a couple gets in with us. I hear Jason say, "She's a badass," but not what the woman had asked as I concentrate on not holding my breath through the squeezing pain. It releases just before the doors open to our floor, and I give the woman a smile as she tells us, "Good luck," when we exit.

"What did she ask when she first got in?" I inquire.

Jason looks down at me with pride in his eyes. "She asked, 'No wheelchair?' with the most astonished look on her face." He chuckled.

"I mean, is that not normal? I'm just doing what the ladies in our class said," I prompt as we approach the nurses' station only a few feet ahead of us.

Obviously overhearing my question, the nurse sitting behind the computer answers me, "No on both accounts. Usually, the mom can't get into a wheelchair fast enough, and normally, what we teach in the classes go right out the door as soon as the labor pain starts. Good job, Mom." She smiles brightly. "Miss Greenwood?" I nod. "Dr. Chavez called and let us know you were on your way, so your room is all ready for you, dear."

She comes out from behind the desk and takes my arm as Jason holds my other hand, and she guides us to room 21. It's much brighter in here than the one I had at Womack, and it's not that the florescent lights are just more lit. There's a lot of natural light coming in through the giant windows on the far wall, and I have a fantastic view of downtown Houston this high up. The bed and gizmos are all on the left side of the room, an open door leading to a bathroom in the far right corner, and several comfy looking chairs and a couch on the wall beneath the windows. Looking behind me after we walk more fully into the room, I see all the things they'll use after our girl enters the world, like the scale to weigh her, and the clear plastic bassinet she'll lie in while they clean her up.

"I have to potty," I tell Jason as they let go of me, and head toward the bathroom.

"Are you having an epidural?" the nurse asks quickly before I have a chance to close the door.

"Yes, ma'am," I reply, my hand gripping the handle.

"Okay, I'll call the anesthesiologist for you then."

"Well, you can hold off for a bit. I'm really not in that much pain," I tell her, crossing my legs so I don't pee on myself as Avary wiggles against my bladder.

"Dr. Chavez will be here any minute to break your water, and that's when the real pain starts as their little head pushes right up against your cervix. If you're going to get an epidural, I would definitely go ahead and get it before he does that," she suggests adamantly.

"Oh. All right then." I nod, and with a squeak as a contraction takes hold, I push the door farther open so Jason can get to me. He's there in a flash, letting me hold onto him tightly as I breathe through it once again. It's an awkward feeling, having to pee so badly plus trying to make it through a contraction, and when it's over, I plop down on the toilet without even waiting for him to exit and shut the door.

I groan with relief and look up to find Jason still standing there, my face heating with embarrassment.

"I don't want to leave you in here by your— What's with the blushing?" He gives me a small smile.

"I just realized you'll be seeing all sorts of crazy shit today, the least of which is me peeing in front of you for the first time." My voice is tinged with a bit of panic.

"Don't you think we're past that, babe?" he asks, his eyebrow lifting.

"Hell no, we ain't past that," I squawk. "Close your eyes. I have to wipe."

He chuckles but closes his eyes, seeing the seriousness in mine.

"You're the mother of my child, the love of my life. What do you think is going to happen?"

I can't help but smile at his profession as he stands there with his eyes closed in the middle of the small bathroom, my big pregnant ass on the toilet, reaching behind myself to flush the toilet so he doesn't see my pee when I stand up. "There should be boundaries, ya know? Some things left a mystery, so you still see me as this, like, sexy woman instead of too... human, I guess. I don't know..."

"Baby, I think you've done fell off your rocker. Can I open my eyes now?" he asks, his accent thick as he grins.

"No, I haven't! Not to bring him up at such an intimate time for us, but Aiden used to come into the bathroom, where I was happily relaxing in the bathtub reading, and would plop his dumb ass down on the toilet and poop! Right there in front of me! At first, it was like, okay, cool. We're that comfortable with each other. But *very* soon after, it was like... what has been seen cannot be unseen. There's shit that should stay a mystery, quite literally. Keep a little mystique. Just like I don't want you to watch when she comes hurtling out of my hooha. Yes, you can open your eyes." He does, and then I reach my hands up for him to haul me off the pot.

"What? I'm watching my kid be born, babe. There ain't no stopping me from—"

"You can watch her be born, but I don't want you to actually see her come out of my va-jay-jay, Jason. Do you not remember that video we saw? It does something to a man. It's one thing to watch someone else on film doing it, but if you were to see *me* do it, stretched like that, seeing a whole baby coming out of *me,* you won't be able to look at me down there and see anything but that. And sorry, but I like you looking at my ladybits and seeing it as a sacred love shrine, not the functional body part that pee and babies come out of, not to mention other stuff. Let me keep a little bit of my sexuality and dignity. Please."

Something I said, or maybe the panic in my voice, causes him to pull me to him in a comforting hug. "Okay, babe. If it's that important to you, I won't look."

I breathe out a heavy sigh of relief. "Thank you." A moment later, I feel his body shaking with silent laughter and pull back to look up at his face. "What?"

"Sacred love shrine?" He grins ear-to-ear, and then it's like saying it out loud breaks the dam and he throws his head back and laughs.

"Shut up, Robi-ho," I growl, and he continues to chuckle as he leads me out of the bathroom. "We need to call Buffy and Nay." I told them I wanted them to be in the delivery room with me and Jason a few weeks ago, and they were thrilled. Plus, Josalyn will be going home with Buffy for the couple days I'll be in the hospital.

"And my parents," he adds as the nurse comes back into the room, a tall man in blue scrubs following behind her.

"I'm Dr. Reynolds, and I'll be your anesthesiologist." He reaches out to shake our hands. "Rebecca here said your contractions aren't that bad, but she explained about what happens after the doctor breaks your water, correct?"

"Yes, sir. So I'll be taking that epidural," I say with a frantic nod.

"Okay. No one is allowed in the room while we do it, so, Dad, this'll only take a few minutes, if you'll just step out—"

"Hold up," I interrupt. "Not even he can be in here with me?" My heart starts to pound inside my chest. I did not sign up for doing *any* of this on my own.

"No, ma'am. It's against policy. Just the doctor and a nurse can be in the room when placing the epidural," he explains.

"Don't worry, honey. It only takes a minute and then he can come right back in," the nurse, apparently named Rebecca, tries to calm me.

Unlike me, Jason keeps a cool head. Knowing they won't budge on the matter, he takes my face in his hands and tilts my head back to gain my attention. "Babe, it'll only a minute. I gotta run down to the car and get our bags anyways. And I'll call Buffy, tell her to call Nay, and then I'll call my parents. Then it'll be a party up in this place. Okay?" He looks at me with those perfect chocolaty eyes, and everything seems to come into focus. I can do this. Just one pinch and it'll be over.

"All right," I breathe with a nod, and he kisses me gently before heading out the door, which closes on its own.

"Now, honey. You aren't going to hurt me. You squeeze all you want. I can take it. We're going to sit you on the edge of the bed here, and you're gonna drape yourself over my shoulders and hunch over. Did you get an epidural with your other baby?" she asks as I move to sit where she told me.

"Yes, but I was in so much pain from being in labor for so

long that I really don't remember feeling it when they did it," I explain.

"Well, since you're not in that much pain this time, you may feel it, but it'll go numb so fast you won't even have time to say 'Ouch.'"

A few minutes later, I'm resting in bed, watching my contractions on the monitor, and Jason comes into the room carrying our bags.

"I called everybody. Buffy and Renee are on their way, and Dad and Mom will be up here with Josalyn in about an hour," he tells me, and the doctor walks into the room after knocking softly on the door. He's followed in by Rebecca, who comes to stand beside my upper body, while he stays at the foot of the bed.

"How you feeling, dear?" Dr. Chavez asks, putting on gloves he pulled from his pocket.

"Great," I reply, feeling Jason push my hair out of my face.

"If I recall what you said before, your doctor broke your water last time too, didn't they?"

"Yes, sir."

"All right. So you know it's a piece of cake. I just use the amnihook to nick a little hole in the sac and the fluid comes right out. You don't feel a thing." He gets on a stool and the nurse picks up my dead-weight legs, bending them at the knees and letting them fall all the way open. In PE class, we would've called this 'butterfly position' only my feet are farther apart so the doc can insert the amnihook. Several absorbent sheets, which look like puppy house-training pads, are placed under me, and before I even know it's happening, I'm already cleaned up and being tucked back under the blanket.

"That's it?" Jason asks, a look almost like disappointment on his face.

"Most of the time, it's not like it happens in movies. No big explosion of water," Rebecca explains with a smile. "Now y'all just sit back and relax, and let's see how the little one reacts to her waterbed being gone."

I lie back and use the remote on the bed to tilt myself farther into a lying down position to get some rest. I'm suddenly very tired after getting up so early, and I figure I can get in a little nap before our families get here.

I come to in a panic, grabbing at my chest, feeling like I'm suffocating. I can't get in any air. I'm drowning, but I'm not underwater. My lungs refuse to work, and my arms flail in my terror. When I get my eyes open, I see Jason lunge toward me from where he was standing with my sisters-in-law and my niece Brooke. I can't even speak. My nails tear at my gown, trying to pull it away from my throat. I try to sit up, but I can't move anything but my head and arms.

Before Jason can even fully get the word, "Help," out, Rebecca is there on my other side and takes hold of my right hand, wrapping her other arm around my back, and pulls me up into a sitting position. She tells Jason to hold me there, and with his arms around me, I watch as she uses the remote to sit the bed up, each second ticking by feeling like an hour without being able to breathe. My eyes are watering, and my lungs burn for oxygen.

Rebecca takes my face in her palms and forces me to meet

her stern gaze. "You can breathe. You may not be able to feel it right now, but you are inhaling and exhaling perfectly fine." She lets go with one hand to point to something on the monitor. "You see that? That is your oxygen level. You are okay. The epidural just went too high up your spine with you lying down, and any minute, it's going to shimmy back on down, and you'll feel right as rain. Okay? You're breathing, hun."

I close my eyes and try to feel my lungs unfreeze as I consciously pull in air through my nose. I can feel the coolness enter through my nostrils and down my throat, but not fill my chest. But I know the air couldn't have gone anywhere else but into my lungs, so it calms the panic enough for the minute it takes the numbness to go away, and I relax back against the bed.

"Well, that was exciting. You okay, kid?" Buffy asks, coming over to hug my neck as Rebecca leaves the room.

I swallow thickly and nod. "Yeah. That was fucking scary as hell."

"I think I gotta go clean out my drawers," Jason says quietly, and Buffy lets out her loud, boisterous laugh.

"Did you shit yourself there, Jason?" she asks, cackling, which makes me smile.

"Holy fuck." He presses one of his hands to his heart and bends over, bracing himself with his other hand against his knee, locking out his tattooed arm. "I don't think I've ever been that scared before." He stands up and reaches across the bed to fold me into his arms, kissing my neck where he buries his face, and I feel him inhale me.

"You?" I scoff. "I woke up feeling like someone was trying to off me with a pillow over my face!" Renee and Brooke come over to the bed and give me kisses on my cheek. "When did y'all get here?"

"Just before you started flopping around like a fish out of water," Renee says, and I turn to look at Jason. "Are your parents here with Josalyn yet?"

"Not yet, but they should be here any minute," he replies, still not letting go of me.

"Well I guess that's all the nap I'm gonna get. Baby, can you hand me my makeup bag out of there?" I ask, pointing to the big black Playboy bunny duffle bag I had packed all my stuff in.

He finally releases his death grip on me to walk over to the couch to retrieve the small pink bag that holds my makeup, bringing it back over to the bed, where I unzip it and pull out my compact.

"Are we serious right now?" Buffy asks, giving me a crazy look. "Are you really putting on makeup in your hospital bed while you're in labor, Kayla?"

"Yes. I want pictures, and in all the ones I got while I was having Josalyn, I seriously look like I could've walked onto the set of a zombie movie without stopping at the makeup trailer first and fit in just fine with the rest of the undead," I explain, adding a little blush to my pale cheeks before brushing on a light coat of mascara.

"I think I've seen it all now," she replies, and goes to plop into one of the chairs.

Just then, I notice there's someone else in the room with us, and as I catch sight of where he is and what he's about to reach for, the monitor starts beeping like crazy. "Bret! No!" I shout, right before my nephew's curious and destructive fingers have the chance to grab a hold of the IV attached to the machine behind Jason.

Rebecca comes bursting through the door, apparently alerted by the racket the monitor attached to me is making. She comes over and punches a button on the screen, then asks me if I'm okay before adding, "You're blood pressure just skyrocketed." That's when she spots my rambunctious little nephew making laps around the stand holding the IV bag.

"Can I ask for one of y'all to take him out of here? We can't have anything or anyone in here that can make her blood pressure rise like this," she asks the room.

"Brooke, why don't you go out to the waiting room and sit with your brother?" Renee prompts, and my niece sighs but takes Bret by his hand and leads him out the door.

Rebecca notices the makeup brush in my hand and looks at me with laughter in her eyes. Before she even has a chance to ask, I explain to her what I told my sisters about my awful pictures from my last labor and delivery. "Fair enough," she replies, and I barely have my bag zipped when in walks Jason's mom and dad, Josalyn holding her papa's hand. I nudge Jason with the bag, silently asking him to put it away before they see it. One, his mom would scold me and tell me how silly I'm being for worrying about the way I look at a time like this, and two, his dad would tease me relentlessly.

"How you doin', babe?" Dad asks, coming up to the bed to smack a kiss on my forehead.

"She's six centimeters, so four to go," Jason cuts in, and I shoot him a look. "She checked you right before Buffy got here.

You don't remember?" At the shake of my head, he adds, "You responded to her asking if she could check you and everything. You must've been out of it. Remind me to ask the doc for some of these drugs to take home with us." He wiggles his eyebrows at me and I smack him on the chest.

"As if you'd need to use them on me," I whisper-hiss in his direction, trying not to let his parents hear, but his dad chuckles, so I know he did. Hopefully Mom was too far away though.

"Mommy!" Josalyn chirps and reaches her little arms up. Dad picks her up so she can lean over the bed rail and give me a hug.

"Hi, my baby doll. Guess what?" I prompt.

"What?" she whispers.

"Your baby sister will be here in a little bit. The doctor just has to get her out of my belly."

Her eyes widen. "How they gon' do that?"

I look over at Jason, my teeth pulled between my lips, not knowing what to say.

"They're going to unscrew her belly button. What did you have for breakfast, big girl?" he quickly changes the subject as I snort at his answer.

"Pancakes!" she replies, clapping her hands. "Papa made dem and let me pour da syrup!"

"Oh, my goodness. Were they delicious?" I ask her, smiling at her excited face.

"Supah delicious!"

I can barely handle how adorable she is, with the little gap between her two front teeth and cheeks glowing from how big she's grinning. Dad sets her back on her feet when she spots Nay and Buffy on the couch beneath the window, and she runs over to them and throws herself into Buffy's open arms.

"How's it been? Smooth sailing since you called last, bud?" Mom asks Jason.

"We had a scare with the epidural working a little too well, but the nurse fixed it within seconds. They couldn't have a more attentive staff. Everyone's been great. The doc broke her water, and she almost immediately dilated two more centimet—"

"Oh, shit! We need to call *my* parents!" It dawns on me suddenly, but Buffy puts me at ease.

"I called your mom as soon as I got off the phone telling Renee it was go-time. Your dad said to tell you not to push until midnight so Avary can share a birthday with him."

"Push what?" Josalyn asks, her sweet face looking at Buffy, waiting for an answer.

"My buttons," Buffy growls, tickling my two-and-a-half-year-old's belly, making her squeal with laughter, effectively diverting her attention from the conversation.

"All right, baby. Why don't you come with Mimi and Papa, and you can play with your cousins in the waiting room?" Dad asks Josalyn, and knowing she'll get to play with Bret and Brooke, Josalyn runs over to him and grabs a hold of his hand, and they leave the room.

A few hours later, after catching a couple of quick catnaps between dilation checks and goofing around taking pictures with my crazy sisters—my favorite being Renee getting into a football stance at the foot of the bed, pretending like she's going to catch the baby when she shoots out—Rebecca comes to check my progress once again.

"Wow, you're at like, nine and a half." She pulls the rolling stool over with her toes and sits at the foot of the bed. Placing her fingers back inside me, she says, "Give me like, half of a push, hun."

I hardly bare down at all when Rebecca squawks, "Stop! Stop! Don't do anything. Don't push. Don't sneeze. Don't even breathe. I gotta get Dr. Chavez now!" If it weren't for the happy-excited look on her face, that would've probably scared me, but as she speeds toward the door, she throws over her shoulder, "This baby's a'coming fast!"

And just like that, I'm sent into the same panicked feeling I had when the other nurse told me Josalyn was ready to be born and it was time to push. My heart starts pumping, and I get really scared suddenly, but this time...

This time I feel warm, strong fingers interlace with mine, and then my hand is lifted to pillow-soft lips. Warm breath blankets my icy knuckles. My hand is uncurled and my palm is pressed to a stubble-covered cheek, and then the most handsome face on the planet is lowered into my line of vision, with eyes the color of Hershey Kisses locking with mine, filled with more love, pride, and excitement than I've ever seen before.

"You've got this, baby," he says, just loud enough for me to hear. "You're so strong, and perfect, and beautiful. Look what a badass you've been all day. And I don't think there's ever been a more gorgeous woman in labor in the history of ever." He grins, making his whiskers tickle my palm. When I catch his contagious smile, he leans forward and runs the tip of his nose along mine and I close my eyes. "I won't look, babe. Don't worry about that. I promise I won't, so get that out of your head. And I'm not gonna scream a countdown in your ear."

My eyes open at this, meeting the mischievous glint in his. I can't believe he remembers me telling him that story about Aiden, and how I wanted to stab him in the jugular.

"I love you so much. And there's no one in this world I would rather have as the mother of my baby." He leans down to kiss me, pulling back to brush my long ponytail back over my shoulder.

The door opens, and even though Dr. Chavez is striding swiftly into the room, Rebecca excitedly hustling in behind him, he still has that same calming bubble around him that sucks you in like a vortex as soon as he nears. With the love of my life by my side, my silly sisters jumping up and down by the windows, my peace-inducing doctor at the foot of the bed, and my badass nurse at the ready next to him, my fear subsides, and determination and anxiety to meet our daughter takes me over.

In a hushed voice so low it makes everyone in the room silence in order to hear the important words coming out of his mouth, Dr. Chavez says, "As soon as the contraction starts, you'll push as we count to ten. If the contraction is still going when we reach it, you'll take a deep breath and go again. We'll break between contractions and start all over again until this princess makes her grand entrance. You ready, Mom? Dad?" He glances between me and Jason, and we both nod. "Okay, good. Dad, will you be cutting the cord?" he asks.

"Yes, but I promised her I wouldn't look when Avary is coming out," Jason replies, squeezing my hand.

"Completely understandable, and in many cases, a wise choice. I don't need anyone fainting in my delivery room." The doctor smiles, which brightens his darkly tanned face. "So what we'll do," he takes the sheet gathered at my waist from where they'd lifted it from my feet so they could check me, "is keep this right here across your knees, and as long as Mr. Robichaux can contain his curiosity as he's promised to do and not peek over it, he won't be able to see anything. Stay right up there by her head and pull her knee back, and it'll make a little tent for me to work under. Who wants to hold your other leg, Mom?"

"Me!" Renee yelps and raises her hand as she hurries around the bed to get to my right side.

"Bitch," Buffy coughs behind her hand and then smiles. "I'll be the photographer." She turns the digital camera on and aims it in our direction."

Renee sticks her tongue out at her then gets a grip on my leg, mimicking Jason's stance. With my thighs being grasped behind my knees and my feet in their opposite palms, it gives me good leverage when it'll be time to push, which is apparently now.

"Here we go, folks. Ready. Go. One, two, three..." Dr. Chavez continues the countdown in his soft, soothing voice as I bear down with all my might, and instead of joining in with the chant, I hear Jason next to my ear whispering, encouraging me, telling me I'm doing great and how beautiful I am, thanking me for giving him this wonderful gift. And it's not like in the movies. I don't want to yell at him or call him hateful names for 'doing this to me'. No, instead, I want to absorb every word he's telling me, which I'm hearing not only with my ears, but with my heart and soul.

This baby is being born into a room full of nothing but love and quiet, tranquil welcome. At the end of the first set of ten, with a glance at the monitor, the doctor tells me, "Deep breath," which I immediate gasp for, "and push. One, two..."

Bearing down once more, I don't even hear them reach 'five' before an overwhelming sense of relief fills me as Avary exits my body, making me feel both empty and full at the same time. Dr. Chavez stands, lifts Avary over the sheet across my knees, and lays her on my stomach, where Rebecca immediately starts rubbing her clean with blankets while somehow simultaneously suctioning her nostrils and mouth. I wrap my arms underneath the squalling baby girl and pull her up higher onto my chest and immediately burst into tears. How could I possibly have thought I wouldn't love this tiny thing with every fiber of my being? My mom was right. The moment my eyes landed on her miniature, scrunched-up, pissed-as-hell face, my heart grew twice its size.

I'm so enamored with her I miss it when her father cuts her umbilical cord, my focus never waning until I feel Jason kiss my cheek, and I turn my face to capture his lips. "She's so tiny," I sob, looking back down at Avary, and my heart clenches when I see his hand reach toward her and his finger run gently down the bridge of her itty-bitty nose.

"She's gorgeous, like her momma," he tells me, his voice tight, and I glance up to see his eyes and face are pinched with barely-contained emotion.

Rebecca picks her up, saying she only needs her for a moment while she weighs her, and very quickly, as promised, brings Avary back, now wearing a soft striped beanie on her head and swaddled securely in a clean blanket. Wrapped up like this, her little cheeks look so chubby, and since she's stopped crying, I can really get a good look at her.

"Oh, my God, she's a mini Jason," Buffy says, leaning over the side of the bed next to him. I see his body jolt at her words, and to my astonishment, it's as if a dam breaks inside him as his eyes fill with tears and immediately spill over. It's only the second time I've ever seen my unwavering badass boyfriend cry, the first time being when he got drunk during one of his trips to visit me and professed his undying love for me in an alcohol-induced stupor, in which I had responded by laughing so hard I almost puked.

But this... there is nothing humorous about this. What I'm witnessing right now is the physical response of a grown man being brought to his knees by a six-pound, fifteen-point-seven-ounce baby girl—a real man's response when they see their child for the very first time. All that hard-acting, take-no-shit attitude went right out the window, and what's left before me is my soul mate with all of his walls pulverized and blown away. And it's a beautiful sight.

The next hour is a blur as first Jason holds Avary for the very first time, my heart filling nearly to bursting seeing him hold our baby with such gentleness and care, and then Renee and Buffy take turns getting their fill of newborn baby smell. Jason's mom and dad come in with Josalyn, who had been taking a nap in the waiting room and was not happy about being woken up. Red-faced and sweaty, she passed up wanting me and reached for Aunt Buffy, who gladly took her out of her papa's arms so he could hold his newest grandbaby before handing Avary to Mimi. Lastly, Brooke and Bret came in to meet their cousin, and the hustle and bustle of excitement died down as Buffy took Avary into her arms to let Josalyn meet her sister.

Still out of it from being woken up from her nap, my big girl only gave a small smile and Avary a kiss on her cheek before lying her head on Buffy's shoulder, looking like she was ready to fall back to sleep.

"I think that's our cue to get going," Buffy tells the room as she hands Avary to Jason, nodding at Renee, who gathers Brooke and Bret after kissing the baby one last time, hugging me and Jason, and then taking Josalyn's overnight bag from Dad.

Jason's parents leave soon after, and we're finally left alone with our new bundle for a few quiet minutes. All we can do is stare at her. She really does look just like Jason, with her full cheeks and insanely long dark eyelashes.

"She's got your nose, thank God," he says quietly through a chuckle.

"I can't get over how little she is. She's the same exact weight as Josalyn was when she was born, but I'm so used to seeing our big girl that I forgot how tiny she used to be."

"Let's see her hair," Jason prompts, nodding at the beanie on her head, so I reach over and pull it off, and instantly, my eyebrows pull together.

"Tilt her closer to me?" I ask, and when he does, I lean

forward and cock my head to the side. "Is that just the light reflecting off her shiny black hair, am I delirious, or is that a grey streak in the front?"

He brings her head closer to his face to inspect the top of her hair, shifting side-to-side to see it at different angles. "That's definitely a grey streak. Jeez, punkin', was being born so stressful it gave you greys?" he asked her softly, placing a sweet kiss to the strands in question.

"Hmm... that's pretty cool, actually. Just like Rogue from *X-Men*. Plus, it's her mommy's favorite color." I smile. But then a flash of my childhood enters my head and I tell Jason, "Kids are so mean. They'll tease each other for any-damn-thing. I hope she likes it about herself and doesn't end up dyeing it."

"Nah, Daddy's gonna teach her to be a badass and take no shit. If anybody tries to pick on her, she'll knock their ass out. Isn't that right, baby?" he coos at her, and then Rebecca comes into the room after a light knock on the door.

"We're just waiting for them to put the final touches on your postpartum room, Miss Kayla. Do y'all have any questions while we wait?" she asks.

"Yeah, actually. How'd you do this swaddle so tight? What's the trick? We practiced on the dolls during Josalyn's sibling class last month, but mine kept coming undone." As the words leave his mouth, he's reluctant to give up his hold on Avary when Rebecca reaches out and takes her from him. I hide my smile, loving the overprotectiveness he already feels for our girl.

Laying her at the foot of my bed, she unwraps Avary, who sleeps right through it all as Rebecca gives Jason a lesson on the perfect swaddle. "And then, once, she's all baby-burritoed, you can hold her really any way you like. Like, cradling her..." She demonstrates the way Jason was previously holding her. "...or my personal favorite, the football hold." She spins Avary's tiny body in her arms, pressing the baby's chest to her side, her legs tucked behind Rebecca's back. In this position, the nurse can hold Avary's head in the palm of her hand, needing only one hand to hold her, leaving the other one free to get anything she might need done. I used to hold Josalyn like this sometimes while breastfeeding until she got too heavy to hold with one arm, and knowing Rebecca is a L&D nurse who works with and holds multiple babies every single day, I didn't even blink at the way she comfortably and confidently moved my newborn around like she weighed nothing.

Jason, on the other hand, looks like he is about to annihilate the poor woman. His feet are spread shoulder-width apart, his body tense, almost like he's ready to pounce, forearms rippling as his hands ball into fists at his sides. Daddy doesn't like his baby girl being tossed around like a football, apparently.

Seemingly oblivious to Jason's battle-stance, Rebecca flips Avary around once again and holds her out, saying, "Now you give it a try."

It appears to disengage his building anxiety, and he reaches out to take her, tucking her under his arm like the nurse showed him. "Wow, that is a comfortable hold," he says after a few moments, his body visibly relaxing.

There's another light knock on the door before a different nurse comes in pushing a wheelchair, letting us all know my room for the next forty-eight hours is ready. In the blink of an eye, and without my boyfriend seeing, the nurse removes my catheter and guides my feet through the openings in the padded fishnet underwear I'm to wear until I take a shower and can get into my own comfy granny-panties we brought in our hospital bag. The feeling in my legs has slowly started to come back. They still feel fat and heavy, like your lips when you get Novocain-ed at the dentist after a filling, but I can move them and could probably stand up with help.

Jason looks between the baby in his arms and me, and I see the sheer panic of not knowing what he should do written all over his face, so I put him out of his misery. "You take care of our nugget, baby. These ladies know what they're doing. They won't let me hurt myself."

He nods, but still comes around to the other side of the bed to hold the wheelchair steady while the two nurses help me swing my legs over and get my footing before I attempt to stand. I brace myself, remembering the excruciating pain I had after I gave birth to Josalyn when the epidural started to wear off, but I'm happily surprised to find there's not even a twinge of discomfort. They get me turned around and assist me while I lower my bottom slowly and carefully into the seat of the wheelchair.

CH♠PTER Sixteen

What stands out to me in the next several hours is how very different this experience is, going through it with a man who loves me unconditionally, who cares about me more than anything else in the world. The only time Jason leaves my side is when I ask him to go get me something, which isn't very often, because this hospital is treating me like a queen. After Jason—giddy as a schoolgirl—pointed out that Avary was born on the 21st, in room 21, at 4:21p.m., we realized it was well past time for dinner.

Using the call button at the side of my new bed, they directed me to pick things from the different sections of the menu conveniently located on the stand next to me. I picked a garden salad with ranch from the soup and salad section, and a cheeseburger for my entrée, but when I couldn't decide between seasoned French fries or a sweet potato as my side, they said they'd send up both at no extra charge. "We take care of our moms while you're here," the woman on the phone explained. Finishing up my order with a chocolate brownie as my dessert, she estimated it would be delivered to my room in about twenty minutes, which would give Jason enough time to run down to the cafeteria to get whatever it was he wanted so we could eat together.

Now, as I sit up with Avary cradled in one arm, I nurse her as I eat my burger one-handed, having told Jason no when he tried to take her from me so I could 'eat in peace.' I needed the distraction of my dinner to get me through the initial pain of breastfeeding. I didn't miss this feeling whatsoever. Mentally telling myself I just have to make it through the first four days before it would get easy again, I dip my French fry in ketchup and take care not to drip it on the baby.

When all three of us are finished eating, I push the rolling food tray from where it was hovering above my thighs so I can place Avary between them to change her diaper. Jason hands me a fresh one and some wipes, and as I lift her miniature booty out of her soiled diaper, she wastes no time peeing all over my lap.

"Seriously? I thought it was only baby boys who were supposed to pee on you when the cold air hit their little pickle," I gripe then laugh.

"Well, you said you needed to take a shower anyways, so now you have no more excuses to put it off. Time to take care of Mommy," Jason says, and after I have her clean diaper in place and her wet nightgown changed, he presses the button on the side of the bed.

"Nurses' station. What can I do for you, Miss Greenwood?"

"Hi, we'd like someone to take the baby to the nursery for a little bit now so I can help her mom take a shower," he calls out.

"Perfect timing, Mr. Robichaux. It's time for her heel-prick and hearing tests. When you're ready for us to bring her back, just let me know. Sending someone now," she replies pleasantly.

"Thank you," Jason says, and I hear the line disconnect.

Within a minute, one of the nurses who had been in and out of my room doing various checkups on both me and Avary comes to get her, placing her in her clear bassinet and wheeling her out of the room.

"All right, babe. Let's get ya clean." He comes around to the side of the bed and holds out his hands for me to take. I stand carefully, still not believing I have absolutely zero pain after just giving birth. It's like I'm waiting for the ball to drop and all the agony I felt last time to suddenly hit me all at once.

Jason keeps a firm hold of me as I slowly shuffle into the spacious bathroom, and then closes the door behind us. Trying to rein in my self-consciousness as he helps me undress under the bright fluorescent lights, I do my best to ignore the heat of my cheeks as he tells me to put my hands on his back while he bends down to remove my super snazzy long blue socks with grippers on the bottom that they'd put on my feet. But I grow dizzy with embarrassment when I'm left in nothing but the nude, padded fishnet undergarment and grab onto his shoulders.

"Don't," he growls, and I look into his intense gaze. "Don't you dare be embarrassed right now, babe. You just gave birth to my baby. *My* baby. Something I never dreamed I would ever have. You are the most beautiful, perfect creature I've ever seen in my life, and today, your beauty in my eyes grew a hundred-fold. Nothing I see as I take care of you right now—not your body, not the blood, not this sexy ass pad-thing they put you in, nor the highly attractive granny-panties I'll help you into when I get you all clean and dried off—will make me look at you any differently."

I can't help but laugh, which brings a mischievous sparkle into his eyes, and I reluctantly nod.

He turns his face to kiss one of my hands on his shoulders and then keeps his gaze locked on mine as his fingers grip the waistband of the underwear. "I'm not looking, babe. Promise," he assures me, and I keep my balance, stepping out of them as his eyes stay on my face. He folds them up, steps on the pedal of the biohazard trashcan beside the toilet, and tosses them in, never once looking at them.

To my surprise, he swiftly undresses, and then grabs two towels off the rack, placing them on the toilet lid next to the shower opening. I wasn't expecting him to bathe with me. I see there is a stool inside the shower, just like at Womack, and I explain what I did last time, how the nurse taught me to fold up a towel, place it on the shower seat, and soak it with hot water to sit on while I cleaned myself. He follows my instructions quickly and holds me around my waist as I step inside the wide stall and sit down. Although I don't have pain from the birth, the hot towel is soothing, helping me relax as Jason takes out our toiletries from the bag sitting on the floor beside the door.

In these moments, as Jason lathers and rinses my hair, even following my directions to leave the conditioner in a few minutes before he washes it out, and then uses my loofa to clean the rest of me, I've never felt more loved and taken care of in my whole life. And when he takes the showerhead down once more to rinse away all the sweet-smelling suds then follows the stream of water with his lips, kissing nearly every inch of my body, including my now-deflated and squishy belly, I fall even more in love with him.

Kayla's Chick Rant & Book Blog
December 24, 2009

Merry Christmas, everybody! I'm on winter break and finally had a spare second, so I thought I'd stop in and give y'all an update on everything that's been going on before I get on with this busy day I'm about to have. Plus, Jason is making me want to kick his ass today, and I decided to lock myself in the bedroom for a little bit, since playing on my blog makes me feel better. I swear on my BOB, if he doesn't get out of this foul-ass mood he's in, I'm gonna flip my shit and go postal on his ass. It's Christmas! I know I fought tooth and nail to get the hot, broody, tatted-up bad boy, but damn.

Thank you for all your kind words in the comments under the pics I posted of our little nugget. It's been a rough few months. As usual, Avary woke up about thirteen times last night to nurse and take her Gripe Water. I'm so ready for her to grow out of her colic. You'd think at four months old it would have gotten better by now, but no. My poor girl has the worse acid reflux I've ever seen in a baby. I guess God started me out with an easy, perfect child first with Josalyn before testing my strength with my new little one. I haven't had a good night's sleep since a few months before Avary was born, because she moved around so much while I was pregnant. And yet, I still woke up in a fantastic mood, because, well, again… it's Christmas!

When we got up this morning, Jason barely spoke to me while we got the girls dressed, made breakfast, and ate at the kitchen table. He didn't even look at me or try to cop a feel when I changed into the cute outfit I'm wearing to Tony and Buffy's house tonight. I don't know what's crawled up his ass, but he better get over it soon.

Buffy has welcomed us in with her family's tradition of Bring-Your-Own-Crab for Christmas Eve dinner. She and Tony will be making a prime rib and the sides, and then she told us to bring all the crab legs we want to eat, and they'll cook them up when we get there. We're… at least *I* am super excited about it. I can eat my weight in crab legs. It was one of the first things Jason and I ever bonded over, our love of the delicious seafood.

A pain in the ass to eat, but so worth the effort.

Anywho, this is what I've been up to for the past few months:

End of August:

My semester started a week after I gave birth, and I quickly had to drop two of my classes, which I will take during the spring semester and be able to graduate in June. Doing two physical education classes in one semester just was not going to happen, so I kept my Yoga I class and dropped my weight training one. I've really been enjoying learning yoga, so I think next time I'll take Yoga II instead of something different.

Funny story:

Soon after we got home from the hospital with Avary, exhausted and with sore boobs, she woke up for what had to be the eightieth time one night, screaming her little brains out after I had just gotten her to sleep maybe an hour before. Jason, trying to be comforting, reached over to rub my back right as I was bracing myself for Avary to latch onto my nipple, which felt like it would fall off at any moment because she'd been overusing them so much, and it's like his hand electrocuted me. I probably looked possessed by the devil himself as I yelled, *"Don't fucking touch me!"* and then immediately burst into tears as at the exact same moment I was overcome with shame for screaming at my loving baby-daddy for trying to make me feel better and Avary grabbed ahold of my raw areola with her razor-like gums. I sat there, bawling my eyes out, and then cried even harder as Jason got out of bed and left the room, and I felt like the worst human being on the face of the planet.

But then he came back, and he was carrying a tray. There were two steaming washcloths rolled up next to a big glass of 'red stuff', our codename for Fruit Punch flavored Crystal Light, which we'd been drinking for months like it was water from the Fountain of Youth. There had been nights during my pregnancy when we'd go on 'Wal-Mart dates', when we'd walk the aisles of the superstore late at night when I couldn't sleep or just needed to get out of the house. We came home several times with party trays full of pepperoni, salami, cheese, and crackers, and make a fresh two-liter jug of our red stuff, and we'd sit in the middle of the bed just the two of us and finish off the entire snack tray and the whole container of drink.

When he sat the tray next to me on the nightstand, I saw he had also brought me two Reese's Peanut Butter Cups, and my emotions seesawed between loving him with every fiber of my being and hating myself for being such a psycho bitch.

Seeing Avary was now asleep, but just using my poor boob as a pacifier, he gently picked her up out of my lap after I unlatched her, swaddled her like a pro, and then put her back in her soft, white bassinet beside our bed. He then unrolled the two washcloths, squeezed them to make sure they wouldn't burn my skin, and then as I leaned back on my pillow, covered my aching breasts with their soothing heat. He sat on the edge of the bed next to me and unwrapped my Reese's Cups, handing me one like he would a painkiller, and after I ate it in one bite, he gave me the glass of red stuff to wash it down with. After doing the same with the second, he removed the now-cool washcloths and handed me the lanolin cream out of my nightstand drawer so I could slather on a much-needed coat to my nipples.

He got back into bed after helping me get my arms back through my sports bra and giving me two fresh breast pads out of the bathroom, and then pulled me to him to rest my head on his chest, his arm securely around my back.

"I'm so sor—" I tried to apologize, but he cut me off.

"Don't even worry about it, baby. I love you. Get some sleep."

One day, I will write a romance novel, and the hero I create will be based solely on him. My real-life book boyfriend.

Even if he is being a dick today.

September and October were hectic. A lot of schoolwork for me, and Jason going to work during the day and a class at night at our school. His parents, now both retired, didn't mind watching our girls one bit while I went to my classes during the day. There was a lot of playing and taking care of our kids, but the biggest event is after a couple of months of searching for the perfect one, we finally found a house of our own. Obviously, we couldn't afford it ourselves, but his parents had been toying with the idea of buying a house and renting it out. We went to what had to be thirty different houses in Friendswood, but everything was either too much work as a fixer-upper, which was the only thing that fit into our price range for a home in the coveted suburb, too small, or in an area that was prone to flooding.

Finally, our real estate agent talked us into looking at a house in the next suburb over, Pearland, literally ten minutes from the

Robichauxs' house.

It. Was. Perfect.

Three bedrooms. Two bathrooms. And extra room off the living room I could turn into my library. I felt it was the one as soon as we walked in the door.

The paperwork and everything took about four weeks to go through, and we moved in last month. It feels like we're a real family now, just the four of us and our yappy little dog. Life is good.

November:

We got settled into our house before piling into my minivan—yup, I traded in my Malibu for a Family Assault Vehicle, in which Jason made me a baby pink box for my twelve-inch subwoofer so I could bass out (no judging)—and driving to North Carolina for Thanksgiving. It was a wonderful trip, and a much-needed vacation.

Which brings us to now. Jason's parents are making the forty-five minute trek to Kingwood tonight too. I think it was so sweet of Buffy to invite them along. The woman has five brothers and sisters, and now four kids of her own, so it's understandable she loves to be surrounded by a big family during this time of year, especially with her own family scattered states away.

My dad has flown in to spend Christmas in Texas, while Mom stayed behind to be with Granny and the rest of her side of the clan, so I'm thrilled to see him when we get there tonight. Add them to my nieces Aspen, Amanda, and Abigail, and my nephew, Alex, and it'll be a very loud, boisterous, and fun-filled evening with the Greenwoods. I hope Jason's parents, Steve and Barbara, are prepared!

Now if only my Grinch of a baby daddy would perk the hell up.

CHAPTER
Seventeen

"Do you want me to go now to the grocery store to get the crab, or do you want to just grab it on our way up to Kingwood?" I ask Jason, who is zeroed in on TruTV at the moment, lying on his stomach in the middle of our two-year-old's bed at MiMi and Papa's house, while Josalyn straddles his butt and brushes his dark hair. The image they make is adorable, but he's pissing me the hell off with his bad attitude today. We came over to his parents' house about an hour ago so they could follow us up to my brother's later.

He sighs like I'm asking him to get up and run a marathon, making my blood pressure rise. I can't fucking stand it when he sighs. It's an instant way to make me go from happy to stabby in zero minutes flat. He sits up on his elbows and runs a hand over his sexy scruff before looking up at me, where I'm leaning against the bedroom's doorjamb. He's lucky he's so freakin' hot.

"I guess go get it now, since they'll probably close early on Christmas Eve. Grab a bottle of your wine too to take with us. And a bottle of my shiraz," he says then turns his attention back to the TV, basically dismissing me.

"Oh, yes, Master. Anything you like," I huff out, turning on my heel and exiting the room. I grab my purse from the couch, where it was sitting next to Mom, and open it to make sure my wallet is inside, sticking my phone in after turning the ringer on.

"Avary is napping in her crib. Jason wants me to go ahead and get our crab from the grocery store. Do y'all need anything while I'm there?" I ask the Robichauxs. Steve sits up in his dark green recliner, the leather squeaking under his weight as he shifts to pull his wallet out of the back pocket of his jeans.

Handing me a twenty, he asks, "Yeah, honey, will you grab me a tub of their fresh guacamole? Will you look on top of the fridge and see if we still have tortilla chips? If we're running low, a bag of those too, please."

"Sure, Daddyo. You need anything, Momma?" I turn to Barbara, seeing she's trying to think of something she's missing for tonight.

"Oh, pecans. I got everything to make the sweet potato casserole, but forgot to grab the pecans to go on top. That should do it," she replies.

"Alrighty, I'll be right back. And if you can, see what's got Jason in such a pissy mood. Maybe he'll tell his momma, 'cause he's certainly not telling me." Receiving a nod accompanied by a look I can't decipher, I head to the kitchen to check on Dad's chips. Seeing he's almost out, I add them to my mental checklist of stuff to buy at the store.

I walk out to Jason's green Altima, half expecting him to run out to kiss me goodbye and apologize for being a dick, but he doesn't. So, I hop in the car and drive to HEB, my favorite grocery store. It's way different than the Food Lions I grew up shopping at. It's like the mothership of all food shopping establishments. It has absolutely everything under the sun, even a self-service olive bar. I can't stand olives, but it's pretty freakin' cool it has a whole buffet designated to every olive under the sun, prepared in just as many different ways.

I grab a shopping cart and head into the store, grabbing a tub of Dad's guacamole, snatching a bag of his tortilla chips off the end cap as I make my way to the enormous wine section. I find my bottle of moscato quickly, knowing exactly where it is, and then spend the next ten minutes trying to find a bottle of Jason's shiraz. Heaven forbid I choose the wrong one. I don't want to put him in an even fouler mood.

I have no idea what's gotten into him. We were absolutely great last night, after he'd gotten home from work. We had cuddled up to watch a movie after eating dinner and putting the girls to bed. After a typical Avary-disturbed night of sleep, I woke up super excited about getting to spend a four-day weekend with my man, and he woke up acting like someone had peed in his Cheerios. I honestly have no clue what could've happened to make him so grouchy.

I weave through the crowded aisle of last-minute Christmas shoppers to find Momma's pecans and then to the fresh seafood section to get our crab legs. Seeing they're on sale for six bucks a pound, I grab us ten, knowing we can put away at least that between the two of us, check out, and hustle to my car to head back to the Robichauxs'. When I pull in, Jason is in the driveway, waiting to help me bring in the groceries. Before I can even open the door myself, he's there, looming over me in the driver's seat.

I don't have time to ask him what he's doing before he seals his perfect lips with mine, taking my breath away when he dips his tongue inside. My every sense is filled with all things Jason —the smell of his deliciously masculine cologne, the sound of his ragged breaths, the now familiar and comforting taste of his irresistible mouth, and, when I open my eyes as the kiss slows, the sight of his ridiculously long eyelashes that splay nearly to his cheekbones.

When I can finally speak, my voice is breathless. "Well, hello to you too."

"I don't like you leaving me in a bad mood. I'm sorry I've been a dick today. I've got... a lot on my mind," he says gruffly, still leaning over me inside the car, his chocolate brown eyes twinkling with an emotion I can't quite place.

"Whatever it is, baby, you can talk to me about it. You don't have to bottle it up inside," I prompt, but he just shakes his dark head.

"Nah, I'm sure I'll be fine tomorrow," he tells me vaguely, and then disappears from in front of me as I hear him pop my trunk.

I grab my purse out of the passenger seat and get out of the car, and when I shut the door, he's there beside me, holding the plastic bags and peeking into the one with the wine bottles. I hold my breath until he looks up at me with a small smile.

"You always know exactly what to get me." He leans down and places a quick kiss on my lips, making my heart thump in my chest at his approval.

"I hope you think the same thing when you open your Christmas presents tomorrow," I say and he nods.

"Ditto, babe. Fucking ditto."

Despite the brief reprieve in the driveway from his foul mood, shortly after loading up into his Altima for the drive to Kingwood, Jason returned to his grumpy state. Before we could back all the way out of the driveway, his parents waiting to back out after us from the garage to follow us up in their red Toyota Highlander, Jason slammed on the brakes and threw the car in park with a curse. He opened his door and was jogging toward the house before I even had a chance to ask what he'd forgotten.

After a moment, I saw him exit the house and turn to lock the door again, walking over to where his dad sat in the driver's seat of the SUV, his window now rolled down. A few quick words I couldn't make out and a nod from Jason later, his dad reached out the window to pat his shoulder, and then Jason made his way back to the car.

I didn't bother asking what that was all about, knowing I'd just be brushed off, so for the entire drive to my brother's, I let him be, trying my best to let the radio pass the time.

By the time we get to Tony and Buffy's house, I nearly explode from the car, trying to escape the suffocating tension. God, I love this man, but his mood swings give me fucking whiplash. I hope once we get inside and he hangs out with Tony for a while, he'll lighten up some. My big brother is quite a moody guy himself, but for some reason when the two get together and start talking guns and History Channel shows, they are as happy as clams.

I let Josalyn out of her car seat, while Jason detaches Avary's carrier from its strapped-in cradle, and his parents' Highlander pulls in behind us. I keep an eye on Josalyn as she runs up to the door, stands on her little tiptoes, and rings the bell, and then I grab the plastic grocery bags, plus the gift bags for my nieces and nephew, out of Jason's trunk.

I hear the door open and Buffy's sweetly lilted voice as she says to Josalyn, "Well, hello there, sweet girl! Merry Christmas, baby!" and my daughter's giggle as she throws herself into my sister-in-law's arms. And then I wait for it... aaand there it is. Buffy's laugh is still so infectious. You'd never imagine such a boisterous sound would come out of such a tiny, pretty thing. It's loud and full of uninhibited joy, and immediately puts me in a lighter mood, the tension easing from my tightly strung body.

I greet her with a kiss to her cheek as she sets Josalyn back on her feet and takes the bags out of my hands. Following her through the foyer and into the kitchen, I help Buffy empty the bags on the counter, where she has everything already prepped for the crab legs.

I turn and look through the huge bay window and spot my big brother manning the grill as usual, and see my dad sitting in a chair next to him. I feel a smile split my face as I watch him pull a piece of meat from the tongs Tony holds out to him, knowing Daddy can never wait until dinnertime to taste the food. I hear Mom's voice in my head, *"Mike, there won't be any food left to put on the table if you don't stop sneaking it!"*

"I've got this, if you want to go see your dad," Buffy tells me, so I head through the breakfast area, and into the living room, where the French back doors sprawl across an entire wall before stopping at a fireplace, its mantel full of framed pictures of the entire Greenwood family.

I glance over to the giant L-shaped couch, where Jason is taking Avary's tiny squirming body out of her carrier. I can't help but feel my heart swell as he cradles her in one arm while carefully straightening out her pretty, red satin Christmas dress I put her in before we left the house. His eyes come to me as he leans down and kisses the top of her head, the grey streak at the front a stark contrast to the rest of her pitch-black hair. Nothing but love fills his gaze on me, and it makes me hopeful his bad mood has already lifted.

I turn the knob on the door to the back yard and step outside, pulling it shut behind me. There's not much of a difference in temperature between the inside of Tony's house and out here, since he likes to keep it arctic. Being in Texas, though, it actually got up to the mid-seventies today, but it's gotten much colder since the sun has gone down. As I step up to my big brother and twine my arms around his middle, he engulfs me with his six-five frame.

"Merry Christmas, kid. The drive up okay?" he asks, rubbing my arms rapidly to get the chill off.

"Merry Christmas, Nony. Yeah, the drive was fine. Traffic wasn't as bad as I thought it would be," I tell him, stepping over to my dad, who stands waiting with his arms spread wide.

"Hey, Daddy!" I wrap my arms around his neck and feel his

beard tickle my face as he lays a kiss on my cheek.

"Hey, baba-doll. Where are my babies?" he asks, looking around me to peer in through the kitchen's window.

"Inside. Josalyn is probably attached to Aspen, and Jason just got Avary out of her carrier." I barely have time to finish my sentence before he's headed into the living room.

That man loves babies. And it's a good thing too, since he now has ten grandkids between his four children. There have been quite a few back-to-back the past several years. First, Jay and Renee had Bret in 2005, then I had Josalyn in 2007, Tony and Buffy had Abigail in 2008, and just over a year later, I had Avary a few months ago. When I got on the phone with Dad after I had her, the first thing out of his mouth was, "You couldn't wait one more day, so she and I could share a birthday?"

Tony snaps me out of the memory as he lifts the lid of the grill, letting out a plume of smoke. "You all right, sis?"

"Gettin' there. I'm hoping once Jason gets around his buddy, he'll get out of his foul mood. He's had a stick up his ass all day, and I have no idea why," I confide.

"Ah, I'm sure he's fine. More than likely just stressed out because he's got a new baby and it's your first Christmas down here. It can be overwhelming for a guy," he says.

"How so?" I tilt my head over the giant prime rib he's cooking, inhaling the delicious scent of the seared beef.

"Well, before, he only had to worry about making himself happy. Now, he's got a whole family of his own to make sure they are taken care of. He's probably worried the gifts he's gotten each of you aren't good enough, or that he hasn't gotten you enough, period. Or maybe he's overwhelmed about it being his first Christmas with his own family in your new house. It's basically his first time being the man of the house, not the kid, right?"

He looks at me with his always bloodshot but still beautiful blue eyes, the same eyes all three of my brothers share with both of my parents. I doubt Tony's body even realizes what time zone he's in right now. He's constantly travelling all over the world for his job.

"True, I didn't think of that." A sense of relief washes over me that it could be something as simple as masculine pride that's weighing on my boyfriend's shoulders.

I watch Tony use an obscenely sharp knife to cut a slice of beef off then lay it on the plate sitting on the table next to grill. He halves it, pops one into his mouth, and then holds out the other piece to me with a fork. I devour it velociraptor style and moan as the flavor bursts in my mouth. One does not leave my big brother's house without a painfully full belly of the best food imaginable.

"That's amazing. Mom's not here, so you don't have to burn it," I say, knowing if she were here he'd have to cook at least part of it well done. The rest of us like our beef, at most, medium rare.

"Damn straight," he agrees, and I chuckle before heading inside.

When I walk into the kitchen, Jason's Mom is flapping around the kitchen, trying to help Buffy, who, by the look on her face, would obviously prefer to have her workspace to herself. Anything Momma asks if she can help with, Buffy turns her down politely and laughs, shooting a look for help at Jason and his dad. Steve finally catches it and tells Barbara, "Hey, Mike is in the living room with Avary. Why don't we get out of Buffy's hair and see what he's been up to?" taking her hand and pulling her in that direction.

"Well, only if you're sure you don't need any help," she aims at Buffy.

"Oh, I'm positive," she replies with an enthusiastic nod, and as the older couple leaves the room, my gaze locks with my sister's and we both split up laughing. "Bless her heart."

"God love her," I add, shaking my head. Being retired, the woman doesn't know how to *not* try to take over everything anyone else is doing. If you don't cut her off at the beginning, your project will suddenly become hers. I don't think she realizes she does this; she's only trying to be helpful.

With Josalyn upstairs playing with her cousins and Avary with her grandparents, I sit down at the kitchen table and take a minute to relax. When I look over at Jason, I see he's sipping on a glass of his dark red wine.

"Wow, you didn't wait long, did you?" I raise a brow at him, and he looks down into the liquid.

"I figured if I'm going to drink, I better do it early so it wears off before we go home. Don't worry, baby," he adds, seeing the expression on my face. "I'm only going to have a glass or two, and after I eat, I won't be able to feel anything. If I do, I promise I'll tell you and you can drive home."

I can only have a glass or two myself, since I breastfeed the baby, so what he says appeases me. If having some wine will aid in lifting his Scrooge-like mood, then he can have the whole damn bottle for all I care.

"Would you like a glass, Kayla?" Buffy asks from behind her counter, and when I look up, she's glaring at Jason.

"Oh, yeah. Sorry, babe. You want some of your wine we brought?" Jason hops up from the table and moves to open the bottle of moscato with the corkscrew sitting next to Buffy's baby pink KitchenAid mixer. I've threatened to steal it several times, but I always get laughed at. One day...

"Yes, please. It's warm, so will you throw a couple of ice cubes in it? I don't understand how you can drink that dry-ass wine, especially with it not cold. I don't like to have to drink water behind my wine in order to wet my tongue again."

"I love the dry reds too, but I like to add Sprite to it and make it a wine spritzer," Buffy interjects, opening the oven and sliding the pan of crab legs in before shutting it again.

"I've never tried it like that before. Maybe that would make it bearable. You do your crab in the oven?" I ask, fascinated. I always learn cool things in the kitchen every time I come to Buffy's.

"Yeah, it's so much easier than trying to boil them in a big pot on the stove, especially since we're doing so many."

I watch as she pulls several sticks of butter out of the refrigerator, unwraps them, and puts them in bowls. She sits them next to the stove, assumingly so they'll be close by to melt in the microwave above it once the crab is ready.

Jason closes the freezer and walks toward me, my heart jumping a little. After everything we've been through, I doubt I'll ever get used to him being my man, here to do things for me as simple as pour me a glass of wine. Even after our yearlong

long-distance relationship, moving to Texas to be with him, and having his baby. The two and a half years before that I had to spend without my soul mate was… terrible, to say the least. Thinking I would have to live without him… It's still surreal I'm here, with Jason, and I'm his girl.

Well, woman now, I guess. We've been through and have grown up so much since I first fell for him that I can't really be called a girl anymore. It's been nearly five years since I first met him. I can remember that night so vividly, like it happened only hours ago instead of half a decade. I can almost smell the engine oil mixed with his cologne as he changed the starter in his old Chevy truck. I feel the same scattering butterflies erupt in my stomach, remembering the first time our eyes locked over the hood as he wiped his hands on a shop rag.

"What's that face?" he whispers in my ear as he leans down and places the wine glass on the table next to me. "What are you thinking about, baby? Because that look is making my dick hard."

At my gasp, he chuckles and sits back down in his seat. I know the heat in my cheeks is visible when Buffy looks over at me and shakes her head. Letting out one of her laughs, she playfully gripes, "You two! Not at the table where my kids eat!"

CH♠PTER Eighteen

An hour later, after setting up all the pots and pans full of food with serving spoons and filling glasses with ice, we all line up and pile our plates with everything from the crab legs we brought, to Buffy's homemade stuffing. We set the kids at the table in the kitchen, and the grown-ups sit down at the table in the dining room. Avary went down for a nap upstairs in Abigail's crib a few minutes ago after I nursed her, so I can eat in peace. I turn the volume on the baby monitor up so I'll be sure to hear it if she cries.

"You want a refill, Jason?" Buffy asks before she sits down, and they exchange a look I barely catch before it disappears.

"Yes, please," he replies, handing her his glass. She quickly moves through the doorway into the kitchen to pour him more wine before returning and placing it in front of him.

Looking at him closely, I don't really know what emotion I see on his face. He doesn't look like he's in a bad mood anymore. He almost looks anxious. Nervous, even. He flexes his hands as he rests his wrists on the edge of the table, and he takes some deep breaths as he looks down into his lap. I really hope being around so much of my big family isn't freaking him out.

I reach over and grasp his hand, and when he looks from my grip up into my face, it warms my heart to see him visibly relax. He smiles at me then lifts my knuckles to his lips, placing a gentle kiss on them before squeezing my fingers then releasing them.

The next hour is filled with the sounds of cracking crab legs, moans of appreciation, humorous banter, and of course, Buffy's laughter, followed by everyone else's.

"I'm going to go wake Avary up and bring her downstairs so there might be some hope she'll sleep tonight," I tell Jason, standing from the table when I'm finished stuffing myself.

"I got your plate, babe," he says, waving my hands away from my mess. There wasn't a single leg left out of the ten pounds of crab I bought. I lean down and kiss him quickly on the lips before walking through the kitchen, out to the foyer, and up the carpeted stairs. I turn right at the top and quietly open Abigail's door, not wanting to startle Avary awake.

After gently rubbing her back and petting her chubby cheeks, she slowly awakens, and when she looks up to see who's loving on her, her dark chocolate eyes, the same as her daddy's, sparkle as she sees it's me, and her face splits with a wide, toothless grin. "Hey there, sleepy head. Did you have sweet dreams, baby girl?" I coo, picking up my little bundle and putting her to my chest. I smooth out her red satin dress and bury my nose in her neck, breathing in her baby scent.

"We're about to open presents downstairs. You want to go see all your family?" I ask her.

Her response is another giant smile, and her answer satisfies me enough that we make our way back downstairs.

"Gimme my grandbaby," my dad says, holding his arms out. "But give her to me backwards. They like to see what's going on, ya know."

I hand Avary to him with her back to his front, and he wraps one arm across her chest and places his other under her butt, so she's basically sitting in his grasp. I've watched him hold all eight of my nieces and nephews this way, and it makes my heart swell to see him hold my own daughter this way, the same way it did when he used to hold Josalyn.

He bounces her a few times, and when she giggles and drools, I know she's good. It's like she remembers him from when we went to visit him, Mom, and Granny last month in North Carolina for Thanksgiving. Or maybe she just senses that PopPop loves her to death.

Suddenly, the room fills with bodies of all shapes and sizes. From the miniature ones of Abigail and Josalyn, to the tall ones of my boyfriend, brother, and Steve, mixed in with the medium ones of my nieces, Amanda and Aspen, my nephew Alex, and Buffy and Barbara. We all pile onto the couch, giant leather ottoman, and the floor, waiting anxiously while Buffy plugs in the Christmas tree and dims the overhead light.

Jason sits beside me on the light tan suede couch, and I feel him stretch and put his arm behind me along the pillows. I lean into him and kiss his neck before reaching forward to tighten Josalyn's ponytail, where she bounces on the ottoman next to Abigail.

"Okay, babies. I'm going to hand each of you a present, but don't open it until everyone has one, got it?" Buffy says from where she's kneeling next to the lit tree.

"Got it!" all the kids say in unison, making all the adults grin as we watch Buffy read the labels on each of the gift bags and wrapped boxes, passing them out to who they belong to.

When all five kids have one in their hands, and Barbara holds one for Avary next to my dad, he calls out, "Rip and tear!" like he has at every birthday and Christmas as far back as I can remember. Suddenly, the room is filled with the sounds of paper being demolished and the children's excited squealing, making my cheeks hurt I'm smiling so big.

"Oh, my gosh! Aunt Kayla, this is *awesome!*" my seven-year-old niece, Aspen, shouts.

"Bring it over here. Let me show you," I tell her, and she wobbles over on her knees from the other side of the ottoman. "Look, it just looks like a toy ATM machine, but it's really a piggy bank that locks and keeps count of your money for you." I point out the instructions on the back while she plays with the buttons.

"That's perfect for her!" Buffy enthuses. "She's a little money hoarder. She doesn't spend a dime of her birthday, Christmas, or Tooth Fairy money—says she's saving up for a car."

"I remember you saying that. Saw this and had to get it for

her." I laugh, and Aspen tackle-hugs me against the pillows of the couch, giving me a big kiss on my cheek. I love this sweet girl so much, just as much as my blood-related nieces and nephews. She's literally Tony's redheaded stepchild, which made me giggle the first time I met her. She's so amazing about playing with her much younger cousin Josalyn, who worships the ground she walks on.

She crawls off my lap and into Jason's, giving him the same treatment. "Thank you, Uncle Jason!"

I'm so proud of him when he squeezes her back and tells her, "You're very welcome." Growing up an only child, he's had to get used to all the little ones in my family. And the big ones, for that matter. He was a little shell-shocked the first time my parents and brothers gave him hugs. I have a very affectionate family. We don't even end phone calls without saying I love you.

Just as Aspen moves away, we're being attacked by my one and a half year old niece, Abigail, and Josalyn, who want us to help them open their Fisher Price toy and Barbie doll. When I get Josalyn's Barbie out of the package, I lean close to her so she can hear me over the chaos. "Don't take off her clothes, okay, baby? We don't want to lose them before we can get her home." The child loves changing her Barbie dolls' clothes.

"'Kay, Mommy," she agrees then turns to Abigail's toy to help her figure out what it does.

My dad comes over next, handing Jason the baby and another Fisher Price toy so he can open his own gift from us. Avary wiggles in his arms, and I lean over and get myself a slobbery kiss before I hear Dad's, "Oooooh, chocolate-covered cherries. My favorite!" Taped to the front is a card with enough money inside for him to go see a couple of movies, his favorite pastime. "Thanks, kids." He stands and plants a kiss on top of not only my head, but Jason's too, and I can't help but giggle at Jason's befuddled face.

The adults agreed only to get gifts for all the kids instead of each other too, since we have so many little ones between us, so I'm very surprised when Aspen calls from beside the Christmas tree, "Aunt Kayla, there's one for you under here!"

I turn to look at her, her curly auburn hair glowing all around her where she's reaching beneath the tree. She's only seven, so maybe she's reading it wrong and it's something under there for my brother's family's Christmas morning tomorrow.

But sure enough, when she walks over to me and hands me the big white envelope, my name in cursive is scrawled across the front. "Thank you, baby," I tell her, and open it up.

As I start to read it, it seems odd that it sounds so romantic. I mean, I love my brother and his wife a lot, but the card says things like, *For me, the best Christmas gift this year will be having you by my side,* and *Christmas comes once a year, but the love I have for you only comes once in a lifetime.*

It's not until I get down to the bottom and see Jason's normal handwriting, instead of the fancy cursive on the envelope, that I realize it's not from Tony and Buffy.

"This is from you?" I look over at my handsome boyfriend, my face and voice full of surprise. "I thought we were going to exchange gifts tomorrow. I didn't bring yours," I say, a little disappointment tingeing my words.

"Just read the rest," he says quietly, lifting his chin toward the card.

I look down and read in his neat handwriting, "Go upstairs to the kids' bathroom. I love you, Jason."

I think for a moment with my eyebrows furrowed, and then it dawns on me. "Oh, my gosh! You actually remembered! You got me my Victoria's Secret Snowplum shower gel, body spray, and lotion, didn't you?" I bounce up and down on the couch and then wrap my arms around him. It makes sense he'd put it in the bathroom for me to find, seeing how they're body care products. I've been begging him for it for over a month, because it's a limited edition scent that only comes out around Christmastime.

I don't even give him a chance to respond before I leap off the couch, round the corner of the living room into the foyer, and bound up the stairs two at a time. When I get to the bathroom at the head of the steps, the motion sensor light flips on and I take a look around. There's nothing on the counter... nothing in the sink... nothing on the toilet lid... nothing in the bathtub except for the kids' shampoos.... I don't see a Victoria's Secret bag anywhere. I look down and see the cabinet under the sink is slightly cracked open, so I reach for the knob and pull it open. What I find instead isn't a basket full of yummy smelling products, but yet another card.

Across the front, it says, *Kayla, open first then go downstairs.*

Sliding it out of the envelope, I laugh at the two reindeer on the front, who are both skating toward a big hole in the ice. Pointing at it, one of the reindeer says to the other, "Look out...

ice hole!" and the other one is turned to glare at him, saying, "What did you call me?"

When I open the card up, I jump and almost drop it when Jason's voice starts talking to me, which in turn shuts off what he had obviously recorded previously. Now that I'm expecting it, I reopen the card and listen to my man's deep, sexy twang.

"Merry Christmas, baby. I love you so much. Your Christmas hunt's almost over. Just go back downstairs for your next clue."

Shaking my head, with a big, goofy grin across my face, I tuck the card back in the envelope and head back down the steps. My soul is happy, hearing so much of my big family gathered in one place as they chatter and laugh, but suddenly, as my feet trot down the stairs, I hear everything suddenly go absolutely quiet. Even the Christmas music Buffy had playing is silenced.

With my eyebrows pulled down, I round into the living room from the foyer... and my heart stops.

Standing in a giant group of loving faces, everyone is staring at me with huge smiles where I just entered, all except my Jason, who is in front of me.

Down on one knee.

A black velvet ring box lifted toward me.

His gorgeous face and twinkling eyes full of mischief and adoration.

I've got tunnel vision. All I see is him. It all makes sense now—the grouchy mood, the undecipherable looks between people today, his nervousness at dinner. Everyone already knew but me. His attitude today was because he was so tense, anxious, his big plan all laid out and ready to go.

His sexy lips are lifted into his crooked smirk, the first I've seen all day. His scruff has been allowed to grow for a few days, and the darkness of his cheeks make his eyes look even brighter than normal, the chocolaty brown of his irises a shocking contrast to the stark whiteness surrounding them.

I glance down, and the elegant ring box in his masculine, rough hand stands out against the backdrop of his green and white striped polo shirt I insisted he wear to look festive. His dark jean-clad knee presses into the white carpet, while his elbow rests on his other one.

He starts speaking, and all other thoughts leave my mind as I listen to his voice, the voice I've loved since the moment I first met him as he cursed at his truck. It wraps me up like a warm winter blanket, comforting, feeling like I could be engulfed by it forever as it soothes me. Yet my heart still pounds ferociously in my chest. I bet if I looked down, I'd see my bright red shirt moving with its beat. But I can't look away from my beautiful man.

"Kayla, we've been through hell and back. But that's what matters—we made it back to each other. You are the one who got away, but then came back to me. You are my soul mate, the one I was made to be with. I don't deserve you, but I'll spend every minute of the rest of my life earning you if you'll spend it with me. Will you marry me, baby?"

I come out of my stupor as soon as the question leaves his mouth, and I throw myself on top of him, wrapping my arms around his neck and laughing as he stands up. With a squeaked, "Yes!" the room erupts in applause, congratulations, and the sounds of cameras going off. As I finally pull away far enough that he can slide the ring on my finger, tears sting my nose as I look at what he picked.

He remembered. He remembered from years ago when I described my dream ring. The checklist is all there. Pear shaped center diamond. Smaller diamonds circling the band. Dainty, not gaudy, so it wouldn't look stupid on my tiny hand. It's perfect, just like my fiancé.

My fiancé.

Oh, my dear God, Jason Robichaux is my fiancé.

With that thought, I wrap myself back around him and laugh-cry with my face buried in his collarbone. He has to hold me up for a moment until I hear Josalyn's tiny sweet voice next to us, asking, "Daddy, why is Mommy crying?"

I unlatch myself and bend down close to my beautiful girl, holding out my hand for her to see the ring. "Look, baby. I'm crying because I'm so happy. Mommy and Daddy are getting married."

"Really? Just like Cinderella?" she says, her eyes wide.

I chuckle and kiss her chubby cheek. "Yep, just like Cinderella. And just like Belle and the Beast too. You know that's Mommy's favorite," I try to get her on a different subject, so she won't be worried about my tears anymore.

"Yep! I think Avary's favorite is Jasmine and Aladdin, because she never cries when I watch that movie," she tells me seriously then turns and runs over to my dad, who's holding her sister once again, and she runs her hand gently over Avary's soft hair. "Is Jasmine your favorite princess, baby sister?" Josalyn asks her, and Avary lets out an excited squeal, kicking her legs and making Josalyn laugh as she turns to me with a proud look on her face. "See?"

"I think you're right," I reply, and seeing her attention is now distracted by PopPop, I turn back to Jason.

Looking down at me with that smirk still in place, he asks, "How about we gather up our babies and head on home? I think it's about time to seal the deal with some engagement sex."

"Engagement sex? Is that the same as make-up sex? Because you totally owe me some of that too," I tease.

"What do I owe you make-up sex for?" he questions, linking his arms around my waist and pulling me toward him with his hands on my ass.

"You've been a douchecanoe all day today!" I hiss. "You totally owe me."

"Wow, engaged not even five minutes and you're already calling me names and making commands." He shakes his head, and then bursts out laughing when I punch him in the gut.

His face turns soft as he looks back down at me, and I hold him tighter as he confesses, "I'm sorry I've been a dick today, babe. I was so scared something or someone would fuck everything up. I wanted everything to be perfect. And then at the very last second, I realized I was about to drive off and leave the ring."

I smile, understanding that's what he must've had to run back into his parents' house for before we left. "Well, it all turned out perfect. I had no idea. It was the best surprise ever. I seriously thought maybe you'd propose on New Year's, because you know that's my favorite holi—"

"I know," he interrupts. "And that's exactly why I didn't wait until then, because you would've been expecting it." He grins.

"Sneaky bastard." I lean up and kiss his lips, and then Buffy orders us to pose for some pictures, which she and Jason's mom snap several of.

I hold back my laughter when my dad pulls Jason into a big hug, not a man-hug he's used to getting from other men, and my face softens when Jason hugs him back just as hard. "I promise I'll take care of her," I hear him say, and it takes everything in me not to tear up again in front of my kids.

Soon, we gather up the girls' gifts, Avary's diaper bag, and my purse after giving rounds of hugs and kisses, wishing each other a Merry Christmas. When we load up the car and back out of my brother's driveway, I take a second to soak in the Christmas lights decorating his house, knowing this moment in time will be saved in my memory for the rest of my life.

Lying in bed, still catching our breath from the

engagement/make-up sex we just had, I look at the ring on my finger, where they're twined with Jason's. Keeping my voice as serious as I can, I lay it on him, because that's just how we are, and I love it. "So...wait a minute. Are you telling me you didn't get my Victoria's Secret Limited Edition scent, fucker?"

When he doesn't make a sound, not even a little laughter, I look up at him with my head on his chest, seeing he has his lips pulled between his teeth, and he's looking everywhere but at me. Then his eyes come to mine, and he mumbles, "Whoops," to which I reply with a poke to his ribs.

"I swear to God, if one of my presents in the morning isn't a bag full of body goodies, after I've been reminding you for over a month, I'm going to kick your ass."

He chuckles, squeezes me to his side, and places a kiss on top of my head. The last thing I hear before drifting off to sleep is him whispering, "My sexy fiancée. I love it when you get all feisty."

Fiancée is my last conscious thought, and then I'm fast asleep.

CHAPTER Nineteen

Kayla's Chick Rant & Book Blog
April 8, 2010

Let the record state that *I* wanted to elope. I would've been perfectly happy taking a nice little getaway to Vegas, doing a quickie wedding at a little chapel like Marky and Kim did, and then spending a few days going to shows and relaxing by a pool. But alas, Jason roped me into planning a full-on big-ass wedding, because unlike me, he had "never been married before, and it's going to be the only wedding I ever have, because I don't believe in divorce, so I want to do the whole, big shebang." And with those beautiful brown puppy-dog eyes looking down into mine, that's how the cookie crumbled. Since this wedding was mostly for him, though, I made him help me with every aspect, right down to the dress, because I felt I should wear the dress he would want to see me in. Plus, he proclaimed to be the wedding-dress-picking-master, having picked "the one" for a couple of his friends before.

I found a couple I liked on DavidsBridal.com, planning to go try them on the next day, and showed them to him on the site. He came across one he absolutely drooled over, but when I saw what the model looked like who was wearing the dress, I told him, "Sorry, baby, that model has curves for days. The dress won't look that good on me, because I don't have those tits or that ass." He shrugged and said he'd go with me to see the dresses in case there were any in the store they didn't have on the website.

I tried on the dresses I'd written the style numbers down for, but none of them flipped my skirt. We were about to leave, when Jason called from between two rows of fluffy puffs of white, "Babe! I found that dress I liked! And they have it in your size!"

I sighed, but turned around and walked to where he was, grabbing it out of his hand after he took it down from the tall rack. "I've already forewarned you it's going to look ridiculous on my flat chest. No making fun of me when you see how terrible it looks after seeing it look so good on that runway model," I griped, but he just swatted my ass as I turned to walk back into my dressing room.

I slipped it on over my head, buttoned the halter around my neck, and zipped it up to where it only reached a third of the way up my back, fitting my body like a second skin. When I looked into the mirror, I shook my head at my reflection. In the words of Captain Jack Sparrow, *there'll be no living with him after this.*

The dress was perfect.

The one.

And he had picked it out off a website.

Fuck.

When I exited the dressing room, he didn't even bother hiding his smirk, knowing he had been spot-on, and when I stood up on the pedestal under the spotlight in front of the giant mirror showing my every angle, I watched as the smirk changed into a different look altogether. One that made me feel like a goddess. Yep, this was 'the dress.'

Having only two classes during this last semester of my college career, I had enough time during the day to plan the entire wedding, which we set for April 17th. Mom's church was booked for the ceremony, the Knights of Columbus hall was reserved for our reception, and we will be having Angelo's Italian Kitchen catering it. I found a wonderful woman, Tanya, on Craigslist offering her photography skills for free if we'd sign a release for her to use the pictures in her portfolio, which I thought was an incredible deal. My bridal portraits she took turned out beautiful, so I know she'll be able to capture our wedding perfectly.

Calla lilies are the running theme of my all black-and-cream wedding. Jason's mom and I, along with Aunt Pat and several of their church friends, have spent countless hours putting together the decorations for the pews and centerpieces. I found a fantastic sale on fake calla lilies at Hobby Lobby for all the décor, but we'll have real ones for me and my bridesmaids' bouquets and the men's boutonnieres.

One of Mom's friends, Miss Patsy, recommended a DJ she'd used in the past, who also offered things like a disco ball and laser lights, and after interviewing him and seeing some of his past events in pictures, we hired him right away. Miss Patsy was known in the church for being an amazing cook, and she offered to cook all the food for our Rehearsal Dinner. That, I'm very much looking forward to. We're having it right in the Robichauxs' living room. Mom swears up and down the living room is big enough to fit several round tables and chairs into the space, so I have full faith there will be enough room for the whole wedding party.

We had so much fun going to get the guys fitted for their tuxes. I instantly fell in love with Jason's childhood friend, Big John, who lived up to his name full-heartedly. When thinking of that guy, five b-words come to mind: big, beautiful, black, bald, and bearded. We became instant friends when we discovered each other's mutual love for all things nerdy. I may not be a big gamer like him, but he was highly impressed with my knowledge and fondness for superheroes, vampires, and all things supernatural. Jason's work-buddy Bubba would be our other groomsman, to match my number of bridesmaids. Logan would be flying in from California to be our best man, but he didn't need a tux since he'd be wearing his fancy Marine uniform.

First, we went to eat lunch at Black Eyed Pea, Big John and my blossoming friendship growing exponentially when he discovered my love of soul food, being from North Carolina. There were a lot of black-jokes being tossed around between the boys, which made me terribly uncomfortable. I never joke about things like race because I'd never want to offend or hurt anyone's feelings; it's just who I am. But when Big John started throwing in his own, the tension left me. I didn't join into the banter, but I certainly laughed at what they were saying, trying to top each other with their inappropriateness.

Then we went to Men's Wearhouse. That was an adventure. Finding a tux to fit Big John's 6'3" 450-pound frame was quite the feat. Jason was determined to have the fancy coats with tails, and it was hilarious watching the crazy men turn into little boys playing dress-up.

Buffy drove herself, Renee, and Brooke down to my side of town to go to David's Bridal to find their Bridesmaid dresses, but seeing how the least expensive dress was $125, and knowing I was on a strict budget and that I didn't want to put any of them in jeopardy by making them buy a dress they'd only wear once, I decided to go out on my own to find something more fitting. They just needed to be nice 'little black dresses', so I didn't think it would be too hard. I ended up hitting the jackpot, finding two of the same super cute black tiered dresses in Renee and Brooke's sizes for $15.00 each at Ross, and then after sending Buffy a picture of them, she found one just as nice for herself. It's different than the ones I picked, but I actually like that they won't match, since she is my matron of honor.

My mom and dad will be here in a few days, and then we'll have the wedding rehearsal and dinner the night before the ceremony. It's been very stress-free. I don't know why so many women turn into bridezillas while planning this stuff. It's been nothing but fun for me. Of course, having so much help from Jason's mom and all her church friends has made it that way. I can't help but snigger to myself each time one of them says something like, "Oh, I'm just so happy Jason found a good girl to make him settle down," or "We never thought he'd be the family-man type," or "Who knew he'd be the first of all his friends to get married and have babies. We thought he'd be the last, if it ever happened at all." It made me feel like one of my romance novel heroines, the good girl who tamed the bad boy. Well, I better get off here. We're going to Spec's to place our order for the bottles of wine and the keg for the reception.

A keg at a wedding reception...

Only in Texas.

April 17, 2010

Today is the day I've fantasized about since the early months of 2005, when I fell for my soul mate and let my mind wander to that dangerous land of What If. During those days, I had no idea of the crazy journey I would go on in order to finally arrive here. On that rugged and treacherous path, I fell into sinkholes, the lowest of low-points in my life, but also came across mile-markers with picturesque views I would never want to un-see. And without those heartbreaking miles, I don't think I would appreciate reaching my destination as much as I do at this moment.

I woke up this morning beside my fiancé, and kissed him, knowing the next time we were in that bed together, it would be as husband and wife. Up until then, we had broken almost every tradition. He had picked my dress; we stayed together the night before the wedding... and who knows how many more. But that is when the rule breaking would end. When I left the house with my mom and my little girls to meet my hairdresser, bridesmaids, and Tanya, the photographer, at the church in the bridal parlor, I wouldn't see Jason again until I was walking down the aisle. We met this morning two hours before everyone else was supposed to get here, since Angie was giving us all intricate up-dos.

Another amazing find, I met her at my school. She's in the cosmetology program at San Jac. I don't have any hesitation going to the women training to be stylists, because their every snip of the scissors has to be approved by their instructor. Plus, a haircut, highlights, wash, and blow-dry is only $40.00, compared to the outrageous prices some of these fancy places charge. I had been assigned Angie for my trim and highlights a couple of months ago, and she did such a great job that I asked her if she was any good at doing up-dos. She showed me some of her work, photos taken for class assignments on mannequin heads and a few people, and they were all gorgeous, so I came back to her to do my style for my bridal portraits.

When I asked her to do it once more for my actual wedding,

plus Buffy, Renee, Brooke, and my mom's hair, she jumped at the opportunity, needing this kind of event as a credit for her cosmetology license. As instructed by Angie, we all showed up with 'dirty hair', which she said was much easier to style than a freshly washed mane.

Wearing jean shorts with my lacy white and baby blue garter around my thigh, and a button-up pink plaid shirt so I wouldn't have to pull one over my head and risk messing up my do, I applied my makeup in the brightly lit dressing room of the parlor while Angie pinned, curled, and sprayed every strand into place. When she was finished, I handed her a bundle of miniature porcelain calla lilies that she wove through one side of the style. I'm just not a veil kind of girl.

The rest of the ladies each took their turn in the hot seat, Angie styling their hair while I did their makeup, recalling the rules I'd learned during my pageant days, making sure our faces wouldn't look washed out under the bright lights. When all of us were done being made up and primped, Angie gave us hugs and left, because she had another bride's hair to do that afternoon.

"Did you bring the stuff?" Buffy asks conspiratorially, raising her eyebrow and glancing down at my hands.

"Yeah. We need to get it on before Jason's mom comes in. If she catches us before it's all done, she'll throw a hissy until we wipe it all off," I say quickly, rummaging through my makeup Caboodle until I find what we need. We hurry out of the dressing room and into the main room of the parlor, and I run over to the door to lock it. "Whatever you do, do not open this door. Especially if it's Jason's mom. Everyone allowed in here right now is already here, so please don't unlock this door for any reason until we're done getting dressed and ready." The girls around me, including Tanya and her assistant, all nod.

"First order of business... this." I hold out the gleaming bottle of black nail polish for everyone to see, and the first thing I notice is the mischievous look in my niece's eyes.

"You know she's going to shit herself, don't you?" she asks, receiving a stern, "Brooke!" from my mom.

"What? It's true." She shrugs.

"You're in a church, Tadpole. Watch your language," Mom tells her, reaching over to swat her playfully on her butt.

"That's why we have to hurry up and get it on and dry, then get completely dressed, bouquets and all. That way she can't make us take it off. We wouldn't want to risk getting nail polish remover on our dresses, now, would we?" I smirk.

I love my soon-to-be mother-in-law. God knows I do. But that little woman can be one controlling, opinionated bulldog when she wants to be. If she knew I want all my bridesmaids and I to have matching black nails, which I think looks super cute against the cream-colored calla lilies, she'd throw a hissy fit. Shit, she even gave me hell when she saw it on my toenails last night, knowing I'm wearing open-toe heels today. I was able to cool her jets a little by telling her no one would see them since my wedding dress is floor-length, leaving out the part it would soon be on my fingers as well.

We all sprawl out in the middle of the floor, my babies thinking it's hilarious that all the grownups are down on the ground with them, as they giggle and crawl all over us while we try to carefully apply the polish to our nails. Avary reaches for my garter and tugs, making little grunting noises as she tries to get it off me, so I slide it down my legs and put it around her like a headband.

As each chick finishes getting painted and dry, they move into the dressing room to change into their dress and heels. I wait as long as possible after mine are done, making sure they are completely dry before attempting to get into my ivory dress, which Buffy helps me step into, trying our best not to wrinkle the freshly steamed satin. When the halter is clasped and the back is zipped, I sit down so she can buckle my strappy cream shoes, the low heels easy for even me to walk in.

Suddenly, the door handle to the parlor jiggles, and we all hold our breath as if whoever is out there will somehow be able to break the lock. When there's a light knock, Buffy goes over to it to move the dark piece of fabric covering the small, narrow window and peaks out. It must be someone important, because she closes the curtain back and opens the door.

In walks Aunt Pat and her daughter, Ginger, carrying the vases holding all of our bouquets, right on time. I stand up and walk over to the table they set them on to take a closer look.

"Oh, my gosh, they turned out beautiful!" I cry, wrapping my arms around Pat's shoulders. "You did an amazing job."

She had taken the ivory satin ribbon I'd found at Hobby Lobby and wrapped the long stems of several calla lilies into bundles, and then had used the thin black velvet ribbon to form a crisscross pattern down their length. The results are clean, classy, and elegant, and with our black-tipped fingers wrapped around them, it'll give us all just a touch of my quirkiness—the girl who likes to wear Payless shoes with my Coach bag and

Marvel Comics T-shirts. I like what I like. What can I say?

"You look wonderful, honey. We were just dropping these off really quick, since I knew you'd need them for your pictures. We need to run home and get dressed," she tells me, giving me a one-armed hug, and they quickly exit the room.

"Now what?" I ask the room; we still have about an hour and a half before the ceremony begins.

Tanya speaks up. "Now, we take wedding party photos. I'll start with all you girls, and then go take some with the guys. We do the full party together after the wedding."

"Sounds good. Where should we do them?"

"I found some places outside, and also inside the sanctuary, where I can pose y'all in some really fun shots." She turns to her assistant. "Will you go tell the guys not to leave their dressing room? We don't want to risk the groom seeing the bride. Tell them we'll come get them when we're ready to do the groomsmen shots."

The assistant returns, and holding open the door, she lets us know the coast is clear. We spend the next forty-five minutes taking pictures outside in the beautiful spring weather, inside the church, where we take a really cool shot of me on the floor in my dress, with it spread out all around me, as Tanya snaps photos standing on the balcony above. The photo shoot ends after taking fun pictures all over the sanctuary, my favorites being the few we take of me playing the piano while my bridesmaids act as backup singers. I especially love the one of just the three of them bracing their elbows on the piano as each girl either covers their eyes, ears, or mouth, copying the Three Wise Monkeys portraying 'See no evil, hear no evil, speak no evil.' I might have to print that one out and hang it in the house.

We scamper back into the bridal parlor, making sure not to be seen by anyone, since people have slowly started to trickle in. Hopefully, being mother of the groom, Barbara will stay with Jason the whole time before the ceremony instead of venturing into the girls' side. As I catch a glimpse at the time, seeing we only have about thirty minutes until everything begins, my nerves start to get the best of me, and I really don't feel like hearing any crap about something as insignificant as my nail color. I might turn into that bridezilla I was wondering about a couple weeks ago.

Tanya tells us she's going to take the groomsmen pictures and the next time she'll see us is when we're lining up to walk down the aisle. My heart gives a tremendous thump at that thought, and when the door closes behind her, I collapse onto the couch to take a breather from all the excitement.

There's a knock on the door, and my blood pressure skyrockets, but then Buffy opens the door to my smiling big brother, and I sigh with relief. Tony lumbers into the room carrying Abigail, followed by Aspen, Amanda, and Alex. They make the perfect distraction, my nieces dancing around the room with Josalyn, Alex picking up and snuggling Avary, and Buffy snaps a few pictures of all the shenanigans while I watch them all play.

Before I know it, there's a light tap on the door, and Renee answers it after seeing it's the wedding coordinator the church provided.

"All right, everyone. It's show time!" she says, clapping her hands together. "Everybody who isn't part of the wedding party needs to make their way to their seats, and all my ladies need to follow me. The guys are already in position at the altar."

"Oh, God," I breathe, and my mom takes a hold of my hand.

"You're all right, doll," she tells me, rubbing my bare upper back with her other palm.

I take deep breaths as I watch my brother pick up Avary, knowing he's taking her to Jason's parents to walk down the aisle. When he and his kids file out the door, the coordinator motions for us to follow them, and soon, she's lining us up in the proper order outside the wooden and glass doors of the sanctuary.

I try to peek through one of the windows to watch as my dad walks my mom to the altar instead of to her seat in the front pew, wanting to see the beginning of my sand ceremony. I had never heard of it before until I read about it in a bridal magazine a couple months ago. On a tall, round table up on the altar is a glass jar, and six small glasses, three filled with white sand, and three filled with black sand. Right now, each of our parents will pour one of the glasses of sand into the jar, alternating the two colors, and when we are pronounced husband and wife, we will make our way up the steps and pour our own sand into the jar, topping it off with a sealing lid, so I'll be able to keep it forever.

I can see Jason's dad holding Avary on his hip as he pours his glassful into the jar, and then the husbands help their wives down the steps, and my dad heads back up the aisle toward me. He looks so handsome in his dress uniform, and you bet your sweet ass he's been bragging constantly that he can still fit into it, even after retiring from the Navy over twenty-five years ago.

When my hand is wrapped around my dad's bicep, his warm hand squeezing it to him tighter over the back of mine, I watch as first Brooke then Renee start down the aisle, the wedding coordinator whispering, "Go," when it's each person's turn. Buffy goes next, which leaves no one else in front of me except my little girl, who looks beautiful in her ivory satin dress, holding her ivory basket decorated with the same black velvet ribbon wrapped around my bouquet. Josalyn's been holding the coordinator's hand this whole time, and when I wasn't spazzing out inside my head trying to take in everything going on, I caught glimpses of her awe-filled face, hearing her tiny voice tell Brooke, Renee, and Buffy how pretty they look, and how I look like 'Cinderelly'.

The woman bends down to Josalyn, and I hear her tell her, "Just like we practiced," and she lets go of her hand.

I see everyone's face light up with a huge smile as my big girl makes her way down the aisle, reaching her little hand into the basket and pulling out a single petal to carefully place along the path. She stops to smile and wave at my brother, Jay, and my nephew, Bret, her favorite cousin, before continuing her flower girl duty. When she gets to the front pew, I see her turn around, and then I hear the entire crowd burst into laughter as she heads back up the aisle to place a few more petals after seeing she had missed a couple spots. Seeming satisfied with her work, my little perfectionist then walks back to my mom and takes her seat next to her.

Immediately, the organist begins playing Pachelbel's "Canon in D", and my hand tightens even further around Dad's arm. "Don't let me fall, Daddy," I whisper, adjusting my sweaty grip on my bouquet. I'm surprised the calla lilies haven't withered from my nervous abuse.

"I've got ya, baby girl." He pats my hand then kisses me on my cheek, his tidy mustache tickling me and making me smile.

The congregation suddenly stands as a whole, and next thing I know, my dad is walking me down the beautiful church aisle, decorated with calla lilies and strings of black beads wrapped around the end of each pew. I hardly know anyone here, so each time my sight finally lands on one of my brothers, my nieces and nephews, and eventually my mom, a little bit of my nervousness lessens. Especially when I spot Marky and Kim, who give me blinding smiles and excited waves, which makes me giggle.

Finally, I'm down what seems like a mile-long aisle, and I look up to see Jason grinning while wiping his eyes. He looks gorgeous in his long-tailed tux. I watch as he turns around to say something to his groomsmen, who all chuckle and nod at each other, before Jason turns back toward me. And then I'm in front of him, my dad placing my hand in Jason's before kissing my cheek and then patting him on the back.

"What was that all about?" I whisper to him, my heart finally chilling out a little having him near.

"They made a bet I would cry when I saw you. The jackasses won," he replies just as quietly, and I lift my face up to grin at the handsome men before me.

To the far right, Bubba, who I've never seen in anything but jeans and fishing shirts, looks wonderful as he stands next to a towering Big John, who looks red-carpet perfect in his tuxedo with the white of his shirt against his chocolate skin. And then there's Logan, who flew in from California yesterday, just in time for the wedding rehearsal. I don't think there ever was a man who looked better in a uniform. His 'Marine stuff', as I called it yesterday, making him give me a dramatic growl, is utterly perfect, not a speck of lint anywhere in sight, as if the particles themselves are scared to come anywhere near the big, badass giant of a man.

As Jason leads me to our spot in front of the minister, the rest of the world suddenly disappears except for the three of us... until it's the complete opposite. The ceremony becomes a blur. I know I repeat things and respond how I'm supposed to, hearing Jason do the same, but I'm mostly aware of other things. The emotion quivering Jason's voice. Big John's bright white teeth smiling from over Jason's shoulder. The way Logan stands perfectly still, making me imagine that's what he looks like in formation with his Marine brothers. Bubba's perfectly manicured goatee. The photographer snapping photos from the second-story balcony. Avary baby-babbling from the front pew. Buffy fidgeting near me, as if her feet are hurting in her heels.

My ADD is off the charts, just like it used to be when I went to church every Sunday when I was younger, only right now, I don't have my favorite older friend Traci keeping me occupied. Back when I was a kid and she was a teenager, she used to hold my hand and push back my cuticles, telling me it'd make my nails grow faster, or play tic-tac-toe on the edges of the Sunday bulletin with me to keep my mind and mouth quiet during Mass.

Instead, I feel Jason take my hands into his, as if he can sense I'm about to start panicking because my mind won't shut the hell up. Knowing we're the center of everyone's attention right now, literally up on a stage with everybody watching, it's like it's amplifying my whirring brain. This is one of the reasons I stopped participating in pageants. This is also one of the reasons I had wanted to elope somewhere, just the two of us, but I gave in so he could have his big church wedding. Jason knows anxiety can overwhelm me when my wandering attention starts getting the best of me, and I'm grateful when he leans forward to whisper, "I'm here, baby," as the minister recites the excerpt from Corinthians I chose for the ceremony.

Forcing myself to focus on my hands in his and what the pastor is saying, soon, rings are on fingers and I'm being kissed, and I breathe a sigh of relief. We pour the final two layers of sand into the jar, walk back down the stairs, and I feel all the tension leaving me with every step I take past the applauding audience.

I know your wedding should be one of the happiest moments of your life, and really, truly it is. I can't imagine being any happier than in this exact second, knowing I am Mrs. Jason Robichaux, but I'm also ecstatic the ceremony is over. We wait in the bridal parlor for a few minutes until almost everyone has left. They'll be meeting at the Knights of Columbus hall a few miles away for the reception while we take our family and full wedding party pictures. It takes about half an hour to get every group shot we can think of, the only hiccup in my smile being when Barbara tells me, "I can't believe y'all put that shit on your nails." But my grin soon returns when Buffy gasps and scolds, "Barbara! Language. You're in a church," making the older woman grumble under her breath before walking away.

Now... *now* I can relax. And I finally let all the nervous energy leave me as we hop into my van to head to the hall for the reception, where the wedding party will meet out in the gardens to do a few more fun shots before Jason and I are introduced as husband and wife.

But when we arrive, I'm shaky from my emotional roller coaster today, and I feel like I might faint if I don't get some food in my belly, so Tanya tells us we can wait until later to take the rest of the pictures. We wait for everyone else to go in before us, and soon, we hear the DJ over the speaker system introduce us, so we walk through the door, where Jason twirls me and dips me, planting a kiss on my lips, and the room explodes with everyone's applause.

"You want me to make you a plate, babe?" he asks as he stands me upright.

"Nah, I can get it. But I'm not waiting. I don't care what the right order of business is at these things. I'm getting my food *now*," I reply as the smell of Italian dishes hits my nose, making my stomach growl.

He holds my hand as we walk past tables of people wanting to stop and congratulate us, Jason pausing only long enough to tell them he's gotta feed his bride before she passes out. Soon, I have a plateful of lasagna and garlic rolls and a glass of sweet tea in front of me at my special spot at the front table, and I waste no time digging in. When I feel halfway human again, I look around to find my people. My mom is next to Josalyn, helping her eat her spaghetti, and Buffy is feeding Avary a bottle.

Since I'm done inhaling my food, the DJ calls Jason and me

up for our wedding dance, which is to Lady Antebellum's "I Run to You". He leads me through a two-step around the dance floor, and when the song ends, the DJ invites everyone else up to dance. My nieces come out with his little cousins, and when tiny little Natalie sees I'm finished dancing with Jason, his Aunt Melissa lets her loose to come up and talk to me.

In the sweetest voice ever, she asks with awe in her eyes, "Are you Cinderella?" I can't help but laugh, since Josalyn had told me I looked like the princess earlier today.

"No, baby girl. You don't remember me? I saw you at Christmas, remember? Those are my little girls," I tell her, pointing at my kids at the table. She follows my finger with her eyes then looks back at me and nods.

"Will you dance with me?" she asks, which surprises the heck out of me. Before this conversation, the child had never spoken to me before, even when I'd given her a Christmas present when they came to the Robichauxs' house this past year. It had been cool seeing all three of the new babies together; Lisa, Dianna, and I had them all within a couple months of each other.

"Of course." I curtsy, and her face explodes with the biggest smile I've ever seen on her adorable face. I spend three songs dancing with her before Aunt Melissa comes and rescues me so we can do the money dance. I had never heard of this dance before, but as people started coming up to me with cash to spin me around the dance floor for a little while, I didn't question it until Jason's dad stood in front of me with a $100.00 bill.

"Why are people giving me money?" I laughed as he led me into some fancy swing moves I had seen him do with Barbara in the living room.

"It's a way for anyone who really wants to dance with the bride or groom to guarantee they get a turn. The money is usually for helping pay for the honeymoon," he explains, and I look down at the wad of cash in my hand when Barbara's brother, Uncle Robert, cuts in. He's probably my favorite one of Barbara's relatives. He's flamboyantly gay, reminding me of Jack from *Will & Grace*, and the shit out of his mouth makes me crack up every time he visits. Plus, my girls love him. I end up stuffing my cash down the front of my dress so I can have my hands free, making him laugh.

Out of the corner of my eye, I see Marky walk up to Jason and hand him a dollar, and I nearly double over with laughter as they try to keep a straight face while they lead each other through a dramatic waltz, ending with Jason dipping my brother. And when he stands him back up and pats him on the back with a laugh, Jason turns and nearly runs into Tony, who's leering down at Jason from his 6'5" height, an evil grin on his face as he holds out his dollar bill. Jason reaches up with a pout to take the money, and as soon as it's out of Tony's grasp, I nearly choke on my spit as I suck in air when my brother reaches around Jason's back, slaps both hands down hard on his ass cheeks, and pulls Jason to him, the laughter finally coming out of me in a yelp when Jason mirrors the position, holding Tony to him by his butt.

"Now that's what I'm talking about," Uncle Robert says from beside me. If I'd been drinking anything, it would've been the perfect set-up for a spit-take.

Next, it's Logan's turn to dance with me. "Sorry if I step on your feet," he warns, but it's all for show. He leads me through a perfect two-step, complete with twirls and a dip at the end that leaves me grinning ear-to-ear.

By the end of the money dance, Jason made over a hundred dollars more than me. Probably because I spent most of the time watching him spin around the floor with Big John and a few more people.

The rest of the evening is spent dancing, drinking, eating cake, and visiting with everyone. A notable moment was when a bunch of Barbara's church friends complimented me on our black nail polish, saying what a cute and quirky idea it was and how classy it looked with the black and ivory theme of the wedding. I couldn't control my face when I smirked at her as her face dropped at their comments. I blame it on the wine.

We took all the fun pictures we could come up with out in the garden and in the gazebo, and lastly, little Bret caught the garter, and Amanda caught the bouquet. After that, people started trickling out until all that was left was our immediate family and the rest of the wedding party.

By this time, I could barely hold my eyes open, so Jason's dad told us to go ahead and leave all the cleanup up to them. Jason and I loaded the girls, both sleeping, into their car seats, and my mom squeezed in too, my dad deciding to stay behind to help fold up chairs and tables.

We get the girls in bed and I kiss my mom goodnight, and when I plop onto our bed, watching Jason as he undresses, I start to laugh.

"What is it?" he asks, smiling at me as he loosens his bowtie.

"It's just like in one of my favorite movies, *Just Married,* when Brittany Murphy and Ashton Kutcher get to their honeymoon suite and she's too sleepy to consummate the marriage." I pout out my lip and paraphrase what she says, "My parents are going to know I'm not a virgin anymore, and they're going to know you're the one who deflowered me!" and I burst out laughing at my own joke.

"Babe, we have two kids. I don't think that's going to be a problem," he snarks, finally getting all the tiny buttons on his shirt undone. "Plus, I'm tired as hell too. We'll do our consummating tomorrow." His dress pants drop to the floor and he steps out of them, leaving him in only his boxer briefs and his white undershirt. He walks around to my side of the bed and holds out his hands for me to take then pulls me up.

I reach behind my neck to undo the hooks of the halter while he wraps his arms around me, taking hold of the zipper and sliding it down. I place my hands on his shoulders as he holds my dress low enough for me to step out of, and I hear him suck in a breath when he sees the bright blue thong I'm wearing.

"What?" I ask mischievously.

"I'm suddenly not so tired," he answers, laying my dress across the foot of the bed before taking hold of my hips and pulling me to him.

"These were my 'something blue'. Which apparently are going to match your balls tonight, because I'm about to fall asleep on my feet," I tease, my arms looping around his neck to hold myself up. He envelops me in his warm embrace, kissing my lips before allowing me to melt onto the bed behind me.

"Will you grab a hanger for the dress? I don't want it to get all wrinkled. God only knows if it'll ever be worn again. Maybe I'll save it for one of the girls," I ramble, feeling my eyelids grow heavy.

"Yeah, babe. But first, lift your legs up," he tells me, and I groan as I pull my legs up onto the bed. I feel his hands at my ankles, undoing the little buckle of my shoes, and when he slides them off, I wiggle my toes, feeling a couple of them pop. Damn high heels.

With my eyes closed, I hear him move to the closet, return to the bed, fabric rustling, and after a minute, I feel him slide into bed next to me. As soon as he wraps his arm around my waist and presses his nose into the back of my neck, inhaling me like he always does, I fall asleep, a smile on my face.

EPILGUE

Kayla the Bibliophile
Blog Post: November 14, 2013

I've finally finished transferring all of my old posts from
Kayla's Chick Rant & Book Blog to my Kayla the Bibliophile
one. Reading some of those old posts brought back a lot of
memories, and the reviews made me want to restart a couple of
my favorite series. It also made me want to pick back up with
my diary type posts, which I haven't done since my wedding.
So let me start out by recapping what's happened since then...
well, the condensed version at least.

In May 2010, we went on our Honeymoon in Vegas. *snort
We had a blast, stayed at the Carriage House, went and saw
Mystere, the greatest damn Cirque du Soleil ever, and ate... and

ate... and ate some more. My kinda vacation.

Also, I graduated college *finally*, and I kept one good friend from my entire college experience, Tina, who was in my Yoga II class during my last semester. She was hilarious, had really cool tattoos, and loved to read, like me, so we were instant friends. Book friends are the best friends, which I've now made many, many more of since starting my Kayla the Bibliophile Facebook page, but I'm getting ahead of myself.

The next month, I began working at GNC again after being hired on the spot since I was a rehire. I was starting to get cabin fever being at home all the time, and Barbara volunteered to watch the girls during my shifts that Jason was working too. I think it was around that time Jason got his job at Turner Industries. It wasn't anything too great, just working as a helper in the pipe fabrication shop, but since then, he's moved his way up and into the office, and now he's doing drafting, using all the AutoCAD skills he learned in school.

No big, important life changes happened again until June 2012, when I quit GNC and started working at Legacy Gymnastics as the Office Manager. It was amazing being able to bring my kids to work with me, them hanging out in the office just like I used to do at my mom's job at the church. They even got to take gymnastics classes as one of the benefits. There was a lot of downtime, since how I was only really busy in between the recreational classes, when parents would either register their kids for classes or need to fix something on their account. So while classes were in session, I did a lot of reading, Facebooking, and playing on Pinterest.

After saving up the money, I went and bought an iPad 2,

which opened up a whole new world in reading for me. I had fought for so long, not giving in to the e-book phenomenon, staying loyal to printed books exclusively, but with the first flip of the electronic page in iBooks and the Kindle app, I was hooked. One day, I heard whisperings about a book called *Fifty Shades of Grey*, which I only picked up because it was fanfiction of my beloved Twilight series. I had never read a series that wasn't paranormal before, so I didn't have high hopes.

Boy, was I wrong. The series absolutely consumed my entire world for three days straight. I only left my bed and my bathtub long enough to throw some food at my kids before returning back to my reading cave. And when I had finished the third book, I seriously didn't know what to do with my life. I started researching, trying to get my next fix, attempting to find something that would affect me the way EL James's books had, and after a lot of duds, I finally found one. *Bared to You* by Sylvia Day blew my mind, so much so that I needed to tell the whole world about it.

October 2012, at work, instead of getting on Pinterest and scrolling the Popular board, I logged onto Facebook and figured out how to create one of those pages you can "Like". I named it Kayla the Bibliophile, after having fallen in love with the word after learning it in Karen Marie Moning's Highlander series. I'm definitely a person who loves and collects books, so the name fit me perfectly. Many of my friends and family members always called or messaged me, asking what they should read next, especially after not having my old blog to refer to. I hadn't kept up with it in a couple years, so I sent them all a link to the page so my posts would show up in their newsfeed whenever I would write a new review.

Then, the unthinkable happened. One of my very favorite authors, Dakota Cassidy, saw my review for *The Accidental Werewolf*, and she shared it and my page with her readers, and my following shot up to 100 likes overnight! What an adrenaline rush that was! Not only did I have more people to share my love of books with, but one of my idols had actually noticed me. It was almost as great as when I went to Kerrelyn Sparks's book signing at Katy Budget Books and got to meet the woman herself.

And then it happened again, and again, authors sharing my reviews after I'd post them, and soon, new authors who were publishing their own work, which I learned were called indie authors, started contacting me, asking me if I would like to read their book in exchange for an honest review. My mind was blown. Authors wanted to give me their books just so I would review and post about them? Score!

That's when I met an Australian author by the name of Belle Aurora. The name immediately caught my attention in the sea of review request messages, because of my obsession with Belle from *Beauty & the Beast*. She asked if I'd like to read her debut novel, *Friend-Zoned*, and I instantly said yes after reading the blurb. My enthusiastic messages while reading, and my review, were the beginning of our beautiful friendship.

Not only did I start blogging again, but I also started following and supporting other blogs, including one I'd been in love with since 2009, Maryse's Book Blog, which I found on the internet when I needed the reading order for Sherrilyn Kenyon's Dark Hunters series, and a new one I became addicted to, Smut Book Club, now known as Shameless Book Club, because of its creator Angie Lynch's fantastic book recommendations and hilariously naughty sense of humor. I love the comradery between people with the shared love of reading. I even made friends at small, single-author signings around Houston, running into the same two readers, Amanda Cantu and Shawna Stringer, at Katy Budget Books. We realized we had the same taste in books if we kept fangirling over the same authors, so we became Facebook official.

Seeing that most author interviews consisted of a lot of the same boring questions, I came up with a list of seriously risqué questions, "Dare to Tell the Truth with Kayla the Bibliophile". I wanted it to feel more like sitting down with a group of your girlfriends, having some drinks, and talking about boys. I contacted as many of my favorite authors as I could think of, requesting an interview with them, warning them it wasn't the average 'What made you want to become an author?' type questions, and surprisingly, a ton of them thought it was a great idea and sent in their answers. Making it a weekly post, it became widely popular, and I suddenly had authors contacting *me*, asking if they could do the interview!

Scrolling through my newsfeed, I came across a book by an author named Red Phoenix called *Brie Learns the Art of Submission: Submissive Training Center*. With its ultra-sexy cover and the author's unique profile picture—she's a redheaded hottie who always wears a mask—I just had to read it. I signed up for my first 'blog tour', in which the author gathers a bunch of bloggers to review and post about their book to get one big burst of attention, hopefully reaching a good amount of new readers. This one was run by Stephanie's Book Reports, and as soon as *Brie* arrived in my inbox, I started reading... and didn't stop until I had consumed the entire series. Little did I know it had started out as a serial—short novellas released in increments—and I was just lucky enough to catch it when it was being published as a full-length novel. I don't know how I would've handled having to wait for the next serial to come out only a few addictive chapters at a time.

I was obsessed with a capital O with this book. Like, even more so than with *Fifty* or *Bared to You*, and I was inspired. I identified with the character, Brie, so much that I felt like I could portray her, and it didn't hurt that we had the same physical attributes. So I made a profile on Model Mayhem and found a photographer who was looking for a model to add photos to their portfolio. Mike Fox wanted to try his hand at boudoir photography, seeing its rising popularity after discovering he was damned good at taking headshots and senior portraits, and he just so happened to live right down the road from me.

My mom was visiting me the week Mike and I set up the photo shoot, so she went with me. I hadn't modeled since I was a teenager, so I was super nervous, but Mike put me at ease from the get-go. Along with his hilarious wife, Angi, and their three teenaged kids, they are all actors in the small theaters around town. As animated and jovial as he was, he had no qualms getting down on the floor and striking the sexy pose he wanted me to try while directing me throughout the shoot. With Angi acting as his assistant, there wasn't a single wardrobe malfunction or a hair out of place, and we got all the pictures I wanted, including one kneeling on rice—a BDSM punishment we learned in the book—suggested by my blogger friend, Crystal, of Crystal's Many Reviewers. That one was painful... so painful, that when Mike's dogs heard me groaning, they came to see about me, and he got a cute candid picture of me playing with the pups with the rice spread out all around us.

As a surprise for Red Phoenix, when it was my date to post for her blog tour, not only did I include all the buy-links, the book's description, and an almost manic raving review, I also posted the pictures I had taken as Brie. She absolutely loved them, and I could tell that my fandom truly touched her, and so began my friendship with one of my very favorite authors on the planet.

She invited me to join her private group, Club Red, where her readers could openly discuss the books and everything inside them without fear of judgment. One day, Red posted a contest in the group, to see who could create the best quote pic, where you find a picture that reminds you of a certain line from the book, and you make a graphic/collage. My competitive nature kicked in hardcore. That signed paperback would be mine! Suddenly, I was in competition with this Sara chick, who was putting out just as many quote pics as I was, everyone else left in the dust—probably because they have lives—but instead of hating on her, I couldn't help but admire the graphics she was creating.

Everyone on Red's fan page voted, and thankfully, I won that gorgeous book to add to my collection, and Sara messaged me to congratulate me. And I think we ended up messaging back and forth for like three hours that night. We were instabesties, with an almost identical taste in books, and I loved her sense of humor. Not too long after that, I asked her if she'd like to join my blog to help me keep up with all the interviews and review requests I was getting, and so Sassy Sara came to be.

Around the same time I had met Red, I had gotten a review request from an author in New York named Danielle Jamie. Only her request was a little different than others I received. She had found my blog and saw that I lived in Houston, and she asked if I would read her books and give her names of places to add to the story, since she was basing the series in Houston, TX. Seeing it as a new challenge to mix things up, and the author was too sweet for words, I told her yes and began reading the Savannah Series. This was a whole other challenge than what I had originally thought, because before then, I had never read an unedited book before. I had always received Advance Reader Copies that had already been through the editing process. Keeping in mind she was still working on it, I didn't let the editing issues effect my enjoyment of the book, but being a grammar-Nazi, I couldn't help but fix punctuation and minor issues that were easily noted by highlighting them on my iPad. It was actually thrilling finally putting my degree to good use, considering how I had taken extra English and writing classes when I first started college.

When I sent her the document back, I sent it with a note that read,

Please, don't be offended, but I'm kind of crazy when it comes to mistakes in books. I know you haven't gotten it edited yet, and I've included some Houston-based restaurants and places Brooklyn and Savannah could go

in your story, but I've also taken the time to edit the rest of the story for you too.

Instead of being offended, Danielle was ecstatic, and I breathed a sigh of relief. In exchange for some fancy handmade hair bows from the children's boutique she runs, Bailey Booper's Boutique, for my little girls, she had me do another read-through when the story was complete, just to make sure she had gotten all the details right, and asked if I'd edit her next book when she was done writing it. My answer was a resounding, "Hell yes!"

A few weeks later, I read a book called *This Man* by Jodi Ellen Malpas and fell in love with the over-the-top Alpha hero, Jesse Ward, and his heroine, Ava. Around the same time, Mike contacted me, asking if I'd like to be his guinea pig for some things he'd learned in a photography tutorial—the perfect opportunity to take another picture starring as a book character I loved. In my favorite undies and a lace-sleeved shirt, a paperback copy of *This Man* in hand, we got a great shot of me as Ava. When he sent me back the edited version, I added the quote, "Always in lace," to the picture, a line Jesse always tells his woman, and sent it to Jodi in a message. And just like Red Phoenix, she loved it, thanking me profusely and even sharing it on her page.

I told her how much I loved her books and asked if she'd like to do my interview, and after reading my raving review— complete with a British-to-American glossary, since she had used some words I had no clue what they meant, forcing me to google them, and thought my American followers would appreciate the help—she readily agreed. I couldn't help but grin when she called me "cheeky" for asking such invasive questions.

My next obsession came in the form of CJ Roberts's *Dark Duet*, by far the darkest books I had ever read. In my review, I stated, 'It's like CJ somehow got inside my brain and wrote a story that would make the most sinister, kinky parts of me evilly grin with glee.' I had no idea there were books out there like these, telling stories that I wouldn't even confess to my best friend I fantasized about. After researching, trying to find more in this dark genre, I found a few more and quickly devoured them, including Aleatha Romig's *Consequences* and CD Reiss's Songs of Submission series, which led to another photo shoot with Mike, adding three more characters to my photo album, Olivia, Claire, and Monica.

Now that there were five, I figured I needed a name for this niche of my blog, especially since no one else was doing it. I dubbed it The Book Girlfriend Series. Everyone else seemed more concerned with the leading men in books, but to me, I found that if I didn't like the heroine, then I didn't like the book, so it was my way of paying homage to the women in my favorite stories.

Chatting with my Australian author friend, Lola Stark, one day, I told her about what I had done for Danielle's book, and she asked if I'd like to read through her debut novel, "Tattered Love," before ARCs were to go out. I inhaled that book in a day, which tells you how much I loved it, since I'm a pretty slow reader, and when I sent her my notes back, she was impressed I had found that in the beginning of a scene, her hero Mace had been wearing a blue shirt, but when he was undressing to molest the hell out of the heroine, Scarlet, his shirt was green. It had been through her editor and several sets of beta eyes, and no one else had caught the blooper.

The next day, Lola sent me a message telling me that her editor, Becky Johnson, wanted to expand her company, Hot Tree Editing, and wanted to take on another editor, and that she told Becky about my find in her book. Lola told me if I was interested, I should contact Becky about the position. I did right away, and Becky sent me two chapters of a book, telling me to "edit it the way I think it should be".

Opening the document, I went through it, correcting punctuation, adding in missing words, restructuring sentences to make it flow better, and checked and fixed details of continuity. When I sent it back, I was super nervous, since I really wanted to impress this lady, who at the time was an English teacher who ran her editing company on the side in Australia. When she wrote me back, though, my heart nearly leapt out of my chest. "Please, work for me!" the message had said. "You caught over 200 revisions more than the other people I was interviewing. You have the job if you want it!" And so I became a Senior Editor at Hot Tree Editing.

I started helping to perfect such authors' works as Lila Rose, Milly Ly, Aurora Rose Reynolds, and yes, even my first author friend, Belle Aurora, plus many, many more. I was being paid, real money, to do something I loved, a job that wasn't even a job at all. Sure, it's a lot of work, and it takes a lot of time and brain power, since I want to do the best job I can for these authors' babies, but it's the dream job I never even thought to dream, never thinking something so amazing could happen to me, the girl who didn't have a clue what to do with her life besides be a wife and mother.

Over the years, I told many of my author friends the story of how Jason and I met, fell in love, lost our way for a while, and then finally ended up together in the end, and each one always said, "Man, you should write that as a book!" especially Danielle, who told me I married my real-life book boyfriend. I always laughed it off, thinking I'll never have the time, especially now, working full-time at Legacy in the evenings, editing during the day, and blogging, not to mention being a mom and wife, even though it's been my dream since I was twelve years old to write romance novels. But who knows? Maybe one day.

Last month, I went to my very first big author signing, Naughty Mafia in Las Vegas. I don't think anything will ever compare to the excitement I felt meeting so many of my favorite authors at one time. A few months ago, I saw it being advertised on Facebook, and after talking to Marky, he said I could stay with him and Kim at their new house in Vegas if I was able to attend. Jason told me to go for it, which set everything in motion. For my blog, I had an idea to contact all the authors who would be signing and asked them to participate in my Dare to Tell the Truth interview, and I would feature an author each day as a countdown leading up to the signing. A ton of them agreed, and I figured since they did my interview, which tended to stand out among the rest, I might have a better chance of them recognizing my name when I met them in person.

I became Facebook friends with quite a few of them, and

after I got back the interview from a new-to-me author named Erin Noelle, I hurriedly sent her a request. Her answers were hilarious and shameless, and I felt an overwhelming urge to be her friend. Weird, I know. As soon as she approved my request, I saw that she lived in Texas too, but she didn't have the city listed, so I messaged her, and the conversation went a little like this:

Kayla Robichaux: Hi, Erin! I'll be flying to Vegas for the signing from Texas too!

Erin Noelle: Really? What city are you in? I'll be going the Thursday before the signing. My sister is coming with me!

Kayla Robichaux: I live in a suburb of Houston. How fun! I'll be going first thing Friday morning. I hope I have time to go to one of the shows on the strip. I went to Mystere a couple years ago, and it was AMAZING!

Erin Noelle: I live in a suburb of Houston too! I'm in Pearland. My sis and I are going to Zumanity while we're there. You should come with us!

Kayla Robichaux: Holy hell! I'm in Pearland too! And that sounds like a blast. Count me in!

Erin Noelle: No fucking way! Little did I know when I was doing your interview that you were right down the street!

And little did we know how literal that statement was. We live exactly one street away from each other. Our kids even go to the same school. We quickly made plans to meet at the nail salon between our neighborhoods Wednesday before the signing, unable to wait until we got to Vegas.

As I stepped out of my van, she got out of her little blue Mini Cooper at the same time, and it was like a scene from a movie, when twins who were separated at birth see each other for the first time. Our heads comically tilted to the side as we looked at each other, and I mumbled, "Do you see what I see?"

"I'm kinda freaking out right now," she replied, and from that moment forward, we referred to each other as 'Twinnie'. After getting our nails done, we hugged each other goodbye and made plans to meet up at the hotel as soon as I landed. She also gave me homework, demanding that I read a book called *A Table for Three* by Lainey Reese on the flight. I swear to God, from now on, when Erin gives me book recommendations, they will go to the top of my To Be Read list, because that book was hotter than Hades.

As payment for editing Danielle's second book, she offered to make me a tank top with my blog name on it to wear at the signing, and when it arrived in the mail, I knew it was perfect—hot pink, with Kayla the Bibliophile in bold black script across the front.

Even more exciting, Danielle decided to go to the signing too! We were so anxious to finally meet each other, the embodiment of her bestie characters Brooklyn and Savannah, that she took a cab from the Hard Rock Casino Hotel—where the signing was being held, and where she was sharing a room with other attendees—and met me in baggage claim right when I got off the plane. I quickly dubbed her 'My Little Nugget', the tiny woman only coming up to my collarbone. But what she lacked in height, she made up for it with spunk, and Lord, do I love her! My first mission after meeting Erin for breakfast was to find Jodi, who had flown in all the way from 'London-ish'. I had to hug her; everyone else, I could (impatiently) wait until the signing.

After messaging Jodi on Facebook, she replied, telling me she was at the pool, so Danielle and I went and put on bathing suits—don't even get me started on how I had to borrow a bikini from a girl three sizes smaller than me, and had to walk sideways with my ass against the wall because there was more crack than a whore house—and went in search of the British beauty. Danielle finally spotted her after we made no less than ten laps around the giant outdoor pool party, and I tackle-hugged Jodi before getting a poolside picture with her. My face hurt from smiling so hard during my fangirl moment.

I could write an entire novel on every second of my trip to Vegas, but I'll spare you all the details. But here are some notable highlights:

*Meeting Aleatha Romig at the registration desk before anyone else noticed she had arrived.

*CJ Roberts freaking out when I got up to her table and she read my shirt with my name on it. She let me grab her humongous boobs in thanks for my review and for the picture as her character Olivia.

*Jodi Ellen Malpas—in a pretty white lace dress—crawling under her table to get to me in order to take a picture of the two of us in our matching Converse.

*Seeing other authors freak out when they met some of their own favorites, including Danielle, when she got to hug SC Stephens and Gail McHugh.

*Hearing the loudest, most contagious laugh from across the entire ballroom, following the boisterous sound until I ended up at table, where an adorable blonde author was cheering on a race... a vibrating dildo race. Asking one of the people in the extremely long line who she was, I received a wide-eyed guffaw before the reader told me, "Tara Sivec! If you've never read her, you have to, like, now! You will never laugh so hard in your life as you will reading her Chocolate Lovers series!"

I had been excited to meet the authors I already knew. For some reason, it never even occurred to me I might find someone new to read. I ended up standing in the long line to meet Tara, not knowing if I would ever get another opportunity to, and told her I was looking forward to reading her work. She talked to me like we were long lost friends, treating me no different than she would her number one fan, and it made me want to read her stuff as soon as I could get my hands on it.

When I did get to read it a few days later, I found that the reader I had talked to in line was not exaggerating. It is literally the funniest series I have ever read in my entire life.

During my night out with Erin and her sister, I told her mine and Jason's story after she asked about my family, and just like the others I'd told, she said I should definitely consider writing it down, if not to publish, then at least for my kids to read one day. She went on to tell me she'd do it as a trilogy if it were her, because it sounded like it would need that many novels to tell the whole story; otherwise, it'd end up being a 300,000 word book.

Before we said our goodbyes, I told her how much I loved her book recommendation of *A Table for Three* and asked what I should read next. She was very adamant that I read Tymber Dalton's *The Reluctant Dom*, which I downloaded on my

Kindle app before my flight home to Texas. I'd never been turned on, happy, and sad, all at the same time before, but the author managed to evoke all those feelings inside me with her beautifully written masterpiece.

After spending so much time with my author friends that weekend, I have to admit my fingers have been itching to try my hand at writing. And like Erin said, I wouldn't have to publish it. I could do it just for fun. She told me that's what her Book Boyfriend series had started out as, just a fun story she wrote for the book club she was in, and they talked her into self-publishing it. Next thing she knew, she was a *USA Today* best seller. I'd never expect anything like that to happen to me, but nevertheless, the thought of someone asking for my autograph the way I did at that author signing is pretty thrilling. Like I said before, who knows? Maybe one day.

June 14, 2014

I feel sneaky, like I'm doing something I'm not supposed to and going to get caught and then in trouble for it. I finished my edit for Aurora Rose Reynolds, and I don't have another one for a couple days, so I don't know what to do with my life. Josalyn is at school, and Avary is at mother's day out for the next four hours. Idle hands, and all that jazz.

I ask for a booth near an outlet when I walk into the Denny's next to Baybrook Mall, and when I sit down, I order the dish Gavin got me hooked on all those years ago—the club sandwich with fries and a bowl of ranch.

I lift the screen of my laptop and open a new blank document, closing my eyes for a moment to think back to my first days in Texas in 2005. I place my hands to the keyboard, take a deep breath, and my fingers begin to type of their own accord...

Prologue

Kayla's Chick Rant & Book Blog
Blog Post 1/23/2007

I'm a happy person, damn it! I'm happy sober; I'm a happy drunk, and I smile until my cheeks hurt. I'm so freakin' perky all the time. I always get invited to everyone's parties; I never get scrolled over when people are looking through their phones to see what's going on. Everyone loves for me to be around because I bring no drama. I'm shameless, and will make a fool of myself to make everyone laugh. I don't say these things to be conceited; I say it to show you how unlike me it is when I tell you...
I cried myself to sleep again last night. I cradled my swollen belly in my hands and rocked myself back and forth praying in a whisper, "Please, God, make him love me. I know you put

us here to be together. Just make him realize it. Please!" The
last word came out on a sob. I swear I'm not a horrible
person, as I laid there crying over another man while I'm six
months pregnant with my husband's baby.

I will never say what happened was a mistake. I believe
everything happens for a reason. I also believe in soul mates.
But what if one person finds their soulmate and the other one
just refuses to acknowledge it? Can you be happy with anyone
else? Or if once your soul finds its other half, are you doomed
to long for them?

These are all questions I've asked myself since I left Texas a
year and a half ago, since I left the man I know I'm supposed
to share my life with. No, I didn't leave him. He told me to go.
He told me there was no reason for me to stay since my
semester of school ended. That's when happy, perky,
shameless Kayla snapped.

The End of Our Beginning

A Note from the Author

The Blogger Diaries Trilogy was truly based on my real life story with my husband Jason. While books one and two were completely accurate, I took creative liberties with book three, and to be fair, I thought I'd spill the beans here.

About a month before I found out I was pregnant with Avary, and then moved back to Texas, Jason's mom, Barbara, discovered she had stage 4 lung cancer. She had never smoked, and was a health freak—except when it came to chocolate—so it came as a devastating shock. When we found out I was pregnant, it's like it took her hard head and turned it into steel. If she was going to fight for her life before, then she became the Mohammad Ali of cancer patients when she learned she had a grandbaby on the way.

Doctors gave her six months to live, which meant she wasn't even supposed to make it to the end of my pregnancy. She surpassed those odds and got to see Avary be born. Not only that, but the reason we decided to have the wedding only four months after

Jason proposed was so she could possibly see her son get married. That little woman blew those odds out of the water once more by taking their six months and stretching it to four years, all because, in her words, she had her two granddaughters to live for. My only wish is that she could've seen me finally find my place in the universe, in this crazy book world, but I know she's watching—and critiquing—my every move from above. Miss you, Momma.

Next, I decided to write who we WISH could have been at our ceremony, our best friend Logan. In reality, Logie was deployed to Afghanistan at the time of our wedding. In our wedding program, we listed him as the best man, but had a childhood friend of Jason's stand in for him. Thankfully, he came back safe and sound.

I've gotten many reactions to my story, from people absolutely loving it, identifying with it, all the way to people calling me crazy (and other, more colorful names) for putting my life so nakedly out there. I've gotten a few questions from readers and friends over and over, so I thought I'd answer them here.

"What does your family think?"

My family is nothing but proud. They think it's amazing that I not only wrote a whole book, but an entire series. I come from a very open and supportive family, so I'm lucky in that respect. Every member I wrote about in the trilogy is exactly the way they are in real life.

"What about your kids?"

I have a cleaned up version of my stories to one day give my kids when they are older, so they can read about their Mom and Dad's tale.

"What if something happens to your marriage?"

There are all sorts of acronyms in the book world that I've learned over the years: MM, MFM, FF, BDSM, PNR...HEA being my favorite, for Happily Ever After. My friend Sierra Cartwright introduced me to one I'd never heard of, HFN, or Happy For Now. At the time these stories were written, all the feelings put into them were genuinely true. But from past experiences (the ones you read in books one and two) I know shit happens. I've learned from those past relationships and am no longer that naïve twenty-year-old, and much more the realist. If something ever happens to my marriage, it doesn't change our beginning. So maybe my trilogy isn't an HEA, but it's definitely an HFN.

"Will you write fiction after your trilogy is complete?"

Yes! I already have some stories floating around in my head, and one that I've already got plotted out. I just have no idea how long it's going to take to write it, since I've never had to *make up* a story before!

ACKN♠WLEDGEMENTS

My acknowledgements seem to always be as long as my books, so I'm going to try to calm my tits a little bit this time!

I made a very special friend when I first started writing *Wish Come True*. It began with someone tagging me in a brilliant painting, one of Belle getting tatted-up by Beast while reading and sitting on a pile of books. I immediately messaged the artist, Joel Santana, aka themaddhattr, and asked how I could order a print and told him I would be pimping him on my book blog, since I have a minor obsession with Belle—says the girl who now has a huge tattoo of the princess that covers her whole forearm. He was tremendously appreciative, and it blew me away that someone with such incredible talent was so humble. We ended up having a ton in common with our love of comic book and Disney characters, and musical inspiration, and started sending each other links to the songs he would paint to, and I would write to. Thanks to him, this book was written with Blackmill's "Evil Beauty" blasting through my headphones, which seemed to make the words pour out of me. Follow him on Instagram at

@themaddhattr. You won't be disappointed!

This was the first time I wrote with a buddy. TK Rapp met me every day at our Dunn Bros Coffee and busted out words for her book while I plucked away at mine. Just having her presence across the booth from me was a blessing, not to mention her laminated writing cheat sheets.

Franci Neill, my PA extraordinaire…where do I even begin? She's the human version of my Adderall. She keeps my head on straight when I need it to be, and takes care of my author page so I can concentrate on writing and editing. I don't know what I would do without her. Thanks to her, I even got included in the 'They Literary Lived Happily Ever After Volume 2' t-shirt campaign! She's a miracle worker, and an angel.

Heather Lane, as always, I couldn't survive without our venting talks. They might not be as frequent as they used to be, since she's a big-time trailer magician and I'm always either writing or editing (idle hands are bad), but it's a comfort just knowing she is there whenever I need to rant. She never fails to make me laugh my ass off when I need it.

Becky Johnson. God. Y'all have no idea how excited I was to write the epilogue, when I could finally tell you about my godsend, my amazing boss and editor. A dream came true last October, when she flew in from Australia for my author signing and I got to squeeze her in person. There's a video on my page of us meeting in real life, and those tears are real. Shit, I'm tearing up right now just remembering the experience. Love you, Becky!

JC Cliff is not only an incredible writer, but she's an incredible person too. I've been lucky enough to be her editor since her first book, and she's formatted each one of mine. There has never been another person I've met who is so selfless, always willing to help me, no matter how hard it is, no matter how much of an inconvenience it might be, and no matter how much effort it's going to take to make me and her blonde ass understand what the hell is going on. We figure this shit out together. Love you to the moon and back.

Lainey Reese makes me feel like I'm the greatest writer on the entire planet. Now, I know it's important to have critical people on your team to make you better at whatever you do, but it's also really fucking awesome when one of YOUR favorite authors truly admires your work. When she's done sending her messages after reading my stories, I feel all my hard work is worth the effort.

Rebecca Allman works with me at Hot Tree Editing. She was a final beta reader on the last book, and unknowingly read book 2 without having read book 1. It was thanks to this booboo that I put the giant warning in the front of books 2 and 3. But even not knowing the full story, her feedback was incredibly helpful, and I ran to her, asking if she'd like to read the first one so she could learn what was really going on. From there sparked a friendship I now couldn't live without. She's my Aussie bestie, and the nurse from this story is named for her. She is the most hilarious person on Earth, and you can thank her for the wordage "cunty asshole" in *Wish Come True*, which my best friend Logan and I use on a daily basis now after a story Rebecca told us about a magpie that clearly had a death wish.

Speaking of Logan, I have to thank him the most, more than anyone else, for this book getting written. For the past several months, Jason has been working out of town in Corpus

Christi, only getting to come home every few weekends. Not wanting his girls to be left alone—and not wanting me to absolutely lose my shit trying to do everything on my own *plus* write a book—he recruited Logan to be man of the house, in exchange for home-cooked meals, laundry service...and apparently a nurse after he had surgery. Which I'd do all over again in a heartbeat for all he does for us around the house...even though he was a giant— yeah. Thank you for all you do for me and the girls. You're the only reason these last six month have been bearable.

Erin Noelle, my most trusted author friend, my Twinnie. There's nothing I can't tell or ask her without getting complete honesty and great advice back. We may look alike, but her brain works *way* better than mine sometimes. There's something to be said about the wisdom she's gained in the six years she's been alive longer than me. We'll be friends forever...because she knows too much. After reading this book, she gave me straightforward feedback that not only made me feel good about this piece of work, but also my writing ability itself, and I'll be forever grateful.

Thank you to my beta girls, Kolleen, Stacia, Brittany, Melody, Andi, Franci, Tina, Rhonda, Theresa, and Jamie. And thanks to everyone in my private reader group KD-Rob's Mob for all the hilarious posts and support!

Finally, Jason, thank you for showing me what a real-life romance could feel like. Thank you for inspiring a hero worthy of his own trilogy. And thank you for encouraging me and helping me make my dream of being an author come true.

Made in the USA
Columbia, SC
11 January 2020